A BLOODY RITE OF PASSAGE

The Shoshoni landed hard on his back, the wind knocked out of him, and for a few seconds his reflexes jammed. He struggled to rise. Lone Walker leaped astride the brave, arm raised. The brass guard of the cutlass gleamed in the sunlight, then the blade swept down to skewer the Shoshoni and pin him to the ground.

Jacob watched this without moving; in truth he hardly breathed as Lone Walker began to sing a death chant for the man he had killed. And when the Blackfoot had finished, he stood and, noticing Jacob close by, walked over to the boy. The warrior's wise sad eyes searched the youth as if they were peering into his very soul.

"Why did you help me?" Jacob asked.

"Would a father not help his son?"

"My father is dead!"

"My son is dead," Lone Walker spoke calmly. He reached out and lifted the boy's hand that held the knife and placed the point of the blade against his own chest. Jacob could take his life. The horses, the weapons, everything was his for the taking. All Jacob had to do was kill the Indian standing before him.

D0019480

IN
THE SEASON
OF THE SUN

by
Kerry Newcomb

BANTAM BOOKS
NEW YORK · TORONTO · LONDON · SYDNEY · AUCKLAND

IN THE SEASON OF THE SUN
A Bantam Book / February 1990

ISBN 0-553-28332-4

Published simultaneously in the United States and Canada

Bantam Books are published by Bantam Books, a division of
Bantam Doubleday Dell Publishing Group, Inc. Its trademark,
consisting of the words ''Bantam Books'' and the portrayal of a
rooster, is Registered in U.S. Patent and Trademark Office and in
other countries. Marca Registrada. Bantam Books, 666 Fifth
Avenue, New York, New York 10103.

PRINTED IN THE UNITED STATES OF AMERICA

KRI   0 9 8 7 6 5 4 3 2 1

For Patty, Amy Rose, and P.J.,
with all my love.

Acknowledgments

Books don't get finished without the love and support of special people. I offer my love and gratitude to Ann and Paul Newcomb, my beloved parents; Aaron Priest, my agent; and my terrific editors, Greg Tobin and Linda Grey. I would also like to offer thanks to my friends . . . especially to the children of Saint Rita's Catholic School for their hugs and joy and the gift of being part of their lives.

Thank you, All-Father.
May I walk the Great Circle of Life Singing.

PROLOGUE

March 1829

Lone Walker's song began as a whisper, quiet and fragile like the breeze that set the brittle stalks of buffalo grass trembling. As the sun broke free of the horizon and washed each distant hill in molten gold light, the voice of the Blackfoot deepened and grew resonant. His singing pulsed like blood in the veins and brought life to the stillness, to morning; it summoned the power of air and water and earth so that the world would not die.

Lone Walker outstretched his arms in the tribal sign for "day." In his left hand he held a ceremonial arrow, its flint-tipped shaft banded with red and black markings and circled with a leather strip from which dangled a raven feather. His right hand slowly uncupped and he sprinkled the earth with sacred meal.

> "All-Father, Great Spirit,
> Your power is astride the hills.
> See it burn the tips of the grass.
> See it chase the darkness from the sky."

A prayer on the wind, a voice fading, reverberations cease; the words are gone, but the mystery remains.

Lone Walker turned his finely formed features away from the breeze and felt the wind's cool breath upon his naked back. He dusted the last of the sacred meal from his palm and then, closing his hand, touched the thumb and index finger together in the sign for heart and brought his hand to his breast.

1

"O Sacred Wind,
Flow through me.
Lead this one,
Guide this one on his journey.
I follow the vision.
The earth beneath my feet is good.
The wind is good.
And though my heart is heavy,
I will follow."

The Blackfoot warrior lingered atop the mounded earth, allowing the warmth of the newly risen sun to seep into his bones. He smiled as a couple of prairie dog pups raced up the gentle slope toward him. Suddenly their black tails raised in alert and the two pups stopped, aware of the man's presence. They scampered down the mound and raced for the protection of the closest burrow. The pups paused at the freshly dug entrance to stare at the man on the hillock, who had made no move toward them. Since he posed no threat, the chattering pups resumed their play. Such a chorus of yips alerted half a dozen other prairie dogs, who emerged from the tunnels dotting the plain and joined in the fun.

A bright yellow meadowlark rose out of a cluster of tall filmy weeds and took to the air, exuberant in flight, its flutelike trilling carried away on the wings of the wind.

Lone Walker nodded. It was time for him to leave as well. He retraced his path down the north side of the hill to the coulee where he had made his camp. His mountain ponies stamped the earth as Lone Walker approached. The ground underfoot was cropped clean where the tethered horses had grazed during the night. The pinto neighed as the brave approached; the bay whinnied and shook its head.

The Blackfoot sang softly to the beasts, "Be gentle, be gentle," and the animals quieted. Lone Walker proceeded to cover his scarred torso with a beaded buckskin shirt that hung to just above his knees. His leggings were of the same soft-brushed hide and adorned with a triangular pattern of beadwork down the sides of his calves and thighs, a design mirrored along the hem of his fringed shirt. The beadwork brought his thoughts back to Sparrow Woman, his wife, and his heart ached to hold her in his arms again, to ease her suffering. Yet he too suffered. During the Hard-Faced Moon, his tears had mingled with hers as he carried the body of his only child to the Hill of the Dead and placed his lifeless frozen body upon the burial scaffold.

Young Bull had drowned in the twelfth winter of his life. Death had stolen him away from his mother and father, and there would be no other children. Sparrow Woman had walked in a dream and heard the All-Father tell her she would remain barren. How great was her grief.

But Sparrow Woman was not the only person who spoke with dreams. Lone Walker too had journeyed in the realm of the spirit and had listened as the Above Ones instructed him to take up his war shield and lance, his elk horn bow and quiver of arrows, and ride away from the Piegan Village nestled in the heart of Ever Shadow. Only in such an undertaking could he free his soul from black sorrow. Lone Walker did not understand how this might come about nor did he ask why. But a wise man heeded his dreams.

Lone Walker looked north and in his mind's eye imagined the sun brightening the serrated ridges and snow-capped summits of Ever Shadow, pictured in his memory morning breaking clear and fine in the valleys and on the people who lived there.

His people. His wife.

"Sparrow Woman, I have your heart with me," he whispered, hoping in some miraculous way to ease her suffering across this vast distance.

Then Lone Walker smothered the last few embers of his campfire, gathered up his weapons and blanket, and swung up onto the back of the bay. The brave dug a smooth flat stone out of his buckskin pouch, spat on one end, and tossed it to the ground a few feet in front of him. The stone landed with the moistened end pointing south.

It was good enough for Lone Walker. He nudged his heels against the bay's flanks and the mare immediately started forward. The pinto obediently fell in behind.

Lone Walker no longer wondered how long the journey

would last. And yet he was certain he would know when it had ended.

He followed the spirit trail which led him into the heart of the rolling plains, a vanishing figure beneath an eternity of blue sky sweeping down to meet the yellow grass, a man alone with his sorrow and his song.

PART I

Sun Gift

1

April 1829

"**Y**ou got more nerve than a cracked tooth, Jacob," Tom Milam said to his older brother as he retreated to a safe distance and glanced over his shoulder as if expecting to see their father come striding toward them from the bluff overlooking the Platte River. His gaze lingered a second or two before returning to Jacob and the rattlesnake that was coiled in the middle of the deer trail.

At thirteen years, Jacob was shooting up in size; one day he would be as big boned and broad shouldered as his father. Jacob brushed a strand of sun-bleached gold hair out of his eyes, waved a forked stick in the rattler's face, and jumped back as the brown-and-black-banded reptile cracked like a whip. It missed its mark by inches and immediately coiled again, tail rattling and tongue flicking in the direction of the thirteen-year-old.

Ten-year-old Tom Milam was slim and dark, as quick and wary as a fox, in truth the bearer of his mother's attributes. He lifted the rifle Jacob had set aside and pointed it at the reptile. The gun barrel wavered, for the long gun was heavy as hell for him to hold. Jacob caught a glimpse of his brother out of the corner of his eye.

"Put it down, Tommy," the older boy remarked. "You're as like to hit me as ol' Beelzebub here." The snake struck again and Jacob once more leapt out of harm's way. This time as the snake retreated to coil anew, Jacob attacked. He darted in and with a flick of the wrist pinned the rattler to the ground, catching the snake's lethal head in the fork of the stick. Jacob reached for his "Arkansas toothpick," a knife

7

with a fourteen-inch blade of double-edged steel. One quick flash of steel and Jacob lifted a headless length of meat that writhed and twisted in his grasp. The rattler's severed head bared its fangs, a reflex that death had yet to still. Jacob opened a pouch hung at his side and dropped the remains of the snake inside.

"What do you aim to do with that?" Tom grimaced.

"Eat it," Jacob replied matter of factly. "And make a belt of its hide."

"You gotta be kidding," Tom said.

"Injuns do all the time," Jacob explained. "That's what Kilhenny told me, and seeing as he's part redskin, he ought to know."

"Well, I ain't eating no snake, so we better hunt us up a buck or buffalo calf or even a plump rabbit," Tom said, his mouth watering at the thought. He looked over his shoulder, southward toward the Platte River where the Milams and four other families had camped for the night. "Maybe we better not wander too far. You never can tell, we might run into some Injuns." Tom brandished the rifle, though it was much too big for him.

"What would Injuns want with us," Jacob scoffed.

Tom looked up at his older brother, a grin on his face. "That snake of yours. An Injun'd rather eat rattler than plum pudding any day." He laughed aloud, worked the rifle behind Jacob's legs, and gave a shove, then scampered off as Jacob landed hard on his bottom in the buffalo grass.

"Tom . . . you!"

But Tom was running flat out and Jacob could only crawl to his feet and race after him. Tom was quick, fleet of foot, and possessed the boundless energy of a jackrabbit, but Jacob's long-legged gait offset his younger brother's speed and he quickly closed on his prey. Tom managed to glance over his shoulder and spying his brother, started laughing uncontrollably and blundered into a covey of quail that exploded from the yellow grass and tripped him up. Tom tossed the rifle aside, almost impaling himself on the barrel, and tumbled out of sight and groaned in agony.

Jacob rushed toward the huddled shape of his brother. Tom

lay curled and suffering as Jacob slid to a halt and knelt at his side.

"For God's sake, Tom, what happened? Where are you hurt?"

"Oh, Jacob, I think I busted it," Tom moaned. The side of his face was matted with dirt and strands of grass, and his eyes rolled up until only the whites showed. He clawed at his chest and managed to open his shirt.

"What's the matter?" Jacob repeated, really worried now.

Tom fumbled with the buttons of his shirt, reached inside, and gasped. "See for yourself, Jacob. It's broke."

Jacob was momentarily torn between staying by his little brother's side or running back to the Platte as fast as he could to fetch his father and the other men from the camp. John Beaufort knew some healing and Kilhenny, the scout, had claimed to patch himself a hundred times. "Lordee, Thomas, where's the break, your shoulder, ribs . . . what?"

"Worse," Tom replied sadly. "See here." He held up an ornately carved clay pipe he had pilfered from his father's belongings. He'd intended an illicit smoke here in the privacy of the prairie. But his fall had shattered the stem and chipped the bear's-head bowl. "Pa'll kill me for sure."

"A busted pipe!" Jacob blurted out, realizing he had been duped once more. "Why you . . . little . . . lying, no good . . ."

Tom laughed in his face, even when Jacob gave him a good shaking and tried to rub his face in the dirt. Unfortunately for Jacob, his brother's impish humor was contagious, and he rolled off the smaller boy and lay on his back and had a laugh at his own expense.

"You really think I was dying?" Tom asked. "Did you really?" His blue eyes twinkled merrily.

"I ought to make you eat your weight in dirt for scaring me like that, Tommy." Jacob rolled on his side and stared at his brother. "You got the devil in you, Tom. And you better grow out of it, for it will do you no good."

"Now you sound like Pa. Always preaching and such," Tom scowled. "Me . . . I'll take a life like Coyote Kilhenny's. Now there's one for you. Just think of all the places he's been and the things he's done."

Jacob sighed, realizing it was futile trying to talk sense into his younger brother. Tom had been tagging at the scout's coattails ever since Kilhenny had signed on in St. Louis. Where the other children seemed afraid of the brutish frontiersman, Tom was a moth drawn to the flame. In turn, Kilhenny basked in the boy's attention. An ordinary man like Joseph Milam, their father, could hardly compete with tales of Indians and wild escapades across plains and deserts and mountains. Oh, Jacob too stood in awe of the scout. But Jacob was more cautious in his affection. His bronze-eyed gaze softened and he patted the younger boy's arm. Then he stiffened and a frown knotted his brow. He placed his ear against the ground, following the example set by Kilhenny weeks earlier. Tom started to speak, but Jacob waved him to silence and slowly raised himself up to a kneeling position and straightened, then rose to a crouch and eye level with the tall grass. He thought he had heard the tremor of approaching horses or buffalo. He hoped for buffalo and fantasized returning to camp with enough meat for all five families. Wouldn't father be proud?

Dreams of a successful hunt died aborning as a war party of braves crested a swell in the rolling landscape and plunged on toward the bluff in the direction of the wagons.

Jacob's blood froze in his veins as he watched the war party gallop through the tall yellow grass and pass within fifty yards of the thirteen-year-old. He counted seven half-clad men wearing buckskin leggings, their naked torsos wildly painted in garish designs of red and black and yellow. The warriors brandished circular shields of willow and rawhide and carried rifles and war lances, light bows and long-shafted war clubs. Raven feathers were braided into their hair and into the manes of the horses these proud fighters rode. The horses themselves bore the markings of each warrior's charm, a red hand, a jagged smear of yellow and black, a crimson circle, all designed to give the animal quickness in battle and stamina in pursuit.

Jacob ducked out of sight, then caught Tom and pulled him down fast as the smaller boy was attempting to see.

"Blast it, Jacob, how am I supposed to see if you won't let me?"

Jacob clamped a big hand over Tom's mouth and cut him

off. He pinned the smaller boy to the ground and as Tom struggled, whispered, "Indians." Tom grew still.

"Friendly?"

"I don't know," Jacob said. "They don't look it. There's seven of them all painted up and headed toward the river."

"Ma...Pa...we got to warn 'em." Tom fought against Jacob's restraining hold.

"They weren't traveling as the crow flies," Jacob said. "I reckon I can outrun 'em and beat 'em to the camp if that's where they're bound." Jacob pulled off his pouch, shot box, and powder horn and laid them alongside his brother.

"What am I gonna do?" Tom asked, his once mischievous countenance wide eyed and openly afraid.

"Keep out of sight, you'll be all right." Jacob patted him on the shoulder. "I'll be back for you. I want to see you explain to Pa about how you broke his pipe." He grinned and tousled the ten-year-old's hair.

Tom scowled and tried to look angry, but as Jacob started to leave, he reached out and caught his older brother's arm.

"Jacob...are we always gonna be brothers? Forever?"

Jacob paused for a second, then worked an antique gold ring off his finger. It was a single strand fashioned into a serpent. His father had given it to him on his thirteenth birthday with the admonition, "Keep the serpent coiled around your finger and it'll never wrap itself around your heart." Jacob opened Tom's hand and placed the ring in the palm and closed the fingers.

"Forever," Jacob said. Then he scrambled to his feet and darted away, hitting his long-legged stride through the wind-stirred grass.

"I'm sorry I scared you and pretended to be hurt," Tom called in a whisper. He chewed his lower lip a second and shrugged. "Well, not really." He grabbed up the rifle that was too big for him.

The sun crept upward in the sky. Tom cursed the tears glistening in his eyes. He clutched the ring tightly in his fist and waited.

On the last day of his life Joseph Milam took advantage of his sons' absence and rolled atop his wife, who whispered sharp protests that the families in the other four wagons might hear their lovemaking. Joseph laughed softly and entered her, promising they wouldn't hear if only Ruth would hush and enjoy the brief moment of privacy allotted to them on this wondrous spring morning.

Joseph sighed in pleasure.

"Where are the boys?" the dark-haired woman asked even as her legs wrapped around her husband's thick waist.

"Jacob went hunting and Tom just had to tag along," Joseph said. Sweat glistened in the rolling musculature of his shoulders and back.

Joseph Milam and four other families had pulled their wagons beneath a bluff within a stone's throw of the Platte River. The area was teeming with wildlife, and the lure of fresh venison had been too great for young Jacob to deny. For once, Joseph was grateful for the boy's sense of adventure.

"I think the Beauforts are up and about."

"Still in their bedrolls," Joseph explained patiently. He kissed her cheek, her shoulders, tried to cover her mouth with his, but she twisted aside.

"What about Kilhenny? He's always at hand, always watching."

"Oh God," Joseph muttered and slumped against his wife. "Coyote Kilhenny is our guide. We hired him. He's supposed to be watchful. That's his job." Joseph worked over onto his side and felt his passion diminish. "We've come this far to build a community where all men will be equal. A place where there will be no slavery, a place for each and every person to start life anew. Yet how can any of us start over if we bring our old fears and suspicions and prejudices along as baggage?"

"But the way he looks at me . . . ever since leaving St. Louis . . ."

"You are a remarkably beautiful woman. A might talky— but beautiful." Joseph pulled up his trousers and fastened them about his waist and, patting the blanketed form of his wife, started to crawl out of the end of the wagon. "Very well. Shall I remain celibate until we reach the site of New Hope? Kilhenny tells me we ought to reach the high plains by the end of the month."

"I'm sorry, Joseph," Ruth began, wanting to explain her lack of desire had nothing to do with him. "Stay with me. I don't care who hears us." But her husband merely brought his fingers to his lips, silencing her.

"I'll be back, woman. Just as soon as I've sent the half-breed out to round up Jacob and Tom. What excuse will you be using on me after that?"

"None at all," Ruth said, holding the blanket open for him to glimpse her softly rounded thighs. She modestly covered her womanhood with the hem of her nightgown.

Joseph scrambled out of the wagon. He stood, transfixed for a moment by the sweep of the sky, an airy ocean of cobalt blue on which floated mammoth mountains of clouds severed from earth. This was a vast and beautiful land, fertile enough for a man and his dreams to take root. Joseph Milam, a fool said some men, a malcontent said others—he wore such labels proudly and welcomed scorn—was built large and powerful, but his true strength was of the spirit.

That same spirit had drawn four other families to journey with him out from the confines of Virginia society. Spirit and dreams had led him onward, to St. Louis and upriver to the Platte. Courage and a trust in divine providence held him to his course. He would find the perfect site and set down the foundations of New Hope with its promise of freedom and fresh beginnings.

Kilhenny, who had been hired on in St. Louis, had found them a good camp here in the bend of the Platte. It was early morning, a foreshadowing of sunlight glimmering in the eastern sky, and, save for a lone inquisitive pup, everyone else had yet to rise. Normally the camp would have been the scene of furious preparations for departure, but Kilhenny had convinced the families to rest a day and allow the horses and livestock to nourish themselves on the sweet green shoots of grass sprouting up to replace the brittle golden stalks of yesterday.

The five Conestogas nestled in the lee of the bluff looked like a small flotilla of sea-going ships anchored in an ocean of grass—five prairie schooners with canvas tops for sails and great iron-rimmed wheels to roll across the windswept vastness of the plains and teams of big-boned sturdy horses to

pull the heavily loaded wagons. A good day to rest, Joseph
Milam thought as he noticed the blanket-covered forms of
fathers and sons asleep beneath each of the wagons. Womenfolk required the comfort and privacy found within the faded
blue-and-red-trimmed walls of the Conestogas.

Joseph Milam turned his attention from the wagons and the
smoldering remains of the cookfires to the half-dozen horses,
ground hobbled and kept close at hand to be used to round up
the other wagon teams busily grazing the meadow here in the
bend. Trees obscured the river here, but the rush of water was
unmistakable. It was through this stand of white oak and
willow that Coyote Kilhenny, their half-breed guide, emerged.
The dark-eyed product of a Scottish father and Shoshoni
mother, Kilhenny had grown up on the frontier and, at
thirty-two, claimed to have ranged the wilderness from the
Apache rancherias in Old Mexico to the Cree villages in
Canada. He was a broad, solid-looking man with shoulder-
length red hair and a rust-colored beard that concealed his
coppery features. His appearance was more that of a savage
Indian than a highlander. He wore buckskin trousers and a
hide shirt. A bone-handled hunting knife jutted from his
beaded belt, and another leather belt draped from his left
shoulder across his chest held three .50-caliber pistols, loaded
and primed.

He waved a leather hat in Joseph Milam's direction and
moved with astonishing quickness for one so large. As he
reached Joseph's side, Kilhenny seemed surprised to see the
leader of the families up and about.

"We've long days ahead, Mr. Milam. You ought to be
resting while you've got the chance." The guide waved
toward the trees and the river beyond. "I've been setting up a
net yonder in the river. Reckon we'll be havin' us a fish fry
today, huh?"

"It would be a pleasant change from beans and sidemeat."
Joseph Milam noticed Kilhenny's demeanor darken. The
half-breed frowned as he stared past Joseph. He had noticed
the empty bedrolls beneath Joseph's Conestoga.

"Where are your boys!" the guide snapped, his gaze
sweeping the camp.

"Hunting," Joseph replied, puzzled by the sudden change

in the man's manner. "They climbed the bluff and headed out
onto the prairie. They're afoot; I doubt they'll wander far.
Still, I hoped you might keep an eye on them for me."

Kilhenny's expression grew conciliatory. The half-breed
wiped a scarred hand across his beard. "Didn't mean to bark
at you, Mr. Milam. Guess that's why they call me Coyote. It
just makes my job easier if I know where everyone is."

Joseph Milam nodded; he wasn't easily offended and,
anyway, the guide made a lot of sense. Joseph considered the
woman waiting for him in the wagon and wondered if he
ought to go to her or remain on watch until the half-breed
returned from his rounds.

Kilhenny seemed to read his thoughts. "Go on, man,
there's nothing to worry about. I've made the rounds."

"Well ... I don't know...." Joseph stammered, torn between a sense of duty and his desire. A sudden flurry of
activity above the treetops silenced Joseph Milam in mid-
sentence as half a dozen meadowlarks erupted into flight. A
raccoon scampered out of the underbrush, brought up sharply
at the edge of the clearing twenty yards from the wagons, and
then beat a hasty detour along the fringe of leafy underbrush.

Joseph had enough savvy to know the camp was about to
have visitors, and a cold shiver ran the length of his spine as a
number of possibilities flashed through his mind.

"Damn it," Kilhenny muttered beneath his breath.

Joseph glanced at him, perplexed at the guide's behavior.
The half-breed made even less sense when he brought a
finger to his lips in a silent warning for Joseph to be quiet.

"I better warn the others." Joseph started toward the
Conestogas, brushing aside Coyote Kilhenny in the process.
But the guide's hand shot out and caught Joseph by the arm
and spun him around.

"Not a word and there'll be no trouble." Behind Kilhenny
twelve men materialized out of the shading oaks. Two of the
party were white men, dressed in much the same fashion as
the guide, plainsmen in buckskins, lean and hard looking.
The younger of the two was bald and a gold ring pierced his
right ear; the other concealed his silvery hair with a plaid tam
that was adorned with beadwork and a single eagle feather.
This man's weathered features were arrogant. The bald man

seemed apprehensive, but the shotgun in his hand was steady
even though he swung back and forth as if he were trying to
watch all the wagons at once. The rest of the men were
Shoshoni, ten muscular dark-faced warriors brandishing an
array of bows and war clubs. The faces of the warriors were
streaked with red clay the color of blood. One of the warriors,
a brave of obvious authority, spoke in his native tongue. The
bald-headed man with the ring in his ear stepped forward.

"I tried to hold 'em up, but Walks With The Bear took it in
his head to come on."

Coyote Kilhenny wagged his head and acknowledged those
behind him but never took his eyes off Joseph Milam. The
half-breed pulled a big bore pistol from his bandolier.
"The old sod in the tam is Pike Wallace; he knew my father.
The one next to Wallace is Skintop Pritchard. Now don't be a
damn fool, Joseph. Me and the boys aim to wake the others,
take what we will, and send your people on their way."

Joseph Milam knotted his fists. They were betrayed! A
dream, ended, came crashing down around him. All of
Joseph's hopes . . . New Hope. The name reverberated in his
mind, mocking him now, louder and louder until he could
bear it no longer.

"Now I don't like much what I see in your eyes, my
friend," Kilhenny said. "A peaceable man like you is licked
before he's begun." He cocked the flintlock and centered the
weapon on Joseph Milam's chest.

Joseph counted the men at the edge of the clearing. The
families in the wagons just might have a chance if they were
warned. Joseph Milam grinned and started toward Kilhenny.

"You think because I'm a man of peace I won't fight for
my dreams," Joseph said. His thoughts were of his boys and
Ruth and gave him the courage to do what must be done.
"You're the fool, Kilhenny, and a black-hearted one at that."

"Stand or die, Joseph Milam," the half-breed warned. His
finger tightened on the trigger.

" 'Be strong and courageous,' " Joseph said, quoting Scrip-
ture. " 'There is a greater power with us than with him.' "
Joseph slowly closed on the guide, who stepped back as he
approached. " 'With him is only the arm of flesh, but with us
is the Lord our God to help us fight our battles.' "

Joseph lunged, clawing for the half-breed's throat. Kilhenny cursed and squeezed the trigger. The gun in his hand roared and jetted black smoke and fire, which singed the chest of Kilhenny's attacker.

Joseph Milam landed on his back, trying to comprehend what had happened. His chest was blackened and singed by gun smoke, and from a gaping wound blood seeped like an overflowing volcano rimmed with pink froth. There was more gunfire now, but it sounded so distant. Joseph heard a woman scream and prayed it wasn't Ruth. He hoped the rest of the families were giving a good account of themselves. Sun in his eyes. Overhead, a bank of lazy clouds adrift. *God, how far away the sky!* It was as if he were sinking into the earth . . . no, into some vast and timeless river, flowing on, flowing . . . ever . . . on . . . .

Jacob watched silently as his father died. He stood like a statue, numb in his tracks, and sucked in a lungful of sage-scented air. He saw the white men and Shoshoni emerge from the trees and advance on the wagons; he saw Coyote Kilhenny block Joseph Milam's route to the river beyond the trees, pull a gun from his bandolier, and aim it at Joseph; and Jacob saw his father try a last desperate attack, forcing the treacherous trail guide to fire and alert those still asleep to the danger.

Jacob wanted to scream, but he couldn't find his voice; he wanted to run, but his legs were rooted in place. So he watched from the bluff, not more than fifty yards away, as Joseph Milam was blown backward against the hard earth, his arms splayed wide, looking more like a cast-off rag doll than the man of power and commitment he had been in life.

Kilhenny's henchmen led the Shoshoni in the attack. All need for stealth was gone now and only a sudden vicious assault would assure them of victory. Pike Wallace waved his tam like a banner and loosed a wild highland yell as Skintop Pritchard and the Shoshoni opened fire. As flames jetted from muskets and rifles, Walks With The Bear echoed Pike Wallace with a savage war whoop of his own. Bullets rent the canvas wagons and splintered wood as the startled inhabitants of the prairie schooners staggered into the dawn's light, some of them critically wounded and blood staining their bedclothes. Some of the men and women took up their guns and fired into the mass of warriors sweeping down on them. As brutal hand-to-hand fighting broke out among the wagons, the war party that had ridden past Jacob and Tom arrived at a gallop, following the sound of battle.

The six braves rode pell-mell into the fray. They fired rifles and loosed arrows as the settlers tried to make a stand. One woman, a short, thickset matron, gathered her children around her like a mother hen her brood.

"Mrs. Beaufort," Jacob muttered beneath his breath. Her husband, a man of average height and stature, a schoolteacher whose talents were more for debate and intellectual exercise than combat, vainly struggled to reload his rifle. Skintop Pritchard ran up to him and knocked the rifle from the teacher's grasp. Beaufort staggered back, unable to comprehend a man of such violence. He tried to reason with the renegade. Pritchard only grinned and gutted Beaufort with a long-bladed knife.

A Shoshoni brave scattered the children around Mrs. Beaufort and silenced the screaming woman with a brutal blow from his war club.

Jacob looked away and spied Ruth Milam, nearly naked and kneeling by her husband's corpse, directly in the path of the onrushing horsemen.

"Mother!" Jacob shouted. "No! Run! For heaven's sakes, this way." He waved his arms and tried to attract her attention. He was running along the bluff now, trying to get into her line of sight. She stood over her dead husband and faced the six braves bearing down on her. She raised a long-barreled pistol, aimed, waited a moment, then squeezed off the single shot.

One of the warriors doubled over, flailed at the mane of his war pony as if to pull himself aright; then tumbled to the ground. It was only a matter of seconds and the remaining five reached the woman. Ruth calmly awaited them and her small delicate frame disappeared beneath the flashing hooves of the horses.

"No!" Jacob screamed as his mother was obscured in a momentary swirl of dust that the wind at last brushed away to reveal a shapeless huddled form skewered on a war lance. The mounted braves rode straight for the wagons. "No!" Jacob screamed again and dragged his knife from his belt. Too much, he had seen too much. He would fight and he would die this day, but first, by heaven and hell, he would exact revenge.

The earth trembled beneath his feet and he whirled around to find a mounted warrior bearing down on him. Only then did reason temper his fury and he remembered counting seven braves out on the prairie. And here was the seventh. The brave rode a pinto stallion. The Shoshoni horseman carried a war shield and a rifle. Raven feathers fluttered from the brave's black hair. His face was garish behind a mask of red and yellow markings, and on his shield was the design of a yellow hand with black fingers.

Jacob's knife blade flashed in the sun. Thirty feet away the warrior leaned forward and leveled his rifle as he charged the youth.

"Come on, you red devil!" Jacob shouted, tears streaking his dust-caked cheeks.

The rifle belched smoke and flame. Jacob tried to duck and heard the roar of the gun an instant before the slug slapped against his skull. Searing pain, the world tilted crazily and shattered into a million pinpricks of light, each a miniature sun burning against a backdrop of blackest night. Then the darkness grew and one by one engulfed the tiny iridescent stars until at last only one remained.

2

      " 'And in that day there shall be a great shaking in the land of Israel,' " Kilhenny read aloud. " 'So that the fishes of the sea and the fowls of the heavens and the beasts of the field and all the men that are upon the face of the earth shall shake at my presence and the mountains shall be thrown down and the steep places shall fall and every wall shall fall to the ground.' " The half-breed closed the worn leather-bound Bible and shading his eyes gauged the hour of the morning by the sun looming balefully in the eastern half of the sky like the blank unseeing eye of one of those Coyote had betrayed.

He lowered his gaze to take in the carnage, the lifeless twisted bodies strewn amid three smoldering wagons. The remaining two had been spared the torch. The Shoshoni had loaded one with goods, the other with their captives, five children ranging in age from four to nine. The Indians had the horses as well and were already departing for their village beyond the Green River far to the west and north of the massacre site.

Kilhenny tossed the King James into the nearest fire. "Well, Joseph Milam, you had your shaking too. And by your own hand is the deed done." Coyote watched as the flames that had charred the wagon frame lapped greedily at the pages of holy words. "I planned to strip you of goods and money and be on my way. You forced me to start the ruckus, and see what it bought you and your kinsmen. Nothing but early graves."

"You talking to that wrecked wagon, Kilhenny?" Skintop

Pritchard rode up leading Coyote's horse. Blood caked the right sleeve of his shirt. Old Pike Wallace had doctored the younger man's wound and cauterized the ruptured flesh with gunpowder.

Pike Wallace walked his own mount up alongside his bald companion. The older man led a string of horses taken from the massacre site.

"The younker here is fit enough to ride. The slug passed clean through. I burned the hole and sealed it off. And durned if he didn't seem to enjoy it," Pike added with a wag of his head.

Skintop Pritchard laughed aloud and straightened in the saddle. His grin revealed a row of yellow crooked teeth. He tugged at the gold earring in his ear and appraised Kilhenny.

"How much we take off these bastards?" he asked.

"There was nary a bastard among them," Kilhenny remarked. Now that the melee had ended he could afford regrets. The slaughter had sickened him. Still, Milam had made his own bed and now he'd rot in it. Coyote spat the taste of slaughter, of burned flesh and spent powder, from his mouth, wiped a hand over his rust-red beard, and swung astride his horse. Walks With The Bear, the Shoshoni war chief, noticed him and left the wagons to ride across the clearing toward the half-breed. A couple of other braves followed him and helped themselves to the horses Pike had taken charge of.

The Shoshoni handed Kilhenny a leather pouch.

"As we agreed, my brother. I take the captives, the horses, and the guns. Here is more of the white man's trade stones." The war chief pointed to the pouch Kilhenny held. "I found this tied about the neck of one of the children." Walks With The Bear looked at the other two men, his expression inscrutable behind his mask of war paint, then back to Kilhenny. "It has been a good day, my brother." His chest swelled and he breathed deeply, taking in the stench of charred wood and dry blood, sage and the dusty odor of the beckoning plains. "You ride to Wind River with us?"

Kilhenny shook his head and gestured to the south. He hefted the pouch, unfastened it, and peered at the contents.

Probably another three or four hundred dollars, he estimated, liking the weight of the silver dollars.

"Me and the boys'll drift on down to Santa Fe," Coyote told the Shoshoni leader. "And have us a time." He dropped the pouch into a saddlebag and tied it shut, the combined savings of Joseph Milam's party.

Walks With The Bear raised his war shield, its markings of red and black dabs of paint smeared with dirt. The rawhide surface of the shield was pocked from a stinging barrage of bird shot. Walks With The Bear twice struck the shield against his rifle.

"Your enemies are mine, Coyote," he said and whirled his horse around and galloped after the members of his war party, who had already begun to string out along a trail, driving the captured horses up from the corpse-strewn campsite.

"We really headin' for Santa Fe?" Pritchard said, licking his lip.

"I said we were," Kilhenny replied. "Just as soon as I check things out."

"What things, laddie," Pike Wallace inquired. He wanted to waste no time in fleeing this place of death.

"Milam's two boys, Jacob and Tom, went hunting. Reckon I better find 'em. No tellin' what they may have seen," said Coyote Kilhenny. And the half-breed rubbed a hand over his red beard and waited for the war party to wind upward out of sight.

Then he motioned for Pike Wallace and Skintop Pritchard to follow him. Kilhenny's partners were anxious to leave the carnage behind. And they'd follow Coyote anywhere; after all, he had the money and only a fool would let the half-breed out of sight.

It didn't take long to find Tom Milam. The ten-year-old boy was breaking a path through the tall grass with the barrel of his rifle as Kilhenny and his men skylined themselves on the bluff overlooking the Platte River camp of the Milam party. Smoke from the burned-out wagons still clung to the air, discoloring what would have been an azure backdrop.

Tom Milam halted and shielded his eyes, fearful he had

stumbled onto more of the war party that had passed him a quarter of an hour ago. He turned to run, determined he would not be captured like the poor helpless children riding in the stolen wagons. Then young Milam recognized the rust-red beard and broad-shouldered silhouette of the Milam guide and started toward Kilhenny at a run.

"I kill him now?" Pritchard grinned and cocked his rifle.

Kilhenny watched the lad come running, waving, calling Coyote by name. Tom was a good listener, the only one of all the Milam party to fall completely beneath the half-breed's spell.

"Coyote?" Pritchard said. "I can down him from here."

"Put the rifle away," Kilhenny said. The smaller man looked across the stock of his rifle in surprise. "The hell you say?"

"There's been enough killing today," Kilhenny replied. "Ain't you had your fill, man?"

"It's crueler to leave the boy out here alone. He'll starve for sure," Pike Wallace spoke up. He ran a hand over his leathery countenance. "Listen to me."

Kilhenny nudged his horse's flanks and the animal started to descend toward the plains. "The boy's coming with me," he said.

"What? Are you crazy?" Skintop Pritchard blurted out in astonishment.

"You heard me. And that's the way of it," Kilhenny retorted as his companions walked their mounts abreast of him, Pritchard to his right and Wallace to his left and the boy coming at a run, even closer. "Lower your gun or answer to me, Skintop."

Pritchard stared at the larger man and finding no trace of weakness in the half-breed's iron gaze, lowered his rifle and eased the hammer forward.

"We'll take him with us," Kilhenny repeated, turning toward Pike Wallace. The silver-haired man shook his head and sighed, staring past Kilhenny. "All right, you old bastard. Have your say. But it's a waste of breath."

"I knew your father; I was close to him as a brother. I killed the grizz' that sent him under, dug his grave with my knife and hands," Pike Wallace said, doffing his tam as he spoke. He slapped his leg with the hat. "So damn if I won't talk to you like your father would and say, 'Mark my words, there is black luck in this, worse than any Irishman's.' You kill a man, then take his son for your own. Black luck, and you bring it on your own head."

Kilhenny listened, then without a word rode at a canter up to the boy who emerged onto the trampled grass.

"Coyote! I seen 'em . . . Injuns! Must've been a hundred of 'em at least," Tom exclaimed.

"Where's your brother?" Kilhenny said, studying the terrain.

"I don't know. We spied us a war party. Jacob run off to warn Pa. I heard gunshots, then the Injuns came back. What's it mean, Coyote, what's it mean? Was there a fight?"

Kilhenny scratched at his beard, speculating as to Jacob's fate. The boy never reached the camp. The Shoshoni probably intercepted and killed him.

"Who are they?" Tom asked, apprehensive. He pointed to Wallace and Pritchard who waited a few yards away.

"Friends of mine," Kilhenny said. "They came to help but alas too late. Your ma and pa are dead. Jacob too, most likely, and the rest of the families either killed or taken captive to be raised as Injuns."

Tom Milam's head sank forward onto his chest and his shoulders bunched together; a shudder passed through his small wiry frame, then another. His knuckles whitened as he gripped the rifle.

But he did not cry, and when he looked up, his red-rimmed eyes were free of tears.

"What'll I do?" he asked in a small voice.

"You can ride along with me if you've a mind to," Kilhenny gruffly suggested.

Tom's features, though grief stricken, grew hard and shrewd beyond his years. "Depends on where you're bound," the ten-year-old remarked, wiping a forearm across his eyes and nose.

Kilhenny threw back his head and loosed a bellowing laugh. The kid had more spunk than most men. He held his hand out, caught Tom's arm, and dragged the youth up behind him.

"Wherever the hell we want to." Kilhenny took the rifle from Tom and pointing his horse south, rode like the wind, away from the river and smoke, the circling vultures, and the site of his treachery and black deed.

Jacob reached for the speck of light. He clawed his way out of darkness and the speck grew and grew, it widened and dispelled the darkness and shot through his skull and joined with a sudden searing pain.

Brighter and brighter.

A throbbing skull, pain searing his leg.

A backdrop of brilliance filled his eyes and delineated a patch of shadow, something large looming over him.

"Ahhh . . ." Jacob sat up and his right hand, still holding his Arkansas toothpick, slashed the air. The shadow screeched and flapped its wings and fluttered down the slope. A second shadow defined itself and Jacob looked up into the bare red face of a vulture. The carrion bird's hooked beak jabbed at the boy's eyes. Jacob raised an arm to defend himself, then swatted the persistent creature with the blade of his knife.

The vulture loosed a vengeful cry and headed down to the blackened ruins of the camp, where the scorched ground bore a less lively dinner, something a host of other vultures had already discovered.

Jacob sat upright, winced, and cradled his blood-caked forehead where the bullet had clipped his skull and plowed a furrow through his yellow hair back. He stared down at his pants leg where the nankeen cloth was torn to reveal a nasty wound. The turkey vulture had gouged a chunk of flesh out of his calf.

He closed his eyes and gritted his teeth and managed to subdue the nausea sweeping over him. Then he stood, but his legs buckled and he fell on his hands and knees. He stood again, fell again, forced himself to try yet again, and this time the world ceased its spinning. His stomach cramped, but he resisted the sickness and took a halting step, then another, dry brush tugging at his legs, the earth beneath his feet giving way and threatening his balance.

A horse whinnied and emerged from the trees, and Jacob recognized one of Beaufort's breed mares, a brown horse brought all the way from Virginia. The animal favored its wounded right foreleg as it caught scent of Jacob and started toward him across the smoldering clearing. Several vultures eyed the mare as a future dinner.

Jacob stepped onto the blackened ground and glanced around him, the enormity of the massacre and the desperation of his predicament slowly sinking in.

"Mama . . . pa," Jacob croaked. He stumbled forward and scattered a cluster of predatory birds. The vultures rose with great wingspans, six feet from tip to tip, in patient, lazy spirals.

In their wake the charred remains of Joseph and Ruth Milam were mercifully unrecognizable. Burned meat clinging to white bones, nothing more. But Jacob remembered where his parents had fallen. Seeing what fire and vultures had left, he doubled over and ran back toward the slope, and crawled hand over foot up the trail to the top of the bluff. Gravel stung his hands, slivers of shale nicked his flesh; but he reached the top of the bluff, fell to his knees, and losing all control, retched. Sobbing, he heaved until his gut was empty.

God God God God, a prayer of one word repeated in his mind. He could form no other appeal, reduced as he was to utter simplicity by such a staggering loss. A shadow fell across him; he expected another damn buzzard and was surprised to find the mare had followed him up the slope.

Jacob straightened and clambered to his feet and walked, careening like a drunkard, to the animal. He caught hold of the mare's long brown mane and pulled himself up astride the horse. The nervous animal sidestepped and trotted onto the plain. Jacob, riding bareback, kept his legs in a tight grip on the animal's middle.

The boy guided the mare through the tall yellow grass and retraced the path to Tom. A quarter of an hour later Jacob brought the mare to a halt where Tom should have been. But all that remained of his younger brother's presence was the satchel with the butchered snake. Jacob shaded his eyes and scanned the terrain.

"Not little Tom, please, God, no," Jacob said softly. "Tom! You hear me!"

"Tom!"

An echo was the only answer borne on a lonely breeze.

3

Jacob Milam ate raw snake and watched the campfires a quarter of a mile away gradually lose their luster as the cool evening hours wore on and the Shoshoni braves and their prisoners drifted into sleep, a frightened and fitful rest for one, a sleep of victory for the other. Jacob cut and skinned another morsel of meat and plopped it in his mouth, the bloody juices slaking what had been a terrible thirst. All day he had resisted the fresh-killed reptile, unable to countenance the idea of making it his dinner, but hunger had proved the best seasoning. In the darkness where he crouched below a hillock and made a cold camp, Jacob Milam dined on snake and was grateful for the meager sustenance.

He stared at the distant camp and imagined the braves raiding the supplies, gorging themselves on bacon and smoked ham and dried apples and jars of sweet preserves.

Jacob hoped Tom had gotten his share. Maybe Tom wouldn't want to be rescued and trade peach preserves for raw rattler. Jacob laughed at the notion. He had to bite down on his forearm to keep from making a sound that might carry to the Indian camp. His wounded head throbbed all the more and the laughter turned to weeping and tears rolled down his cheeks as the nightmarish morning replayed itself in his mind's eye, first, the treachery of Coyote Kilhenny, the murder of Jacob's father, the assault on the wagons, the trampling of his mother in the dust...

When Jacob could bear it no longer, he reached for the double-edged knife of his father, over a foot of steel flashing silver in the moonlight, and its lethal weight gave him courage. Anger replaced grief, and the tears ceased as his mind wrestled with a plan.

But nothing came of the effort. His world had totally changed in the course of a day. There was no going back. And his future was a matter of what might happen the next minute rather than in a lifetime of dreams and expectations. He fought his first battle then, waiting alone in the night, a boy struggling with his fears.

Jacob peered once again toward the distant fires. The camp was quiet now. Earlier there had been gunfire and wild savage cries. Now, a disturbing stillness. Perhaps Beaufort's corn liquor had been discovered, uncorked, and distributed among the braves. The boy hoped every red heathen had drunk himself into a stupor because the only plan he had was to walk into the Shoshoni camp and find his brother and run like hell.

No, ride like hell. He glanced at the brown mare cropping the grass nearby. The poor wounded animal had carried Jacob this far. But young Milam had not forced the crippled animal to anything more than a steady walk as he followed the trail left by the wagons. The Shoshoni war party was westward bound and unconcerned with haste. The attack on the wagons had been thorough, every adult man and woman killed; there was no one left to pursue them.

"No one but me," Jacob muttered. He groaned and untied the makeshift bandage around his head and decided against replacing it with another strip of cloth torn from his shirt.

"Well, I'll never outrun those murderers on foot," Jacob continued aloud, "so I'll just have to steal one." *No, two,* he mentally corrected. *One for me, one for Tom.* Free Tom and then? Run. Hide. Try to stay alive. Return to St. Louis? Maybe. But Jacob wasn't sure he could find St. Louis. The immensity of his predicament was overwhelming. Better not to think.

First things first, Jacob told himself. Finding Tom and stealing a couple of horses out from under the noses of a Shoshoni war party was enough worry for one night. He took a deep breath, stood, sheathed his knife, and patted the mare good-bye.

* * *

A night draped with a thousand shadows, a lonely landscape of rolling hills and coulees sharp cut and opening with stark abruptness beneath the feet of the unwary traveler...

Jacob learned caution by experience; he almost broke his neck as he stepped over the edge of a narrow draw and landed half-way down the incline, legs splayed wide and one hand caught in a thicket of scrub brush. After the first wave of pain subsided, he allowed himself to slide the rest of the way down the gulley. He rested for a few moments. He was dizzy. That worried him. And he suffered nausea. He wished he could lie somewhere and not stir for a week.

Jacob allowed himself a few moments rest, then clambered out of the gulley and limped toward the Shoshoni camp. The boy could count the horses grazing on the plain about twenty yards from the clearing and campsite. He closed on them, choosing his steps wisely as he moved in toward the stolen wagons. The red glow of embers guided him; fitful tendrils of a firelight were a beacon as the boy crept nearer, rounded the circle of horses, and approached the camp on all fours.

The buffalo grass was trampled here and he made his way almost noiselessly to the edge of the camp. He fought his aching skull, his painful leg. He hardly dared to breath and came to a halt just beyond the light of the campfires.

The children were clustered in a single wagon and the sound of their whimpering moans as the little ones tried to rest all but broke his heart. Was Tom there? Jacob searched the huddled forms asleep on blankets or bare ground and eventually made a count of nine braves. Their faces were still painted, but the markings were faded and streaked from sweat. These braves looked to be a formidable lot, even in repose, short, lithe, muscular men clad in buckskins and armed to the teeth, unconscious, yet they seemed to be listening and aware of their surroundings. Jacob frowned, realizing Kilhenny wasn't among them. He would like to have plunged his knife into the ruffian's heart. Suddenly a form materialized right in front of him, and Jacob gave a start and clawed for his knife before recognizing the person crawling out from beneath a horse blanket that had helped to conceal her.

She was fifteen years old and her name was Nadine

Beaufort and she froze, catching sight of Jacob staring at her from the shadows. Then she recognized him. Clutching the blanket and the remnants of her dress about her half-naked torso, she crawled toward Jacob Milam.

She started to speak, but Jacob motioned for her to be quiet and led her back into the darkness. A horse whickered behind them on the prairie and the faint call of a coyote lingered on the night air. Nadine paused, listening to the coyote, her gaze as distant as the fading cry and as mournful. Her pace was weak, her steps unsure, and from time to time she bent double as if in extreme pain.

"Jacob . . . I thought you were dead," Nadine whispered. Jacob didn't answer; he was too busy staring at the poor girl. One eye was swollen shut. Her lips were puffy and bruised. Dry grass clung to her tangled brown hair. Her ripped dress hardly covered the girl at all. Once they reached the tall grass, Nadine sobbed and buried her face in her hands. "I've been used so, Jacob. They've had their way with me. All of them."

The boy, though two years younger, stood as tall as the girl and he stepped forward to take her in his arms. His cheeks grew red at her revelation and he tried to ignore her nakedness.

"Don't cry, Nadine, please. We've got to be strong," he said softly and stroked her hair. "Is Tom in the wagon with the other children?"

"Tom's not here," Nadine said, puzzled. "I was sure you both had been killed."

Jacob's spirits plummeted. *Not here! Tom had to be here. If not, then where?*

"What about Kilhenny?" Jacob asked, his tone darkening.

"Betrayed us," Nadine sobbed. "He and his friends are the cause of this." The girl shook her head, confused. "Kilhenny didn't come with us. He stayed behind with his friends."

Kilhenny certainly had not been around when Jacob had regained consciousness. So he had left. Had he found Tom and taken him?

"We've got to free the others, Jacob. Bring up your folks and my ma and pa," Nadine proclaimed. She smiled. Jacob's blood turned cold at the expression on her face. He could see clearly now even in the faint moonlight and could tell the girl's sanity was nearly shattered. She'd been beaten and raped and seen her parents hacked to death . . .

"Nadine, I came alone. There's no one but me." Jacob tried to cover her mouth, to quiet her. It was the worst thing he could have done. The girl's eyes widened. She tore loose from his grasp and ran off though the tall grass. As she ran, her plaintive cry filled the night, calling for her mother and father.

"Oh God," Jacob muttered and ran after her as the Shoshoni camp came sluggishly to life. The boy freed his knife and crashed through the buffalo grass in the direction of the horses. He gave no thought to stealth, not with Nadine running wild and hollering at the top of her voice. Back in the clearing, the braves staggered awake and fired a couple of rounds at the shadows as the captive children yelled for help. The poor innocents actually thought help had arrived.

Suddenly the Beaufort girl's outcry ceased. Maybe she'd returned to her senses. Not that it mattered now with all hell breaking loose at the wagons, Jacob decided as he charged through a break in the tall grass. At the sight of the horses dotting the moonlit plain, Jacob's spirits soared; he sighed in relief just as he stumbled over the body of Nadine Beaufort. The boy managed to slide to a halt. He sank to one knee and crawled to the fallen girl's side.

She lay on her back, her white flesh ghostly pale in the night, legs straight, one arm outstretched, the other draped across her small breasts. A shattered war club lay close by, glistening.

"Nadine?" Jacob said aloud and touched her head. He drew away in revulsion as his fingertips sank into broken bone and blood and brain tissue.

A war cry shattered the night and a Shoshoni brave leapt out of the grasses. Jacob fell back, startled, and the brave landed atop him and knocked the breath out of the boy. Iron-hard hands closed around his throat and the brave grunted as if in pain, then started to squeeze, a look of victory in his eyes that transformed by moments into an expression of astonishment, then dismay.

Jacob couldn't breathe and his head wound began to bleed

anew and throbbed with the intensity of a red-hot coal burning a fiery path along the side of his scalp.

He couldn't breathe! Not at first . . . then the pressure lessened . . . yes . . . the iron hands grew malleable . . . Jacob swallowed at last and now the crushing pressure eased from his larynx. The Shoshoni brave whose duty it had been to guard the horses pushed himself aright and stared with a dulled expression at the knife in his belly—Jacob's knife that he'd landed on by accident.

The big blade jutted from his belly and Jacob's hand clung to the grip. The Shoshoni grabbed young Milam's wrist and pulled, but he lacked the strength to free himself from the double-edged "toothpick." He shuddered, doubled over, and fell on his side. Jacob kicked out, freed the knife, and got to his feet. He sucked in a lungful of air, his heart hammering in his chest. He stared at the bloody knife he held, at the man on the ground, then at the tall grass. He heard the noise of pursuit—dry grass being trampled, war whoops ringing out— drawing closer.

Something moved behind him. The boy whirled and started to slash out, but he froze in his tracks as a small, sturdy-looking mount, a gray stallion, raised its head, nostrils flared to catch Jacob's scent. Fate had chosen a steed for the frightened thirteen-year-old. He ran to the animal and freed its forelegs from the rawhide hobbles of its owner. The horse shied and tried to run, but Jacob caught his hand in the mane and by the stallion's lunging gait was swung astride the animal's back. Gunfire roared. The orange flames stabbed toward Jacob and spooked the stallion that was already startled by the unfamiliar-smelling boy clinging to its back.

The stallion flattened its ears and galloped off into the night carrying Jacob Milam deeper into the howling wilderness.

4

The ceiling of clouds came with the morning and had seemed impenetrable until noon when Lone Walker paused to survey the surrounding landscape, an immense and lonely windswept plain transfixed now by a single golden beam of sunlight escaping through a momentary rift in the dark cloud cover. Lone Walker remained motionless, a silent spectator to the phenomenon of sunlight and approaching storm.

The bay shook its head, long mane whipping out, and the pinto shifted its stance. Lone Walker sensed their wariness. It was an angry sky and he would do well to find some sort of cover, yet in this sun-stained moment found a magic to renew his sagging spirits. The Blackfoot no longer knew how many days had passed since he had ridden from Ever Shadow. His features were seamed and serious, his eyes worn from watching too many sunsets and sunrises, his limbs weary from wandering. Lone Walker had begun to question the purpose of the Above Ones who had set him on this journey in the first place.

The stream of sunlight bathed a knoll and perhaps as much as an acre of ground around it. The buffalo grass glowed and when the wind blew became like a sea of yellow fire lapping at the base of a rock-strewn, barren knoll. And on this bald hillock rising out of a sea of grass, a figure lay sprawled, his arms outstretched, his shaggy hair the color of the sun-washed grasses.

Lone Walker frowned, then recognized at last what the sun had revealed to him. He started the bay toward the knoll. The Blackfoot's heart throbbed in his chest, all his senses alert, as

he tried to discern between illusion and reality. A nudge of
his heels and the bay broke into a gallop, and Lone Walker
loosed a wild cry that rang out over the storm-threatened
land. Lone Walker's journey was at an end.

A hundred yards became fifty then halved again until Lone
Walker himself was bathed in the same pool of light as the
unconscious boy at his feet. As the wind whipped the dust
away, the Blackfoot swung down from the bay and turned the
boy over and then gasped, realizing he had found a young
white boy who appeared to be nearly the same age as Young
Bull when he died. The Blackfoot straightened and searched
the surrounding landscape, but saw no one. Nothing stirred
save the windswept grasses stretching onward to meet the
thunderheads darkening the horizon.

The pool of golden glowing light narrowed as the clouds
overhead rearranged themselves to eradicate the escaping
warmth of the sun. At last, only the brave and the unconscious boy remained illuminated on the hill.

Lone Walker knelt, placed his ear to the boy's chest, and
ascertained that the young white man lived. But how had he
come to this spot? By horse or afoot or perhaps as a gift of
the sun? But a white skin, mortal enemy to the Blackfoot!
Maybe the Above Ones were crazy this day. Yet what was a
man to do but accept the way of things.

Lone Walker turned the lad over and scooped him up in his
arms. "Sun Gift," he said. "My son."

5

Jacob opened his eyes, surprised that he still lived. As the world slowly slid into focus, he remembered riding for his life, clinging bareback to the Indian pony. His head no longer throbbed as it had during his night ride, no longer seeped blood to blind him, and the nausea that had finally caused him to lose his grip on the animal seemed to have abated.

He was alive. And except for a dull headache and an empty stomach, he felt all right. Jacob's vision cleared and overhead he saw the woven grass roof of a makeshift shelter. He shifted his frame on the blanket under him. Thunder rumbled. He heard droplets of water splashing in a puddle near the entrance, a crawl-through blocked by a blanket. On closer inspection the shelter appeared to be made of hastily woven grass covered by a blanket. The interior was circular, about four feet from floor to ceiling and perhaps six feet in diameter.

A water bag made from buffalo gut had been left close at hand along with a portion of dried meat on a swath of rawhide. Jacob reached for the water bag, then froze, realizing for the first time he wasn't alone. In the dull and meager daylight filtering through the entrance Jacob spied Lone Walker, asleep on the other side of the water and provisions.

The thirteen-year-old fumbled at his waist searching in vain for the knife his father had given him. Suddenly the Indian stirred and the blade of the "Arkansas toothpick" flashed in the gloom. Thunder cracked and Jacob started despite himself.

"You have slept for a day and a night and part of this day. I thought you might die. Instead the All-Father has returned you to life," Lone Walker said in Jacob's own tongue. The

36

boy did not budge an inch, expecting twelve inches of cold steel to plunge into his heart. He felt too weak to defend himself.

"I am Lone Walker," the Blackfoot said, his long black hair framing his dim silhouette. Jacob gingerly touched his forehead and discovered a cloth bandage, moist with a paste of ashes and herbs.

Indians had murdered his mother and father. Hatred welled in his heart, rose to his throat as bitter as bile. In his hatred, he could find no reason for why this savage had tended his wounds.

"It will heal," Lone Walker continued. He leaned forward, his dark eyes peering into Jacob's. "The wounds here, inside, only the coming and going of the moon can mend."

Lone Walker could read the fear, the hatred, and the mistrust in Jacob's expression. The Blackfoot reached over and placed the knife, hilt toward the boy, alongside Jacob's blanket. Then Lone Walker stretched out on his own blankets, lay back, and listened to the wind blow and the rain fall. It had rained for much of the time since his finding the boy. Luckily, the brave had remembered passing the crudely built shelter and backtrailed to find it. He had ground-tethered both his horses and knew they would weather the drenching rainstorm, for the animals had been bred to a harsh environment.

"You are weak," Lone Walker said. "Take food and drink and try to rest more. We have a long way to go." The brave rolled on his side—his back, defenseless, to the boy. He lay still, pretending to sleep, but listening, and every sense alert to threat.

Jacob stared at the knife and his hands closed around the hilt. He wanted to avenge his parents, everyone he had seen murdered. And Tom, yes, his brother too for whatever had happened to him. And here was the opportunity. He rubbed a forearm over his features, felt again the carefully wrapped bandage. He looked down and saw the wound on his leg had also been cleaned and wrapped tight. The boy was confused. He wanted to lash out, and yet he did not move, could not move. Why? Gratitude toward a red heathen, maybe one of the very bastards who had trampled Jacob's mother.

Reason and emotion warred, with neither one victorious.

He returned the knife to his belt. He gobbled down a morsel of jerked antelope meat, found it delicious, and finished what had been left for him. He drank long and deep from the water bag, set it aside, and lay back on the ground that trembled at the thunder. Jacob shuddered, closed his red-rimmed eyes, and tried to plan. Maybe he could not bring himself to kill his red-skinned benefactor, but Jacob intended to escape and if he stole the brave's food and horses in the process, so much the better. He waited . . . and listened . . . and waited for the storm to break, for the rain to cease, for the right time to act.

Jacob woke, saw he was alone in the prairie shelter, and wondered how long he had slept and where the Indian had snuck off to. *Why wait to find out?* His head no longer ached. He sat up and, encouraged, resolved to escape. Quickly as he could, Jacob gathered up the water bag, and his own pouch and wrapped the blanket he had slept on around his shoulders. He crawled out of the lodging and stood in the light of a clear blue sky, a bold sun burning on high, rain-freshened air fragrant with sage, a day to glory.

Lone Walker, a few yards away, sat facing a campfire. He was a short, solidly built man in buckskin leggings. His long unbraided hair streamed in the wind as he busily cleaned and gutted a jack rabbit. His voice rose and fell in lilting tones; he sang softly a prayer of thanks to the rabbit's spirit for nourishing the Indian. Jacob couldn't understand but found himself transfixed by the red man's hypnotic voice.

Lone Walker hung the fresh-killed meat on a spit above the fire. Blood sizzled and dripped onto the coals. He turned and spied Jacob and motioned for him to approach. Jacob looked from the brave to the pair of horses grazing out on the plain and back to the roll of hard muscles cording the warrior's shoulders and chest.

Jacob's legs almost gave out on him. He dragged one foot in front of the other and drunkenly lurched toward the fire. He might be as tall as Lone Walker, but the thirteen-year-old found little comfort in the fact. A man like this Indian could easily overpower a thirteen-year-old boy, especially one weakened from blood loss and exertion.

So Jacob did as he was told and made his way to the

campfire and sat facing the brave, the fire between them. Jacob's hand was firmly clasped around the wooden handle of his knife.

"You still fear me?" asked Lone Walker.

"No," Jacob lied. "How do you speak English so well?"

"I have not always lived in Ever Shadow. I have wandered, alone, like you, Sun Gift."

"My name is Jacob," the boy retorted.

"Jay-cub," Lone Walker repeated. "Jacob . . . Sun Gift . . ." He nodded. "It is good."

"I kinda know what you're saying and I kinda don't," Jacob said. His voice sounded dull and hollow. Too much had happened too soon. His mind could no longer comprehend the tide of rapidly changing events that had swept him away from every security and comfort and love he had known. Everything confused him, the fierce contrast of sun and sky, the limitless horizon, the long-nosed, rust-colored features of the warrior squatting across from him.

Kilhenny, damn his soul, had said no Indian could be trusted, that behind their inscrutable features there burned the blackest intentions. So had said Coyote Kilhenny, the Judas. And here was an Indian who looked at him with an expression that seemed utterly frank, a savage who had saved his life. Lone Walker spoke strangely but was hardly threatening. Jacob didn't know whether to stay by the fire or run like hell.

The aroma of sizzling meat decided for him.

While the rabbit on the spit turned golden brown, the Indian produced a handful of flat cakes made from dried chokecherries mixed with meal. Jacob found them delicious. He watched with unabashed curiosity as Lone Walker produced a basket-hilted cutlass, its blade shortened to no more than eighteen inches in length. He split the rabbit with the cutlass, half for the boy and the rest for himself.

"Where'd a fella like you come by that?" Jacob asked, staring at the shortened cutlass.

"Long ago," Lone Walker said, eyes gleaming. "When I walked in a dream."

Jacob tore a mouthful of meat from a leg bone. His cheeks bulged as he chewed, and as the juices rolled down his chin, he wiped them away on his shirt sleeve, then paused, hearing his mother in his mind admonish him for such poor manners. The memory saddened him. He cocked his head to one side, swallowed the food in his mouth, and narrowed his bronze eyes and stared belligerently at the Blackfoot.

"Do you ever say anything that anybody understands?" Jacob grumbled.

"Yes." Lone Walker looked over Jacob's shoulder. "Our cookfire has attracted a guest."

Jacob turned and sharply inhaled as he spied a horseman in the distance, looming closer, riding at a gallop through the glistening grass. Lone Walker picked up his elk horn bow and fitted an arrow to the sinew string. Jacob hadn't even noticed the bow lying in the grass. Its horn shaft was wrapped with hardened rawhide and an eagle feather dangled from either end of the weapon. But the horseman, an Indian with raven feathers braided in his hair, halted just beyond the range of Lone Walker's bow, raised his rifle, and called for the Blackfoot to put the bow aside. Lone Walker sighed and placed the weapon on the ground at his feet. He moved away from the bow but toward the cutlass nearby.

The Indian cautiously approached. Jacob's eyes widened in alarmed recognition. The mounted brave's features were garishly streaked with red and black war paint. He carried a rifle in one hand and a shield in the other. On the shield had been painted a yellow hand with black fingers. This was the brave who had shot Jacob and left him for dead!

Jacob forced his knees to quit shaking. He was frightened but resolved not to show the fear tearing at him. Here was one of the killers who had massacred the Milam party. Kilhenny had escaped and the other renegades too. Jacob's mother and father were dead. Perhaps Tom as well. Now this brave had come to finish the job. So be it. But he wasn't going to take Jacob Milam without a fight.

"He is Shoshoni," Lone Walker softly remarked, glancing at the boy. Then he returned his attention to the man on horseback, who spoke haltingly in the Blackfoot tongue using a common form of signing to fill in the gaps. The Shoshoni spoke in a clipped, angry tone of voice, gesturing from time to time at Jacob. When the man paused, Lone Walker took the opportunity to explain.

"His name is Black Feather. He tells me that you killed his brother and stole one of Black Feather's horses and that he found the horse a half day's ride from here and it was dead."

In the dark of night Jacob had ridden blindly into a prairie dog village, a portion of prairie virtually riddled with burrows and mounds. The gray had caught its hoof in a burrow and broken its leg, and Jacob had been forced to slit the animal's throat to put it out of its misery. He had stumbled through the morning hours and collapsed on the knoll where Lone Walker had found him.

Black Feather continued to speak. Jacob watched him and studied Lone Walker's expression as well, for he was suspicious of both men. Black Feather concluded his speech. Again Lone Walker interpreted.

"He intends to take you to his village where you will be his mother's slave to make up for the life you took."

"And if I won't go?" Jacob asked as he stepped away from the campfire. Black Feather's horse moved toward the boy, forcing him to retreat onto the plain. Jacob saw a couple of scalps, one in particular, a bloody knot of long brown hair that reminded Jacob of poor crazed Nadine Beaufort.

Suddenly the fear left him and in its place welled fury and a thirst for vengeance. Jacob's eyes flashed with fiery hatred as he stared up at the horseman looming tall and terrible in his war paint and buckskins, with his war shield and rifle. As Jacob backed away, feeling the brown stallion's breath on his cheek, the thirteen-year-old slipped a hand in his pouch and closed it around the dried remains of the rattler he had killed in what seemed like a lifetime ago. He searched and found what he wanted, grabbed ahold of the reptile's tail, dragged it from the pouch, and gave the "rattles" a furious shake right underneath the stallion's nose.

Black Feather's steed reacted like any good mountain pony. It reared back, pawed the air, pitched, bucked, and swung about in a circle so tight that Black Feather was thrown completely clear. Jacob too had to leap out of harm's way. The Shoshoni fell on his shoulder, and with the skill of an accomplished fighter rolled and scrambled to his feet, rifle still in hand. The rawhide shield had broken on impact as it cushioned his fall. Black Feather charged through the dusty wake of his startled horse. The Shoshoni loosed a blood-chilling cry and raised his rifle as Jacob, his own knife in hand, cocked an arm as if to hurl the double-edged blade at the Shoshoni. The rifle barrel loomed ominously large, centered on the boy's chest. Jacob steeled himself for the shot.

The next second, in a blur of motion, Lone Walker dove through the air and knocked Black Feather off his feet. The rifle spat flame toward the sky as the two braves struggled to the ground, kicked clear of one another, and scrambled to their feet.

Black Feather swung the rifle like a club. It was a vicious swipe that would have caved in Lone Walker's skull had he not darted out of the way. The Blackfoot lunged in with his shortened cutlass. Black Feather parried and metal clanged as the rifle barrel glanced off the hilt of the cutlass. Both men retreated a step, each waiting for the other to commit himself. Black Feather feinted with the rifle butt, slashed with the barrel. Lone Walker lunged inside and caught the rifle in the middle of the barrel, then threw himself backward, dragging the Shoshoni forward. Lone Walker planted his right foot in Black Feather's gut and flipped him over.

The Shoshoni landed hard on his back, the wind knocked out of him, and for a few seconds his reflexes jammed. He struggled to rise. Lone Walker leapt astride the brave, arm raised. The brass guard of the cutlass gleamed in the sunlight, then the blade swept down to pin the Shoshoni to the earth.

Black Feather groaned and clawed at Lone Walker's shoulders, then his hands fell back to the ground, his arms outstretched and limp.

Jacob watched this without moving. Still in a state of shock, he did not speak. In truth, he hardly breathed as Lone Walker sang a death chant for the man he had killed. And when the Blackfoot had finished his prayer song, concluding with a chant of thanksgiving to the All-Father for his victory in battle, he stood and, noticing Jacob close by, walked over to the boy. And the warrior's wise sad eyes searched the youth as if they were peering into his very soul.

"Why did you help me?" Jacob asked.

"Would a father not help his son?"

"My father is dead!"

"My son is dead," Lone Walker spoke calmly. He reached out and lifted the boy's hand that held the knife and placed the point of the blade against his chest. Jacob could take his life. For this moment Lone Walker was completely defenseless.

The horses, the weapons, everything was his for the taking. All Jacob had to do was kill the man standing before him, shove the knife home and be done with it. But the knife wavered in his grip and Jacob lowered his head and turned away. His shoulders bunched and his whole form seemed to shudder as he fought back the tears. Then he let go and cried for his parents and his inability to avenge them, for Tom, and for himself, because he was truly lost now.

The Blackfoot warrior crossed to the young boy's side and placed his hands on his shoulders. Jacob straightened, and the tears subsided. He knew then, he had done the right thing. The hatred in him burned, but it no longer consumed.

And Lone Walker spoke.

"Now my son is alive," he said. "Now your father is alive."

PART II

Tom Milam's Story

6

November 1840

On the Feast of All Souls, the celebration of the dead, it was business as usual along the Road of Kings in Santa Fe. Men drank themselves into oblivion or were helped along the way by pistol, knife, or cudgel in dark alleyways or bleak stalls. Men whored and reveled in fantasies realized for the gleam of a silver coin. And in no establishment along the Road of Kings was the laughter louder, the music more gay, or the women more willing than at Ma Cutter's Cibola Cantina. If the sins of the world could have been distilled into a drink, it would have been bottled and served at Ma Cutter's.

The Cibola was a sprawling single-story hacienda with a high-ceilinged spacious saloon dominating the street facade while the other three sides of the square offered rooms for the discriminating gentleman who wished to consort with one of Ma Cutter's girls. Brick walkways crisscrossed the courtyard in the center of the Hacienda and were lined with luminarias. In the center of the grounds, where a whole side of beef turned on a spit over a pit of fire, Ma Cutter herself, a broad-beamed wench, personally supervised the roasting steer. Her red hair was piled atop her head and pinned in place. Her cheeks were powdery and seemed unnaturally pale. Her eyes were quick and darting as she took in the surrounding scene. Now and then she paused to castigate a slothful servant or to caution one of her girls, "her doves," to be extra nice to a particular individual.

Tonight, her worried gaze was fixed for the most part on the saloon. Even for its size the place was crowded. She could imagine the scene, smoky rafters overhead while at the

bar her usual patrons must worm their way through a human
barrier of the most dangerous sort, a host of free trappers
down from the Sangre de Cristos and some even from as far
as the Wind River range to the north.

Ma Cutter was so busy calculating the damage such wild
men might inflict on her furnishings she never noticed the
buckskin-clad form of Coyote Kilhenny stealing up on her.
Clasping her immense stern in a fierce hold, Kilhenny thrust
his groin against the folds of her velvet gown and rubbed
against her fleshy buttocks and bellowed his pleasure.

Ma Cutter almost leapt into the fire pit in surprise and
started to reach for the butcher knife she kept secured in a
sheath dangling from her apron. Then she recognized Coyote
and slapped at him with her large wooden basting spoon
instead, a much less lethal weapon.

"Now here's a woman for me!" Kilhenny roared. His
rust-red hair was slicked smooth against his skull; his beard
glistened with water and smelled of vanilla. Time had streaked
his beard with silver, but his shoulders were unbowed, still
hard as stone, and he laughed and turned Ma Cutter in his
arms and even managed to lift all two hundred twenty pounds
of her a couple of inches clear of the ground. "Keep all them
skinny little gals you run here," Kilhenny said. "They be
schooners, Ma. But you, ah, now you're a Spanish galleon."
He nuzzled the fleshy rolls of her neck. Ma Cutter laughed
and grabbed him by the chin whiskers and kissed him on the
lips.

"You lying honey-dipped old half-breed bastard," Ma
said. "Maybe tonight I'll just make you draw to a long suit,
call your bluff and see if you're"—and she grabbed his
crotch—"up to it."

"I'd die happy." Kilhenny winked.

"Just as long as you didn't go limp," Ma Cutter cautioned,
then she slapped him on the rump with the spoon and
returned her attention to the meat. "Now be off and see to
your men. And mind you, Coyote Kilhenny, I hold you
responsible for any damage to my property, be it a bed or a
bedmate. Be warned, Don Rafael Rodrigo, our new alcalde,
has little use for Anglos. Worse, he is too damn devout and
wishes to close the Road and drive us out."

"The good folks of Santa Fe would never stand for that."
Kilhenny took a knife from his belt and peeled a strip of meat
from the roast. Red juices dyed his chin. "Don't worry, I'll
keep clear of Rodrigo. I'd hate to ruin my welcome hereabouts."

"Wait till it's cooked," Ma Cutter complained.

"It's dead, it's done." Kilhenny grimaced, stuffing the
morsel into his mouth. He pinched her left buttock and
sauntered off toward the saloon.

"Hey, where's that boy of yours? You haven't let the
redskins put him under have you?" Ma Cutter called out.

Kilhenny paused, turned, and flashed a grin. "The only
Injun I've seen put Tommy under was a Paiute squaw and she
put him under her blanket. Made Skintop mad as a mud
dauber in a drought too 'cause he fancied the squaw for
himself." Kilhenny stroked his beard and wagged his head,
remembering how Tom and Skintop had almost come to
blows over the Paiute girl. He wasn't sure exactly whose life
he had saved that day in August. Skintop was strong and
mean, but Tom, at twenty-one, was slim and wiry, quick as a
shadow, lethal as a snake.

"Send him around to me, I'll show him how good life can
be," Ma said with a wink of a painted eye. She laughed and
bathed the beef from a clay tureen of drippings and hummed
along with the melody of a balladeer whose sad lament
floated on the still night.

Coyote Kilhenny entered the saloon and inhaled deeply,
taking in a lungful of tobacco smoke, spilled whiskey, and
blood. There was also the musk smell of Ma's belles, an
assortment of young girls of every shape, size, and complexion, from a chunky lass with paste-white features to a slim,
sultry mulatto. Indian girls and brown-skinned senoritas with
raven eyes went from table to table, man to man, flirting with
one, cajoling another until a man would pay any price for half
an hour of pleasure.

Especially a young man.

Kilhenny searched the crowded interior for Tom and managed to catch a glimpse of a familiar plaid tam as a crowd
gathered around a table and began shouting bets to one
another, presaging some contest. Kilhenny wormed his way

across the crowded room, his eyes still ranging over the Mexican and Anglo faces of Ma Cutter's patrons.

A roaring blaze in the fireplace case a host of wraithlike silhouettes upon whitewashed adobe walls draped with serapes and reed mats. One end of the mahogany bar was dominated by a crystal bowl filled with hard-boiled eggs. Along a wall and free for the taking were clay cook pots of frijoles and rice, and stoneware platters of fresh-baked tortillas made from stone-ground corn flour, stacks of them steaming and fresh from the hearth oven. A plump *mamacita* waited with ladle and plate to serve Ma Cutter's patrons.

Kilhenny's stomach growled. A nubile young girl, no older than sixteen, danced past him, her lace bodice pulled low, her shoulders bare, and the coffee-colored mounds of her breasts threatening to burst the fabric. Aye, he was hungry for that too, he paused to reflect, before edging past her undulating hips and heading for the gamblers.

He made his way to the table where Pike Wallace, his silver hair tucked in his tam, wiped a hand on his buckskin shirt and then tapped his fingers lightly on the sides of three clay cups.

"One cup, two cup, three cup," he said. He glanced up, spied Kilhenny, and winked. "One has the pea, my friends. One out of three. But which one, eh? Put your money on the table and take a guess. I cover two to one. You can't get a better deal than that. Try your luck. Is there an hombre here with guts?" Pike shuffled the cups around on the table and picked one of them up to reveal a dried pea. "See? I just won. And my lanterns ain't what they used to be. One of you sharp-eyed sons ought to be able to do as well, hey?"

A Mexican vaquero took a seat opposite the old trapper and placed a stack of pesos on the tabletop. The *vaquero*, a stocky man who reeked of pulque, grinned at his compatriots and hooked a thumb in his belt and motioned for Pike to switch the cups.

"I am a man of courage, Senor," he said and lifted a bottle of the milky-looking liquor to his lips and drank deep.

Coyote Kilhenny had to marvel at Pike's dexterity. Kilhenny knew what to look for and he still missed the moment when Pike slipped the pea in between the middle fingers of his right

hand. He'd conceal it there until someone demanded to have
every cup overturned and then the pea would mysteriously
appear beneath one of the cups. Kilhenny was tempted to stay
and watch Pike at work, but with a new alcalde running the
city, and a morally righteous one at that, he was determined
to remain on his guard. He was hungry and tired and didn't
want to be booted out of town for failing to control his men.

The *vaquero* touched the top of one of the cups, Pike lifted
it up, and the men around the table shook their heads and
decided which they would have chosen. The *vaquero* lit his
cigarillo and tossed another couple of pesos on the table. His
compatriots, hard men all, applauded and leaned forward to
study Pike's flashing hands as he maneuvered the cups across
the rough surface of the table.

"Where's Tom?" Kilhenny asked, edging closer to his
partner.

"Romancin', what else is he good for?" Pike chuckled and
sat back to allow his latest victim to choose a cup.

"What about Skintop?"

"I ain't his keeper neither," Pike grumbled. "Neither of
them two is my worry."

"It'll be your worry if there's trouble. The rurales saw us
ride in together this afternoon. We could all wind up as the
alcalde's guests in the calaboose."

The vaquero lost again and, demonstrating a bullheaded
belief his luck would change, tossed a few more coins into
the center of the table. The vaquero tugged at his pencil-thin
moustache, his stare intense as he studied Pike's every motion.

Kilhenny leaned close to Pike's ear. "Better let him win
one, old man, or he'll be making you eat your tam, feather
and all."

Kilhenny straightened and left the table. He was elbowing
his way to the bar when one of Ma Cutter's mestizo servants
tugged at his coat sleeve and after getting the half-breed's
attention pointed to a trio of uniformed men standing near the
entrance to the saloon.

Two of the men wore short coats, close-fitting tailored
wool trousers tucked into high-topped black boots, and japanned leather helmets. Braidery adorned the red-and-white-
trimmed coats. The pistols tucked in their leather belts and

sheathed sabers added authority to their appearance. The third man was attired in a similar uniform, though he sported a good deal more braidery and his round belly, protruding like a bay window over his feet, gleamed with shiny gold buttons from his chest to his waist. He stood no taller than five feet in height. His hair was close cropped and the black sprinkled with silver, his bushy sideburns almost totally silver. His leather dragoon helmet sported white metal fastenings and a black plume, a rather dashing addition that seemed incongruous in so corpulent an individual.

The festivities slowed, the cacophony of voices lowered in volume, and the music ceased as Don Rafael Rodrigo's presence became known.

The alcalde seemed to enjoy his effect on the cantina's inhabitants. He surveyed the interior but ventured no further than the doorway. He did, however, summon a servant to his side who darted across to the bar and returned with a hard-boiled egg for the diminutive mayor.

As Kilhenny approached, Rodrigo stepped outside and the half-breed trapper followed him. In their wake, the cantina returned to life, the denizens within quickly attained the level of celebration they had so quickly abandoned.

Rodrigo stood aside and studied the luminaria-bordered Road of Kings with obvious disdain for the cantinas and bordellos. He turned to appraise Kilhenny, who stood half a foot taller than the alcalde and broader in the shoulders as befitting a man who had spend most of his life in the wild. Rodrigo did not seem impressed by the half-breed's physical presence; after all, Rodrigo was the alcalde, the mayor of Santa Fe and the commander of the garrison as well.

"So you are Coyote Kilhenny. I am Don Rafael Rodrigo, alcalde of Santa Fe and in the absence of our glorious governor, Don Manuel Armijo, I am acting as governor as well."

Kilhenny noticed another dozen soldiers standing in an uneven file behind the alcalde. The men waited by their mounts and with envious looks took in the festive avenue where every illuminated window and open doorway offered a glimpse of the pleasures within. Down the Road of Kings toward the heart of Santa Fe, the more respectable citizens of the bustling town carried on their own celebration, marking the Feast of All Souls with a fiesta and in the morning a church service to ask forgiveness for sins committed the night before. The city square and comfortable hotels were off-limits to the rowdy trappers and vaqueros and freight haulers who marched the King's Road.

"I am told you brought three men in with you, Senor."

"Three men and a passel of prize buffalo robes," Kilhenny answered.

"And you will be responsible for the conduct of your compadres?"

"They're grown men," Kilhenny growled.

"And as long as they behave like men, not animals, we will have no trouble, you and I." Rodrigo bit into the hard-boiled egg, chewed and swallowed, and tossed the other half away. "Ah, one thing more. Normally I would not deliver this myself but the governor, my good friend, asked me to present this personally to you. An Anglo freighter brought it from Bent's Fort." Rodrigo snapped his fingers and one of the dragoons stepped forward and passed a leather parchment case to the alcalde, who promptly handed it to Kilhenny. "Governor Armijo and you appear to share an influential friend," Rodrigo added.

Kilhenny untied the case, opened it, and produced a sealed letter that was addressed to him in care of the governor of Santa Fe. The letter appeared to be from one Nate Harveson of Independence. Kilhenny was familiar with the name. Harveson was a successful businessman and merchant who had carried on a profitable freighting operation between Independence and Santa Fe for years. Harveson had interests in the fur trade, New Mexican sheep, blankets, and buffalo robes. *And now an interest in Coyote Kilhenny,* the half-breed thought to himself as he sidestepped into the glare of a nearby window and read the contents of the letter. Its message was brief and to the point.

October 3, 1840

Mister Kilhenny:
Come at once. I will make it worth your while.

Sincerely,
Nate Harveson
Independence, Missouri

Kilhenny folded the letter and tucked it in his coat. He doffed his flat-crowned broad-brimmed hat and bowed courteously to the alcalde. The half-breed was in a generous mood. The money they'd see from the buffalo robes was nothing compared to the likes of what Nate Harveson had to offer.

"I am in your debt, Don Rafael," Kilhenny said.

"I trust it was good news," the alcalde replied, unable to disguise his curiosity.

"Just a bit of gossip from my dear and trusted friend, Nathan Harveson," Kilhenny said, lying with a smile.

"Oh?" Rodrigo was forced to reevaluate the half-breed. Kilhenny's attitude convinced him. Any friend of a friend of the governor's was worth being civil to. "Perhaps you and your men wish to accompany me to the fiesta at my . . . er, the governor's hacienda and depart such sordid surroundings."

"I'll join you, as for my men, I can't seem to locate them," Kilhenny said, scratching his rust-colored chin whiskers.

"No matter. Just so long as they enjoy themselves," Rodrigo purred.

"I don't know about Pike or Skintop, but my nephew Tom could track a good time in purgatory."

Rodrigo chuckled and nodded in accord. "He has an eye for the senoritas, sí?"

"Like a hawk's."

"Well, Santa Fe has many such beautiful women. He will find a senorita to suit him."

"Of that, Alcalde, I have no doubt," Kilhenny said.

7

"Just because you happen to be married to the alcalde of Santa Fe doesn't mean you aren't supposed to have fun," Tom Milam said in a voice as satin smooth as the ribbons he unfastened, as silken as the dressing gown that shimmered in the lamplight and barely concealed Cecilia Rodrigo's voluptuous body. "Ah, you'd be the fairest flower in any garden." Tom worked the hem of her gown up to her waist. "And this the sweetest bud. I don't blame the alcalde for being jealous," he added, lowering his lips to the bud his search had uncovered.

Cecilia Rodrigo gasped, then sighed and settled back against the pillows and stared up at the stucco ceiling of the hotel room, wondering what would happen if she were discovered. She decided—as she closed her eyes and enjoyed the enticement of his kisses—that she really didn't care at all. Don Rafael wouldn't dare punish her. As for Tom, well, the alcalde might jail him, or kill him. And what a pity because the young man was a wonderful lover.

The spasms started deep within her, coursed through her veins like a raging stream of fire; her back arched. "Oh . . . Oh . . . Oh . . ." She pulled the dressing gown up over her head, then reached down and raked his back with her fingernails and caught him by the shoulders and lifted him away from her thighs. "Now," came her coarse whisper. Her eyes became slits; her moist lips and the taut pink crowns of her breasts betrayed her desperate hunger.

"I must have you now," she said in a voice thick with passion. And Tom was only too willing. His blue eyes were hot as a cloudless sky in late summer. His close-cropped black hair glistened with sweat as did his lithe wiry body as he settled gracefully atop the alcalde's passionate young wife.

He entered her quickly, with sudden savage strokes brought her to a second climax, and joined her as she writhed and clawed and called him her sweet stallion, and he wondered how many other lovers she had murmured that same endearment to. Not that it mattered. He hadn't lured her from the fiesta in the plaza for the purpose of finding true love. She happened to be the most desirable woman in the courtyard. That she was the wife of the mayor only added spice to the encounter. Of course, he'd taken precautions should the tryst be discovered. His horse was tethered outside the window, below the balcony in the alley alongside the hotel. Coyote had taught him never to stay in a place that didn't have two ways out. Coyote had taught him a lot more too. But there were some things—and Tom grinned at the notion—that he had picked up on his own.

He nuzzled Cecilia Rodrigo's smooth neck and nipped her shoulder. A murmur of pleasure escaped his lips as he spent himself deep in her and traced a path with kisses from her shoulder to her breasts, returning to her lips and eyes and cheeks and her lustrous black tresses.

"I love you," Cecilia purred.

"You're a liar." Tom kissed her again.

"Lies are best when the bed is warm." She stretched out her arm and patted the pillow beside her. "I want to go to sleep hearing your honey-tipped lies."

"Sleep? When I could be doing this?" He lowered his lips and darting tongue to her breasts.

"Mmm. Better than sleep. But I fear you begin something maybe you cannot finish." She reach down to stroke his leg and after a moment's exploration discovered for herself that he was still hard.

"My sweet stallion," said Cecilia Rodrigo.

If the shoe fits, thought Tom. And he slid between her parted thighs. After two months buffalo hunting on the plains west of the Sangre de Cristo, being with a soft-skinned hot-blooded woman was heaven.

Tom closed his eyes and concentrated on how good Cecilia

felt beneath him. Suddenly, his only worry was if he'd be able to contain the fire he had begun. Senora Rodrigo might blaze out of control and consume him. With her, anything was possible.

In the alley below the window, where Tom's brown mare cropped at the weeds sprouting at the base of the stucco wall, a man materialized out of the shadows. The mare lifted her head, caught a familiar scent, and gave no warning to the man upstairs. Skintop Pritchard had a score to settle with Tom Milam. He'd had no use for Tom as a boy. And less now that he was grown to manhood. Tom had stolen the squaw Skintop had fancied and Pritchard was bound and determined to exact his revenge. He'd bided his time and now in Santa Fe Milam had provided the opportunity for his own downfall.

Pritchard stole soundlessly alongside the mare, with a flick of the wrist untethered the animal, and led her from the alley and down the darkened street toward the plaza where the lanterns lit the night and laughter and music filled the air.

Pritchard quickened his pace, anxious to find the alcalde or one of his subordinates and tell them the terrible news about Senora Rodrigo's infidelity. Pritchard had just entered the plaza when a couple of uniformed dragoons accosted him, noticing at a glance this man in greasy buckskins standing out like a sore thumb amongst the nobility of the Santa Fe community. Pritchard, licking his chops, had started toward a table laden with "*pan dulce*" and clay pitchers of sangria when a sharp command and a drawn saber stopped him in his tracks.

"Hold there," a dark-haired, moustachioed officer ordered and slapped the flat of his steel blade against the hide hunter's chest. "Where do you think you are going, gringo? Back to the Road of Kings or I'll have you chained to the stockade walls."

Skintop Pritchard retreated to the edge of the plaza, his features transformed into an angry mask. No one talked to him in such a fashion. His lips curled back in a ruthless sneer. His hand was halfway to the tomahawk in his belt when the mare behind him whickered and caused him to remember the purpose of his visit to the plaza.

"Your pardon, Senor, but I must see the alcalde, Don Rafael Rodrigo," Pritchard said in his most subservient tone.

"He is not here," the officer said. "I am Captain Elizarro. You may state your business to me and I will relate it to Don Rafael."

"I'll speak to the alcalde myself."

"Not without a tongue, which is what such impertinence will cost you," the captain retorted. The elegantly clad gentlemen and their ladies near Elizarro and the hide hunter moved away from the confrontation, not wanting any part of such unpleasantness. At a gesture from the captain, a pair of stern-faced junior officers joined Elizarro at the fringe of the festivities. The officers were obviously displeased at being summoned from the willing arms of such beauties. Pritchard tried to defuse the situation, holding his hands palm outward in a gesture of peace; a false smile lit face.

"Now see here. I have important news for the alcalde." Pritchard scratched his hairless skull and tried to figure out how things had gotten so much out of hand.

The officers took up position on either side of the hunter. Captain Elizarro, taking courage from the arrival of his men, now advanced on Pritchard.

"I will decide whether your 'news' is important enough to bother Don Rafael with," the captain flatly stated.

Pritchard, glancing at the soldiers surrounding him, finally shrugged.

"Aw, what the hell. You want to be the messenger boy, go to it. I'll tell you. Just make sure you pass it along to the alcalde pronto or it will be too late."

8

Coyote Kilhenny almost made it to the fiesta where gaily lit lanterns were strung on poles and crisscrossed the spacious town square, illuminating the plaza in a dancing glow. Kilhenny had always deemed himself worthy of rubbing elbows with the town's aristocracy. Here was his chance, courtesy of Nate Harveson's letter to the half-breed—here—and then gone. Just as the mayor and his contingent of officers turned onto the Via Publica, Captain Elizarro spied them and galloped straight for the alcalde and reined to a halt alongside the corpulent little mayor.

"Don Rafael, a word with you," the captain said in a grave voice. His horse lost its footing in the dirt and gravel, reared and pawed the air before Elizarro could bring him under control. Kilhenny, unrattled by the man's sudden arrival, eased back in the saddle of the horse he had borrowed from in front of the cantina. Judging from the captain's attitude, there must be trouble somewhere, but Kilhenny doubted it concerned him. He watched as the two men distanced themselves from the company of dragoons, and out of natural curiosity the half-breed tried to overhear what the officer and the alcalde were discussing in such lowered voices. Suddenly, Rodrigo straightened, made sort of a choking noise, sputtered, then wrenched his horse back around.

"*Solados*, follow me!" he snapped. "My apologies, Senor Kilhenny, but you must see to your own amusement!" And with that, the diminutive official lashed his poor mount about the neck and flanks and rode at a breakneck pace down the night-darkened thoroughfare. The dragoons swarmed past the

59

hide hunter, spattering Kilhenny with grit from the wheel-rutted road.

Coyote Kilhenny didn't take offense. The truth be known, he was anxious to hit the trail for Independence. So the half-breed stroked his red beard a moment in thought, then started back the way he had come, determined to allow Pike and Skintop and Tom one night to blow off steam.

Tomorrow morning they'd collect their belongings and start east. It bothered him that he didn't know where Tom and Skintop had wandered off to. Not that Tom couldn't take care of himself. Kilhenny took pride in the boy. He'd raised him on the raw edge of the wilderness. The boy had come of age under Kilhenny's guiding influence. He'd taken his first pelt at ten, his first hide at eleven, his first Injun scalp at twelve. The mountains too had been a hard and ruthless teacher, but the half-breed had grafted his own code of honor and morals on the youth. By the time Tom Milam had reached his twenties he could hold his own with any man, red or white. In a fight, Tom was quick and mean and fierce as a bobcat. Oh, he was a wild one and reminded Kilhenny of himself twenty years younger. Kilhenny took pride in the similarity, though it was cause for concern. Twenty years ago Coyote Kilhenny would have ridden into Santa Fe prickly as a hedgehog and looking for trouble. Maybe the kid would show more sense.

Then again, the lad was too much like his father. Unpredictable. Kilhenny felt no remorse for the past. What had happened eleven years ago near the banks of the Platte River had been as much Joseph Milam's doing as anyone's. Once the firing started, there was no way to hold the Shoshoni braves in check.

Kilhenny considered the man Tom Milam had become. No matter his birthright, he was cut from the same cloth as the half-breed trapper. Coyote Kilhenny grinned, sensing the irony, for the one person Tom cared for and trusted the most in all the world was his father's killer.

Life was funny that way.

Tom woke with a start. He hadn't meant to doze off, but the bed had been so warm and the woman so comfortable beside him that slipping off to sleep had seemed only normal. The fireworks in the plaza at the end of the block had awakened him. He looked at the empty place alongside the bed. The candle in its brass holder hadn't burned any lower, so he must have only just nodded off. He looked around the handsomely appointed room with its colorful *serapes* draped like rainbows across the whitewashed adobe walls and the comfortable arrangement of dresser and end table and two wing chairs near the fireplace and there standing naked by firelight, Cecilia Rodrigo, her coffee-colored limbs aglow. She wore a thin silver chain around her neck on which hung a gold-wrought serpent, coiled into a ring.

Tom's hand shot to his throat, then loosing a low growl, he sprang from the bed and toward the woman. Cecilia gasped and backed away and plopped into an easy chair. The ring dangled between her large melon-shaped breasts and as Tom reached for her the woman tried to cover her bosom. But he was too quick and grabbed the chain from around her neck.

"Don't touch this."

"Ow! Bastard. You scratched my ear!"

"You had no right to take it." Tom slipped the chain over his head and paused a moment to study the coiled serpent, his memories slipping back through the years to another day and to a pair of frightened boys whose world was about to change irrevocably. "Brothers forever," Tom said softly.

"I thought you might want to give me something, to remember tonight by," Cecilia Rodrigo pouted.

Tom laughed softly in derision and pulled on his woolen trousers. "Senora, you will have forgotten me before I reach the end of the hall."

The alcalde's wife glanced up as if to offer protest. But she grinned instead and her anger melted away. She was once again the kittenish flirt Tom had danced with at the fiesta and charmed into an illicit rendezvous.

"But my sweet stallion, you are not down the hall yet," she added and invited him to her embrace. When he did not immediately comply, she reached out and caught him by the trousers. He knelt between her thighs and kissed, then shook his head no.

"And I thought you were a man of iron," Cecilia chided, her expression one of playful disdain.

"A man of iron can rust if he's not careful," Tom replied, his blue eyes reflecting the firelight. He cupped her breasts; she sighed. "There is tomorrow, you know. Who's to stop us from meeting again?" A loud hammering shook the door. It sounded like a gun butt battering the wood. "Don't answer that!" Tom finished. He leapt to his feet, grabbed the rest of his clothes, and headed for the balcony and his horse tethered below in the alley.

A gunshot rang out and the door latch blew away. Cecilia screamed and ran toward the bed as wood splinters showered the throw rug. The woman pulled the blanket off the bed and wrapped it about herself as Rodrigo charged into the room. He slashed the air with his saber, then his wild eyes spied Tom leaping like a cat through the window. He demonstrated his agility even more as he bolted over the stone wall and dropped out of sight.

"Husband, he attacked me," Cecilia moaned as the alcalde turned toward the wife. "See the welts," she added, keeping well in the shadows. "He forced himself on me. Thank the saints I am rescued!"

Don Rafael Rodrigo hurried to his wife's bedside and wrapped her in an embrace. He stroked her tousled hair while she wept and sobbed and thanked the Holy Family for her deliverance.

Down below the balcony, Tom Milam landed hard and fell back on his rump, slamming his head against the adobe wall and jarring all his bones. He groaned and tried to stand and heard laughter. When his vision cleared, he was ringed by dragoons on horseback and staring down the barrels of their muskets. His own horse was gone, wandered off . . . no . . . he'd trained the horse to stay put. Well, the animal was gone, and with it, his chance for escape.

He managed to stand, winced at the pain, and rubbed his rear end.

"I am Captain Elizarro, Senor," an officer said from among the soldiers surrounding Tom. "Permit me, *por favor*, to offer you the hospitality of our jail." Elizarro walked his mount forward and into Tom, nearly knocking the young man off his feet. He slashed down with a riding crop and cut Tom's cheek. "And in the morning, I am certain the alcalde will have many things to discuss with you, eh? Many 'painful' memories for you to recall."

The soldiers laughed at the hapless prisoner in their midst. It was useless to resist. So Tom shrugged and suppressed his volatile nature.

"Maybe I will drop by," Tom Milam said. And he wiped the blood from his cheek . . . and smiled.

9

The jailhouse was a solitary, solid building set blocks off the Via Publica, facing a narrow street and set apart from the other buildings that pertained to civic government. Situated about twenty-five yards from the jail, the nearest structure was a barracks for the city's military police, in this case Captain Elizarro and a dozen men. Elizarro could keep watch from his second-floor apartment while his men, quartered below, were close enough to be called upon at a moment's notice.

Two soldiers patrolled the perimeter of the building, keeping a wary surveillance and challenging anyone who approached. The building itself, behind its adobe walls fifteen feet to a side, housed a single room, a broad open space fronted by a heavy oaken door, bolted from the outside, and two small windows, barred and, as the night was cool, shuttered against the chill. It was up to the prisoners within to feed wood to the iron stove and nurse the wick of the single oil lamp. Five cots were scattered about the room. Skintop Pritchard was sprawled across one. He lay with one hand propping up his head, the better to keep an eye on Tom, who was busy tending the fire in the stove and had hardly spoken a word to the trapper for what seemed the better part of the night. While Tom slept, an early morning chill had crept into the room and roused him from his thin blanket and a fitful rest.

At least Elizarro allowed me to keep my clothes, Tom thought to himself. That was more than Cecilia had done. Tom's grin became a grimace and he gingerly touched the cut on his cheek where Elizarro had slashed him. He stirred the embers and added several blocks of wood, coaxing a timid curl of fire into an honest blaze while he relived the previous night's entertainment along with the alcalde's luscious bride and the confrontation that followed. Before her husband, Cecilia had bemoaned her treatment at the hands of Tom Milam. She accused Tom of luring her to the hotel room and locking the door to prevent her escape.

The alcalde had turned livid with rage as he listened to his wife and he believed every word, so blind was the man by his passion for the woman. Well, she was his problem, Tom thought to himself, and good riddance. Her pleasure was nothing but trouble.

Tom finished with the stove and closed the grate. He warmed himself for a moment. He sauntered across to the door and pressed his ear to the wood. He thought he heard snoring. He studied the edge of the door and the hard leather hinges.

"What is it?" Pritchard muttered.

"If I had a knife, I could saw through these hinges," Tom said.

"Well, you don't have a goddamn knife." Pritchard swung his legs to the floor, stood, and walked toward the stove. He was a head taller than Tom and a roll of fat girded his middle. But his shoulders were hard and he carried enough muscle in his arms and thighs to make up for his thickening paunch. He was still a man to be reckoned with.

Tom ignored the man and walked to the shuttered window and peered through a crack in the wood at the pre-dawn sky. He knew Coyote would come for him as soon as he heard of Tom's predicament. The only question was when.

Pritchard squatted down by the stove and glared at the firebox as if it were to blame for his incarceration. Things definitely hadn't turned out the way he had planned. Rodrigo had betrayed him. Elizarro too. The captain had remembered seeing Pritchard ride into Santa Fe with Tom Milam, Pike Wallace, and Coyote Kilhenny. The captain, suspecting some sort of mischief, had ordered Skintop Pritchard jailed until his tale of Senora Rodrigo's liaison with the young gringo had been verified. However, since the senora stated she had been held against her will, then perhaps Pritchard was implicated in the distressing occurrence. At least that was Elizarro's excuse for not releasing Pritchard.

"I ought to have known better," Pritchard growled to himself. "Never trust an Injun or a greaser." He glanced up, realizing he had spoken his thoughts aloud. "What the devil you starin' at?" the trapper asked as he met Tom's unwavering gaze.

"I was thinking."

It was hard to look at Tom Milam, a man's stare sort of tended to slide off. It gave Pritchard an eerie feeling and he began to tense. He wouldn't admit to fearing the younger man. Skintop Pritchard simply identified wariness as a sense of caution. He'd seen Tom fight. Tom Milam had more than held his own in skirmishes with war parties of Navajo and Paiute and Sioux.

"So?" Pritchard retorted.

"Thinking about you, Skintop. I don't like you, and you haven't any use for me either. You used to let me know it too, every chance you got when I was a boy. You were always bullying me. Maybe I ought to thank you for that." Tom leaned against the wall, fished in a pocket of his black *vaquero*-style jacket, and found a cigarillo. He walked up to the stove, forcing Skintop to retreat a few steps. Tom poked one end of the cigarillo into the flames, lit it, and then popped the other end between clenched teeth.

"Your bullying made me determined to learn to shoot and use a knife. I figured the day would come I'd have to put you under. But you're the kind of smart man who knows when to quit hating public and start hating private."

Pritchard's hairless skull began to glisten with sweat.

"You always were given to jabber," Pritchard sneered. But his eyes shifted nervously as he searched the room for a possible weapon.

"I had a funny dream," Tom continued in a soft voice. "And in my dream, the nag I tied below the hotel window didn't pull free and wander off. No, it was led away; taken by someone with not enough guts to put me under himself. It'd be a cowardly thing to let the alcalde's justice settle accounts, wouldn't it, Skintop?"

Tom advanced on the larger man, who gave ground and

backed toward the front door until his heels clapped sharply against the wood.

"You're crazy," Pritchard said. "I didn't do a damn thing."

"I never said you did, Skintop. Just 'someone.' Of course, now that you've mentioned it . . ."

"Back off, Milam," Pritchard warned, fists clenched. "You back off, hear? You ain't got Kilhenny here to stick up for you."

"I don't need him," Tom replied icily. "Give me your best shot, Skintop, and I'll still have enough left to cut you down to size."

"You asked for it!" Pritchard threw a roundhouse punch as he lunged at Tom, who moved to block it. Suddenly there came a terrible roar, a deafening explosion that rattled the roof and blew both men off their feet. The wall opposite the prisoners crumbled into the room in a shower of adobe chunks and shattered timber and a choking cloud of dust.

Tom, his ears ringing from the blast, pushed himself up out of the debris. "That's a hell of a right," he sputtered. Both men were roughly dragged from the rubble and hastily jerked upright by Coyote Kilhenny.

"You lads better come a-runnin' or we'll all be dancing in front of a greaser firing squad." Pike Wallace's voice carried through the settling dust.

Kilhenny stepped around the overturned stove and the burning timbers that littered the floor, and grabbing each man by the scruff of his neck shoved them stumbling and choking out the gap in what remained of the jail's north wall.

Pike Wallace, looking as skittish as the horse he fought, held the reins of three other mounts as Kilhenny brought Tom and Pritchard staggering out of the ruined jail.

'*Alto!*' a uniformed guard shouted as he rounded the corner of the jail. The dragoon skidded to a halt, his boyish countenance frozen in a look of astonishment at the shattered wall.

Kilhenny rose up in front of the young guard. The half-breed's hair and beard were uncombed and gave him the appearance of a wild beast. He growled and drew a double-barreled percussion pistol from the belt draped across his chest and pointed it at the guard, who shrank from the gun sights, dropped his musket, and beat a hasty retreat toward the front of the jail.

Tom found a pair of pistols holstered and draped across his saddle horse. A Hawken rifle also hung by a leather thong looped around the pommel. Tom Milam stripped off the tattered ruins of his coat, freed the Hawken, and instead of following Pike Wallace down the alley, galloped around the jail and headed straight for the barracks.

"Tom!" Kilhenny called, then cursed as Tom raced past. Dawn's gray light illuminated the street as the dragoons stumbled out of their barracks. Several of the men had forgotten their muskets as they emerged, half dressed and bleary eyed. Another of the sentries from the jail shouted up to the officer on the balcony, who stood with a gun in hand, nightshirt flapping in the early-morning breeze.

"Elizarro!" Tom shouted. His cheek still hurt where Elizarro had laid it open. Tom Milam's voice echoed through the street as he bore down on the barracks. Muskets blossomed petals of flame; lead slugs cut the air around him like the whir of angry insects.

Gunfire from the jail sent the bewildered soldiers scurrying toward the safety of the barracks as Kilhenny and Pike Wallace, their smoking shotguns still in hand, reached for their pistols.

On the balcony, Elizarro stood his ground. He fired one pistol and narrowly missed his target as Tom lurched to one side, then brought his horse to a jarring halt. Raised in the stirrups, Tom fired the Hawken, aiming low and crushing the captain's knee with a .50-caliber slug.

Elizarro cried out, spinning on his left leg as his right buckled. He fell against the wall and slid over on his side as he tried to cradle his broken leg.

"Now you have something to remember me by," Tom called out. He wheeled his mount and rode at a gallop away from the barracks as muskets appeared in the windows and doorway. A rattle of gunfire and a storm of musket balls hounded Tom back the way he had come.

Kilhenny and Pike Wallace just barely managed to clear way for him as Tom reached the safety of the adobe walls of the jail. Skintop Pritchard, who had made no move to hinder or help, waited farther down the alley.

"Are you daft, boy?" Kilhenny said as he reloaded a pistol and returned it to his belt.

"You taught me never to owe a man," Tom said as he bit open a paper cartridge, held the round lead ball in his cheek, and tamped powder and cartridge wadding down the barrel of the Hawken. He repeated the process with the lead ball, primed the gun with a metallic cap, and eased the hammer down. "Elizarro owed and I collected."

Kilhenny noticed the crusted blood on the younger man's cheek. Tom wouldn't look so pretty now, but there were worse things.

"You're lucky Rodrigo didn't slice off your *conjónes*," Kilhenny said.

"Are we gonna be gabbin' or gittin'?" Pike Wallace said. "'cause if it's the latter, we better see to it before those soldiers realize there's but the four of us." Pike turned to Tom. "That is, if you're finished a-courtin' the alcalde's wife, your lordship," he added sarcastically.

"She wore me to the nubbins," Tom said.

"Tell him about it some other time," Kilhenny snapped. "Let's ride!" The half-breed brushed past Tom and whipped his animal to a gallop as he cleared the alley and entered a narrow street that wound toward the outskirts of Santa Fe. Skintop Pritchard, Pike Wallace, and Tom Milam fell in behind the half-breed.

Men, women, and children alerted by such commotion emerged from their houses to watch the four ride past. No one made a move to stop them. No one wanted any trouble from such men as these.

Tom could hear the gunfire as the soldiers continued to battle a phantom enemy holed up behind the jail. It gradually died out as the road widened and then disappeared entirely as Kilhenny led them out onto the desert plain. The sun, like a single molten ruby, rose to greet them.

East, Tom thought, and wondered at the reason. But he followed Kilhenny's lead and pointed his horse toward an ever-widening gap in the barren broken hills.

"Where are we bound?" he shouted, pulling alongside Pike Wallace, who rode stiffly in the saddle.

"St. Louis," the older man called back.

"Good. I hear it's full of beautiful women."

"Saints preserve us," Pike Wallace wailed aloud.

Tom only laughed, his voice rippling wild and free. He rode on with the wind in his face and his eyes on the red dawn of a sparkling new day.

PART III

Jacob Milam's Story

10

The land of Ever Shadow was dotted with glacier-carved valleys and lakes seemingly strung together like glistening jewels. Mountains loomed here, great cloud-covered peaks gnawing at the sky and slate-gray cliffs patched with glacial ice and snow shimmering in the sun. Below the cliffs stretched lonesome meadows strewn with stands of aspen and spruce up on the hillsides, fir and lodgepole pines on the flatlands. The hard-packed earth was covered with buffalo grass, luxuriant and nourishing to the bison, mule deer, elk, and bighorn sheep ranging the landscape in abundance.

Beaver, wolf, and bear thrived here as did the otter and red squirrel, the snow rabbit, dark-furred marten, and mountain lion. White men with their maps called this country Nebraska Territory, the northern reaches of the Rockies. One day it would be called Montana Territory and in the years to come, Montana.

But to the Blackfoot, now and forever, this was their land, their country . . . Ever Shadow.

The buffalo burst through a stand of aspen and before the Blackfoot hunters could react, the animal had brought down two of their pack animals. A riderless horse raced away among the shimmering golden-leafed trees as its former owner, quick as a cat, darted for a white-barked trunk and shinnied up toward the safety of the aspen's foliage. The buffalo bull, standing six feet high at the shoulders and eleven feet from snout to tail, shook its furred shoulders and attacked the remaining brave.

Otter Tail, a chunky, good-natured young man in his early twenties, hauled hard on the reins of his horse and loosed a couple of arrows in rapid succession at the enraged bull. The buffalo shook the arrows from its hump, bellowed, and then charged. Otter Tail rode at a gallop for the timber while in the branches above him, the second brave, Yellow Eagle, looked helplessly at the Hawken rifle he had left by the campfire in his scramble to safety. Otter Tail turned and gravely fitted another obsidian-tipped arrow to his bowstring. But the angle was bad and he didn't have an open shot at the ribcage just behind the bull's shaggy shoulders.

Suddenly a shadow fell across him and another horseman joined the fray. The third hunter was dressed like his companions, in buckskins and capote, a hooded calf-length coat made from a heavy woolen blanket and sewn with coarse thread. He was taller by a head than his "red brothers" and his hair, though adorned with an eagle feather and worn long down the back and braided on the sides, was straw colored, not black, and streaked with white at his left temple. He rode a feisty mountain-bred stallion and narrowly missed knocking Otter Tail right off his horse as he charged past and headed for clear ground.

"Jacob Sun Gift!" Otter Tail exclaimed, trying to warn his friend to ride clear. "You cannot face *Iniskim* alone."

This particular bull was a maverick and followed no herd. Now and then one appeared among the valleys of the divide. For one reason or another, such bulls were loners and roamed the far reaches of Ever Shadow fighting any animal that crossed their path. Here was the first maverick Jacob had ever encountered and Lone Walker's adopted son was not about to turn tail and run. He shouted and challenged the bull and when the animal changed course, led it out into the meadow and away from the trees. The bull gave chase, its lumbering gait churning a trail of dust in its wake. Jacob's horse was fleet of foot and easily outdistanced the bison.

Here in the meadow, at five thousand feet above sea level, the air in November was clear and cold. Jacob's breath, like gossamer streamers, clouded about his nostrils and mouth as he taunted his pursuer. The bull needed no such enticement. It lowered its cruel-looking horns and forged ahead. Jacob reined to a halt and waited, his mount obedient to the man on his back. The stallion had played this game before; still it nervously eyed the oncoming bull and tossed its mane in alarm.

"Not yet," Jacob said, tightening his left-handed grip on the reins. In his right hand he thumbed the hammer of his Hawken .50-caliber and propped the rifle butt against his thigh as two thousand pounds of bison bore down on him like a locomotive gone berserk. The earth trembled underfoot. Both Otter Tail and Yellow Eagle called for their friend to escape while he could. Yellow Eagle, being a strong and agile young man, and at seventeen years the youngest of the three, dropped from his perch and limped through the remains of their camp to retrieve his rifle. He took up the weapon and realized to his dismay that he had no decent shot.

Otter Tail, with his bow in hand, shouted his challenge at the departing bull and took up the chase, hoping to keep his yellow-haired companion from committing suicide. Even as he gamely urged his horse to follow the maverick bull, it was too late to help Jacob Sun Gift. There would be a great weeping in the lodge of Sparrow Woman tonight. What madness, what evil spirit had so robbed her son of his senses?

Jacob Sun Gift knew exactly what he was doing. The animal was unpredictable. With most buffalo, a hunter could ride alongside and hang with the animal long enough to make a killing shot. But this maverick preferred fighting to the chase. So he'd have to be outsmarted.

Jacob stood his ground, knowing he'd have to make his first shot count, that at the last possible moment his pony must dart to the side.

And yet, as the bull closed on him, a strange feeling came over Jacob. An inner voice, perhaps a warning. The sensation was overpowering. Even as Jacob Sun Gift tried to make sense out of the premonition, the enraged bison was upon him. Jacob drove his heels into the flanks of his horse. The bull tried to turn with the horse, but its momentum was too great, though its horns raked the pony's rump. Jacob spun the rifle in his hands and took hold of the barrel. For a brief second he could have fired, straight down into the great beast's heart. Instead, Jacob slapped the animal's ribcage with the gun butt.

"*Hai-ya Hai-ya* I count coup on you, buffalo brother," Jacob shouted as he rode clear of the bull. The buffalo stopped in the middle of the meadow and Jacob drew up his mount some thirty feet away from the buffalo. The two adversaries stood motionless, facing each other across the sagebrush. By rights, the maverick should have been dead and awaiting the butcher's blade. Jacob was as surprised as anyone at his actions. Otter Tail halted a few yards behind him and called to his friend.

"Sun Gift, has some crazy spirit touched you?"

"Stay back," Jacob said.

"Great is your courage. Yellow Eagle and I will tell of it in camp. Now use your long gun and we will roast hump meat tonight."

"No," Jacob replied.

"Then give me the gun and I will kill *Iniskim*," Otter Tail said, returning his arrow to the quiver hanging behind him.

Jacob started his horse forward, slowly. The stallion warily eyed the bull. The buffalo snorted and shook its shaggy head and blew steam from its nostrils. Jacob stopped and raised his rifle in the air.

"*Hai-ya Iniskim.* This day we part as brothers. As the Sun gave me life, so I give you life." Jacob ended firing the Hawken into the air.

The report reverberated in the stillness and echoed throughout the valley and the surrounding hills, emerald in their mantle of fir and lodgepole pine, patched with the gold of quaking aspen. And as the sound of the gunshot returned from distant purple peaks, the maverick bull swung around and trotted up the valley. It splashed across a meandering rivulet of icy water, the runoff from a distant glacier whose snowy expanse had carved the valley aeons past. The buffalo paused yet again and glanced over its shoulder at Jacob, its body shuddered and the last of the obsidian-tipped arrows dropped from its scarred back.

Jacob reached up and touched his own face and the legacy of a Shoshoni bullet. Scar tissue, jagged as lightning, seared the flesh above his left eye and disappeared into his hairline.

And as if indeed lightning had touched him, the hair from the healed wound had grown startling white, devoid of color.

Yes, he and the maverick had much in common. Both scarred. Both apart from the herd.

The buffalo bull continued across the meadow, crunching the sage and grass underhoof. Jacob turned about to ride back to camp when a glint of sunlight off metal alerted him to the presence of a stranger in the woods. He studied the expanse of aspen and there, watching motionless in the shadows of the grove, Jacob spied a hooded figure about fifty yards from the campsite. Jacob cursed himself for not watching his backtrail better. He grabbed a cartridge from his buckskin pouch and loaded his Hawken, setting the lead slug in place by rapping the rifle butt against his thigh. Otter Tail, riding alongside him, noticed his companion's concern and studied the line of forest until he spied the figure among the bone-white tree trunks.

"Crow? Maybe a whole war party?" Otter Tail speculated, his voice thick with tension. Nearly gored by a buffalo bull and now attacked by Crow . . . Kootenai . . . who?

"They would have struck by now," Jacob said, hoping to calm his friend. "You not only eat enough for two men, you worry enough as well."

"Then he is alone," Otter Tail grumbled, offended. "And we will have some sport." He studied the adopted son of Lone Walker. "Unless more crazy spirits are speaking to you." His round belly growled and thinking of the bison he sighed. "So much meat to let walk away."

Up ahead, Yellow Eagle, oblivious to the intruder, was restoring the campsite. He limped as he moved about the clearing. As Jacob, now twenty-four, still bore the scars from his parents' massacre, so Yellow Eagle suffered a similar reminder with every step. It had happened only a couple of years ago at a rendezvous down on the Yellowstone River. A number of Blackfeet braves had entered the white men's camp with the purpose of trading a winter's supply of pelts for rifles, powder, and shot. A drunken trapper had quarreled with Yellow Eagle. Without warning, the trapper had pulled his gun and shot Yellow Eagle through the ankle. Red men and white reached for their rifles. When the smoke cleared,

Jacob, Otter Tail, Lone Walker, and a dozen other warriors brought Yellow Eagle away from the Yellowstone, leaving the trapper behind with a bullet in his skull.

From that day forth, Yellow Eagle had no use for *Apikuni,* the white men. Yet his closest friend was Jacob Sun Gift. For a long time Jacob had little use for Indians, yet he called Lone Walker "father" and Sparrow Woman "mother."

Yellow Eagle straightened and waved, then he slapped his rifle, butt first, on the ground miming Jacob counting coup. Yellow Eagle danced in a circle, counting coup on the hard ground and laughing at Sun Gift's expense.

Jacob rode toward his friend and shouted a mock challenge, and young Yellow Eagle hooted and bent over and showed Jacob Sun Gift his backside, adding insult to derision. Jacob continued his act for another twenty yards. Then without warning he jerked savagely on the reins and rode at a gallop straight toward the watcher in the woods.

Otter Tail had to swerve to avoid a collision. The portly brave started after his friend, thought better of it, and rode on toward the campsite, intending to circle around behind their mysterious audience. Yellow Eagle stared at Jacob in surprise. He ceased his clowning and gathered his weapons, primed his rifle, and headed for the cover of a deadfall, uncertain what to make of his friend's behavior.

Jacob crouched low and forward as the trees skimmed past, and he angled to the left and guided his stallion among the trees. A few seconds later he reached the spot where the watcher had been. Jacob's stallion never broke stride as the animal charged through the settling dust and continued down a deer trail after the elusive visitor. The trail offered the quickest means of escape, and Jacob, without bothering to search for sign, gambled instead and in a matter of minutes was rewarded with a brief glimpse of a horse and rider dashing through timber. The horse was a spunky, fleet-footed dun. The rider was wrapped in a coat of otter pelts and wore a gray wolf-pelt and cowl and carried an elk horn bow, a weapon smaller than the ash bow Otter Tail carried. It had less range and wasn't as durable but could be fired from horseback with ease.

Once Jacob had sighted his prey, he knew it was only a

matter of who had the quickest horse. He was already gaining
on the gray wolf and had all the confidence in the animal
beneath him. He'd raised this stallion from a colt. Although
mountain bred and a good climber, the horse stood taller and
had a longer gait than many of the horses to be found in Ever
Shadow.

The trees began to thin and a few minutes later Jacob
emerged onto a narrow, open valley bounded by serrated
ridges topped with minarets of slate-gray granite. Ground
squirrels scampered out of the way of the stallion's flashing
hooves and hid themselves among the buffalo grass and brittle
stalks of yarrow and Indian paintbrush. It was a race now,
pure and simple, and the stallion was winning. Yet even as
Jacob closed, the gap inexorably drew to within arm's reach
of the mysterious rider, he could not make out the horseman's
features other than a hasty glimpse of a boyish profile.

I'll learn his identity soon enough, Jacob told himself as he
positioned himself to leap from the stallion and drag his prey
to the ground. He thrust his Hawken into a rope catch that
circled the stallion's neck, and with both hands free, he
pushed up and away from the stallion's back and for a
moment was airborne. In that same sickening moment the
dun's rider had hauled back on the reins, slowing the animal's
pace. The stallion sped past and Jacob, arms flailing, made a
half-hearted grab for the dun mare's head. Jacob Sun Gift
sailed in a graceless arc and landed face first in a rivulet of
icy water, a ribbon of water no more than a foot and a half
wide. Jacob knocked the wind out of himself and came up
gasping for air and sputtering the water out of his lungs, his
straw-colored braids blazed with white from his scar plastered
to his cheeks and dripping water down his buckskin shirt.

He heard laughter from a higher-pitched, melodic, and
most assuredly feminine throat. He looked up and to his
surprise saw a young woman sitting astride the dun, about
thirty feet away. She was obviously greatly amused by his
bungled attempt at unhorsing her. The wolf-pelt cowl dropped
back on her shoulders and a luxuriant mane of long straight
black hair spilled down to her waist.

"*In-is-saht,*" Jacob said, speaking the Blackfoot command
for "dismount." He stood and wiped the moisture from his

face. The girl's laughter was infectious and Jacob could not help himself, a grin spread across his face.

"*Ki-tut saps,*" the girl called out, telling Jacob he was crazy. The dun pawed the earth and neighed. The girl swung the animal around, revealing a marking on its rump that Jacob hadn't noticed before. It was a spirit sign in the form of a wolf track, four charcoal dabs for the toes and a triangular one for the paw pad.

"Wait!" Jacob shouted. But the girl shielded her features once more with the wolf's-head cowl and started away.

"Where do you live?" Jacob asked and his question reverberated the length and breadth of the valley.

But the young woman continued down the valley until she reached a distant slope. Then, just as Jacob had given up hope, her voice drifted back to him: "Upon the backbone of the world."

And with that she disappeared among the hill's mantle of stately spruce.

In the same instant, Otter Tail and Yellow Eagle rode out from the aspen, backtracking an earlier trail and finding Jacob's riderless horse contentedly grazing. A few anxious moments passed before they caught sight of Jacob standing by the narrow little rivulet of glacial runoff.

Yellow Eagle, mounted at last on a horse of his own, gathered the stallion's reins and followed Otter Tail across the meadow.

"*Ai-ya,* brother Sun Gift, where is our enemy?" Otter Tail called out. He was close enough to notice Jacob's water-soaked buckskin shirt and the strands of hair plastered to his cheeks.

"Gone," Jacob said, holding up his hands in a gesture of helplessness.

"How can it be so?"

"I stopped to bathe. And while I was so occupied, the cowardly dog crept away," Jacob replied. He leapt astride the stallion as Yellow Eagle handed the reins to him. He decided to keep the gender of the "enemy" to himself.

"You count coup on a buffalo, then you bathe while an enemy escapes. Surely the long hunt has weakened your mind," Otter Tail sagely observed. "It is time we return to our village." Otter Tail shook his head, made a clucking sound beneath his breath, and started back to camp.

"I know why you are troubled," Yellow Eagle said and his chest swelled. "Remember, I used to do crazy things. Then I took a wife. Now I am a man of purpose."

"A man of purpose especially when you crawl under the blankets and reach for Little Plume Woman," Jacob kidded.

The smaller man beside him shrugged and would not be convinced otherwise. Yellow Eagle was certain he had put his finger on the truth.

"Yet I say that I have a fine wife and it is good. And Otter Tail will soon have enough horses to ask for my own sister, Good Bear Woman, and it is good. Hear my words, Jacob Sun Gift. The snows are late this year, but Cold Maker will awake. It is time you took a wife to your blanket. Or else you *will* go crazy." Yellow Eagle galloped away, holding his rifle over his head and crying, *"Kai-yi! Kai-yi!"* As if challenging the world.

Jacob watched his friend and thought, maybe you are right. And he glanced over his shoulder toward the hills and beyond, in the far and hazy distance, to where beckoned the cloud-swirled battlements of the Continental Divide, the backbone of the world.

11

Lone Walker's song rode on wings of prayer smoke to the All-Father. He added another lump of dry sage to the fire and a palmful of crushed ferns, a few stalks of bitterroot, and lastly he took a knife to his long black hair, sprinkled with silver now, and trimmed an inch from his braid. He tossed the length of hair onto the blazing embers. The shaman didn't often make such a sacrifice, but this day was special. From the hillside overlooking the Blackfoot village on the banks of Medicine Lake, Lone Walker had recognized the three riders returning home from a week-long hunt. Many young men had left to bring in fresh meat and furs and hides for the coming months of winter. Jacob Sun Gift, Otter Tail, and Yellow Eagle were the first to return. Lone Walker already knew his son had enjoyed good hunting from the clamorous welcome he received. The noise reverberated among the forested hills. From the granite ledge where Lone Walker watched, he made out a lanky, straw-haired rider leading the procession of pack animals through the village and saw the children, women, and elder chiefs emerge from their lodges to greet Jacob and his companions.

Jacob was home. Alive and home and Lone Walker was happy, for he had been plagued by terrible dreams and dire premonitions. He saw Jacob stalked by a lobo wolf and tried to warn his son of the danger, but he was too late—too late as the wolf leapt through a curtain of mist...

The dream was fresh in Lone Walker's mind; it haunted him even now. But he calmed his fears with reason. Jacob was home now. And safe. Perhaps I will walk in the dream

again, Lone Walker thought. And discover the meaning. For it is not what I feared. And my heart is glad.

He watched the smoke spiral lazily upward to dissipate against gray-white battlements of clouds. And he began to sing.

> "All-Father, thank you.
> This is my heart
> Who has traveled to the high country
> Even to the backbone of the world.
> This is my spirit
> Who has traveled to the plains where runs
> The Buffalo, as many as the stars.
> This is my self
> Who has walked the forest,
> Trailed the deer, snared the sleek otter.
> This is my son
> Who has returned with food and stories
> To warm us during the Hard-Faced Moon."

The tendrils drifted toward the heavens until a gust of wind tore the diaphanous strands of medicine smoke and stirred the embers of the fire. Lone Walker smothered the awakening flames with a blanket, then stood and took up the rifle at his side. It was time he came down from the mountain and greeted his son. He smiled, remembering Jacob's first weeks in the village.

The boys had teased and baited him unmercifully. But he had endured and gave as good as he took and eventually won the respect and admiration of his peers, not to mention the elders of the village.

The sun stood at high noon, poised between a break in the clouds high above the village. The sun-washed lodges bordered the north bank of Medicine Lake. Hills sweeping up to barren broken-backed ridges formed three sides of the glacier-sculpted canyon whose sole apparent means of entrance was through the opening to the south. The glacial ice had not only carved the canyon but left an area roughly three hundred yards in diameter covered with cold clear water. Chunks of transparent, blue-tinged ice floated on the surface for much of the year. The lake was shallow, never more than waist deep on a man, and constantly replenished by both spring rains and melting snow.

The sunlight dimmed as clouds, seemingly with a life of their own, swept forward to surround and eventually obscure the sun. The lake below changed from gold to dull brass, then changed again to polished steel patched with albescent patterns of clouds as the waters reflected the sky back upon itself.

Lone Walker started down the path that led to his own tepee on the lakeshore. The conical hide walls bore the spirit signs of bison and elk and horse. There were pictographs of mountains, forests, and the Great Water he had seen long ago when as a young man his spirit quest had taken him beyond the mountains of the setting sun to what the white men called the Pacific Ocean.

Lone Walker paused, enjoying a moment's reverie, recalling triumphs and tragedies of the past, of friends and enemies living and dead. Lost in his thoughts, he failed to hear the approaching horseman. Jacob called out to his father and continued at a gallop up the grassy slope.

"Has my father grown deaf in my absence?" Jacob called. "I have twice spoken your name. Lucky for you I am no Kootenai." The young man dismounted and pulled his blanket from the stallion's back. He whacked the animal on the rump and the stallion trotted off to join the other animals grazing on the slope. Lone Walker, alerted at last, watched his adopted son come toward him.

"Lucky for you I do not mistake you for a Kootenai and string my lance with your yellow hair." Lone Walker grinned and grabbed Jacob by a straw-colored braid and gave a sharp tug. He stepped back and studied Jacob's features.

"You look tired, my son."

"From taking the game from my traps, from skinning the carcasses and drying the meat."

"Was there ever a hunter like you?" the spirit singer replied.

"And I had to be ever on my guard. Many a night I was certain we were being watched and I dare not sleep." Jacob hooked his thumbs in the beaded belt circling his waist. A bowie knife was sheathed on his left side; a tomahawk was thrust through the belt on his right. His rifle had been left outside his father's tepee along with the pack animals. Jacob started to tell of his encounter with the girl, then changed his mind. Maybe later, he decided.

"Did you see any sign of Crow or Kootenai?" Lone Walker asked, observing the mouth of Medicine Lake Canyon. Two braves keeping watch on the slopes to either side of the south pass were prepared to alert the village should any strangers approach in number.

"I saw no enemies," Jacob answered, choosing his words carefully so as not to speak a lie to his father. Once again he resisted the urge to tell of the wolf woman he had chased. Yet even thinking of her, hearing in his mind her soft sweet laugh, picturing her fine, delicate features, set his pulse racing.

"What is it, Jacob?" Lone Walker said, his gaze both wise and gentle. He could sense a change in his son. Something had happened on the hunt. He seemed more pensive, more reflective, than tired.

"Nothing. I am hungry for my mother's cooking." Jacob clapped his father on the shoulder and started back the way he had come, retracing his own tracks in the soft earth.

Lone Walker hesitated, considered pressing the matter. A shrewd smile slowly lit his features. Maybe he should personally welcome Otter Tail and Yellow Eagle and hear what they had to say about the hunt. He had a feeling he'd learn more from them than from his suddenly recalcitrant son.

12

Night took on its purple cloak, like velvet hung with an occasional star, while in the valley below, the twinkling campfires cast shadows on the coppery-colored walls of the tepees. A restive stillness spread throughout the village of the Medicine Lake Blackfeet, a sense of tranquillity and peace permeated the lodges clustered along the shoreline.

Jacob stood at the shore and stared out across the dark cold waters into the very heart of night. He wasn't alone in his vigil. Sparrow Woman stood beside him. She was small and delicately made, almost fragile in appearance, a false first impression, for she was as resolute of spirit as any man. And as for courage, none in the camp could boast of greater bravery. She had fought alongside her husband on more than one occasion to defend her family and lodge. Her silver-dusted black hair was gathered in two thick braids that framed her coppery features. Her eyes were brown as earth, her smile as warm as summer, her cheerful nature as welcome as a rain shower on a stifling afternoon.

"Where are your thoughts walking?" she asked, drawing close to her adopted son.

"Down a long trail."

"What do you see?"

Jacob inhaled deeply, catching the scent of pine and sage, of earth and smoke, the aroma of cherry bark tea and meat boiled with dried currants, *pomme blanche* roots, and corn, a meal fit for a successful young hunter and one that awaited him within Sparrow Woman's lodge.

"I see myself filling my belly with your good food till I burst," Jacob replied, hugging the woman.

"*Kyi-a*," Sparrow Woman scoffed, shoving him away in mock protest. "Your words are pretty as the flowers in the time of the New Grass Moon. Pretty but nothing to lean against."

"Perhaps I was also seeing a young boy, eleven winters past, brought to Ever Shadow and Medicine Lake and given a home to live in and a mother to love as much as the mother who bore him."

Sparrow Woman's eyes grew misty and she was grateful for the darkness that concealed her emotions and helped her to maintain her dignity. But she was of a sentimental nature and Jacob always knew how to make her cry.

"My husband brought a gift from the sun."

Jacob hugged her, then turned his attention toward the village. After so many years, he knew the name of every woman, man, and child, recognized every sight and smell the canyon had to offer. The hurts of the past had paled with maturity. As a boy he had tumbled and fought and clambered his way up the pecking order until he won the respect and admiration of his peers. He had proved his worth and made this land of Ever Shadow his home and the Blackfeet of Medicine Lake his people. And he had been content.

Until now.

Until the first glimpse of a mysterious young woman had roused in him such discontent. He wanted to see her again. Yet how could he find her? The backbone of the world was a vast and lonely place. Where to begin? A man might ride those battlements forever and never spy another living soul.

A clamor of barking dogs rose from the far side of this village of sixty-two lodges. Jacob guessed from the direction of the noise that the dogs must be those of Standing Elk. The elderly head of the Bowstring Clan kept several scruffy mongrels around his tepee in an effort to ward off his daughter's suitors. Red Moon was of marriageable age and had blossomed into a buxom little beauty and attracted the attention of many of the young men. Both of Standing Elk's wives had been killed in an avalanche a year earlier and the duties of caring for the lodge, of root gathering, cultivating, and tanning had fallen to Red Moon. For this reason, Standing Elk was loath to part with his daughter.

"One day soon Standing Elk will have to take a wife." Jacob chuckled.

"If a wife will take him," Sparrow Woman countered. "And put up with his bad temper."

"He will have to mend his ways or one day some clever young buck may lure those dogs away with a bait of fresh meat and return for Red Moon."

Sparrow Woman looked aside at her son and teased him. "Perhaps a young man clever as my own Jacob Sun Gift."

Jacob blushed. Red Moon herself had let it be known she was especially enamored with Jacob Sun Gift and hoped he would brave her father's wrath to call her out to stand in his blanket. She was comely enough, but Jacob had never felt particularly drawn to the girl. Perhaps she was too willing or he was too much the coward, Jacob pondered, then shrugged.

"Everyone is trying to trick me into taking a wife," he sighed. "Even my mother. Have I grown so tall there is no place for me in your lodge?"

"*Saa-vaa!*" Sparrow Woman exclaimed, slapping at the fringed sleeve of his buckskin shirt. "What nonsense you speak." She looked up from the lake and saw Lone Walker standing by the entrance to their tepee. "I see your father. Come and eat, and we will speak no more of your taking a wife."

"At least until tomorrow." Jacob grinned, knowing that when his mother and her friends went gathering roots, matchmaking was always a source of conversation.

"Tomorrow," Sparrow Woman lightly agreed. He knew her too well. Did any woman of the Medicine Lake band ever have such a son? She paused, letting Jacob get a pace ahead of her. He was taller than any of the other braves and though his skin was burned dark, his hair was fair and shone bone white in the feeble moonlight. No, she answered her own question. None had such a son.

Jacob Sun Gift leaned back against his willow-rod backrest and groaned in satisfaction, rubbing the palm of his hand across his stomach. Sparrow Woman, across from him, added another piece of wood to the fire and reached into a parfleche, a rawhide box, and pulled out some sage and dried cedar. She lit them in the fire. Between the fire and Lone Walker's bed was a cleared space of earth, square shaped like an altar. She placed the sage and cedar onto the altar space. A choice morsel of boiled meat had been left on the altar at the beginning of the meal. Sparrow Woman now took this and dropped the offering into the fire.

Once the incense ritual had been completed, Lone Walker brought forth his medicine pipe and filled it with a mixture of tobacco and cherry bark and touched an ember to the bowl. A few seconds later he exhaled a fragrant cloud of tobacco smoke and passed the pipe to Jacob Sun Gift.

Jacob touched the stem to his lips and puffed a moment, enjoying the taste after a hearty meal. The pipe was both pleasure and unspoken prayer. Tendrils of smoke from altar, pipe, and cookfire entwined to drift upward through the vented panel overhead where the poles were joined together. Prayer smoke swept upward on a night wind to the Above Ones, to the All-Father himself.

Jacob Sun Gift returned the pipe to his father, who smoked in silence, staring at the flames and waiting for his son to tell him of the buffalo and counting coup and the stranger they had encountered. Jacob sensed Lone Walker's expectation. It was customary after the homecoming meal for the one who had returned to speak of his travels. It was the way of the Buffalo Horn band and the Cut Willow people farther to the south, and here in the high country the Medicine Lake band too. Among all the Blackfeet ranging the wild country, there existed a common etiquette, a conciliatory tradition that formed a bond between the bands or villages.

Jacob shattered tradition and began not with a tale but a question.

"Is there a Blackfoot village somewhere along the back-bone of the world?"

Lone Walker appeared more than surprised by the question, he seemed alarmed.

"No one lives on the backbone of the world," Sparrow Woman interjected, too hurriedly, Jacob noted. "Our people hunt there, as do the Kootenai and even the Crow and

Cheyenne. But no village can exist in such a place. Too little food and the Cold Maker brings terrible snows and bitter winds.'' As she concluded, Lone Walker nodded sagely in accord. Jacob, glancing from one to the other, was suspicious of them both. He stood and stretched. The beadwork on his fringed buckskin shirt glowed in the firelight. Sparrow Woman had traded several fox pelts to a white trader down on the Marias for a box of gaily colored beads. Both her husband's and her adopted son's clothes were the recipients of her artistry and adorned with diamond-design lengths of black, red, and white beadwork.

Lone Walker stood and faced his son. He gestured toward the entrance flap of the tepee. "Walk with me, my son," he said. The young man shrugged and stepped outside.

Sparrow Woman reached up and caught her husband by the arm. "Husband, what is it? Our son is with us, yet at times his heart seems far away."

Lone Walker shook his head, then tried to smile reassuringly at his wife. He patted her hand.

"I will find out." He shifted his gaze to the scabbarded cutlass dangling from a lodge pole at the foot of his hide-covered bed. "A dream took me to where the sun sleeps and we did not understand then," he reminded, and in amusement added, "Why should we understand our son now?"

When Lone Walker stepped out into the cool night air, he found Jacob Sun Gift standing a few yards from the tepee and watching three young boys at play in the glow of their firelit lodge. One of the boys pretended to be a buffalo while his two friends chased him round and round in the patch of light. Suddenly the "buffalo" halted in his tracks and charged the "hunters," one of whom leapt to safety and in passing tapped the buffalo boy on the shoulder with a willow branch that seemed to be a pretend rifle.

It had not taken long for the episode to become public knowledge. Of course, the buffalo boy was Crow Fox, a nephew to Otter Tail. Still, the whole village would know of it by morning, of that Jacob had no doubt. He turned and studied Lone Walker's expression. The Blackfoot nodded as if reading the younger man's thoughts.

"I spoke to Otter Tail," he acknowledged. "Our people could have made much use of the kill."

"Otter Tail talks too much."

"And you, not enough."

"I knew the kill was important." Jacob walked away from the lodges and once more to the shore of Medicine Lake, whose black and glassy surface appeared as unfathomable as the human heart. Father and son continued together along the shore, moving away from the village readying itself for night.

In the distance, a wolf bayed and on the hillside, the horses, with a will of their own, started down toward the comforting glow of the Indian lodges.

"You're right. A fat buffalo would have filled many bellies," Jacob repeated. "But I could not take its life. I don't know why."

"A man's spirit can starve as well as his stomach," Lone Walker said gravely. "You did well. There is no harm in what you did. The *Iniskim* shared his spirit with you. It is a powerful sign, whether for good or ill I do not know. Let Otter Tail jabber like the crow. He has never learned to obey anything but his belly. A man must listen to more than that." Lone Walker paused and breathed deep, filling his lungs with pine-scented air. "Otter Tail and Yellow Eagle are young. They think they know everything."

"But they don't know that the stranger who watched us was a girl." Jacob described the young woman he had chased and lost. Lone Walker listened intently.

"A girl?" he exclaimed. Jacob's companions had spoken of the stranger, but they had thought it was a man. "What was her name?"

"I don't know." Jacob kicked at a stone underfoot. He brushed a straw-colored strand out of his eyes. "But I intend to find out. She is Blackfoot, I think. And she lives up there, beyond our hills, where the winds call the Cold Maker by name."

"She lied!" Lone Walker scoffed. "No mere girl could live alone up in such a wild place. Better you seek her out among the bands of our people. Perhaps the plains folk count her among their number."

"She did not lie," Jacob retorted. His father's sudden

reaction surprised and alarmed him. It also made him all the more stubborn. "I will look where she told me."

"A fool's search," Lone Walker snapped. "But if you must, wait till the Berries Ripen Moon so you will not run the risk of being trapped by the snows."

"It is too long to wait."

Lone Walker threw up his hands in disgust and strode up from the lake, trampling the dry winter grass in his wake.

Jacob listened to him depart, taken completely off guard by his father and the way Lone Walker had ended the conversation. Did the older man know more than he was telling? Jacob quietly called to him. He received no answer, only the hollow echo of his own voice sounding uncertain and vulnerable in the night.

13

Morning, and a blind old man dreamed of the summer of his youth; thoughts warmed him, ah, the memories of comely girls, flirting girls, teasing girls in the days when he thought he would never grow tired and feeble and sightless. And yet, being blind made it easier to shut out the bothersome world around him—this world of barking dogs, gossiping women, and child pranksters—and enabled him to have a clearer vision of the past. From the vantage point of his infirmity, the old man could study his life and thereby attain wisdom.

His name was Two Stars. And this morning, the world intruded more than usual. He had a visitor...

"Two Stars, may I enter?" Jacob called out.

"Why not? You have already disturbed my sleep," the venerable war chief answered.

Jacob shoved aside the flap and stepped inside and around the glowing embers of the campfire. His eyes quickly adjusted to the lodge's interior. War shields of toughened buffalo hide were set against the wall. And near the old man's wicker bed, an obsidian-tipped lance rested.

Time had shrunk the war chief, rendering his once proud physique stooped and vulnerable, wrinkling his flesh and curving the spine that in his youth had been arrow straight.

Two Stars sat up on his bedding of bearskin and bulrushes and propped himself against a willow backrest. He pulled his blanket around his bony bare shoulders and turned his sightless eyes toward Jacob, who shifted uneasily where he sat on the war chief's right.

"I left a slab of rib meat with Calling Dove," Jacob said.

A large-boned, rotund woman maneuvered her great bulk through the flap and waddling like a she-bear in the Birth-Giving Moon, she crawled to Two Stars' side. She placed a chunk of fry bread in his hand and a clay cup of whiteweed tea she had brewed to ease his back pain. She wore a buckskin smock with leggings, and strips of leather and beads tied her braids. She was thick necked, and round cheeked, and she rarely smiled. The top of her nose was scar tissue, a sign she had been unfaithful to her first husband. Two Stars had shown her pity when the others of her tribe, the plains people, had turned their backs on her. Now with Two Stars enfeebled, she took care of him. Calling Dove made a gesture of hospitality toward Jacob and offered him some tea which the white Indian declined. Calling Dove shrugged and worked her massive bulk back through the entrance, rattling the whole tepee in the process.

"And what do you ask tomorrow, my young friend," Two Stars said, "for the feast you have provided today?"

"Only the gift of your knowledge and experience," Jacob replied. "There is a path I think I must walk."

"What do you want? My eyes are dim; I can no longer follow a trail." Two Stars softened the bread by dipping it into his tea, tore a morsel loose with his few remaining teeth, and relaxed, chewing; a trickle of moisture formed at the corners of his mouth.

"My eyes are sharp. They can see past the tired flesh and bad temper of an old man to the heart of fire within." Jacob leaned forward, determined not to be dissuaded by the war chief's seeming hostility. "I see a heart of courage and a mind wise from the many moons you have roamed these mountains." He sat back and with gentle humor added, "Do not think to deceive me, old one. I'll wager you can still outwrestle the young bucks of this camp. As for the women, *sa-yaa*, Calling Dove looks well satisfied."

Two Stars doubled over, cackling. He slapped a bony knee and spilled tea on his crossed ankles. The laughter triggered a spasm of coughs that the war chief finally brought under control, though not without effort. The tea seemed to soothe his irritated throat.

"Ahh, the foundling son of Lone Walker has poor talent for

lying. Much like Lone Walker himself," Two Stars said, his formidable veneer tempered now with amusement. "You have become a skilled hunter, so I hear. Now you count coup on the buffalo, elk, deer, and when your belly grows empty, you simply call out and the game comes to your lodge to sacrifice themselves." Two Stars nodded sagely, his gray braids dangling as he bowed forward. "Such magic in one so young."

He sighed and finished his tea as Jacob shifted and squirmed, grateful the old man could not see his embarrassment. And Jacob vowed Yellow Eagle and Otter Tail would pay for their loose tongues. Two Stars settled against his backrest and folded his hands across the shallow draft of his belly.

"Let no anger steal into your heart. A man's life is empty without magic." Two Stars scratched at his leathery neck; it sounded as if he were raking his fingernails across a stiff, dried-out hide. He started to elaborate, paused, and decided to keep some memories to himself.

"Can a woman be magic?" Jacob asked shyly.

"All women are magic. But there is good medicine and bad medicine. Who do you mean?" Two Stars' seamed features brightened. "Has a girl caught your eye, you-who-were-not-born-of-us-yet-are-one-of-us. Sparrow Woman will be pleased."

"The woman I have seen is not of our village. Nor of any village it seems." Once again, Jacob described the young woman who had eluded him and who took on the aspects of an apparition the more he described her. And when he had finished, Two Stars tilted his head back, his mouth hung open, and the muscles along his throat stood out as if threatening to rip through the skin.

Jacob stared at the old warrior in disbelief, wondering if the man was dying. Instead, Two Stars gave a loud cry. "And the child, *Saaa-vaaa-hey*! Does he live, still?" The blind warrior's bones creaked as he stood and reached out his hand. "Jacob Sun Gift!" Jacob immediately crossed to the old man's side and offered his arm for support. "Take me to your father!"

"But I don't understand," Jacob protested. He had come to Two Stars for advice. The war chief's reaction had come as a complete surprise. And Jacob was uncertain how to react to it. So he did as he was told and brought the old warrior out of

the sepulchral confines of the tepee and into the morning
sunlight.

Calling Dove looked up from the hide she was scraping and
uttered a sharp protest, ordering Jacob to stop and leave her
husband alone. Her worst fear was that Two Stars might die
and leave her to fare alone among this high country band of
Blackfeet.

"Be still, Cut-nose Wife!" Two Stars cruelly snapped.
"While I live it is good to feel the warmth of the sun on my
face."

Calling Dove dutifully returned her attention to the task at
hand but the war chief's rebuke had deeply wounded her.

Old man and young, blind man and sharp-eyed youth,
continued through the village at an old man's pace. There
were children playing and young girls hurrying to the hillsides
to search for succulent wild roots or to bathe in the lake while
the few remaining young men rode out of Medicine Lake
Canyon to patrol the valley and the pass beyond. The lodge
of Two Stars occupied a spot roughly in the center of the
village and Jacob had to follow a winding path among the
lodges as he guided Two Stars toward the lodge of Lone
Walker.

The Blackfeet highly esteemed the war chief at Jacob's
side; man, woman, and child cleared out of Two Stars' way.
A few minutes later Jacob reached his father's lodge. Sparrow
Woman sat outside, her shadow stretched forth on the brightly
painted walls of the tepee as she busily repaired a moccasin
for her husband. She spied her son and Two Stars, ducked her
head inside the tepee, and a few seconds later emerged to
resume her work. Jacob noticed a horse was tethered nearby
and it hadn't been there earlier when he had left his supposedly asleep father to visit Two Stars. When Lone Walker
emerged dressed for the trail, it only confirmed Jacob's
suspicions that the spirit singer knew more than he was letting
on.

Lone Walker was dressed in buckskin shirt and leggings
and carried a heavy capote on his arm, which he draped over
the back of his horse. Sparrow Woman finished her repair and
Lone Walker slipped the calf-high moccasin onto his bare

right foot. He seemed a bit embarrassed that Jacob had discovered him before Lone Walker had slipped away.

"You're leaving, my father?" Jacob said as he brought Two Stars up to the tepee. The blind man turned toward the sound as Lone Walker replied.

"Yes."

"To the backbone of the world?"

"Yes," Lone Walker answered, unable to lie to his son however easy it would make things.

"I'm going with you," Jacob said.

"No!" Lone Walker was emphatic.

"Stop me." Jacob brushed past the spirit singer and entered the tepee. Lone Walker glanced toward his wife, who held up her hands in a gesture of helplessness.

"Do you think it is she?" Two Stars spoke.

"Then Jacob has told you," Lone Walker said, kneeling by the war chief, his counselor and friend.

"I told him." Jacob reappeared with an armful of trail gear. He carried extra powder and shot, a parfleche of jerked meat, a capote, and a cap made from the pelt of a red fox and adorned with an eagle feather and quill beadwork. "Now someone tell *me* what is going on. I saw a girl. I don't know who she is, but I wish to find her. I think she is of our people, but I don't know her name."

"Tewa," Two Stars said softly, sounding frail yet anxious. "The daughter of my daughter. I have not seen her for fifteen summers. Yet what other young woman of our people lives upon the backbone of the world?"

Jacob sat by the old man's side. The white Indian was confused and showed it. He looked beseechingly at his mother, who at last took up his cause.

"Husband, there is great magic here," said Sparrow Woman. "First, buffalo spirit comes to our son. Then the daughter of the wolf. *Saa-vaa,* you must tell him." She blushed as she rose and placed herself between Lone Walker and his mount. She placed a restraining hand upon his arm and he could not avoid the wisdom in her gaze.

Lone Walker turned to the son the Above Ones had given him to raise. See, was there not magic in Jacob Sun Gift as well? Let mystery speak and mystery listen. The spirit singer began his story.

He spoke of a man called Wolf Lance, a Blackfoot brave, a fierce and terrible warrior in battle, a trusted and honored friend to Lone Walker, for they had roamed the hills together as boys and dreamed their dreams of manhood, of great deeds and fine horses.

Boys became men and one day took wives to make homes together, to bear children. Wolf Lance, in love with a girl named Berry, came to the lodge of Two Stars, her father, and brought gifts of buffalo robes and four fine ponies he had stolen from the Kootenai across the divide. And Two Stars, impressed by such gifts, agreed to allow the couple to marry. Great was the happiness among the Medicine Lake band for Wolf Lance and his bride. Time passed and they were blessed with a daughter, Tewa, named for the Earth Mother.

Four years later, on a stormy night in July, the Berries Ripen Moon, Wolf Lance arrived unexpectedly at the lodge of Lone Walker and entered without being invited, trusting in the love of the man who was like a brother to him.

Even after fifteen years, Lone Walker could vividly remember that night, the very last night Wolf Lance had been among his people. The warrior huddled by the fire, and as he warmed himself, steam rose from the wolf-skin cowl covering his head. Lone Walker saw in a single glance that something was terribly wrong with his friend and he crawled out from his blankets, leaving Sparrow Woman's warm body, and sat by his friend near the trembling blaze.

"I must leave, tonight," Wolf Lance said. "The Above Ones have walked in my dreams and shown me such things . . . I must leave tonight and take my wife and child." His dark eyes, reflecting firelight, seemed afire. He hunched forward, bowing his burly shoulders; his big, strong hands opened and closed as if he were limbering himself up for some mighty struggle. "Do not ask me what has happened. Know only that it is for the safety of all your sons that I go. The All-Father has placed a terrible path before me, yet I must obey, for who cannot?"

"I don't understand," Lone Walker said. He looked over at the slumbering form of Young Bull, his son. How could the boy's life ever be in danger from Wolf Lance, whom they all loved as one of their own flesh and blood?

"I pray you never will," Wolf Lance replied. He lowered his voice and continued. "Hear me now. I will take my family up onto the backbone of the world, where the twin horns of the Buffalo Cap rise against the winds, and there we will live and I will build my lodge. Let none learn of my whereabouts. But if I die, then perhaps Berry and Tewa will seek to return to their own kind. They may need your help."

"How will I know?" Lone Walker said, accepting what he had heard but unable to understand fully his friend's predicament. Yet a man must follow his dream. Lone Walker understood this more than most people.

"The magic will tell you it is time to come looking for me." Wolf Lance drew a knife and gouged the tip of his thumb and squeezed a drop of blood into the glowing embers. "I mix my blood with the ashes of your fire, with the dirt of these sacred hills. I am always with you, my friend." Wolf Lance sheathed his knife, the sorrow of departure etched in his features.

"Surely the All-Father would not see you driven from your people," Lone Walker said.

"No. This is of my own doing. I cannot change the will of the Great One, but I can avoid it. I must try." Wolf Lance took a pinchful of earth from the cleared ground that served as an altar and sprinkled the dirt into a medicine pouch he wore around his neck. A moment later, Wolf Lance scrambled out of the tepee, paused illuminated in a flash of lightning, and then vanished in the thunder-filled darkness.

"That was fifteen summers ago," Lone Walker concluded.

"Fifteen summers I have longed to see them. Now it is too late," Two Stars said. "My eyes have grown dim. Yet to hear the laughter of Tewa again and to embrace my daughter, this too is seeing in a way. One day soon the All-Father will call me to his Far Land and I will ride on the spirit wind. Is it wrong for an old man to wish to hold the hands of his children one last time? Bring them home to me, Lone Walker." Two Stars sat cross-legged; he began singing softly, a song, a prayer of homecoming.

"Tewa," Jacob spoke the name aloud, liking the sound of it. The name fit the willful little sprite he had seen.

"I must go alone," Lone Walker said. "If it was the daughter of Wolf Lance, and the buffalo spirit that came to my son, these are powerful signs. The All-Father's magic is at work." Lone Walker stood and though Jacob towered over him, the warrior's bearing was undeniable, his authority almost impossible to resist. "Alone," the brave reiterated.

Almost . . .

"I am going with you," Jacob answered, taking up his rifle. "Now more than ever, I must." He raised a hand to still his father's objections, but Lone Walker moved to block him again.

"Why?" he asked.

"Because I am part of the magic," said Jacob Sun Gift. The prayer of Two Stars drifted quietly between then. "And I am part of the song."

Lone Walker started to reply, hesitated, then fell silent, his heart heavy with apprehension for his adopted son, sensing an urgent need to depart and dreading what might lie ahead. He turned and started toward his horse.

"Father . . ."

And Lone Walker looked around, first at Sparrow Woman, who shared his fears, then at the blind man singing; his gaze settled on the yellow-haired young man standing in the sun.

"Come with me" was all Lone Walker said.

It was enough.

PART IV

Tom Milam's Story

14

"It appears Nate Harveson sure knows how to have a good time," Tom Milam said in an awed tone as he sat astride his horse. His heavy woolen coat protected him from the bite of the cold north wind as he waited for Coyote Kilhenny to give the orders to ride on down to the two-storied red-brick home and carefully tended grounds of Harveson's estate.

In the distance, a mile and a half to the south, flickered the lights of Independence, a beacon to trail-weary trappers returning from the howling wilderness and an enticement to settlers who had never been west of the Mississippi.

A smooth worn dirt road wound northward from the town. This thoroughfare was aptly named the River Road, for it followed the undulating course of the Missouri River. A secondary drive split from the River Road. It made an elongated loop past the sprawling estate that covered a bluff overlooking the wide Missouri. The river cut a great brown swath westward through the rolling landscape.

Independence was a good-size community of store fronts, shops, and homes of wood and brick ringed by a thick profusion of tents, cabins, lean-to shacks, and wagons. An array of brothels and saloons dominated the river's edge, there by the docks where the riverboats were tethered to the shore, preparing to make a final run to the settlements upriver before the waterway froze over, trapping the stern-wheelers on the periphery of some desolate frontier settlement.

"I'm for Gully Town and a hot woman," Skintop Pritchard said. "I ain't dipped my wick in so long, I swear the

first bona fide female I meet is in for some romping.'' The
jenny they were using for a pack animal brayed loud and
long.

Tom rode clear of the mean-tempered beast and indicated
the noisy animal with a wave of his broad-brimmed hat.
''Here you go, Pritch. I'm not one to stand in the way of
true love. If she ain't hot, a man like you will make her
so.''

The jenny brayed again and kicked with her hind hooves.
Pritchard scowled as the rest of the men laughed at his
expense. ''One day you're gonna go too far,'' he muttered,
fixing Tom in a murderous stare.

Tom Milam only smiled and his dark-featured expression
never lost its cool reserve, his deep blue eyes hard as block
ice. ''I'll make a point of it,'' he replied.

Coyote Kilhenny walked his horse forward and placed his
big girth in between the two men before the face-off got out
of hand. He looked from Tom to Pritchard and stroked his
rust-red beard. His voice rumbled deep in his throat as he
spoke.

''Enough.'' Kilhenny pointed his Hawken rifle at the
estate. ''There'll be time for the gals of Gully Town,'' he
added. ''Maybe even ol' Tam here'll find him a filly he can
saddle and ride. 'Course, we might need to help him climb
aboard.''

''And you can go to hell,'' Pike Wallace said, adjusting his
plaid tam atop his gray head. The wind tugged at his eagle
feather. A snow-white stubble dotted his windburned chin. He
patted his rifle and drew himself erect with all the dignity he
could muster. ''I ain't seen the day when I couldn't hold my
own and more with the likes of you boys.''

A stiff north wind tugged at their coats. All of the men save
Tom Milam wore capotes sewn from five-point Hudson Bay
blankets. Tom's slender, wiry form was hidden beneath a
black woolen coat that hung to his ankles. It was as long as a
duster and had a wide collar that he pulled up to protect his
neck. He tilted his broad-brimmed felt hat back on his
forehead and studied Harveson's estate, his gaze as intent as a
hunter's. He counted seven carriages tethered to whitewashed
posts on the drive fronting the house. The windows of the

house were ablaze with light and when the wind stilled, the tinkling music of a piano accompanied by flourishes from a string quartet carried across the rolling meadow to the men on the hill.

"You lads be on your best behavior," Pike Wallace warned. "I hear Harveson's a man to walk cautious around." The old Scot sounded almost fatherly in his reproach.

"If Harveson was interested in good behavior, he wouldn't have sent for me." Coyote Kilhenny grinned at the men around him. Tom Milam nodded in accord with the man who had become like a father. Kilhenny touched his heels to his horse and the animal obediently started forward.

"Say, about this Harveson," Tom spoke up, appreciation in his voice as he returned his attention to the spacious-looking two-storied home, the groomed gardens, and freshly painted carriage house, stables, and corral that made up the Harveson estate. "I don't suppose he has a young pretty daughter."

"No, but he has a young pretty sister," Kilhenny chuckled. "Though she might as well be his daughter. I've heard there's more'n one hound been chased off with a load of buckshot in the tail end." Kilhenny scratched underneath his fur cap. He dug his fingernails into his shaggy red mane and worked over his entire scalp. Then he cradled his rifle in the crook of his left arm as young Tom rode up alongside.

"Danger's like salt. It only makes the meat taste better." Tom flashed a row of white teeth in a broad, reckless grin; his eyes twinkled and he looked confident enough to dare the devil himself.

Coyote Kilhenny wagged his head in dismay. There was no point in arguing with the lad. He was incorrigible.

"You better rein it in," Skintop Pritchard cautioned, riding behind Tom. Pritchard tugged at the earring dangling from his right ear and scowled as his gaze bore into the back of the younger man's head. "You got us chased out of Santa Fe. Don't close Independence for us too." Pritchard glanced aside at Pike Wallace as if seeking the old one's support. Pike shrugged. He had no wish to be dragged into the argument.

"It's a free country," Tom said, without glancing back. "And I'll graze any pasture that I please."

"You mark my words, one day you'll go too far," Pritchard warned.

"That'll be the day you're left behind to eat my dust," With that Tom whipped his horse to a gallop and charged down the drive.

"Who do you think he is?" Abigail Harveson wondered aloud as she sat with her legs drawn up and her arms wrapped around her knees. She was a winsome-looking nineteen-year-old with pale ivory skin and dark brown hair braided back from her features and caught in a cluster of thick ringlets. Her eyes were green like a forest at dusk, dark and unrevealing. In truth, Abigail was of an unpredictable nature. She stretched and yawned and the earth-tone flourishes of her silk bodice strained to contain her ample bosom. The browns and tans and russet ribbons of her dress flowed from a narrow waist over rounded hips. She watched as the horseman in black rode across her reflection in the window. Her breath fogged the glass pane; the tip of her pink tongue moistened her lips. She shivered, and blamed it on the dampness creeping into the room as the fire died in the fireplace. It had been a boring day up until now. But these rough-dressed characters on the hill had possibilities.

She left the window, walked across the bedroom, and continued on into the dimly lit hall. She noticed Virginia, the household servant, standing at the top of the staircase. The reed-thin young woman seemed transfixed by the music drifting up from the solarium at the rear of the house. Her slim ebony hands were folded on her white lace apron, fingers tapping to the rhythm. Abigail walked up alongside the maid and cleared her throat. Virginia, all of fifteen years, jumped and stepped back in deference to the woman at her side. Virginia had only been with the Harvesons for a week and wanted to make a good impression. "Excuse me, Miss Abigail, I didn't see you. I was just . . . uh . . . just—"

"Listening to the music," Abigail finished, amused. "My brother is a man of many talents."

"Yes, ma'am. I sure like to hear them play." The servant was conscious of her mistress' presence and felt uncomfortable. "I better be tending things." Houseguests meant plenty

of work for Virginia and it wouldn't do for her to get too far
behind. There was no room in particular that she wanted to be
finished with before the music stopped. She turned to head
down the hall. Abigail stopped her.

"Virginia, . . ."

"Yes, ma'am," the girl answered, her tone worried and
body tense as she faced Abigail.

"I don't bite," Abigail said and smiled. "You know . . . you're
free. Like your uncle Hiram is a free man. And nothing is
ever going to change that. I like to think we are a family
here. We have our different jobs, our different roles in
life . . . but we care about each other. Like a family. Do you
understand, my dear?"

Virginia wasn't sure she did, but the woman's warmth was
infectious. "Yes, ma'am . . ." She backed away a step. "May
I see to things?"

"Certainly." Abigail watched the servant hurry down the
hall and wondered if poor Virginia would ever relax. Abigail
didn't think of herself as a witch. Of course Nate could be
most trying at times. He was an ambitious, driven man given
to quick-tempered flare-ups. Abigail, his one weakness, loved
to bait her brother, just to watch him bluster and fume.

A mischievous expression lit Abigail's pretty features.
Though it was Hiram's duty to show guests into the house,
today Abigail intended to replace Nate Harveson's trusted
manservant. The young woman had the distinct impression
that the men she had seen heading toward the Harveson estate
would be far more interesting than her brother's stuffy,
well-to-do friends. Now what would happen if the two parties
should meet?

Abigail couldn't wait to find out.

Tom Milam leapt down from his horse and tethered the
animal to a ring post by the carriages and sauntered up a flat
stone walk to the front door of the estate. He knew Coyote
wanted to lead the way. So Tom glanced over his shoulder at
the three men he had left behind and slammed the brass door
knocker. He tilted his broad-brimmed hat back and let it hang
behind his head by the leather string. He stood with his
thumbs crooked in his belt. The wind tugged at his long coat.

A black scarf trailed from around his neck like some piratical banner in the breeze.

The door swung open. And he saw Abigail Harveson. She was as fine a looking young woman as he had ever encountered. She had all the bearing of a real lady, someone to be watched from afar and never approached. Skin like rare china, lips like cherry wine, a hint of daring in her expression—all this at first glance, he thought he'd take a second.

Behind him, Coyote Kilhenny, Skintop Pritchard, and old Pike Wallace dismounted and left their mounts by the carriages and marched toward the house. They looked anxious to be out of the north wind, Abigail thought. She quickly appraised the young man in the doorway. Black hair, dark blue eyes, a white ridge of scar tissue scrawled on his cheek, he was slim, catlike in his stance; a brace of pistols and a knife jutted from his belt. "You don't look like you play Mozart," Abigail said.

"Why I cut my teeth on him." Tom grinned. "I'm not particular. I'll play with anyone." He touched the brim of his hat. "My name is Tom Milam."

Abigail laughed and stepped aside to allow Tom to enter the foyer. "Bold talk."

"Actions speak louder than words. Want to learn for yourself?"

"Miss Abigail!" A black servant stepped out of the formal sitting room and hurried to the foyer. His hair was snowy white; his features kind and homely. At sixty years old he held himself erect and his broad shoulders belied his advanced years. He was dressed in a brown frock coat and woolen trousers, shiny leather boots and a white coarsely woven shirt buttoned to the throat. A black sash circled his waist.

"See here, Miss Abigail, you aren't to be opening the door to just anyone."

"I'm not just anyone," Tom Milam retorted, turning on the servant who towered over him. Size meant nothing to Tom. "I'm part curly wolf, part grizz'. I move like a panther and got the humor of a snapping turtle."

"My heaven, a whole menagerie," Abigail commented.

"Yes, ma'am," Tom said, turning back to the girl. "Common

decency prevents me from explaining how I take after a buffalo bull.''

Abigail blushed.

"See here," Hiram said, stepping toward the young man. Suddenly, three other heavily armed men crowded through the door. Coyote Kilhenny placed his massive frame between the servant and Tom.

Hiram started to protest anew until Coyote placed Harveson's letter in the black man's hand.

"Where's Harveson?" Kilhenny brusquely asked. He placed his rifle stock on the floor and leaned on the barrel, his arms folded and gaze intent as he noted the wealth of paintings and furnishings in the handsomely appointed rooms beyond.

"In the solarium, sir. Mr. Harveson is performing. If you'll wait in the sitting room, I'll announce you at the first opportunity." Hiram indicated a room to his right with a sweep of his hand.

"We didn't ride all the way from Santa Fe just to wait," Kilhenny exclaimed as he shouldered past Hiram. Pike Wallace fell in step, as did Skintop Pritchard, although not before feasting his eyes on Abigail, who shifted uncomfortably beneath his hungry stare.

Hiram started to follow the three men. He did not like to be treated with such casual disregard. Tom's voice cracked like a whip.

"Don't," Tom said. "They're hard men. You don't want Kilhenny's kind of trouble. And as the letter said, we're expected."

Hiram swung about, hesitated, then glanced at Abigail.

"Hiram, why don't you see to dinner. I'll show Mr. Milam to the sun room." Abigail's little play was getting out of hand. The last thing she wanted was to see the Harveson's family retainer injured in any way.

"Yes, ma'am." Hiram started down the long hall that ran past the stairs and led to the kitchen at the rear of the house.

Abigail and Tom were alone again.

"Aren't you going to offer me your arm, Mr. Milam?"

Tom reached out and snared her; his right arm circled her waist and he pulled her to him. His lips covered hers in a sudden kiss. Then Tom released her. As Abigail staggered back, she slapped him across the face.

"A fair trade." Tom grinned, his cheek reddening from the force of her blow. He bowed and held out his arm, feigning the role of a perfect gentleman.

Abigail, by now thoroughly confused, didn't know whether she wanted to slap him again or walk with him.

Ed Piller and Richard Crane, a banker and a physician from Kansas City, dropped their bows and violin and viola and gaped at the new arrivals. Their wives muttered beneath their breath and clutched silk kerchiefs to their respective noses. Captain Palmer, a riverboat pilot, paused at his cello, looked up in surprise, and growled, "What the devil?" Con Vogel, a muscular man in his middle twenties, set his violin aside and stood. His chair slid back and toppled over and alerted Nate Harveson, who was hunched over the piano keys. He looked up, awareness slowly dawning.

Harveson was a diminutive man with slender limbs sprouting from a round, thick body. His silver hair was combed forward to mask a receding hairline. A prominent Roman nose thrust over a salt and pepper moustache. When he noticed the men crowding the entrance to the solarium, he rose from the piano seat, leaned forward on the piano, and in a cold voice said, "Gentlemen, there had better be an excellent reason for this interruption."

Kilhenny stalked into the room. Sunlight streamed through surrounding windows but cast precious little warmth. The musicians were arranged in a semicircle. Another four straight-backed chairs accommodated Eva Piller, Leticia Crane, Parson Goodwith, and his wife, Charity, who scooted aside as Kilhenny entered the room and made his way through their midst. Skintop Pritchard winked at the parson's young, pretty wife. She immediately blushed and lowered her gaze. The parson glanced at Pritchard, who seemed to dare Goodwith to take offense. The parson coughed nervously and averted his gaze.

Abigail, arm in arm with Tom Milam, appeared in the doorway. Nate saw her and frowned at his sister's unladylike familiarity with the dark young stranger. However, Leticia

Crane and Eva Piller smugly nodded to each other as if some hidden suspicion had at last been confirmed.

"You sent for me," Kilhenny said. His broad frame hid Nate Harveson from the men in the back of the room.

Tom Milam wondered how such an unprepossessing little man could wield such power. Of course, money had something to do with it. But there had to be more to the man than the size of his bank balance. Tom resolved the man bore watching. As did his sister.

"I'm Kilhenny," the half-breed repeated. "I pulled up stakes in Santa Fe for this scrap of paper and don't figure on being kept waiting."

For a moment no one said anything, as if audience and musicians were waiting for Nate Harveson to explode in wrath and fury and order these intruders off his premises. The man's temper was legendary. However, what happened next surprised and even startled those refined guests gathered in the solarium.

Nate Harveson burst out laughing. He threw his head back and laughed aloud with such force he had to support himself on the piano. His fellow musicians continued to stare as if the director of their ensemble had lost his mind.

"Kilhenny . . . yes, of course. You would be him," Harveson finally said in a silken tone. "You are everything I expected. Yes, I can tell at a glance. You'll do. Yes, you'll do very well."

"I'll do what?" Kilhenny asked. He wasn't used to invoking such amusement in people. Fear, yes, but laughter?

"Well, for now, you can spend some of my money," Nate Harveson said. "Ride on to Independence and put up at the River Wheel Hotel. Your rooms are paid for and so's anything you can eat, drink, or bed. Breakfast with me tomorrow morning, here at my house. Say, around ten. We'll talk then." He clapped Kilhenny on the shoulder and waited to see if he had satisfied the renegade. Kilhenny shrugged and ran his fingers through his red beard.

"Tomorrow," he said and, turning, motioned for Pike Wallace and Skintop Pritchard to leave the room. His fierce-looking cohorts did as they were told, much to the relief of the tamer souls gathered in the sunlit room.

Tom started to follow the others, but the pressure of Abigail's hand on his arm held him in place more securely than a chain. She led him to a nearby chair.

"I've invited Mr. Milam to stay awhile. He is an aficionado of good music," Abigail said. "So I have offered him the hospitality of the afternoon." The coquettish smile brightened her features as she sat beside the dark-haired plainsman.

Tom didn't know what the girl was up to, but she was pretty enough to want to make him hang around and find out. The displeasure on Nate Harveson's face was matched by Con Vogel's hard, angry glare. It appeared the brawny-looking German considered Abigail Harveson his territory and Tom Milam a possible trespasser.

So Tom Milam shucked off his coat and hat and nodded deferentially to the musicians. He glanced at Kilhenny looming in the doorway.

"I'll be along," he said.

Kilhenny frowned. He considered insisting that Tom join him. He reconsidered then, thinking it might not be a bad idea for one of his own to hang around. "Keep watch," he muttered in Shoshoni.

Tom, with a sideways look toward Abigail, resolved to do just that.

Nate Harveson was not about to embarrass himself by creating a scene. His sister was as stubborn as himself. Resolved to the situation, he motioned for his fellow musicians to return to their music. Vogel was the last to do so. He grabbed his violin and snapped it to his shoulder, his fingers clasping the neck of the instrument in a stranglehold.

"We will begin at the pianissimo on page two," Harveson directed.

His fingers touched the keys. He tried to concentrate on the music, but his mind was already miles away, fixed on a plan that would not only make him rich but win him power and a mountain empire. Nate Harveson began to play, and though his mind was on the great plan about to unfold, his fingers upon the keys did not make a single mistake.

Tom Milam sipped French champagne and dined on goose liver pâté and found both to his taste. Perhaps it was the quality of the food and drink, perhaps it was the elegance in which it was served. I could grow to like this, Tom thought. But not the tiresome company.

"The renovations on the church are almost complete," Parson Goodwith was saying. "But the salvation of Independence, ah, now there's another matter." The parson, a tall, spare man with thinning hair and a fair complexion, leaned forward; his Adam's apple bobbed as he swallowed. "Tell me, my son, have you been saved?"

"Sure," Tom grinned. "More times than I can count. By these." Milam pulled aside the flaps of his coat and patted the brace of revolvers thrust in his belt. "Save your lectures, Parson. I'm hell bound and thunder wild. The sermon I hear is the roar of my Hawken and I carry the cutting edge of truth in the top of my boot." His hand swept down to his right leg and drew a razor-sharp throwing knife from a scabbard sewn inside his right boot. Lamplight glittered off the blade. Charity Goodwith, standing close by her husband, gasped and covered her mouth. Her cheeks grew red as her hair.

Tom glanced around and noticed he had become the object of everyone's attention. He shrugged and sheathed the blade. Abigail Harveson crossed the room toward him. Con Vogel, a big strapping young man, stayed close at hand, shadowing Abigail, hovering protectively as if guarding a possession. She sipped brandy from a short-stemmed tulip-shaped snifter. The glass looked terribly fragile in marked contrast to the woman who held it. In her green eyes was strength.

"You are too quick to free your blade, Mr. Milam," Abigail said playfully. "You'll frighten the ladies."

"I'm too quick to sheathe it, or so I've been told," Tom replied. He started toward Abigail, but Con Vogel stepped between them, a broad grin lighting his clean-shaven features.

"They say the best knives and swords are made of German steel." Vogel looked down at Tom and flexed his beefy shoulders beneath his burgundy frock coat. He turned and raised his wineglass in salute to Abigail. *"Zum wohl!"*

"Out where the wolves howl, a knife or gun is only as good as the man who uses it," Tom replied.

It was plain to Tom that Con Vogel had no intention of leaving Abigail alone with him. He didn't like backing away from the German. On the other hand, Coyote had cautioned him about getting into trouble at least on his first day in Independence.

"How good are you, my friend?" Vogel challenged.

"Good enough." Tom glanced past Vogel and met Nate Harveson's frank gaze. Harveson was close enough to hear the exchange and realizing he had been caught in the act of eavesdropping, stepped away from the fawning courtesies of Eva Piller and Leticia Crane. The parson quickly took his place. As for the banker and the physician from Kansas City, the two men watched from a distance, equally intrigued by the young plainsman.

"Well, Mr. Milam here seems most confident of his abilities," Harveson said in a silken voice. He took pride in his ability to judge others.

"A man has to be," Tom dryly observed. "Else he never does anything in this world. I figure you'd know that more than most, Mr. Harveson."

Nate Harveson chuckled, warming toward the dark, slender plainsman despite his obvious interest in Abigail. "Well said." Harveson stroked his chin and though a moment. "Now Con here is a known quantity. He is an accomplished marksman. But as for you, sir . . ."

"Perhaps a demonstration would be in order," Vogel suggested. His expression smug, he bowed toward Harveson. "With your permission. What do you say, my friend? Perhaps we might even wager—but what do you have . . . pelts . . . scalps . . . what?"

Tom felt his temper rising and suppressed it. He shook his head. "I'll take my leave, Mr. Harveson. It's been a long, hard ride."

Nate Harveson looked perplexed. He had expected Tom Milam to jump at the chance to prove his worth.

"But what of our exhibition?" Vogel interjected.

"I'm not one of your 'musicians,'" Tom said, addressing Harveson, and then turning to the German, added, "I don't perform on cue."

Abigail laughed and quickly bit her lower lip as Con Vogel burned, his cheeks crimson down to the neck. Before he could manage an adequate reply, Tom brushed past him, kissed Abigail's hand, nodded to Nate Harveson, and walked out of the solarium.

"Perhaps I should show him out," Abigail suggested, taking a step forward.

"He can find his own way, dear sister," Harveson said, tight lipped, his voice stopping Abigail in her tracks.

"Yes," she sighed. "I suspect he can."

15

The dog waited in the middle of the street, holding a severed human hand in its mouth. The mongrel eyed Tom Milam as he paused on the outskirts of "Gully Town," that riverfront section of Independence where vice and lawlessness was a way of life. And a way of death too, Tom speculated, noticing the dog and its grisly snack. Up ahead on Tom's left was a motley array of hotels, warehouses, saloons, and bordellos. On his right was the riverbank with its piers and loading docks piled high with goods to be transported upriver and down, pyramids of crates and boxes to be loaded onto freight wagons bound for Santa Fe.

After a minute, the dog lost interest in the man in the street and with its tail wagging trotted back down the alley from which it had come. Tom made a mental note to avoid that particular section of the riverfront. The River Wheel Hotel was a couple of blocks ahead and Tom headed straight for it. The wind blew cold here by the river and he was anxious to stretch out near a fire.

The street became crowded the further he ventured into the riverfront district. Four stern-wheelers were tethered to the docks by heavy-looking lines of braided hemp rope. Black men and white scurried over the boxes and crates, shouldering their loads and filing back and forth from the docks to the boats. Along the wooden walkway and street was a seemingly neverending procession of outfitters, half-wild trappers, bewildered settlers, bullwhackers, painted ladies, gamblers, and riverboatmen. Gully Town was no place for a timid soul. The fainthearted kept to the more civilized sections of Independence where shops and offices and homes both simple and more ostentatious endured their close proximity to the river district.

It was an unwritten rule that the rabble-rousers Gully Town attracted keep to the riverfront and avoid the more genteel sections of town. And for the most part, the riverfront's populace policed themselves. The law—in this instance, a constable and three deputies—maintained a stern vigilance but refrained from extending their authority into the heart of the sinful district.

Tom reached the River Wheel Hotel in a matter of minutes. The noise from inside the adjoining saloon filtered through the walls. Suddenly the door to the saloon crashed open and two men landed on the boardwalk. One was a buckskin-clad trapper; the other, a coarsely dressed riverboat man. Tom could see they were evenly matched as they staggered to their feet. Music and laughter and obscene encouragements poured through the open door. The trapper slugged the riverboat man and was in turn rocked on his heels by the boatman's vicious uppercut. The combatants continued to hammer each other, standing toe to toe and trading blows until a round-hipped, amply endowed whore stepped out of the doorway and in between the men. Despite the cold, she pulled down the already low-cut bodice of her blue satin dress and cupped her ponderous breasts.

"See here, boys, I'm woman enough for the two of you." She laughed. The trapper wiped the blood from his mouth and gashed cheek. The riverboat man stared at the whore, his eyes puffed and bruised looking. The two men shrugged. The whore held her arms out to them and enfolded the former enemies into her embrace. They carried her inside, and presumably up to bed, amid a chorus of cheers.

"My kind of place," Tom chuckled. He dismounted and called to a young black boy standing nearby.

"How old are you, lad?"

"Ah'm all of nine, suh," the ragtag child explained. "But Ah'm pow'ful willin' for my size."

"Is there a stable round back of this hotel?"

"Yessuh. Mah pappy works therebouts; he keeps things a'right."

"My name is Tom Milam. Now take my horse and tell your pa to see he gets currycombed and maybe a bait of oats. Here's a dollar for your trouble."

"Yessuh!" the boy exclaimed. He took the reins and led the animal away as Tom climbed the steps to the walkway. He paused outside the saloon, just for a moment, and listened to the clamor of sin and celebration—sweet music to his ears.

He hurried inside.

Lantern light and smoke clinging to the rafters obscured the roof beams and the ceiling overhead. The saloon adjoining the hotel was a wide, spacious room crowded with tables and high-back chairs and dominated at the far end by a long walnut bar that spanned almost the entire width of the room. Three overworked and sweat-streaked bartenders served hard liquor and applejack to a score of trappers and mountain men. The scene was bedlam. It was like a rendezvous, where men drank too much, regaled themselves with lies, chased every available woman, and spent themselves in quarrels, tall tales, cheap liquor, and fistfights. Eventually a man could take no more and collapsed unconscious in the nearest available corner. Floor space was at a premium.

Tom picked his way toward the center of the room where Coyote Kilhenny held court. The half-breed sat at a table with half a dozen hard-looking men, all dressed in buckskins, all marked by the howling wilderness in some way, be it a look or a scar or a manner of speech. They were men with the bark on, like Kilhenny . . . and like Tom Milam.

"Ha—Tom!" Kilhenny called out, seeing the wiry, dark youth approach. "Back so soon from the civilizin' influence of Nate Harveson?"

"I wouldn't mind bein' influenced by Miss Abigail," one of the men at the table, Iron Mike, muttered. He was a squat, surly-looking man with thinning hair and a stubbled jaw. The backs of his hands were matted with black hair. He was coarse and when drunk showed a mean streak that made him a dangerous man to be around. But he was a crack shot and on the trail seemed virtually indestructible, a good man to side with in a fight.

"The reverend tried to show me the error of my ways, so I

figured it was time to leave." Tom grabbed a jug of hard cider from the table and tilted it to his lips and drank long and deep. He set it down and wiped a forearm across his mouth. It was a far cry from Harveson's champagne, and the River Wheel was a good deal more rustic than Harveson's fine estate, but Tom felt at home in both worlds.

"Just so long as you didn't wear out our welcome," Kilhenny added.

"Ain't none of our kind welcome up on Harveson's hill," said Spence Mitchell, another trapper. Tobacco juice mottled his white beard. His long, bony fingers were curled around a tankard of rum. "Harveson sent for the lot of us. Put us up here and payin' our way, so I don't like to be complainin'. But damn my eyes, I don't like to be treated like some snake in the buffaler grass."

"We're good as Nate Harveson any day in the week," Iron Mike grumbled.

"Now don't you worry, lads." Kilhenny stroked his red beard. "You'll be the first to know what's going on. Just as soon as I take breakfast with my good friend Nate Harveson."

The men around him scowled. They were jealous of Kilhenny's access to the wealthy trader, but the half-breed had proved himself a capable leader in the past and they were willing, if need be, to follow him again.

One of the bartenders emerged from the back kitchen with a platter piled high with buffalo steaks and squaw bread. Tom joined the throng headed for the bar. The mouth-watering aroma of fried meat permeated the air. Tom helped himself to a couple of steaks and a fist-sized chunk of fry bread, sat with his back to the wall, and drawing his knife, used it for both a knife and fork.

A narrow-waisted woman of thirty-one stepped through the doors separating the hotel lobby from the saloon. She wore a black and gray taffeta dress with a fringe of yellow-white lace at the bodice, wrists, and circling her boyish hips. Her face was thickly powdered and wore a heavy coat of rouge. Tom recognized her at a glance. Junie Routh had run bordellos from St. Louis to Santa Fe.

She entered the saloon and nodded to one of her girls who was busily cajoling Skintop Pritchard into risking his last dollar at the faro table. Sweat beaded Pritchard's brow as he gambled and lost, playing the odds as recklessly as he lived his life. Junie Routh glanced aside, spied Tom hunched over his plate, gave a cry, and headed straight for him.

"Tom Milam, you've been here long enough to grab some vittles and you ain't even given your Aunt Junie a kiss."

Tom stood, a sheepish smile on his face, as the woman wrapped her arms around him and kissed him on the mouth. She pressed against him. Her hand darted down, searching for his groin. Tom maneuvered in such a way that she grabbed a fistful of buffalo steak instead.

"Aaah!" she scowled and dropped the meat, then feigning displeasure, proceeded to lick the grease from each finger. "You always were a fresh boy."

"It's part of my charm."

"Come upstairs and I'll show you charm," Junie Routh invited, her eyebrows arched, her voice thick with sensuality. "Or has that rich little Harveson bitch ruined you for a real woman?" Junie saw she had caught Tom off guard. "Pike Wallace and I split a bottle upstairs. He told me you stayed behind up on Harveson Hill."

"Why, Aunt Junie, I do believe you're jealous," Tom said.

"They ain't your kind of people is all." She ran her fingers along his neck, discovered the chain, and tugged. The coiled snake ring dangled free from his shirt. "You need to keep with family, honey."

Tom's hand snapped up and caught her wrist. "My family's dead," he said, his bloodless features and venomous tone made her draw back in alarm, as if the antique gold serpent had sprung alive, tail rattling, its deadly fangs bared.

A few seconds passed before Tom relaxed and the hardness left his gaze. He shrugged, made a sandwich of his buffalo steak and bread, and set the plate aside. He stepped up to Junie Routh, patted her derriere, and headed for the double doors leading from the saloon to the hotel lobby.

As he walked away, the ring Jacob had given him bobbed against his chest, hammering his heart with every step.

16

Nate Harveson wiped the biscuit crumbs from his moustache and stood. "I have a map in the study. We can talk there."

Coyote Kilhenny shrugged and shoveled the last bite of egg into his mouth. A big hand surrounded his coffee cup and he poured the steaming contents down his gullet. He slapped the cup back on the tabletop, belched, and nodded in satisfaction.

"Your darky can cook for me any day," Kilhenny announced.

"I'll inform Thalia of that," Abigail said from the end of the table opposite her brother

"You do that, missy," Kilhenny replied. It was too early in the morning for him to extract any derision from the woman's remark.

"Eggs are a rarity west of Santa Fe." Tom sopped up the last of the yolk with a morsel of biscuit. "I can't remember when I last had them. These biscuits are fitting as well."

"I made those," Abigail replied, quite pleased. She wore a simple cotton dress buttoned to the neck. Flour smudged one pale blue sleeve. "I used buttermilk in the batter."

"Old Pike Wallace cooks for us," Tom said with a smile. "I swear his biscuits could pass for adobe. You could wall up a jacal with them. Worse is his pie. The filling's not so bad, but the crust is so tough it would take the hide off a mule."

"I'm pleased you find my efforts . . . uh . . . fitting," Abigail replied. She lowered her head and looked up at Tom with a soft doelike gaze. He knew she was playing with him and didn't care.

Nate Harveson loudly cleared his throat, attracting his

sister's attention. "I haven't brought these gentlemen here to discuss the merits of our kitchen." He gestured toward the hall. A black woman hurried in from the winter kitchen and began clearing the table as Harveson strode out of the room and headed up the hall. Two rooms dominated the front of the house, a formal parlor on the west corner and Nate Harveson's personal study on the east side, across the spacious foyer. Harveson led Tom and Coyote Kilhenny into his book-lined study.

Tom hungrily eyed the leather-bound tomes while Coyote Kilhenny openly admired the back wall that was hidden behind muskets and banners and displayed a handsome British uniform, all derived from the battlefields of the War for Independence. A portrait centered among the memorabilia.

"My grandfather," Nate Harveson announced. "That uniform belonged to a British officer grandpa captured at Yorktown. Papaw sent him home to England wearing nothing but a smock." Harveson chuckled as he took his place behind his desk. He noticed what held Tom's attention. "Do you read?"

Tom nodded. "There aren't many books out on the prairie, though."

"I had not thought of you as a man of education."

"I'm a lot of things."

"Indeed. Well then, come here and tell me if you can read this map." Harveson stood back and gestured toward a scroll he unrolled across his desk. Abigail entered carrying a pot of coffee and enough cups for everyone in the room. She placed the tray on a serving table near the door and took a seat.

Kilhenny noticed her and scowled. "We're fixin' to talk, missy."

"Good. Then I haven't missed anything." Abigail smoothed her dress and folded her slim white hands in her lap.

"Where I come from a woman—"

"We are not where you come from," Abigail retorted. "Thank the good Lord."

"Mr. Kilhenny . . . please," Nate Harveson soothingly interjected. He waved the plainsman over to the desk. The trader weighted down the corner of the map as Kilhenny approached.

Tom stared down at the territory outlined on the weathered

paper. He recognized the location of Santa Fe and the various rivers and Indian territories plotted out from New Mexico to the Canadian border. Kilhenny's shadow fell across the map.

Nate Harveson placed the sharpened tip of a dagger on Independence. He then traced a path that followed the Missouri River north and west, through the country of the Dakotas, Cheyenne, Assiniboin. He branched off the Missouri and onto the Marias where he continued to mark his passage through the foothills of the norther Rockies. He stabbed down into the page, burying the tip of the blade into the desk top.

"I intend to take three riverboats loaded with men, materials, and provisions and build an outpost here at the foot of the mountains. I am told the area is teeming with beaver, otter, and a variety of other pelts."

"Sure," Kilhenny grinned. "That's 'cause it ain't been trapped yet. The Blackfeet have a habit of lifting the scalp off any dumb fool who rides into the High Lonesome. You'd need a small army to pull that off."

"I have an army... almost a hundred men, signed on and ready to go at the first thaw," Harveson said. "But I need someone to lead them. Money talks well enough, but there are times brute toughness is the more efficient method of control." Nate Harveson hooked his thumbs in his waistcoat pocket. He strutted around the desk to the window, stared out at the cold sky, then turned his rump toward the cast-iron stove that he used to heat the room. "These men are a tough, hard, unruly lot. It will take someone tougher, harder, more unruly to lead them."

"Like me." Kilhenny stroked his beard and chuckled aloud. "The market's gone and peaked; there ain't no telling how long she'll hold. Enough men could trap them mountains dry in a season and be out before the snow flies."

"Finish, yes," Harveson said. "But be out? No. What I build will remain. I will remain." Harveson returned to the desk and indicated the established states on the map. "What do you see, gentlemen, what do you see?" Harveson swept his hand from right to left, from the Atlantic to the western boundaries of the Louisiana Purchase. "Just look at it, man.

A country, a nation, spreading out and claiming for its own. Wilderness becomes a territory.''

"And a territory becomes a state," Tom observed, his interest aroused. It was obvious Nate Harveson was after more than pelts in this venture.

"Exactly," Harveson said, excitement in his voice. "And if a man places himself in the right place at the right time, there is no telling how much he could accomplish." Harveson's eyes took on a misty quality; his expression grew distant as if he were fixed on some far-off goal and could see it shimmering through a clouded future. "Do you know what a territorial governor is?" Harveson's eyes widened with glee. "He's king of his own personal kingdom. The possibilities are enormous, I assure you, gentlemen."

Kilhenny stared at the map. He scratched at his beard; his breath rumbled in his throat.

"Your money . . . my muscle . . ." Kilhenny said.

"A partnership of sorts. I would be willing to stipend your services and provide you with, say, ten percent of any realized profits." Harveson rubbed his hands together in anticipation.

"Forty percent," Kilhenny replied.

"You must be kidding?" Nate Harveson blurted out. Kilhenny raised his shaggy head and glowered at Harveson like a bull about to charge. "Uh . . . I could see to fifteen . . . uh, maybe twenty percent."

"Thirty percent," Tom interjected. Kilhenny glanced at him in surprise. He frowned. It didn't sit well that Tom had taken the initiative.

"That's a damn high price."

"We're worth it," Tom said. "It doesn't seem that much to pay for a 'kingdom.' ''

Harveson had to laugh. He looked at Abigail. "He has me there, sister."

Abigail nodded and for the first time entered the conversation. When she spoke, it was with a sense of conviction and authority that belied her nineteen years.

"The initial investment is ours. Mr. Milam. And it is a substantial one. I propose we limit your share to twenty percent of the profits realized from the fur trade." Abigail stood and crossed to the desk. Tom backed out of her way.

"After the Harveson Company is established, we can increase your percentage over a period of time until it reaches thirty percent. By then, we should have a bustling settlement. There is every indication that there are substantial mineral deposits in the mountains west of us. My brother and I are hopeful that the company will be developing them as well."

"I ain't never heard a woman talk so much," Kilhenny said. But she made sense. There had always been talk of gold up in the Marias. Trouble was, the Blackfeet killed anyone who went looking. But a hundred well-armed men ought to chase the bastards clean into Canada. "I reckon we have a deal, Harveson," the half-breed said, holding out a beefy hand to Nate Harveson. "I'll keep the lads in line and personally handpick all the rest that'll be marchin' with us. Everyone'll be part grizz', I guarantee."

"Just so long as they know who they work for," Harveson said.

"Oh, they'll know," Kilhenny said. His windburned features split in a good-natured grin that to the wary held as much warmth as a coiled rattler.

"One thing more," Abigail said, folding her arms across her bosom. "I'll be going with you."

Tom felt a rush of excitement. He liked the idea. He'd have Abigail Harveson practically to himself for heaven only knew how long. It was a measure of his ego and his confidence that he completely disregarded the other "hundred" men who would make up the expedition.

Kilhenny glanced disapprovingly at the young woman. She did not wither before his hard stare.

"I have long since given up trying to influence Abigail's decisions," Harveson said, standing by his sister. He held her hand and patted it. "Half the investment is hers, after all."

Kilhenny abruptly shrugged. "Suit yourself."

Abigail shifted her gaze to Tom. "I always do," she said.

Con Vogel watched the plainsmen ride away at mid-morning. He had purposefully remained in the guest bedroom throughout breakfast. He'd had Virginia bring him coffee and a platter of biscuits, which he had wolfed down without tasting. He hit the hall angry but had himself under control by the time he reached the foyer at the bottom of the stairway.

Nate Harveson was still in the study. A cold breeze flowed past the open front door as Abigail stood in the doorway, watching the horsemen vanish down the drive. She turned, closed the door, and read the mood behind her suitor's forced smile.

"There's coffee in the study. Nate's in there too," she said and started down the hall on her way to the solarium. Vogel hesitated, looked at the study, glanced back toward the hall, and allowed his emotions to guide him.

He reached the solarium and found himself in the streaming sunlight. Through the unshuttered windows he saw Abigail, bundled in a cloak of forest green, emerge from the rear of the house and head down a winding cobblestone path.

"Damn," Vogel muttered and then, undaunted, went looking for a coat.

Abigail followed the walk past the outdoor kitchen the Harveson servants used in the warm months of spring and summer. The path curved around the stables and the small but tidy-looking houses of the servants set off east of the corral and then continued to the river, where the walkway climbed the bluffs to a gazebo, round and walled on two sides with an intricate latticework that served both as a beautiful embellishment and a windbreak. The conical roof was topped by an iron weather vane, a black metal fish, that turned lazily into the wind.

Inside, a bench seat bordered the two walls and in the center of the space a wood-burning stove insured the warmth and comfort of any occupant. But Abigail didn't need a fire. She liked the cold. It helped her think.

She stared down at the broad brown swath of river flowing past her vantage point a couple of hundred feet above its silty surface.

Father was dead, mother had abandoned her adopted country and returned to the civilities of her ancestral home in Northumberland, England. The Harveson fortune belonged to her and her brother equally. She could simply withdraw her financial support, and his plans and dreams would collapse in a matter of days. Yet Abigail knew she wouldn't. Living in

Independence, she had been witness to the trickle of visionaries bound for the unexplored reaches of the west. She had heard the stories of trappers, and mountain men. She had listened to their dreams and felt a longing to see for herself this "howling wilderness."

What others mistook for willfulness and irreverence was in part the struggle of the pioneer spirit burning in her breast. She envied the likes of Tom Milam. She wanted to see what he had seen and more. Her comfortable, safe existence was proving tiresome. Nate was right, why not risk it all when greater wealth and more awaited them both, the stuff that dreams were made of if only they had the courage to dare.

The notion of traveling in the company of handsome young Tom Milam intrigued her as well, she honestly admitted. It was easy to be honest in this private place. She looked out across the river and sighed, enjoying her privacy. The crunch of boots on the path alerted her. She turned and with sinking spirits realized her solitude was at an end.

Con Vogel stood in the doorway of the gazebo. A fur cap and the turned-up collar of his knee-length wool coat partly obscured his square-jawed features.

The musician cleared his throat as if to announce himself. Then he entered and crowded her on the bench and stretched out his legs. "What is the matter with you, dear one?"

"Why should there be anything the matter with me?"

"Because you answer me with another question." The musician inhaled, enjoying the rosewater scent, the clean, healthy perfume of her own sweet self. "Remember Boston . . . last year. . . ah, what a grand time we had. How fortunate I was to meet you. I treasure those two weeks. You were gay, so full of laughter. Not like now, so deep in thought. What use, all this thinking? A pretty girl has no need for it."

"You mean I should be content to find a man to take care of me."

"A man like your brother or, perhaps, a man like—"

"You," Abigail finished.

"I can think of no one better," Vogel said. "After all, I am a gentleman. I am not without prestige in my country." He patted her hand. "Come, why do you insist on accompanying your brother? We could be very happy here together. And safe."

"Safe," Abigail repeated, watching the river below eddy and swirl. A log drifted by, half submerged. It bobbed past the bluff on its way toward town and the stern-wheelers moored at the docks. One of its battered branches caught on something beneath the surface of the river and the log twisted in toward shore. It ground into the mud, caught, and held, made a prisoner of the riverbank. The river flowed around and over as the silt began to build up, burying the stubbled branches.

"Abigail, what are you thinking?" Vogel asked.

"I think I shall follow this river. Upriver. I would like to see the wild country men talk of."

Her gaze never left the log, trapped in the mud, safe from the river flowing past. In a matter of weeks it would be buried.

"You cannot be serious."

"I have already informed my brother as to my decision. I assure you, I am most serious," Abigail replied. "I've been dwelling on the matter for days."

"What about me . . . us . . . ?"

"Maybe you should stay here." Abigail stood and crossed to the gazebo's entrance. "You are a big, strong boy with hard muscles and nary a vice. You'll do well, Con, wherever it is safe."

Con Vogel watched Abigail leave, his dark thoughts in stark contrast to the brilliance that bathed the departing young woman in its cold glare. There was anger in him. His dreams dashed, now someone was going to pay. Not Abigail. After all, his relationship with her might still be salvaged. Yes, she had become increasingly distant toward him throughout his visit, but it had taken Tom Milam's arrival to bring things to a head.

Tom Milam . . .

Vogel smiled, at last an outlet for his anger revealed. Tom Milam's very presence had been an effrontery; the situation demanded satisfaction. Con Vogel would have his day, after all.

17

"**J**acob, are we always gonna be brothers?"

"Jacob, are we always gonna be brothers?"

Tom saw his older brother. He heard the stalks of buffalo grass rustle in the wind. He felt the tremor in the earth as the war party rode past.

"Stay here, Tom."

The scene had changed as the years passed. The dream was no longer an exact re-creation of the moment but close enough for Tom to feel the fear again, a young boy's fear, and to taste the dryness in his mouth.

Jacob held out the ring for his younger brother to take. Tom watched the ten-year-old, his own boyish image, take the ring.

Jacob turned to leave.

Don't go! This was new, for Tom usually watched him leave without calling out. *Don't go! You're running to your death! Jacob, no!* The scene unfolded as it always did. Jacob shrank into the distance. He ran for all he was worth up the slope; he was crouched low and his long-legged gait propelled him swiftly away.

Jacob! A last lingering echo died in his sleep, reverberating in the barren hallway of his mind as the darkness closed around and the image of a grassy slope dissolved.

What am I doing here? I don't want to be here. Wake up, you fool.

Another image, another memory. Nightmares stacked one upon the other like children's blocks. Only this wasn't play.

Tom could smell the stench of blood, and his lungs burned

129

from powder smoke. Gunfire and the cries of a wounded man, a Kiowa brave. It didn't matter that the Shoshoni had killed his parents, in Tom's eyes, every heathen savage shared the blame.

The hunting party never knew what hit them. One moment they had been returning to their village with a travois loaded with fresh meat, and the next, two of the braves were shot dead and another two tumbled from their mounts, mortally wounded.

Still, Tom watched himself toss the Hawken aside, leap from behind a slab of granite, and vault through the air. He dragged a brave from horseback and they rolled a few yards down the slope. Gunfire echoed across the hillside. He ignored the sound, his attention centered on the Kiowa, who sprang to his feet and, tomahawk in hand, charged the young man who had knocked him from his horse.

In his sleep, Tom tensed as he had on the slope, watching the brave hurl toward him. He palmed his belly gun, a short-barreled percussion pistol. He thumbed the hammer, and the gun kicked in his hand. The Kiowa flew backward as if plucked from the ground by an invisible snare. He landed hard and doubled up, holding his belly. Blood seeped through his fingers.

Tom crawled to his feet and walked toward the brave and stood beside the warrior. The Kiowa began to sing his death chant through clenched teeth.

"That's right, sing your dying song, you bastard," Tom said as he calmly reloaded. His shadow fell across the man. The warrior's eyes burned with hatred; his features were drawn and pain filled as he watched the man who had shot him.

"Does it hurt?" Tom asked. He stared dispassionately at the man. Blood continued to seep from the wound. A gut-shot man took a while to die . . . and every moment was filled with pain. Tom opened his shirt and dangled the snake ring in front of the dying man's face. He nudged the brave with his boot. The Kiowa groaned in response.

"This is for my family, you murdering red devil. Take your time; die slow."

Farther up the hill, Kilhenny, Pritchard, and Wallace were

rummaging among the dead men littering the hillside. Coyote Kilhenny finished off the wounded braves with a quick thrust of his knife. Tom could have done the same. Instead, he sat by the man he had shot and watched him die.

The warrior at last succumbed—the life light in his eyes dimmed; his breath grew ragged, labored, then ceased.

Tom experienced the warm satisfaction of a job well done. He remembered the feeling even now, months later. And yet there was more, a sense of loss as well, something he didn't understand but felt all the same.

His family massacred, a score of red men had been killed in retribution. Dreams showed Tom what he refused to see in life.

In his dream, Tom sat by the dead man on the slope. He glanced down expecting to find the Kiowa's visage frozen in death. But the dead man had changed. The Kiowa was gone. Tom saw the face of death, but it was his own.

He bolted upright, his hands clawing the empty air, his lips drawn back in a silent scream that reverberated in the back of his skull. The image of his dead self shattered like glass.

The hotel room materialized in the pre-dawn light—faded brown-and-tan-covered walls, a dresser, washstand, and basin, and the creaky brass bed in which he slept. Heat was funneled up from a furnace below, and by the chilly interior of the room and his breath vapor billowing in the air, Tom figured the management was conserving coal.

A cold sweat streaked his features. Tom swung his legs over the side of the bed and stood. The dream had left him shaken. He padded across the cold hardwood floor to the window fronting onto the pier and the silty brown expanse of the Missouri. The night sky grew lighter with the approaching dawn. He had hours yet to sleep. But the dream had bested him. He pulled the room's only chair up to the window, wrapped himself in a blanket, and found the bottle of the house whiskey that he'd been nursing since last evening. He sloshed the contents and sat before the window.

And there Tom waited, for the morning, for an end to night.

18

"Hold still, damn it," Iron Mike bellowed as the girl standing against the wall began to tremble like a frightened bird. Hester was one of Junie's "doves," a dimple-cheeked sixteen-year-old mulatto whore in a camisole and nightdress and stocking feet. Skintop Pritchard had carried her downstairs to settle a bet between himself and Iron Mike. The girl squared her shoulders against the wall. She tried to hold her head still to keep the rum from sloshing over the lip of the pewter tankard balanced on her head. Her mousy brown hair was already plastered to her skull from the first dousing she had received.

"Please Mr. Pritchard," Hester called to the man with the smooth-shaved skull standing alongside Iron Mike's squat frame.

"Shut up," Pritchard snapped back. He winked at Iron Mike. "Go on, Mike, take your best shot and if you miss . . . well, . . . don't hit any part I aim to screw." Iron Mike and the men standing around him laughed at Pritchard's remark.

Distant thunder rumbled outside the walls of the River Wheel Saloon, then rain began to lash the night-darkened windows where the wind drove it under the eaves of the building. In sharp contrast to the storm's sudden noisy arrival, the interior of the saloon was unnaturally quiet. Riverboatmen and trappers steered clear of the girl against the wall and left a wide aisle as Hester closed her eyes and tried to pray.

Skintop Pritchard tilted a jug of home brew to his lips and

poured enough raw spirits down his throat to pickle a calf. He slammed the jug down on the nearest table and howled.

"Yeeeaaahhhhh! I'm a twister with lightning for blood and thunder in my guts. Keep your distance, boys, or Mike here'll part your hair with his Hawken."

"Bah!" Iron Mike raised his rifle to his shoulder and sighted on the tankard.

"A blind man couldn't miss from this distance," Pritchard dryly remarked.

Iron Mike glared at him, then shrugged. He grabbed for the jug and finished off the fiery remains of the River Wheel's house whiskey, a nefarious concoction of corn mash, red peppers, Missouri River water, tonic, and a dash of black powder. "Gawdam, but that stuff'd grow hair on a skillet," the trapper gasped. Then with eyes watering he stumbled to the far end of the saloon. He braced himself against the doorsill until his head cleared. The raw liquor ate at his guts; he'd passed his limit and wanted nothing more than to sleep it off. But he wasn't about to let Pritchard's claim go unsettled. Iron Mike could shoot rings around Skintop Pritchard any day of the week and he meant to prove it once and for all.

"Gimme a mirror. Someone fetch me a mirror," Iron Mike bellowed.

"Don't you worry, Mike, reckon little Hester thinks you look fetching just the way you are," Spence Mitchell called out from a nearby table.

"Go to hell, Spence," Iron Mike retorted.

Spence Mitchell raised a liquor bottle in salute. "I'm on my way," he said. He combed his fingers through his liquor-and-tobacco-mottled beard. His lips curled back, revealing a row of black, broken teeth.

One of the trappers fished for a moment among his possibles and produced a shard of mirror, an irregularly shaped piece showing roughly four inches of shiny surface.

"Here you be, Iron Mike." The man tossed his find to the marksman.

"Thankee, Mr. Schaefer." Iron Mike turned to Skintop Pritchard standing nearby. "Now you'll see some real shooting." He picked up his rifle and settled the heavy barrel on his shoulder as he turned his back to the girl against the far wall. He cocked the rifle; the metallic "click" booming ominously in the suddenly quiet room.

The rifle, pointing back over Iron Mike's shoulder, began to waver as the trapper tried to focus on the image in the mirror.

"Be still, damn you," he yelled, though the girl hadn't budged. He tried to steady the hand holding the mirror, cursed to himself, and wiped his forearm across his eyes as perspiration began to bead his sunburned brow.

"You getting nervous, Mike?" Pritchard said, enjoying himself.

"Wait and see." Iron Mike curled his thumb around the trigger, raised his left hand holding the mirror, and centered a reflection in the glass. It should have been Hester, frozen in mute terror, flat against the wall.

But a man's image dominated the shiny bit of looking glass that Iron Mike held before him. Tom Milam stood in front of the girl, a pistol in his hand and aiming, seemingly so, at the man with the rifle.

"Sonuvabitch!" Iron Mike yelled in horror as Tom fired. The pistol roared like a cannon in the close confines of the saloon. The mirror exploded in Iron Mike's grasp, and the trapper tumbled to the floor, his right ear burned by the slug fanning past. As a glossy mist settled on the floor, Iron Mike's rifle belched flame. The men in the saloon ducked out of sight as the lead ball ricocheted around the room before thudding into a panel of the bar.

"You bastard," Iron Mike roared as he staggered to his feet. Blood seeped from a dozen tiny cuts on his left hand. Slivers of glass jutted from his palm.

Tom ignored him and turned to the girl. "Get out of here."

"God bless you, Mister," Hester said as she passed him the tankard and darted toward a back door.

"Don't bet on it," Tom replied and tasted the rum. He holstered his pistol, drew a second weapon from his waistband, and sighted on Iron Mike as the trapper grabbed for Skintop Pritchard's rifle and swung around toward the young man who had humiliated him. Iron Mike brought up sharply and froze in mid-motion seeing that Tom had another pistol trained on him.

Tom grinned and hoisted the tankard in his left hand. "To your good health, Iron Mike."

Iron Mike nodded, licked his lips, and calculated his chances. He figured he could snap off a shot with the rifle. And get myself killed in the process, he thought. But he didn't hold with backing down from any man.

Fortunately, Junie Routh emerged from the hotel. She burst through the doorway that led to the hotel lobby. One of her girls had run upstairs to warn her of the ugly situation in the saloon. She wore a flowery purple dress with a ruff of lace covering her bodice. Yet despite her finery, Junie arrived ready for trouble. She brandished a broad-bladed carving knife, sharpened to a fare-thee-well, doubled edged and wicked looking. She sliced the air once for effect. "The next one of you jehus that makes trouble, I'll personally cut his pecker off and feed it to the wharf rats."

She looked around the room, searched each man out, and cowed him with her angry stare. In her fury at being disturbed, she resembled more some mad harridan than the proprietor of a hotel and saloon. To emphasize the fact she meant business, Junie tossed a horribly shriveled, leathery-looking object onto a nearby table. "I've done it before."

The men at the table looked in horror at the grisly trophy, gagged, and scrambled toward the nearest exit. Those that remained pretended to fade into the woodwork and tried to focus their attention elsewhere.

Iron Mike returned the rifle to Pritchard and staggered out the door. He disappeared into the stormy night.

"Let's open your pants and make you dance," Junie Routh said, advancing on Pritchard. He dropped the rifle as if it were a live coal.

"We were just having a little fun," he complained, keeping a table between himself and the madam.

"Behave yourself if you ever want to have more," she warned. She glanced toward Tom, who held up his hands in surrender and pocketed his belly gun. Then to defuse the tension, Junie Routh tossed a handful of wooden "Free-Screw" tokens onto the floor. The formerly cowed mixture of trappers and riverboatmen exploded into action and leapt for the tokens, overturning tables, and gouging and punching one another in the process.

She picked up the dried member from the table and crossed to Tom, who started to load the pistol he had fired.

"A poor night for riding," Junie said, noting that Tom was garbed in his long black woolen greatcoat.

"I have business," he said.

Junie Routh thought of Nate Harveson's attractive sister. "Are you certain you don't mean pleasure?"

"Business," Tom replied and drew a note from his pocket and passed it to the madam. "A boy slid this under the door to my room." Junie Routh opened the note and read softly aloud.

Milam,
There is a matter between us that can only be settled on the field of honor. I have no second but await your convenience.
Con Vogel

Junie Routh scowled, and shook her head. "A duelist. I knew his kind in New Orleans." Her gaze narrowed as she studied Tom's brash, darkly handsome features. "Don't take him lightly. He may look like a fop, but I'll warrant he's a crack shot. Remember, looks can be deceiving."

"You're full of warnings tonight, Aunt Junie." Tom patted her plump bottom. He holstered his loaded gun and leaned into her. "By the way, your trophy looks as if it could have come from a buffalo bull."

"Maybe he was a bull of a man," Junie said with a shrug.

"Why'd you cut it off then?" Tom asked, disbelief in his tone of voice.

"Maybe I just wanted something to remember him by," said Junie Routh.

Tom chuckled and headed out the back door, his reckless laughter drifting back with the thunder. Lloyd Mitchell, the bartender, a portly man with brown bushy sideburns and a clean-shaven chin, slid a drink poured from Junie's private bottle down to the woman at the bar.

"That boy's bound for trouble, Miss Junie," Lloyd said. He poured a drink for himself as well. After all, they were friends.

"And wouldn't I like to be along for the ride," Junie Routh sighed and tossed down the drink. She winked at the bartender and motioned for him to refill her glass. "Just wouldn't I."

Coyote Kilhenny and Pike Wallace waited out the rain and kept vigil from the hurricane deck of the *Dew Drop,* a stern-wheel mountain boat leased by Nate Harveson and quartered for the winter here in Independence. With this boat and another like it, the expedition would set forth in the spring and run the treacherous Missouri up into the heart of the north country. Kilhenny's thoughts were on the months ahead when he spied Tom Milam out of Gully Town. He saw Tom in the glare of sheet lightning and called out to him. But to no avail. The downpour obscured his voice. Rain drummed a steady cadence on the roof overhead and formed a veritable cascade that spilled past Kilhenny and Pike Wallace and drenched the bow and main deck below.

Smoke curled from the clay pipes both men smoked. The aroma of tobacco mingled with the stench of ozone in the electrified air.

"Where's he bound, you reckon?" Pike Wallace asked.

"Harveson's maybe," Kilhenny said. "I warned him about that gal, but he's as stubborn as—"

"You," Pike chuckled, finishing the half-breed's sentence. "Tom's cut from the same cloth, mark my words. Even if you ain't his pa." Pike nodded. "And he's the better for it. Tom knows how to keep alive. Not like his real pa, fixin' it so's you had to kill him just to keep the bastard quiet." Pike Wallace colored; his voice trailed off as he realized he had touched on a sore point. "I didn't mean to—" he stammered.

"One day you'll 'I didn't mean to' once too often, Pike," Kilhenny said.

"C'mon, I practically raised you, me and your ma's people," Pike chided.

"That's right. And it would grieve me to have to put you under."

"You wouldn't do that." Pike tugged his tam firmly down on his head and looked out at the rain. "Anyway, I ain't slipped but just that once."

"I raised Tom like my own," Kilhenny said. "Every man likes to think there's a little bit of himself to carry on when he's gone. As far as Tom's concerned, I'm his pa now. He trusts me."

"What about Harveson? Do you trust him?"

"About as far as I can shoot. I aim to watch my back trail. But the situation has real possibilities. The way I see it, we aren't getting any younger. It's time to make my mark." Kilhenny tapped the ashes from the bowl of his pipe. The tiny flecks of fire were extinguished by the rainwater spattering the deck. "Harveson can be a big help. At least his money can."

"See here," Pike said. "Harveson'll have an army around him should you try anything." Pike Wallace continued to puff on his pipe. Wisps of smoke curled around his leathery features and silvery hair.

"Yeah, but I'll be choosing the men," Kilhenny replied, a satisfied smile softening his rough features. "It'll be my army. The way I see it, Harveson has about thirty men already in town. We got three months or so to hire on the rest."

"What do you want me to do?" Pike asked. He wouldn't mind ending his days a rich man. It beat running whores in Gully Town.

"You and Tom can head south. Make a run as far south as the Red River. Offer them buffalo hunters twice what they'll make in a year on the plains. And see if you can round up Walks With The Bear."

"And it'll keep Tom out of trouble as well." Pike grinned. "Oh, he won't like it."

"He'll do what I tell him," Kilhenny replied. "And Iron Mike, Spence Mitchell, and our friend Mr. Pritchard will range north and hire on who they can find. I stay on here and make the rounds of the freighters, riverboatmen, and drifters, and see what I can come up with. There ought to be a few

men among them.'' Satisfied with his plans so far, Kilhenny
pocketed his pipe, and dug in his coat for a stoneware flask of
brandy he had clipped from the bartender at the River Wheel
Saloon. He uncorked the bottle and saluted the night and the
dreary downpour and the golden days that he was positive lay
ahead.

Pike Wallace waited his turn, confident, as always, he
would share in the drink as surely as he would Kilhenny's
dream.

19

Hiram eased back in his chair, closed his eyes, and inhaled the aroma of Thalia's freshly baked corn bread. Thunder rumbled and rain beat against the shuttered windows, but a fire crackled in the hearth and the broad-beamed kitchen table was set with a pot of butter beans, hot coffee, sweet cream butter, and now fresh corn bread.

"What are you thinking, old one," Thalia asked as she worked her ample rear end onto the bench seat opposite Hiram.

"Oh, I'd like me some fresh-picked field corn, roasted and dipped in butter. Bite in and gnaw on the husk till the butter drip down my chin. Man oh man, what I wouldn't give for that and a summer day."

"Well, buttermilk, corn bread, pork hock, and butter beans will have to do you," Thalia flatly stated. " 'Cause it's a long, cold row to hoe till summertime."

Hiram opened his eyes, scooted up to the table, and smacked his lips in appreciation. Thalia had been in a sour mood for days now and he hoped to humor her.

"If there's anything better'n corn bread and butter beans, I haven't seen it."

Virginia entered from the pantry. She held a crock of honey and with eyes lowered, took her place at the kitchen table.

"Seems everyone here has got a cloud hanging over 'em except me," Hiram observed, looking from the maid to the cook.

"It over you too, but you can't see it," Thalia said. She propped her arms on the table. Her chest was all bosom, round and ample; her backside, all derriere. She had a cherubic face and, normally, an easy smile, though it had been hidden of late. "Mr. Nate says he's takin' us all with him upriver to lawd knows where."

"At my age, change is exciting," Hiram chuckled and reached over to pat her plump arm reassuringly. "You've only seen half my years, but you're twice as worried."

"I don't cotton to being murdered by savages. Them red heathen'll scalp us same as white folk."

"Mr. Harveson is taking plenty of men along for protection. And if the ones I met are any indication of the sort, then it's the wild Indian I pity, not us." Hiram sliced a wedge of corn bread, slathered enough butter on it to drip down the sides, and then smothered the wedge in an avalanche of pale green butter beans and a chuck of the smoked pork hock, made tender after several hours of simmering in the bean broth.

"You seen to Miss Abigail's bath, gal young'un," Thalia asked, her gaze hardening. The rotund black woman had been relegated to cook now that she was too plump to waddle upstairs to tend to the rest of the household. Thalia had grown to tolerate the new girl and endured an uneasy coexistence with her for the sake of peace and quiet.

"Yes, ma'am, I took care of it." Virginia nodded, opening the crock of honey and spooning out enough of the amber syrup to cover the wedge of corn bread on the plate. "Is there any buttermilk left?"

"That's the trouble with womenfolk," Hiram good-naturedly said as he passed a stoneware pitcher of cold buttermilk to the girl. "Y'all can't decide when to be sweet and when to be sour, so you're both at the same time. I could never figure it out. It's why I never got married, I reckon," he added with a sigh.

"You men ain't no better," Thalia grumbled, her careful gaze focused on Virginia. "Not too much now; I'll need some for biscuits tomorrow."

Virginia filled a tin cup, sloshing a spoonful of milk onto the table. She ignored the cook's admonition and began to hurriedly devour her plate of bread and honey.

"Spare fixings," Hiram said. "Here, you're a growing girl. Take you some beans and smoked meat."

"Leave her be, old man. She's in a hurry. Her chores ain't finished for this night."

For the first time, Virginia seemed to acknowledge the conversation around the table. She glanced up at Thalia with such animosity in her eyes that the older woman stopped in mid-sentence, shrugged, and concentrated on filling her plate from the bean pot.

Hiram studied both women for a long moment, the fork in his hand poised halfway to his mouth. Both women had him puzzled. Something was going on, but he didn't know what; and neither woman would elaborate further. He shrugged, plopped a morsel of meat into his mouth, and began to chew. His snowy white eyebrows furrowed with his worried expression. Whatever the secret, he'd learn it in his own good time.

He dug into the food on his plate, grateful for a full belly and the security of a cozy blaze in the hearth, while outside thunder rumbled and a shadowy figure detached itself from the rain-washed dark and started toward the house.

"What do you want from me, Con," Nate Harveson brusquely asked. "This is not Europe where marriages are arranged. My sister has a mind of her own, a will of her own."

Con studied the contents of his brandy snifter, swirled the dark amber liquid, and inhaled the fumes. It was heady stuff but no solution to the problem at hand. Almost overnight it seemed his well-laid plans were in ruins.

"You know the kind of men you have hired. You have made a pact with rogues and brigands."

"I know." Harveson settled back in his easy chair and watched the shifting patterns of rain on the windows of the solarium. "I shall miss this room," he sighed. He saw his own reflection in the glass and stood and walked to a window. With his receding hairline and prematurely silver hair, he looked older than his thirty years. He finished his brandy and walked to the piano and ran his fingertips over the keys. He intended to take the instrument with him in the spring.

"And still you insist on bringing your sister along, with such an unruly lot?"

"I can handle Kilhenny and his type. Such men are like a team of wild horses. But I have the reins to keep them under control." Harveson turned and faced his sister's suitor. "Money, Con Vogel, money will keep my wild stallions under control." He chuckled and twirled the tips of his moustache. "My eyes are open. I know Kilhenny's sort. Not the kind one invites to a Sunday picnic, eh? But we aren't going to a picnic."

Harveson reached in a vest pocket and pulled out his watch, dangled the timepiece by its golden chain, then read the time and returned the case to his vest pocket. He yawned and stretched his thin arms, then patted his thickening waist.

"The hour is upon us." He cocked an ear toward the rolling thunder. "Good sleeping weather." Harveson started toward the door, paused, and glanced back at Vogel. "After father's death, my mother returned to England. I don't think she had ever been happy here. She wanted Abigail to accompany her. Abby refused. Adamantly. In that we are alike. Stubborn." Harveson lifted a lamp from a nearby table. He turned up the flame. The light bathed his face, revealing his Roman-like features. "If after months of vacillation, my sister finally has made up her mind to share this adventure with me. So be it. Nothing you say or do will change her mind."

Nate Harveson peered at Vogel and added, "Of course, you may come with us. And maybe we will bring civilization to the wilderness." Harveson vanished into the hall.

Con Vogel could hear the man as he started up the stairs. He was alone now and celebrated by helping himself to the last of Nate Harveson's brandy.

"So be it," he mimicked. Well, the man had left him no choice. He could meet Tom Milam on the field of honor and kill him. And if that damaged relations with the likes of Kilhenny and company, then it was just too bad. Let Abigail travel north then, but without Milam. Con Vogel would be there, right by her side, to win back her affections. Things would be like before.

He downed the contents of his snifter. The brandy spread

warmth to his limbs. He felt better now and wondered just exactly how Tom Milam might respond to his letter.

"Well, he had better not keep me waiting long," Vogel said aloud.

"Can I get you anything, sir?" Hiram said, emerging through a side door that led off to the kitchen. The servant brushed crumbs from his lips and glanced around to see who the fair-haired man had been addressing.

Vogel set the empty snifter on a nearby table. "You can turn down the lights as I leave." He walked over to an end table where Nate Harveson kept a variety of spirits. Vogel chose a small dark glass flask of cognac and without so much as a "by your leave," stalked out of the solarium and tramped down the hall.

Vogel felt his way to the banister, silently cursing the servant who had extinguished all the light downstairs. Maybe Harveson himself had darkened the rooms and foyer. He could be maddeningly frugal at times.

Now if I had his money. . . Con Vogel paused, staring out at the dark but seeing, in his mind's eye, his family's estate house and grounds, the rolling green hills that followed the Rhine. But the third of the sons had no claim on any of the family wealth. His oldest brother had inherited and subsequently dissipated the estate. Con had already left by then and come to America to seek his fortune. He'd known some desperate days at first. Meeting Nate Harveson had been a real stroke of luck. He had hired Con Vogel as his private music tutor. But Con wanted to be more than a musician in residence, ever at the mercy of Nate Harveson's whims. Abigail Harveson had been his ticket out of poverty. Now the days ahead seemed as bleak as the darkness above.

He took the stairs one at a time, measuring his steps, quietly ascending, and when his head cleared the landing, he paused again as the hall above brightened. And he spied Virginia, the upstairs maid, with oil lamp in hand, standing before the door to Nate Harveson's bedroom. The flame in the glass flue burned low; she gave it just enough wick to keep the fire going.

Here in the wood-paneled hall the storm was a muffled

presence, yet the fifteen-year-old girl shuddered and stretched a trembling hand toward the door latch. The door swung open, and Virginia removed her dust cap and clutched it in one hand. She held the lamp before her as she stepped inside Harveson's bedroom and closed the door behind her.

Con Vogel quietly climbed to the upper landing, carefully placing his steps as he started down the hall, and when he stood abreast of the master bedroom, he noticed even in the gloom the door was ajar. The girl had failed to close it all the way. Vogel grinned and cautiously approached the bedroom. A faint sliver of lamplight delineated the edge of the door. And it swung back on its hinges at the slightest touch. He opened the door just enough to see the mirror on the wall to his left.

Framed by the gilded borders of that looking glass, two bodies feverishly entwined, dark flesh and starkly white, hands and legs and sweaty naked torsos, fevered kisses and Nate Harveson's hushed moans of pleasure. Vogel caught a glimpse of dusky flesh by candlelight, then heard a muttered curse and Harveson saying, "Damn it, girl, you didn't close the door proper."

Coverlets rustled. Naked feet padded across the room. Con Vogel was caught off guard and retreated into the hall but not before young Virginia appeared in the door. Her eyes widened with recognition, but she made no move to cover her budding figure. The door slowly, slowly closed at her touch, her eyes locked with the musician's.

The click of the latch startled Vogel from his trancelike state. He continued down the hall only to pause yet again at Abigail's bedroom door. He recognized the bath sounds and heard the woman in the tub softly humming to herself.

Con Vogel thought of Nate Harveson and his servant. Jealousy welled in him and encircled his throat in a merciless grip. For a moment it was a struggle to breathe. Abigail Harveson would be his one day. No one else's, especially not some backwoods oaf like Milam.

He maneuvered uncertainly across the hall to the guest bedroom opposite Abigail's room. The interior of the guest room was illuminated by the flash of distant lightning whose lurid glare lit the balcony window that overlooked the rear grounds of the estate.

Vogel seemed to remember drawing the curtains but could not be certain. He had left a lamp lit. However, the damn thing must have burned out or run low on coal oil. He felt his way to bed. The frame creaked beneath his weight as he sat down on the edge of the big four-poster. The feather mattress was soft and to his liking . . . if only he had someone to share it with.

He considered relighting the lamp on the end table, then decided to hell with it and kicked off his riding boots and loosening his shirt, stretched out on the bed. Thunder growled from afar. The downpour droned on, hypnotically. He folded his hands behind his head, sighed, and allowed himself to relax.

At that moment he felt the skinning knife against his throat.

"Don't move," Tom Milam whispered.

It was a pointless warning. The earth could have trembled, split apart, and the mighty Missouri changed its course and overflowed the entire estate. Con Vogel would not have budged. A knife has its own steely kiss when razor edged and flush against the throat. Tom eased closer to the musician until his breath fanned the man's cheeks.

"Hear me now," Tom began. "There is no field of honor, not here. You call me out, I'll kill you any way I can, anytime and anywhere. The only reason you're alive right now is because you sleep under her roof."

Vogel swallowed and even so subtle a motion caused the knife to bite into his throat and send a trickle of blood from the glimmering steel down his neck to the pillow.

"Now, we can leave things as they are and the next time I come calling it'll be for keeps, or you can take your damn note back and we'll forget this ever happened. Which will it be, fiddle player?"

Con Vogel stared up into that dark, youthful face above him, and never had he seen so hard and cold an expression. There was death in that stare. In the glare of lightning, Tom's eyes were twin obsidian pools set in high-boned features sculpted of brimstone. "Choose . . ."

"I take back my letter..." Vogel managed to gasp in a hoarse voice. "And my... challenge."

Tom nodded but did not ease the pressure, not yet. "Open your mouth."

Vogel did so. And Tom took the letter from his greatcoat pocket and placed the folded piece of paper between the musician's lips. Vogel obediently clamped his teeth shut.

As quickly, the pressure was gone; the bed creaked as Tom slipped off the mattress and melted into the shadows.

"Don't follow me." His tone of voice implied the direst of consequences should the German disobey him.

Con Vogel remained like a statue in repose until he heard the bedroom door open and close. Slowly, he brought his hand up and took the piece of paper from his mouth. Gingerly he probed his throat and winced as his fingertips found the hairline cut. The flesh was sticky with congealed blood. It was hardly more than a nick but hurt like hell.

He lay on his back and stared at the ceiling, his cheeks flush with shame. *I ought to follow him, to hunt the bastard down and kill him for this humiliation*. He pictured revenging himself in a dozen different ways, each image more gruesome than the one before. He toyed with the notion with satisfaction but did not stir from bed.

Abigail glanced up in surprise as Tom Milam walked into her bedroom. His boots left muddy prints on the throw rug. That was the least of her worries as she leaned out from the tub and caught a towel from a nearby chair and held it to her bosom, covering what she could of herself.

Tom grinned at the look of utter amazement on Abigail's face. He walked to the small black iron stove that Abigail used to warm her room as well as to heat water. Tom lifted the heavy iron kettle from atop the stove and carried it to her tub.

"I thought you might need a little extra hot water."

"What are you doing here?" Abigail managed to say. She still couldn't believe her eyes.

"I figured to help with your bath." Tom nonchalantly poured the contents of the kettle into the tub, being careful to keep the spout angled down at the foot of the tub.

"Precious little reason to ride out from town in a driving rainstorm."

"Your comfort was reason enough."

"I need but to raise my voice and my brother will see you horsewhipped and thrown out into the night."

"And yet you speak softly. You do not call for help."

"I don't need help," Abigail pointedly replied.

"Are you sure?" Tom moved with leonine grace along the side of the tub and knelt until his lips were a whisper away from the young woman's mouth. He leaned forward and kissed her cheek, her neck. She tilted her face and his lips found hers.

His arms slid beneath her and when he stood, Tom lifted her in his arms. Water streamed from her nubile form and splashed back into the tub.

Tom turned toward the bed.

"Wait. We can't. My brother . . ."

"He's probably asleep." Tom continued on to her bed and lowered her onto the blanket and quilt.

"But I'm all wet," Abigail protested in a hushed tone.

"So am I." Tom yanked the towel aside. He lowered his lips to her breasts, his tongue flirted with each taut pink crown.

"No." This time the urgency in her voice made him stop. He sat back, puzzled—surprised by her tone and the fact that he had obeyed. He was used to having his way with the fairer sex. A "no" had never stopped him before.

"You feel the same as me," he confidently observed. "You want the same."

"Yes," Abigail said, but she pulled the quilt across her bare legs. "But not here. Not now." She trembled as her own passion slowly subsided.

"When?"

"I'll tell you," Abigail said. And she reached up and touched the scar on his cheek. "You'll be the first to know." There was a hint of amusement in her upturned lips. "When I'm free of this place, this house. And the weight of the past." She sat up and kissed him. "Come to me in the wilderness, where we can be as wild as the river and free as the clouds. Come to me then, Tom Milam."

"And in the meantime?"

"Be my friend," Abigail replied. "Please."

Tom studied Abigail for a long silent moment, then seemed to look through her. And in that trancelike state he glimpsed a gentleness within his own shadowy soul he thought had ceased to exist. It was a vulnerability too dangerous to afford. He could have crushed it, buried it forever, and let the demons of dark deeds have their day. All he had to do was . . .

Abigail's hand touched his and brought him back.

"Very well," Tom said. It was like watching himself from a distance, seeing and hearing someone he no longer knew. Touching her. Being with her. "For now a friend."

PART V

Jacob Sun Gift's Story

20

Jacob Sun Gift bellowed as the icy waters of the spring splashed across his shoulders.

"*Saaa-vaaa-hey!*'" he shouted. "That's cold." He immersed himself in the frigid runoff that spilled over a granite ledge and formed a bitter cold curtain of water.

Jacob wore only a loincloth, and the showering spring washed down the length of his long-limbed, sun-burnished torso. With his blond hair well past shoulder length, he resembled more some wild Norseman until he emerged from the spring and, after drying in the chinook wind, donned his buckskin leggings and beaded shirt. Once again he was Jacob Sun Gift of the Medicine Lake Blackfeet.

After more than a week of waiting out an early blast of winter—freezing temperatures, sleet, and snow—it was a relief to refresh himself in the spring. While Jacob bathed, Lone Walker built a cookfire and placed a couple of grouse on a spit over the flames. He grinned, amazed by Jacob's reaction to the cold springwater. Lone Walker's foundling son had never taken to this morning ritual of the Blackfeet. To the prayer singer it was a sacred ritual to begin each day whenever possible by immersing oneself in the flow of living water.

"*Ho-hey,* Snow Eater, welcome," Lone Walker said as the fierce rush of the chinook wind lapped at the campfire, the flames turning to streamers in the gust. "Keep the passes clear for us," Lone Walker continued, face to the wind. He shifted his gaze to the surrounding peaks and sensed the dismay in his son. In truth, the Blackfoot's own heart was heavy. After the more than three weeks since leaving Medi-

153

cine Lake, they had not even crossed the trail of the elusive young woman Jacob had seen.

Jacob returned to his father's side, squatted down, and pulled on his moccasins. He folded the white rabbit pelts he used for socks on bitter cold days. Worn with the fur turned in, the pelts kept a man's feet toasty warm. No need for them today with Snow Eater on the loose.

Dressed in his buckskins, he left the campsite for a quick circle of the perimeter and to check the snares he had put out the night before. The sun rose golden in the azure sky. The branches of nearby firs trembled in the breeze. Here in broken shadows of the wooded slope, the ground was patched with snow and Jacob left his tracks in that mantle of white. Where the trees thinned, his footsteps raised little clouds of dust on the hard earth. The temperature had warmed considerably by the time Jacob returned to camp with a pair of fresh-killed rabbits dangling from twin lengths of rawhide.

Jacob held up the fresh meat for his father's inspection and then, squatting down against a log, began to skin and butcher his kill. The work went swiftly and soon he had a pair of soft white pelts drying in the sun and a parfleche of fresh stew meat for the evening meal.

Lone Walker announced the roasting birds were thoroughly cooked and the two men feasted in silence. As the Blackfoot ate, he studied Jacob, trying to read the younger's man mood.

"Maybe we will ride through the Buffalo Horns today," Lone Walker said, nodding toward the valley and the twin peaks rising to either side like the horns of a buffalo hat.

Jacob shrugged and continued to eat. And the warm breath of the chinook fanned the embers of the campfire.

"What is it, my son?"

Jacob looked up from his meal, wiped a forearm across his mouth, and frowned, searching for the right words. "A wind blows through my soul." He tossed a leg bone into the flames. "I do not think we will find her, Father. We have already ridden up into the gap before the snows. We found nothing. Not even the remains of a campsite." He glanced down at the charred leg bone as if it were to blame.

"We will find her," Lone Walker replied. He wiped the grease from his hands in the dirt, stood, and walked from the fire upslope, climbing hand over foot until he had skylined himself above the cave and campsite. Like a statue then, rock still on the crest of the ridge, he remained with his arms outstretched to the azure sky. The wind buffeted him. The buckskin fringe of his leggings and shirt fluttered like streamers, like tongues of fire, for each strand was tipped with red war paint.

Lone Walker began his song.

> "All-Father,
> Hear this one who walks the sacred path.
> Lend us your eye,
> My son and me,
> That we may see
> That we may find the end
> Of our trail.
> All-Father,
> Hear me.
> Ride with us, Grandfather.
> Be our sight beyond sight.
> Bring us to the end of the trail."

Jacob sat by the fire and watched his father and felt a yearning in his heart to believe the older man's actions would be of any use. It was difficult for him to trust in magic. Growing to manhood among the Blackfeet, he had watched the shamans work their magic. Sometimes such men were successful, sometimes not. Jacob had always attributed any favorable outcome to coincidence. Not that he held to the fundamentalist beliefs of his birth parents. Their God had failed them, allowed them to be massacred. He had no use for any of the mysteries. He trusted his powers with rifle and bow. He trusted the stride of a good horse. These were things a man could count on.

And yet, listening to Lone Walker alone on the windswept height, even the pragmatic and doubting Jacob Sun Gift felt his heart stir. Whether the Above Ones heard or not, there was power in the voice, power in the man.

The song brought back memories of when Jacob, as a thirteen-year-old boy, had huddled by the warrior's campfire

and heard Lone Walker sing his spirit song. Jacob's heart had
been filled with grief and hatred, emotions that had warred
within him for many a day. But that was long ago; he was a
Blackfoot brave, Sun Gift, son of Lone Walker, and there was
room in his heart only for the people of his village, for a
phantom girl, and, of course, for the wind.

Jacob looked up at Lone Walker and listened as the
warrior's keening chant echoed down the long hills.

Of what use a singer? A song? Jacob straightened, senses
suddenly alert. He cocked his head to one side, then standing
slowly, faced the valley, his lanky frame casting a long
shadow upon the sun-washed slope.

Lone Walker's voice faded. He had heard the same as his
son. Now he waited, vigilant, patient as the sentinel pines
dotting the golden hills.

Wait. Be patient. Be still. All things torturous to a young
man. Yet Jacob endured.

And endured . . .

Then he heard it again. A gunshot and then another.

Jacob and Lone Walker were no longer alone in the valley.
Someone had arrived. Someone in trouble.

21

Tewa rode for her life beneath the fiery glare of the morning sun. Gunfire echoed throughout the long hills and lead slugs like angry bees fanned the air around her. She crouched low on the dun and let the horse's mane lash her face as she tried to make herself less of a target. She glanced over her shoulder at her pursuers, four Kootenai bucks, armed with flintlocks, knives, and war hammers. They had surprised her back up the valley of the Buffalo Horns. She'd had to abandon a fresh-killed antelope and her pack horse in order to save herself.

Tewa's strongly muscled thighs firmly held her astride the galloping horse as she twisted around and loosed an arrow from her elk horn bow at her pursuers. The feathered missile arced through the chinook-warmed air and passed harmlessly among the four braves strung out about fifty feet behind her. The hunters howled and raised their rifles aloft and dared the girl to try again.

The ground underfoot was moist and treacherous from recently melted snow. But the dun was mountain bred, a hardy animal whose powerful legs bore the young woman down the valley. Rifles thundered and a slug burned her shoulder and left a bloody furrow in its wake. Tewa grimaced and reined her charging steed toward the timbered slope. She caught a glimpse of movement out of the corner of her eye, glanced aside, and recognized with sinking heart another couple of Kootenai bucks had emerged from a grove of aspen and were moving to head her off.

Tewa pressed against the dun and urged her gallant mount

to even greater speed. A hundred yards became sixty, then thirty. The shadowing groves of pine and aspen, willow and fir, were a haven, a harbor of safety stretching out to her. All she had to do was lose herself in its emerald concealment.

Twenty yards. Ten. The two braves galloping to cut her off opened fire. Smoke blossomed from their rifles. She did not hear the roar of the guns. She only felt the dun beneath her shudder, falter a step, then regain its stride, blood spurting from its side as, dying, the mountain pony carried her to the tree-lined base of the ridge.

The woman gave a sharp cry of grief mingled with rage as the dun went down. Tewa, daughter of the wolf, kicked free, and hit the ground hard. She rolled onto her back, then slammed against the base of an aspen. She gasped for breath, clawed for her elk horn bow, and scrambled forward on hands and knees to retrieve the arrows that had spilled from her quiver.

She rose up on her knees and fired across the barrel-chested body of her horse as a lone brave ducked beneath the branches of an aspen, spied Tewa's wolf cowl, and raised his rifle. Her arrow caught him in the throat. The buck threw his rifle away and pitched off his mount. His fingers pawed at the shaft in his throat.

Tewa crawled to her feet and scampered away. She moved with all the speed of the animal whose pelt shrouded her dark, pretty features. She dashed straight upslope for a few minutes, a shadow wolf flitting among the trees, and then altered her direction, keeping to where the stand of timber grew the thickest. She paused beneath a stately pine. Part of the trunk exploded, showering her with splinters. She staggered back, momentarily blinded, then resumed her desperate race while the brave who had narrowly missed her reloaded and shouted for his companions to join him.

She scrambled over lichen-covered boulders and rotting logs, she glided soundlessly between the mottled white trunks of aspens and the ashen-hued saplings of ponderosa pine. Golden-yellow leaves crunched underfoot. Gray squirrels scampered out of harm's way.

Tewa paused to catch her breath and get her bearings. Something crashed through a balsam thicket, and the young woman whirled and fired her last arrow, spying too late the glossy black pelt of a fisher as the weasellike animal emerged from the thicket and headed upslope. Tewa groaned and started toward the undergrowth. She had wasted her last arrow and wanted it back.

She'd covered half a dozen yards when a Kootenai brave ran out from around a blind of aspens and all but tripped over her. She swung the elk horn bow and batted the brave's rifle aside. Flame and black smoke spewed from the muzzle, and the rifle ball ricocheted among the trees. The man was a head taller and fifty pounds heavier than the girl. But he was off balance and she hit him low, head-butting him in the groin. The brave gasped for air and fell over on his backside. But the gunshot had pinpointed her location. War cries rang out from three different directions. Tewa changed direction yet again and headed upslope, knowing full well her pursuers had her cornered.

The soft, shallow topsoil became patched with tabletops of gray-black stone. Aspens gave way entirely to ranks of ponderosas whose stately spires trembled in the wind. There was still hope, Tewa realized. If she could reach the top of the ridge, she might find a place to hide amid that jumble of boulders and weather-eroded ledges and cliffs.

She would have to outrun Kootenai though. And that posed a problem if they had kept their mounts. War cries sounded close at hand. No point to standing still and wondering. She broke from cover at a dead run. Thirty yards to her left, the brave she had knocked down and a companion broke through a thicket. They were both afoot. Good. She had been raised in the mountains. No man could match her in a foot race. She sprang onto the sun-washed slope and began the final leg of her ascent at a dead run.

With every yard she climbed, the men on her left fell behind. Her muscles ached, but she never slowed her pace. She gulped in the warm air and willed herself onward. Tewa heard the drum of unshod hooves on the rocky ground and glanced to the right as three more mounted Kootenai bucks galloped toward her. The air rang with their shouts of triumph. Tewa ran with the last of her strength, her heart sinking as she veered toward a pair of massive boulders bordering a narrow gap.

The passage was wide enough to permit a single rider, and if the Kootenai tried to ride through, at least she could fight them one at a time, unless they chose to stand back and riddle her with bullets. She'd have to shame them into coming for her. It wasn't much of a chance. But it was all she had.

Tewa reached the gap and scampered through. The passage was about ten feet long and worn smooth from the runoff of melted snow. Actually the two boulders had once been one huge chunk of table rock that erosion or earthquake had split asunder.

As Tewa reached the opposite end of the passage, an arm shot out and caught her by her buckskin shirt, strangled her cry, and flung her back against the granite wall. A few dazed seconds, then her vision cleared. She raised her hands to ward off this new attacker. Her fingers closed around a Hawken rifle.

"Here!" said Jacob Sun Gift.

The woman stared in wide-eyed recognition at the yellow-haired, fair-skinned warrior who spoke her tongue and dressed as one of her father's people. "And make sure you use it on your enemies, little Tewa."

Seeing Jacob again was startling enough. That he called her by name left her speechless.

"How...?"

Jacob didn't stay around long enough to hear the rest of the question. He scrambled up the face of the rock. Tewa watched him leave, then glanced down at the rifle in her hands. She had been chased long enough this day. She reentered the passage.

The Kootenai were a dozen yards from the gap and closing fast. Their attention focused on the shadowed passageway, they never noticed Jacob positioning himself atop the tablerock. One of the bucks brought up sharply as another horseman entered the fray.

Lone Walker bore down on the first man he saw. He had watched from the underbrush on the far side of the granite wall as the Kootenai braves had chased the hapless girl upslope. Now he attacked with all the fury of a father defending his own. He rode straight at the Kootenai and raised his Hawken rifle. The brave before him brandished a flintlock, its wooden stock outlined in brass tacks. Both weapons spoke as one. Horses collided. Lone Walker and his enemy went down in a tangle of flashing hooves and kicking limbs.

Jacob vaulted from the granite wall as the remaining two horsemen turned toward Lone Walker. Jacob tried for them both but miscalculated his leap. With a sickening snap, the bulk of his weight landed between the shoulder blades and the base of the neck of one brave. The other Kootenai escaped Jacob's grasp and rode out from the shadow of the wall. He wheeled his horse and faced the gap as Tewa fired.

The Hawken recoil shoved her back against the boulder. The Kootenai screamed, dropped his rifle, and galloped down the slope. The buck's left arm dangled uselessly at his side as he hunched forward and rode to safety. Farther down the hillside, the men afoot had already turned and fled.

Tewa strode out of the gap. She shook her fist and taunted the fleeing Kootenai. Her outcry reverberated through the hills. Jacob, for his part, staggered to his feet, happy not to have killed himself. His jaw was bruised from where he had clipped his chin on the skull of the man he had landed on. The Kootenai lay at his feet, his features hidden by his raven-feather headdress. The man was dead, his neck broken.

"If you are not falling off your horse, you are causing other people to fall off theirs," Tewa said, facing him.

Jacob started to offer a retort. His elation at finding the girl was short lived. He looked past her as Lone Walker managed to stand and stumble toward them. The horses stood and shook the dust from their coats. The Kootenai with the brass-tacked rifle did not move. Suddenly Lone Walker veered sharply and braced himself against the granite wall.

Jacob saw the powder-singed hole in the side of the shirt soaked with blood.

"Father!" Jacob brushed past Tewa and reached Lone Walker as the Blackfoot slid down to his knees, scraping his cheek on the granite. The prayer singer looked up, smiled wanly, and collapsed in Jacob's arms.

22

It was the last thing Wolf Lance wanted to see in the waning daylight. While the sun balanced on the forested battlements west of the divide, Tewa led Jacob and Lone Walker through the winding wooded valley and up the steep hillside to a lodge concealed in a grove of Douglas fir. Her father stood by his mount, a chestnut-colored charger, as the horse grazed contentedly. The warrior seemed rooted in place, in truth, he was shocked that his daughter had disobeyed him.

Jacob quickly appraised the girl's father as the trail climbed toward the lodge. He saw a man of average height with sloping shoulders, powerful-looking arms, and broad hands. He moved suddenly, graceful like a wolverine, took up a rifle, then leapt astride his horse, whirled the animal about, and charged down the slope. The man's intentions were openly hostile. Jacob glanced back at his father, stretched out on a travois and apparently unconscious, and rode forward to put himself between Lone Walker and this new threat.

Wolf Lance was dressed much like his daughter, in buckskin leggings and shirt, and wolf pelts draping his shoulders and forming a cowl that concealed much of his features. Wolf Lance brought his horse to a skidding halt in front of his daughter's procession.

"Tewa . . . what have you done?" Wolf Lance blurted out. Dust drifted on the wind. Shadows lengthened on the land.

"See for yourself, Father," Tewa said. She indicated the travois and the wounded brave supine on the makeshift litter.

Wolf Lance looked at Jacob, both angry at the young man's intrusion and quizzical as well, for Jacob was obviously a white man and yet obviously a Blackfoot. Tewa's father recognized the beaded workmanship of the Medicine Lake People, once his own.

"You ease up on that rifle," Jacob said, blocking the way to the travois.

Wolf Lance hesitated, his finger still curled around the trigger of his flintlock. Then Tewa added, "My father, these two saved my life. I was trapped by our enemy, the Kootenai. Jacob Sun Gift and his father, Lone Walker, fought at my side."

"Lone Walker!" Wolf Lance slipped from horseback and brushed past Jacob before the latter could reposition himself on the trail. Wolf Lance hurried to the travois, leaned his rifle against the pine sapling frame, and knelt alongside the wounded man. Lone Walker cracked a feeble smile, his eyes slitted as he looked at his old friend.

"You are not where you said you would be," Lone Walker weakly admonished.

"I lied," Wolf Lance replied, smiling, but his expression revealed his true concern.

Wolf Lance glanced up as Jacob's shadow fell across him.

"He needs much rest. I dug a Kootenai bullet out of his side. But I fear there is poison in him," Jacob said.

"You speak our tongue; you dress and walk like one of the People," Wolf Lance observed.

"He is my son," Lone Walker said.

"That cannot be," Wolf Lance replied.

"He . . . is . . . my . . . son." The man on the travois replied. His voice faded and his eyes closed. He seemed to shrink into his blankets. For a moment the blood chilled in Jacob's veins as he expected the worst. He leapt down from horseback and placed his ear to his father's chest and listened, gratefully, to the beating of the wounded man's heart.

Wolf Lance stood and walked away from the travois to the edge of the trail where it wound from the creek bed in a series of switchbacks that led to the lodge, back up on the hillside.

"They must stay with us, my father," Tewa called to him.

"You don't know what you are saying."

"It's the time of the Cold Maker. Though the valleys are clear, many of the passes are blocked. It is too long a ride to

Medicine Lake. Snow Eater has left. I do not think he will return.''

Wolf Lance knew his daughter spoke the truth. The chinook wind that had howled through noon had died to a whisper with the setting sun, and under cover of encroaching night, a chill stole across the land. If the snows returned and caught Lone Walker and his white son up on the divide or anywhere without adequate shelter, it would mean disaster for both.

"I'm not waiting for you to decide." Jacob remounted and caught up the reins to the travois mount as well and resumed his climb to the Lodge.

Wolf Lance moved to block the trail, rifle in his hand.

"You are rude, *Apikuni*."

Jacob caught his meaning, referring to him as a white robe, one without fur, not quite a true robe or, in this case, a true Indian. "I am Blackfoot. The People call me Jacob Sun Gift. And I am rude . . . to save my father's life." Jacob glanced around at the man on the travois and then returned his attention to Wolf Lance in the middle of the switchback. "I don't know why you chose to live apart from your village. But I tell you this, I'm taking my father to shelter, so fill your hands or get out of the way."

Jacob thumbed the hammer back on his Hawken rifle and started his horse forward. For a moment he actually thought Wolf Lance would fight. The flintlock was cocked. All he had to do was turn and fire. Instead, Wolf Lance retreated a step, then another, and another, and eventually he stood aside and allowed Jacob and the horse he was leading to pass. He looked at his old friend unconscious on the travois and sighed. Wolf Lance could not bring himself to deny shelter to one who was like a brother to him.

Tewa rode up to him, relieved there had been no violence.

"It is good, Father. We have been alone too long. My heart is happy that we are among our own people. There is magic in this. Powerful medicine."

"You don't understand, little Earth Daughter," Wolf Lance said.

"I understand I am happy," Tewa replied and rode after Jacob.

Wolf Lance watched her leave. In stillness came the night.

The trail to the lodge became more difficult, even treacherous. No matter. Wolf Lance knew the way. Powerful medicine, she had said. Bitter medicine, he corrected in his thoughts.

He had lived a long time here on the backbone of the world. After the death of his wife, he taught his daughter to be a shadow like himself, to hunt with bow or snare, to avoid all contact with others—to treat everyone as an enemy to be avoided.

And over the years he had almost forgotten the dream that had forced him to abandon his own kind and live like a phantom in the mountains. Now the Above Ones had taken a hand. There was no escaping what was to be.

Before another spring, there would be grief on the wind and blood would cover the moon.

23

"**M**y mother sleeps there," Tewa said, pointing toward a wooded hill just barely seeming to rise out of the darkness. The high ridges already sported the yellow-golden glow of morning. Feathery clouds dotted a deep azure sky. The chinook wind had lasted but a day. With the night, the temperature had fallen, and this new day had dawned brisk and cold. There was no wind. Jacob did not need a capote with the air so still. And as the sun continued to bathe the valley in its fragile warmth, Jacob was glad he had left the cumbersome coat back in the lodge.

He looked in the direction Tewa indicated and thought he could make out a burial scaffold in a clearing on the opposite slope.

"She died two winters ago," Tewa continued. "I was not so lonely while she lived. My mother told me stories of her people and the village by Medicine Lake."

"It is good there," Jacob said.

"I should like to go someday," Tewa said. "But my father will not permit it."

"Why?"

"His dreams brought him here. They have not led him back yet. Maybe one day," Tewa said with a sigh. She paused in her climb and checked a snare she had set beneath a thicket of chokecherries. She and Jacob had left at first light to make the round of the snares she had set. The trail she had left ran the length of a narrow gully winding away from the house and zigzagging back into the eastern foothills.

Tewa's valley seemed hemmed in on all sides by mountain

ranges. And that was nearly the case save for a narrow gorge that split the humpbacked ridge to the east and a dogleg break in the bald-faced cliffs to the west.

Tewa knelt to inspect the fresh droppings on the path and announced that a small herd of antelope had passed in the night. Jacob shaded his eyes to the sun's glare and studied the rocky battlements that lay ahead. Up near the wall's serrated crest, a dozen or so mountain goats gathered at a salt lick. They maneuvered with sure-footed ease over what seemed impossible ground, their shaggy white fur like patches of living snow constantly rearranging its pattern on the cliff.

"I should have my Hawken right now," Jacob sighed.

"No," Tewa replied. "My father has seldom used his gun. And never in our valley. There are no friends in these mountains, my father would say, only enemies. A gunshot speaks long after the gun has killed. It brings down food but calamity as well, alerting our enemies. My bow shoots swift and true and silent."

"Your bow," Jacob scoffed. "A woman's place is in the village or gathering roots, making shirts and leggings for her husband. Hunting is a man's work. Trapping or stalking game is no task for a mere girl."

"*Saaa-vaaa-hey!*" Tewa exclaimed, straightening. "I will show you what is woman's work." She trotted down the trail and away from Jacob. Tewa moved with expert grace. She ran effortlessly, her elk horn bow swinging in her left-handed grasp, her wolf-pelt-draped shoulders bowed forward.

"Wait! Tewa, wait!" Jacob called after her. She was heading straight for the cliff where the mountain goats had arranged themselves around the lick. She'd have to work her way in awfully close with a bow that had such short range, Jacob thought. Just climbing the cliff face would be treacherous enough. Stalking across that weather-worn granite without spooking the animals was next to impossible.

Jacob cursed himself for his own stupidity and resolved to follow the girl. Maybe he could keep her from breaking her fool neck. Jacob hefted his own willow-wood bow and started down the path. By the time he'd covered fifty yards, Jacob had come across three snares that Tewa had set and there were plump rabbits in two of them. So much for the trapping skills of this "mere girl." Jacob sighed, feeling the guilt of his thoughtless remarks settle on him like a black cloud.

If Tewa were injured proving her worth, it would be Jacob's fault and none other's. He broke into a run, hoping to overtake her. He had a long stride, but Tewa knew the lay of the land and the quickest route to danger. He only hoped he could catch her.

Wolf Lance stepped into the shadowy recesses of his lodge. It was built of hand-hewn timbers, mud chinking, and stone, built like the fair-skinned frontiersmen constructed their lodges down in the Wind River range. Wolf Lance had been to rendezvous long ago. He had watched and learned from the trappers.

Now he waited for his eyes to adjust to the dim interior. Sunlight streamed through gaps in the chinking like buttresses of gold holding up the walls; sunbeams rooted to the floor. The floor was covered with hides, the walls too in some places. A crudely fashioned door hung ajar on its cracked leather hinges.

"Your lodge has no circle of life," Lone Walker dryly observed, his voice issuing from the darkness.

Wolf Lance glanced around at the four walls. True, a tepee had no walls; as in a circle, beginning and end were the same. But the winters at this altitude could be brutal. "Sometimes it is better to abandon the circle of life and live than to walk in it and freeze to death."

"Sometimes it is better, when the Cold Maker comes, to ride down from the mountains and be with your people again." Lone Walker lay upon a bed of buffalo robes and was semi-reclining on a willow backrest.

Wolf Lance crossed to his side and held a water bag out to the wounded brave. The water bag was made from a length of buffalo gut, and Wolf Lance wore it across his shoulder like a bandolier.

"I have brought you living water, my old friend," Wolf Lance said.

"Your woman has you well trained," Lone Walker said. Then he remembered what he had earlier overheard, that Berry was dead. "How did she die?" he asked, the weak smile fading as he accepted the water bag. But he could only use one arm, so Wolf Lance trickled water into his mouth.

"Does it matter? You, of all people, spirit singer, should know."

"I ask for the sake of Two Stars, her father," said Lone Walker.

"He still lives?" Wolf Lance exclaimed.

"And takes a woman to his bed. He has a warrior's heart."

Wolf Lance softly laughed, set the water bag aside, and sat by his friend. He lifted his gaze to the buffalo-robe bedding on the other side of the campfire. Unable to build a fireplace or chimney, he had been forced to peel back a rawhide section of the roof to draw out the smoke whenever a fire burned. It was an efficient system, much more so than the vented flaps of a tepee. There on the robe she had trembled with fever and there, after many days, she had died.

He spoke of her death, his voice wavering at times, for deep within he felt the blame of her death. She had been gentle and kind. She had followed him, trusting in the reasons he had taken her from her family and friends. She had trusted.

And now she was dead.

"Why did you leave?" Lone Walker said.

"Why did you follow?" Wolf Lance replied.

"*Saa-vaa*. Talking with you is like following a game trail over stone. I return to my cookfire with an empty belly." Lone Walker winced as he tried to reposition himself. It only set his bullet wound afire with pain.

"Where is my son?" Lone Walker asked.

"How can a white-skinned one be your son?" Wolf Lance scoffed. Realizing he had responded with another question, he said, "He is checking the snares with Tewa, my daughter."

"And you do not wish him in your daughter's company?"

"It is not time for her."

"It is past time, my friend."

"Not for Tewa!" Wolf Lance hadn't meant to sound so angry. He softened his tone. "She has known only her father and mother. She is innocent of the wiles and tricks young men play. He will fill her head with nonsense. No longer will my daughter be happy here; she will long for her own people."

"Is that so bad?" Lone Walker said, his voice weaker now.

His eyes closed. His breathing grew steady, though from time to time he groaned in his sleep.

Suddenly he coughed and opened his eyes. He seemed to look right through Wolf Lance, as if he could see to the very heart of the man. Wolf Lance's blood ran cold before the spirit singer's harsh stare. Sweat beaded Lone Walker's brow and his flesh felt hot to the touch. Even when Wolf Lance touched the wounded man's forehead and cheeks, the wide-eyed gaze never wavered. Wolf Lance wanted to run from those eyes that peeled away his own thoughts and motives and fears and left him naked and even afraid.

As suddenly as it began, the wounded man's eyes closed again and his rigid muscles relaxed. Lone Walker's firmly muscled limbs settled into the bedding. He slept.

Wolf Lance, trembling, crawled to the door and staggered out of the cabin. He gulped in lungfuls of the thin air, his breath clouding before him. He looked down upon the valley that had begun as a haven but became a prison. His mind in turmoil, he shuffled forward into the sunlight. Overhead, an eagle drifted on the upper wind currents. It appeared to dangle from the firmament as if the All-Father had hung it in place as a permanent ornament.

"You should not have come," Wolf Lance said, emotion building in him. He felt trapped by these mountains, like a wolf caught in a snare. Cornered. No way out. He tilted back his head and cried aloud. It was a purely animal sound that tore from his throat and reverberated down the valley. A cry of fear, a cry of rage. His arms were outstretched, his lips drawn back to bare his teeth, his legs splayed and firmly rooted.

The cry of the wolf ended at last. And in its place came the calm of knowing he would do what had to be done.

He was ready.

Lone Walker asked too many questions. One day soon he must learn the truth. And on that day, it would be too late for any of them. They were claimed by the dream, now.

"My dream," said Wolf Lance in a whisper heard only by the earth beneath his feet and the breeze that plucked the branches of the firs—the silent earth, the quiet wind.

* * *

Tewa paused beneath a ledge of lichen-splashed granite and inched her way across a slide of gravel and the twisted broken trunk of a pine. She had stolen from the concealing forest and, keeping the ledge between herself and the salt lick, had managed to come within bow-shot range, about a hundred and fifty feet up the face of the ridge. The ascent was steep but not sheer. The greatest danger was the spill of loose shale just at her feet. Not only was it treacherous to climb across but the slightest misstep could cause a noisy cascade of gravel tumbling down the tree line.

The ledge that had served to mask the movement now became a liability, for it blocked her shot. She would have to clamber around the ledge to bring the mountain goats in sight. She'd have to risk spooking them; there was nothing else for it. Tewa leaned forward in a crouch. She held her elk horn bow and a black-feathered arrow in one hand. She placed another arrow between her teeth and started to climb, then froze after her first step. She spied Jacob on the ridge wall, farther to the right. He was following a less precipitous route that offered a good deal more cover. She had considered the course as well, except that the boulders played out about seventy yards from the lick and Jacob would have to cross virtually barren rock to close in on the lick. And even then, with the animals downwind, Jacob would spook them.

Jacob waved to Tewa, above and to his left, concealed in the shadows beneath the ledge. Tewa watched as he made a gesture as if he were shooting a bow. She stared at him, uncomprehending. He pointed at her and then at the goats above and repeated miming a bow shot.

She nodded in understanding. He wanted her to be ready to use her bow. For what? She had no target. The ledge blocked her. As long as the animals stayed by the lick, they were safe from her bow. Unless something drove them out into the open. Something or someone. Tewa worked her way to the opposite corner of the ledge. It was slow going. She took extra care to work herself into position. Once the animals above caught sight or scent of Jacob Sun Gift, they'd try to escape by scampering out of range of the oncoming hunter. Some were bound to cross Tewa's line of fire.

Down below and off to the side, Jacob waited for Tewa to

position herself at the farthest corner of the ledge. Once she was poised and obviously ready to take a shot, Jacob stood and loosed a wild war whoop and waved his hands in the air as he charged the herd.

The mountain goats seemed to move as one. They sprang from the lick and bounded out of harm's way. Some took to a direct ascent. Others chose an easier course, an all-but-invisible trail that ran the length of the ridge.

Tewa darted out from behind the ledge as a plump-looking ewe leapt past. The Blackfoot huntress skidded to a halt; the bowstring twanged, sending a black-feathered shaft to its mark. The animal's legs buckled and it nosed down into the shale. Tewa braced herself, fitted a second arrow to the string, and started to shoot when the ground beneath her gave way. She lost her balance, fired wild, and fell away, rolling head over heels in an avalanche of gravel.

She landed on her back, arms and legs spread wide to still the spinning world while she struggled to catch her breath. A face blotted out the morning's glare. She recognized the sound of Jacob's voice and as consciousness returned, she began to understand what he said.

"Are you all right?" He spoke in an urgent tone, the expression on his face mirrored the concern he felt.

Tewa frowned; she was embarrassed by her fall. She had intended to impress Jacob with her ability. Instead, the young woman felt she had only succeeded in making a fool of herself. Jacob hauled her to her feet. Tewa freed herself from his grasp and proceeded to dust herself off. She had lost her wolf-pelt cowl and her black hair hung free. She looked up, daggers in her stare as Jacob laughed.

"I can hunt as well as any man!" Tewa indignantly stated, anger in her voice.

"Better than most." Jacob folded his arms across his chest as he studied her. "I was a fool to say otherwise. There is only one place for a warrior."

"And where is that?" Tewa inquired, exercising fragile control over her hot temper.

"Alongside the one who has opened his blanket to her," Jacob replied.

"I . . . I do not know of such things."

Man and woman stood in awkward silence, grown quite unexplainably ill at ease by the subject of the courtship ritual. Jacob at last broke the uncomfortable tableau. He pointed past Tewa. "See what the little wolf has brought down."

Tewa turned and spied the ewe she had shot, lying on the slope. Blood splotched its snowy coat where Tewa's arrow jutted from the animal's heart.

The mountain goat was just over four and a half feet from nose to tail, a solid-looking animal, well muscled and ready to be rendered into cuts of meat once it was carried back to camp.

"A good kill, little she-wolf. As true a shot as any I've seen," Jacob said, leading the way. Tewa paused to retrieve her elk horn bow. She had dropped the weapon to keep from breaking it during her fall. As she approached her kill, Jacob dabbed his hand in the animal's blood. He straightened and reached out to Tewa.

"Let me see your hand," Jacob said.

Tewa looked at him in surprise, then uncertainty gave her cause to frown. A breeze tugged at her long black hair. In that molten-gold brilliance of high-country sunlight, Jacob felt his inner workings flip-flop at the sight of her.

Tewa extended her hand. Jacob dabbed the blood from his hand onto her palm. Then he cupped her hand in his.

"Together we have walked the mountain. We have killed that we might have life. We return to the lodge, together. And it is good," Jacob said.

Tewa could feel the warm moisture of the blood between them. She could feel the beat of Jacob's palm. It warmed her as well. Given to solitude, she would have been tempted to draw away and rebuke him for such a liberty. Now she felt strangely drawn to him, compelled to speak, to make at least some token reply. She willed herself to say something. Anything was better than standing here with a hollow core for a stomach. And wondering. Wondering. Wondering.

"It is good." A tremulous smile brightened her features. And the heart of Jacob Sun Gift soared.

24

Fever set in. It lasted three days and broke the fourth. During that time, Lone Walker was never alone. Jacob spent much of the time at his father's side. He kept a fire burning and an extra blanket close at hand when the chills set in. He bathed his father's brow and even managed to get him to eat some weak broth once in a while. Tewa and Wolf Lance offered to help and managed to force Jacob into a little rest, but, for the most part, Lone Walker was cared for by his son.

So it happened on the fourth day, Lone Walker opened his eyes and saw Jacob seated beside him, slumped forward, his head rising and falling with each breath. Jacob stirred, then continued to snore as Lone Walker rose upon his elbows. He did not know how much time had passed, nor did he really care. Being alive was all that mattered.

Lone Walker studied the interior of the lodge. There were willow backrests and many pelts. A willow frame in the corner was covered by a buckskin shirt that Tewa had begun to decorate with the last of the beads and porcupine quills and tiny colored stones no bigger than buttons that she had found in her travels. The girl and her father were both gone. Lone Walker sniffed the air, inhaled the mouth-watering aroma of rabbit stew, and managed to sit up. His wounded shoulder sent a stab of pain coursing through his body as a warning against too much movement. But if Lone Walker practiced restraint and kept his movements slow and deliberately paced, he found the wound bearable. The stillness was a nuisance though.

Lone Walker slid over to the fire and helped himself to the

stew, taking a bowlful of the bubbling broth. Using a wooden spoon, Lone Walker noisily began to eat. He slurped the broth and devoured the chunks of meat, wild onion, and fry-bread dumplings floating in his clay bowl.

"Father," Jacob blurted out, abruptly awake. He hurried to Lone Walker's side.

"I can feed myself," Lone Walker snapped, unintentionally gruff. "It has been many years since I sucked at my mother's breast." He cocked a weary glance at Jacob's tired, worried features. If the young man was wounded by his father's remarks, he did not show it. "How many mornings have I slept through?"

"Four," Jacob replied.

"Ah. Too much sleep. I'm as stiff as an old grizzly after his winter sleep."

"And you growl like one," Jacob added, daring his father's bad temper.

"*Saa-vaa,*" Lone Walker muttered in disgust. "Was there ever such a son?" Then with a hint of a smile he reached over and patted Jacob's arm. "Such a faithful son?"

"Where is Tewa and Wolf Lance?" Lone Walker asked.

"I am here," the girl said, stepping quietly through the doorway. She held the beginnings of a buckskin shirt. Behind her, through the momentarily open doorway, Lone Walker could see it was beginning to snow. Large feathery flakes dotted the air, drifted silently to earth. Tewa's wolf-pelt cowl glistened with moisture; droplets gleamed like diamonds against the gray-black fur. She brushed the pelt aside and squatted by the campfire.

"It is good to see you living," Tewa said.

Lone Walker noticed she and Jacob seemed to be purposefully avoiding each other's glances.

"I am happy as well." Lone Walker attempted to reposition himself. The movement sent a sharp stab of pain through his shoulder and down his back. He groaned and fell back against the willow backrest. Both Jacob and Tewa came to his aid, one on either side of him. Each tried to support him and in so doing their hands met, then closed one upon the other.

Lone Walker waited for Jacob to help him sit up. He looked up at his son, at Tewa. Man and woman dutifully returned to the task at hand. But what Lone Walker had seen gave him cause for concern. He was old enough and perceptive enough to know when two are called together. He had walked the same path, as a young man, and taken Sparrow Woman to warm his blanket, his lodge, his life.

Tewa crawled over to one side and began stitching, with quill needle and sinew thread, on the buckskin shirt. There had been no time for being alone with Jacob since the hunt. He had remained at his father's side and she had tried to wait with him. Wolf Lance was always finding something for her to do. Still, every so often, she would find some excuse to join Jacob in the lodge. There by his side, she learned how he came to Ever Shadow and the Medicine Lake village. And she had spoken of her own life, lived in solitude, as if in hiding, from what? A dream? Yes, a dream and nothing more.

The door to the lodge burst open as Wolf Lance made a dramatic entrance, and from the accusatory look on his face he was expecting something more than what he found . . . Lone Walker both awake and alert, Jacob at his father's side, and Tewa on the opposite side of the fire.

"I—I have seen to the horses. There is shelter and food for them in the corral." He kept the horses hidden in a grove back up the valley in a small box canyon whose entrance he had sealed and secured with a makeshift fence. The animals had been kept in a meadow, where they could roam free and graze at will. But as the weather worsened there was no choice but to drive them into the box canyon. He gave Jacob a final suspicious glance and then turned his attention to Lone Walker.

"My heart is glad to see you looking stronger." Wolf Lance stretched his hands out to the fire. "Cold Maker is coming. Soon you must be ready to ride."

"My father hasn't the strength to sit up by himself, much less ride a horse." Jacob spoke in a flat, unemotional tone of voice. "And we are staying here until he can ride."

Wolf Lance ignored the younger man. He fixed his attention on Lone Walker, who seemed to read the mind of Tewa's father. "We will leave tomorrow," he said, nodding sagely.

"Father, no," Jacob protested.

"I have said it."

"No. I will not permit you."

"Permit? Am I your son now? Every day we risk being trapped here. Now I have spoken. We leave tomorrow and the matter is ended." Lone Walker hunkered down in his blankets and tried to rest.

Tewa started to offer her protest, but a sideways look in her father's direction cautioned her to keep her opinion to herself. In truth, Tewa knew her motives were selfish. She enjoyed having Jacob around, although she was too shy to admit that fact to his face. The emotions, the feelings, his nearness aroused left her very confused.

"Do not worry," Wolf Lance said. "This storm will not last. The passes will be clear." He stood and returned to the door, yanked it open, and disappeared outside. "I will bring firewood," he called over his shoulder.

Jacob rose and followed him. He found Wolf Lance in the grove of firs at the side of the house. Tewa's father was busy gathering wood from a pile of dry kindling he kept stacked among the firs to keep the timber dry. Wolf Lance straightened and still had to look up at Jacob, who towered over him.

"I thought you were Lone Walker's friend," Jacob said, barely controlling his anger. He was without a coat and the cold cut right through him. Melting snowflakes soon matted his yellow hair, turning it the color of wet straw. His breath clouded the air.

Wolf Lance already held an armload of wood. Now he stood as one transfixed. He made no reply. Indeed he no longer even looked at Jacob. His gaze appeared to focus on something in the distance with such an expression of horror that Jacob finally had to turn to see for himself what dreadful thing commanded the brave's attention.

In a matter of seconds, he understood. For through the snowfall's thickening swirls, Jacob could make out the far slopes and the jagged ridges, risen out of the broken landscape, whose summits were obscured now in thick gray clouds. A storm raged in the passes. At such an elevation the wind would howl and kick up a blizzard, and the snow would come down in blinding sheets.

"Too late," Wolf Lance muttered, a mixture of sorrow and

despair in his voice. By morning, the passes to the east would be completely blocked. The Above Ones had tricked him. Cold Maker had played him for a fool.

"Looks like we are all trapped now," Jacob said.

"Yes," Wolf Lance replied. And the look in his eyes was as bleak as the storm raging above the timberline. "Trapped . . ."

25

Snows came. White powdery flakes covered the earth, melted, froze again in layer upon layer. As days became weeks, the snow in the passes piled too deep to walk in unaided.

Tewa and Jacob worked together on this the eighteenth morning since he had come to the valley. Jacob fashioned snowshoes made of birch while Tewa finished tanning an elk hide using a mixture of buffalo calf brains and liver to draw out the glue in the hide. The buckskin, once smooth and soft to the touch, would furnish enough material for three pairs of moccasins. Tewa had already fashioned a needle from a piece of goat's leg bone. Elk sinew would be her thread.

Tewa enjoyed Jacob's company. As he spoke of the Medicine Lake village, her heart would pine for an end to her father's self-imposed exile. She wanted to be among her own people again, to gossip and laugh with other girls her own age, to feel a part of the world again as a person and not some wild creature hiding out in the heart of Ever Shadow.

Despite Wolf Lance's every objection, she had grown to accept Jacob as one of her own kind, though his long hair was burnished gold not black and his sunburned skin, bronzed not dark and coppery. And why not accept him? Jacob walked the path of the People. The ways of the Blackfoot were his ways, their dreams his dreams. A man like the legendary Lone Walker, he who had crossed the backbone of the world in his youth and seen the Great Water at the edge of the world where the sun sleeps, if even such a man as this could call Jacob "son," then Tewa knew it was right for her to accept the handsome young man called Sun Gift as one of her own kind. It was enough for her to trust him, to like him, and in the end to feel the stirrings of an even more powerful emotion. Being near him made her feel hot and cold all at once, to feel desperately tense and troubled and yet light-headed in the same breath.

She tried to hide all these emotions from Wolf Lance, who kept coming up with excuses to keep Tewa from finding too much time alone with Jacob. He made a point of accompanying her whenever Tewa left to check her traps. If she chose to scout the valley or range the ridges for sign of any intruders, Wolf Lance was there, shadowing his daughter, always in sight, unobtrusive but impossible to ignore.

But today Tewa and Jacob planned to give her father the slip. Jacob finished his work first, donned his snowshoes, and walked away from camp. He followed a trail leading north. Half an hour later, Tewa left to check on the horses. She did so, and afterwards, once the young woman was hidden in the shadow of the firs, she darted out of sight. Wolf Lance and Lone Walker were working on their own snowshoes and never noticed a thing until it was too late to call her back.

About an hour later, on the forested ridge above camp, Jacob and Tewa rendezvoused. They grinned like mischievous children who had just outwitted the adults. Jacob had an extra pair of snowshoes strapped to his back. He carried his Hawken rifle and, beneath his capote, Tewa's elk horn bow and a quiver of obsidian-tipped arrows.

"Now, little she-wolf, where will you lead me?" Jacob said. He pulled the cowl of his long coat up to cover his head. The heavy woolen capote kept him safe from the cold wind. Losing himself in Tewa's dark-eyed gaze helped to raise his temperature as well. Whatever feelings had drawn Jacob into the mountains in search of the young woman had intensified now that she was near. All the better that she sought out his company. He wanted to speak to her of what was in his heart, but he didn't have the words.

"I will show you a special place," Tewa said, pulling the wolf cowl around her features. "Who can tell when my father will not shadow us again?"

At the mention of Wolf Lance, Jacob glanced around, half

expecting to see the older warrior come riding at a rough gallop through the snow.

"Does he fear for your safety with me? And he seeks to protect you?" Jacob asked.

"Maybe he hopes to protect you."

"From who?"

"Me," the young woman replied, enjoying Jacob's confusion.

"Well then, I hope he fails." Jacob sheepishly lowered his eyes and found something on the ground to stare at. When he looked up, Tewa was smiling. She turned and started up the ridge. The snow wasn't as deep on the slope and except for the cold thin air the climb wasn't arduous. Jacob was more than happy to keep to a switchback trail. When it broke from timberline, they were well above the lodge and all but out of sight of the two older warriors silhouetted against the sun-patched ground out front.

Wolf Lance finished repairing the woven center of his snowshoe. He glanced toward the grove of trees and the horses cropping the shoots of grass sprouting through the snow. Tewa's absence bothered him. Normally, he would not have been alarmed by her disappearance, but with this white man who pretended to be a Blackfoot lurking about . . .

"My brother, your thoughts follow a troubled path," Lone Walker said.

"They follow my daughter," said Wolf Lance.

"With children, it is often the same thing," Lone Walker chuckled. He reached for another strand of birch wood peeling to weave into his snowshoe frame. "Trouble and joy," he added, and winced as his newly healed wound protested the suddenness of his actions.

Wolf Lance stood and crossed to the side of the lodge where a bow and quiver of arrows hung from a branch stub. He slung the quiver over his shoulder.

"You worry too much," Lone Walker said. "No doubt Tewa has gone to check her snares and set them again if need be." Lone Walker started to rise. "I will come with you."

"You move too slow," Wolf Lance said. "It is none of your concern. She is my daughter."

"And he is my son," Lone Walker retorted, knowing full

well what his old friend suspected, that Jacob and Tewa had conspired to be together. Why else would Jacob be so interested in hunting on a day when there was already plenty of meat all ready to roast. As for Tewa, anyone with eyes could see the horses were fine.

Lone Walker studied the slope behind the lodge and imagined just about where the young couple might have crossed paths. Wolf Lance took a rope made of braided horse hair and started back through the campsite. Lone Walker moved to block his path.

"Let them be," he said. "Remember how it once was with us, when we were younger and called to the girls to stand with us in our blankets. Give them this moment, for my son and I will be gone soon. We will try our luck in the passes."

Wolf Lance did not reply.

"Where is the harm? I am able to ride. Soon, Jacob and I will be gone and leave you to your exile," Lone Walker said. "Let them be. It is the way of things, the All-Father's will if they are together." Lone Walker brought his face close to his friend. "The All-Father led my son to Tewa. Now let them walk the same path if only for a little while."

Again Wolf Lance made no reply. He brushed Lone Walker aside and started toward the grove where the horses grazed. Lone Walker, ignoring the pain flaring through his shoulder, caught Wolf Lance by the sleeve of his wolf-pelt coat and spun him around. Jacob's father was angry now. He'd had his fill of mystery, of his old friend's open hostility toward Jacob.

"Give them time."

"Time?" Wolf Lance scowled. "My daughter has never known a man. Only her father. Time? For your white-eyed son to fill Tewa's head with foolish talk? Time to turn her against her father? Take her to his blanket?"

"You have been gone too long, my brother." Lone Walker spoke in a conciliatory tone, trying to reason with this unreasonable friend. "Is it so terrible if my son and your daughter are two called together?"

Wolf Lance started to reply and hesitated, his eyes growing moist, then he seemed to shrink in on himself. He pulled free of Lone Walker but only to slump onto a log near the campfire.

"Yes," he replied. "And even worse, I fear." He stared at the flames of the campfire. Smoke rose in lazy spirals, grayish white against the stark blue expanse of the sky. He watched the flames flutter and dance and in their constant motion found the courage to speak what had been locked in his heart since he had first fled to the backbone of the world.

"I walked in a dream, long past, when Tewa was but a child," Wolf Lance began. His expression seemed distant, as if, to relive the dream and share it, he must cleanse himself of all emotion. "I saw my daughter, grown like a flower in the time of the New Grass Moon, blessed by the All-Father with beauty and gentleness and courage. And great was my happiness. Until the Above Ones revealed to me the path I must walk. In my dreams, Tewa left my side and stood in the shadow of another man, one who opened his blanket to her."

Wolf Lance reached out toward the flames and warmed the palms of his hands. Then he reached beneath his wolf-hide coat and brought out a tomahawk, its Green River iron blade smooth and sharp. He held the short-handled ax aloft, his grip tightened around the wooden shaft, then, with a savage downward sweep, he buried the blade inches deep in the ground.

"It was given to me how I must kill this shadow man. It was the All-Father's will I must fight him. And try to kill him." Wolf Lance looked up at his friend. "And one thing more was shown me on the last night I spent among my people: the ground covered with blood. White snow and blood and Cold Maker's wind howling lost and lonely among the hills. This was my vision, that I must battle all the men who would seek my daughter. I must change my name to Slayer and kill the sons of my brothers—your son, too, Lone Walker, even your son."

Wolf Lance stood and returned the tomahawk to the beaded belt circling his waist. He held out his hands and shrugged. "That night I fled. I came to the backbone of the world and did not change my name to Slayer." The warrior in exile looked toward the horses and for a moment considered trying to track his daughter. Yet, with sinking spirit, he realized things were already beyond his control. If indeed the Above Ones had brought Jacob to this valley, then so be it.

He glanced at Lone Walker and saw the look of horror in that noble brave's face.

"I cannot counsel against the will of the All-Father," Lone Walker slowly replied. "I followed a dream to the Great Water at the edge of the world. But to take the life of one of our people, what kind of vision quest is this?" He struggled to understand his friend's terrible dilemma.

"Perhaps when I have shed blood the Above One will be satisfied and I will be free," Wolf Lance said.

"Freedom at the price of one of our own," Lone Walker reminded him. "It cannot be a good thing."

Wolf Lance nodded, trying to show concern, but an idea had formed. He brightened, having realized Jacob was no Blackfoot. No matter what Lone Walker said. *Has the All-Father provided a way for me to return to my village after all? If blood must be shed, why not that of a white man, a pretender?*

"No!" Lone Walker blurted out, reading Wolf Lance's intent in the expression on his face and in his eyes. "Do not even think it."

But the warning came too late.

The vastness of distant peaks and scalloped ridges held many wonders: forested valleys, icy creeks fed from the runoff of glaciers, cliffs eroded into shapes to match the clouds.

By noon Tewa had brought Jacob to the lower slopes of a battlement that from a distance resembled the snarling visage of a bear partly masked with snow. Lodgepole pines and groves of aspen framed the "muzzle," which like the rest of the "head" was naked granite, carved by the elements into the face of a beast. Jacob followed without question. He didn't much care what the destination was as long as Tewa walked at his side. The bitter breath of the north wind did not dissuade him. His heart felt light and impervious to any gloom. Happiness, however, did not make him careless. He had hunted with Lone Walker much too long to be caught unawares in enemy country. And so it was that he glimpsed a tendril of what appeared to be smoke curling above the treetops ahead, and he lunged for the young woman and

caught her arm and pulled her back behind a dense stand of
aspens whose stark white trunks were bent and crooked from
the snows of past winters.

"Someone's camp," Jacob muttered, gesturing in the direction of the smoke with his rifle.

Tewa softly chuckled and motioned for Jacob to continue
on through the woods with her. Jacob fell in step alongside
the woman. He trusted her but cocked his Hawken all the
same.

Fifteen minutes later the trees thinned where the shading
pinos choked out the aspen. The source of the smoke was at
last revealed. White gossamer tendrils spiraled upward through
a narrow aperture just beneath the snow-packed "eye" of the
bear. About ten yards below the aperture the shadows gave
way to a patch of darkness that could only be the mouth of a
cave.

"Come," Tewa said and broke into a distance-eating gait
that left Jacob far behind. But only for a moment. He started
after the woman, his long-legged stride quickly closing the
gap. His yellow hair streamed behind him, his upper torso
leaned into the run. Tewa glanced over her shoulder and
began to laugh. She won the race to the cave by a length and
darted inside—a flash of a smile, a toss of her long black hair,
and she was gone.

Jacob had to slow down to keep from breaking a leg as he
ducked into the gloom. He almost lost his footing and slid to
a halt on the rocky floor as his eyes adjusted to the dimly lit
confines of the antechamber. The cave angled back into the
hillside. Jacob heard the sound of flints struck together, then
the crackle of flame. Amber light delineated a narrow, shoulder-
width exit from the antechamber. He heard Tewa laugh again
and, at a loss as to what else to do, worked his burly frame
through the back exit and stepped into the torchlit room
beyond. Here was a chamber roughly over fifty feet in
diameter. Thirty feet overhead, the ceiling bristled with
stalactites. Stalagmites rose from floor to roof, their rocky
veneers sculpted aeons past by an underground stream that
was no more than a pool of water eleven feet across in the
center of the chamber.

For all the underground beauty of the cave, the first thing

Jacob noticed was the warmth. He'd already begun to sweat. He peeled off his capote and buckskin shirt. Steam rose from the surface of the underground spring and drifted up, as if drawn by the column of light streaming through the rent in the ceiling, the aperture Jacob had spied from outside.

Tewa had already shucked her leggings and coat and wore only a soft doeskin smock that hung to mid-thigh. She was no longer laughing. She moved silently to the edge of the spring and stepped down into the pool's warm depths. As the water rose above her knees, she hesitated, then pulled the smock up over her head and tossed it onto her other clothing. She finished lowering herself into the pool, her long hair floating on the surface as the water climbed to her rounded breasts. She waited for Jacob.

The sight of her, like this, left him aroused. There was no hiding it as he removed his clothes and padded barefoot, to the pool. The water was hot as he worked his way toward her through the water. Tewa moved to him, emerged streaming from the water to stand naked before him. Droplets of water clung to her like tiny jewels.

She reached out and touched his eager flesh, tracing a path that led to his chest and neck. She stepped into him; her breasts, like hardened buds, brushed his chest.

"You are very beautiful," she said in a whisper.

"Stand with me," Jacob said with all the longing in his heart, and he opened his arms. He held no blanket; all he had to offer was the strength of his embrace.

It was enough for Tewa.

26

Jacob and Tewa returned to the lodge shortly after dusk. A full moon lit the way across the snow-covered earth. Against a sky scattered with star jewels, gossamer clouds trailed like ghostly bridal veils, passing south on the gentle wings of the wind.

"And if my father is angry?" Tewa asked. Having tricked Wolf Lance, she was willing to bear the brunt of his anger yet dreaded it all the same. She did not understand her father of late, he had become a stranger to her. Still, she loved him, would always love him, even now, in her fear and uncertainty. How would he react to her decision to end her exile and return to Medicine Lake?

"Then let him be angry," Jacob said. "We are called together. You and I. And I will not leave unless you are by my side." Tewa placed her hand in his and then trudged across the glade to the lodge. Jacob pulled the door open and they stepped inside, leaving the cold night air behind.

Lone Walker, squatting by the fire, looked up from the elk ribs he'd been roasting over the flames. He was alone in the lodge and on recognizing the young man and woman seemed relieved, though the revelation of Wolf Lance weighed heavy on him. He lifted the ribs off the fire and with his knife hacked away portions for himself, Jacob, and Tewa.

"Where is my father?" the woman asked as she and Jacob fell to their knees around the comforting fire.

"Gone to bring in the horses," Lone Walker said. There was a makeshift corral in back of the lodge where the animals were kept at night. "Don't worry. He's already eaten his fill."

"I must speak with him," Jacob said from his place by the fire. He looked up at Lone Walker, studied the warrior's expression. Jacob felt as if he could keep no secret from the man. "When we leave, Tewa is coming with me."

Lone Walker had suspected as much. In fact, from the moment he had set out with Jacob in search of the wolf girl, Lone Walker had sensed this inevitable development. But he hadn't foretold the danger involved. Wolf Lance was a man to reckon with. Jacob, for all his size and strength, was no match for a seasoned fighter like Wolf Lance.

"I have no wish to eat," Tewa sighed. Suddenly the sound of a galloping horse could be heard from outside. The lithe young woman sprang to her feet and hurried through the door, clutching her wolf-pelt coat about her shoulders as she plunged into the wintry night. Jacob rose and started to follow her, but Lone Walker reached out and caught his arm. A moment later Tewa returned, looking confused, her cheeks flush from the cold night air.

"My father . . . is . . . is gone," she stammered.

"A man knows what he knows," Lone Walker said. "What he does with that knowledge is something else again." The Blackfoot brave motioned for the two young people to sit by the fire. He reached into the parfleche he carried at his side and brought out a pinch of a powdery-looking mineral, which he tossed into the cookfire. Bright, livid orange flames flared for a moment, then died. Lone Walker wafted a silky black feather through the trailing vapors. He lifted his gaze, fixed on some faraway point now, and spoke.

"Hear me. And I will speak to you of men and dreams . . ."

Morning came. It etched the rims in gold, then sunlight poured down the broken slopes like spilled honey. The grove of trees where Wolf Lance had passed the night fractured the dawn's fiery glow into shafts of sunburst yellow that roused the warrior from his slumber.

Wolf Lance had camped back in the woods well out of sight of the lodge. He'd weathered the night in the old way. First he'd dug a shallow depression in the earth, as long as he

was tall. Then he'd built a fire and when he had a good
supply of coals, extinguished the flames and scattered the
glowing chunks of charred wood all along the depression.
He'd covered the coals with a bearskin robe and settled into
the warmth. Another covering of pelts for a blanket and Wolf
Lance slept snug and warm. And much too long, he scolded
himself, for he had wanted to be waiting at first light, ready
to do battle the moment Jacob stepped outside. He had no
love for what was about to happen, but a man must follow the
path set before him by the Above Ones.

Wolf Lance moved out across the snow. He cupped the
frozen moisture to his face and neck. His charger, ground
hobbled among the aspens nearby, whinnied at the sight of the
brave. Wolf Lance scrubbed his chest, gulped in a lungful of
that brisk cold air. He exhaled, his breath clouding the air and
trailing off through slanted shafts of sunlight. Wolf Lance
said, "It is a good day to die."

He knelt down and gathered up his buckskin shirt, quickly
pulled it over his head, and then pulled back his bedding to
reveal the charcoal-lined pit in which he'd slept. He dipped
his fingers into the ashes, mixed in a little wood, then drew a
black streak across his eyes and another higher up on his
forehead. He dabbed charcoal onto either hand. And he was
satisfied. Now he was marked as one who followed a dream
path.

Wolf Lance took up his Hawken rifle and checked to make
sure it was loaded and primed. Then he left his camp and
returned to his horse. The animal tossed its mane and called
to him as he approached. The Blackfoot spoke soothingly and
pressed a soot-blackened hand to the animal's buckskin-
colored neck, leaving an imprint on the horse.

Wolf Lance freed the horse from its hobbles and swung up
on the buckskin's back. Reins in hand he turned his mount
and rode out of the woods and back to the lodge. He followed
a deer trail that ran the length of the valley before climbing
over the divide. The trees thinned in a matter of minutes and
the lodge angled into view.

The warrior headed straight toward the clearing in front of
the lodge. He had picked the time and place to fight. Wolf
Lance wore no coat. He wanted to be free for combat. His

long black hair streamed away from his features. His expression was tight lipped and betrayed no emotion as he held his horse firmly in check. The animal wanted to run but was forced to trot through the snow, its hooves throwing up ice-crusted clods of dirt.

About sixty feet in front of the lodge Wolf Lance reined to a halt and waited, knowing he must have already been spotted a hundred yards back. He waited. And waited. And the sun crept upward in the sky. The wind died, leaving the cold to settle on the land. Sunlight warred with winter's chill. Against the clouds whose imperceptible drift made them seem stationary, over the man alone and the lonely land, swept the silent shadow of a golden eagle.

The Blackfoot lifted his eyes to that noble minion of heaven, the lord of the backbone of the world, aloof, predatory, circling silent, watchful, and waiting to swoop down on some unsuspecting prey.

"Enough," said the man on horseback. He raised the rifle over his head and shouted. "*Ho-hey!*" The cry echoed down the valley. "Jacob Sun Gift!" The hills repeated the name. "Come and fight me!"

Was Lone Walker holding back his son? Surely not even the spirit singer would stand in the way of the All-Father.

"Jacob Sun Gift. It is a good day to fight." Wolf Lance waited. He shifted uncomfortably astride his horse. The stillness had taken on an eerie quality. He glanced around, made nervous by the lack of response. "Is the son of Lone Walker a coward?"

Only an echo and then the awful silence once again.

"Come and fight!" Wolf Lance roared. Anger welled in him like an ember in his heart suddenly burst into flame. "Bring your gun and horse. Face me here!"

Wolf Lance drove his heels into his mount and wheeled the startled beast around and galloped across the clearing at an angle that brought him to the side of the lodge where he could see the back of the structure and the makeshift stockade abutting the granite cliff to the rear of the lodge.

Empty. The stockade had held half a dozen horses. It was empty. Wolf Lance leapt down from his horse and charged the log dwelling he had built with his own two hands. He hit the door, shoulder first. It slammed back and he staggered into the room, tripped on a clay bowl, and tumbled to the floor. He rolled through the cold ashes of a dead fire and swung his rifle around to cover the shadows that seemed to leap out toward him like so many tormenting demons.

The cabin was empty. And had been so for hours. Wolf Lance kicked aside a willow backrest, ravaged the pelt bedding with his rifle barrel. He noticed something else, then. All the dried meat was gone from its string against the far wall.

"Tewa!" the warrior shouted as he spun on his heels and headed for the door. He burst into sunlight, brought up sharply as he noticed for the first time the various sets of tracks in the snow. They had meant nothing to him before. But now—he studied a trail that wound down the valley. "Tewa!" he called again and listened as the name carried back and grew fainter with each repetition. "My daughter," he said, his own voice diminished. "They have turned you against your father."

He looked back at the lodge. The trail food had been taken. And all the snowshoes were gone from their pegs on the outside walls. Everything to keep him from immediately following. And they could keep fresh horses under them and cover twice the distance as a man astride one poor, tired mountain pony.

"I see your hand in this, Lone Walker, my old friend." Wolf Lance muttered bitterly. He watched as his horse headed toward familiar pasture. Well then, let the animal graze, grow fat on the last of autumn's grasses poking through the snow. Wolf Lance stared off toward the mouth of the valley and the way he must go. He did not need to track them. "So be it," he said. He had ridden the trail in his mind often enough. Now his heart grew hard as stone, his very being one grim resolve.

"I will come home."

27

She was Sparrow Woman. She was Lone Walker's woman. And she had grown to live with waiting. A week or a season, the pain was the same. The longing too. And yet stoic acceptance had become as second nature to her over the years. Her husband was a man of dreams, of quests, a spirit singer whose life must ever be divided between home and the journey. Lone Walker's life was mirrored in his name.

It was the time of the Hard-Faced Moon, and snow blanketed the village of the Medicine Lake People. Sparrow Woman wrapped herself in an otter-skin coat. She had sewn it with the pelts turned inward to protect her from the cold. The air was bitter and still, and the ashen clouds hung heavy on the land, muting natural sounds of village life. There were no children at play among the tepees. No proud young men galloped their horses across the surrounding meadow to impress the unmarried daughters of the tribe. There were some people afoot: several moved out to bring the horses closer into the village while a few women headed down to the lake.

Sparrow Woman had already made one trip to shore to bring fresh water to her lodge. But she had chosen to repeat the brief trek to the water's edge, this time to bring living water to the lodge of blind Two Stars. Calling Dove, the old one's cut-nose wife, had been ill of late. Though recovering, the woman was still too weak to bring the customary living water to her own lodge. Sparrow Woman had willingly accepted the chore. She enjoyed her visits with Two Stars. He reminded Sparrow Woman of her own proud father, who had gone to the All-Father many years past.

Sparrow Woman walked from her tepee and followed the path she had earlier left in the snow. Soft wet flakes settled in her footprints, gradually obscuring the passage, but she knew the way by heart. The dogs were quiet, chased into hiding by the gloomy overcast sky and the ever-present cold.

The wife of Lone Walker moved quickly, she was anxious to be out of the weather herself. She was not even tempted to visit any of her friends along the way. The task at hand was of sole importance. She lowered her head and plunged through the gray gloom, and gradually the press of lodges thinned and the level ground inclined. Sparrow Woman chose her steps wisely now. A clay water jug dangled from a rawhide rope clutched in her left hand. The jug belonged to Two Stars and woe to the woman so careless to break it.

The ground underfoot had eroded and the slope was broken and irregular, but Sparrow Woman took her time and descended the last few yards to the ice-rimmed lake. She knelt by the edge of the lake, set the jug aside, and drew a war hammer from her belt. The weapon was Lone Walker's and consisted of a sturdy oak shaft approximately two feet in length, the hilt wrapped in rawhide and crowned with a water-smoothed oval chunk of granite half again as large as a man's fist.

The woman didn't bother to try to locate the hole she had made earlier. It was quicker, simpler to crush the ice-glazed surface close at hand. A single swipe of the war hammer and Sparrow Woman had a miniature pool in which to lower the clay jug. By the time she had filled the container, a couple of other women, alerted by the sound, approached through the settling snow.

"I have broken through here," Sparrow Woman called to them. As they neared she recognized Little Plume Woman, wife of Yellow Eagle. Good Bear Woman, Yellow Eagle's sister, hurried past Little Plume Woman.

"See, I told you. It is no wild bear, only Sparrow Woman breaking through the ice."

"I wasn't worried," Little Plume Woman replied, too defensively to be believed.

"You were," Good Bear Woman chided. "You are so funny." The smaller of the two tilted back her head and had a good laugh. She was a pretty girl with dimpled cheeks, round ample hips, and a full bosom made for nursing the young. As yet she was unmarried but ever hopeful that Otter Tail, Jacob's friend, would find the courage to stand before her father and offer him gifts for the hand of his daughter.

"I am not nearly so funny as the sight of an unmarried woman waiting for big belly to marry her. Otter Tail will never have enough horses or pelts for your father." Little Plume Woman spoke in a clipped tone of voice. Hers were sharp features, high cheekbones and thin lips drawn back in a humorless smile. Her chin was pointed; her neck, long and regal. Yellow Eagle, despite his game leg, had proved himself an excellent provider. In battle, he called no man his better. Little Plume Woman was proud of him and proud to share his blanket, proud to have been called together in union with him. She enjoyed sharing this happiness and pride with her spinsterish friend.

"Otter Tail will ask for me. He only waits to trap more pelts, that my father will be pleased with his offering," Good Bear Woman retorted.

"And while the two of you argue, Cold Maker seals the pool of living water I am leaving behind!" Sparrow Woman said, interrupting the quarrel. Listening to such nonsense made her glad she was no longer a young maid, fresh as a sapling, struggling for a place in the sun. She stepped aside as the younger women hurried down the bank. Water sloshed from the jug as she made her way up from the lake. The gray gloom lost no time in muffling the voices of the women at the water's edge.

Snowflakes fluttered against her cheeks and glistened in her thickly braided hair and planted icy kisses on her forehead. She wished she had brought a shawl to cover her head. But wishes were as dust in the wind, unable to be grasped and quickly forgotten. She pressed on, pretending to ignore the cold. In truth, her thoughts went far beyond her own discomfort, rising like prayer smoke to the western mountains to the husband she loved and to her beloved adopted son, the two most important people in her life. They searched the backbone of the world for what? Ghosts? The answer to a mystery?

This winter storm was as gentle as a pup compared to the

wild winds and terrible storms sweeping down from the peaks to trap the unwary hunter in the passes. She feared for husband and son, yet refused to believe the worst. After all, Lone Walker had told her long ago, "*I will return to you. I will always return to you.*" She had believed him then when love was young. She could do no less after these years of knowing him and feeling love flower like some eternal bud that refuses even the deadly grasp of winter, that remains and continues and nourishes and endures.

Sparrow Woman hesitated before the lodge of Two Stars. She drew a corner of the entrance flap aside and announced herself. She heard the old one cough and between spasms he bid her enter.

The interior of the tepee was warm and offered blessed relief from the ever-present cold. The tepee wasn't as large as that of Lone Walker, being only about fifteen feet in diameter, but it certainly provided adequate comfort for the blind one and the younger outcast he had taken to wife, Calling Dove.

"I have brought you living water," Sparrow Woman said and placed the jug on a willow-wood stand.

"I am grateful," Two Stars sighed. He sat near the fire and fed a couple of thick gnarled branches to the flames. Sparrow Woman marveled that he did not burn himself. But then, the old man possessed many skills. There was none in the village to match Two Stars in arrow making. His were the straightest shafts; his always flew true to the mark.

Sparrow Woman crawled across to Calling Dove's side. She smiled wanly, her normally robust form seemed shrunken into the pallet on which she lay.

"Have you taken any of the food I left?" Sparrow Woman asked.

Calling Dove nodded and indicated a nearby bowl that had once been filled with stewed meat, bread, and broth. Meat juices formed a glaze on the inside.

"I am stronger today," Calling Dove replied. She pulled a woolen blanket up across her immense bosom. Her round, scarred face wore an expression of gratitude.

"But not strong enough to attend to the one who opened

his blanket to her," Two Stars said in a wounded tone. "I am
but a poor sightless man, alone and helpless—"

"As a sly fox," Sparrow Woman finished the sentence for
him. Several parfleches of jerked meat and wild tubers and
dried berries were arranged near the old man's bedding, all
gifts from other people in the village. Two Stars was loved
and respected by all, his wisdom a welcome addition to any
council or gathering of tribal elders. Still, he loved to elicit
sympathy for his sightless state.

"I have frozen my fingers and braved the Cold Maker's
wrath to bring you living water. What more would you ask of
me?" Sparrow Woman asked merrily.

This morning his bones ached from the bitter press of
winter and Two Stars' mood remained as gloomy as the
landscape he could no longer see.

"You could bring word of my daughter and Wolf Lance.
You could tell me that I might embrace my granddaughter
before I die."

"I have heard nothing." Sparrow Woman knelt alongside
Two Stars and warmed herself by the fire. "You will have
your granddaughter, your Tewa."

"I fear they are all lost; now your dear ones as well as
mine."

"No," Sparrow Woman said. "Do not even think it."

"Don't you?"

"No."

"Why?" Two Stars turned his sightless eyes toward her.

"Because I am the woman of Lone Walker. And when he
leaves, he takes my heart with him. I would know if my heart
were lost."

"Do you never fear?" asked the blind man.

"Always. But never more than I love."

"The sun has set many times since Lone Walker and Jacob
Sun Gift rode from Medicine Lake," Two Stars glumly
recalled.

"Then today is a good day," Sparrow Woman said. "Cold
Maker has hidden the sunrise and sunset. We will not need to
count them." She stood alongside the old one and touched his
shoulder.

"The time grows close when I will enter the Great Circle

and see the Above Ones and stand before the All-Father. If only I could believe that I will hold the flesh of my flesh before I die.''

The longing in his voice was no pretense, Sparrow Woman realized. How she wished she could find the right words to comfort him. His seamed and wrinkled countenance was like a map of life: here, a line of suffering; there, his brow bore the scars of anger and violence; and see how his leathery cheeks were creased from laughter.

''Believe in my husband. I did, and he brought me a gift from the sun.'' Sparrow Woman squeezed his bony shoulder, then, with a reassuring smile toward Calling Dove, she walked out of the tepee and into the thickly falling snow.

How peaceful here as if the village were deserted. She heard only the noise of her own passing as she returned to her lodge. The wind began to increase, gusting gently, swirling the precipitation and building drifts against the north side of the lodges. A baby's hungry outcry pealed through the deer-hide walls of a nearby lodge. Sparrow Woman noted with relief that she wasn't alone, after all, in this snow-shrouded landscape.

She picked her way through the village, using the decorated walls of the lodges as guideposts. She kept the cluster of tepees that belonged to the Kit Fox Clan to her right. To her left, the Bowstring Clan had adorned their lodges with pictographs of battles, of warring braves armed with bows and loosed arrows rampant against a background of buckskin.

She turned back toward the outskirts of the village and after what seemed a lifetime, stopped about thirty feet from her tepee. She looked past her lodge to the snow-swept expanse that stretched back down the valley. She remained motionless as if entranced by something unseen out beyond the storm, something that waited and watched.

She wanted to cry out, to alert the village, and yet she held her tongue. She was loath to give herself away. Her throat felt tight as if she were gripped in a stranglehold by some invisible giant. But she had to find the will and the strength to warn the village.

Perhaps her senses were playing tricks on her. She could not see or hear, try as she might, beyond the earthbound clouds. And yet Sparrow Woman felt to the depths of her being the approach of a stranger out of the gray clouds and swirling gloom.

'*Now!* An inner voice warned her. *Run!*

And still she held her ground, rooted in place by the turmoil in her breast. Fear no longer gripped her. She had misjudged her premonition. A new emotion welled within her, threatened to burst, became impossible to contain. She mouthed a name, no louder than a whisper—didn't she yell it—then started forward, a single hesitant step. One followed another as ahead—and the distance was deceiving—riders materialized out of the storm, as if conjured by the wind and wishes, the answered prayers of an aching heart.

Sparrow Woman ran toward them, casting aside all dignity, and called their names.

"Lone Walker, my husband, Jacob, my son."

They saw her while the lodges of the village were but ephemeral shadows hidden behind veils of wind-whipped snow.

Jacob held back and rode alongside Tewa. He reached out and took her hand in his. "We are home," he said.

"Home," Tewa repeated as if sounding the word for the first time. She tightened her grip, taking comfort in Jacob's certainty and strength.

Lone Walker rode on ahead, reached down and caught Sparrow Woman, and lifted her into his arms.

28

Sing a song of flesh and oneness, of ripe desire, of hunger and thirst and sweet appeasement. And yet, to be lost in love is all the singing and all the song a man or woman needs.

Lone Walker sighed contentedly and rolled on his side. Sparrow Woman nestled her warm, silken thighs against him, and with every breath her breast, insistent, pressed and slowly rekindled in him an earlier, spent passion. Four days ago, he had come down from the lost places, the far-removed places, the windswept passes and high mountain meadows. He had brought Jacob home, and Tewa.

Lone Walker remembered with satisfaction the expression on Two Stars' face as the old one embraced his granddaughter. And Calling Dove, though weak from her illness, had fussed over Tewa with motherly concern. Word had spread throughout the village, and well-wishers had defied the winter storm to welcome Two Stars' granddaughter. Lone Walker grinned, recalling how Jacob complained that far too many young men had noted Tewa's arrival. They called her She-Wolf and Warrior Woman, for she dressed like a brave and rode as well as any warrior, and on the very first clear morning had displayed her talents with bow and rifle. Then again, was it any wonder that the daughter of the legendary Wolf Lance should be so skilled?

"Where is our son this night?" Sparrow Woman asked, sighing softly in her husband's arms. The crackling fire underscored her question. Their shadows, entwined, danced upon the buffalo-hide walls of the lodge.

"Where else?"

"Two Stars' again."

"And taken his blanket and willow flute." Lone Walker glanced past his wife's shoulder at his son's shield and rifle and willow backrest. "He has left something behind for us to remember him by."

Sparrow Woman frowned. Her displeasure was apparent. Her limbs tensed. She no longer responded to Lone Walker's caress.

"You wished for him to no longer be alone. Now when he plays his pipe and invites a woman to his blanket, you frown and grow sour as green honey. What song is it that can find the truth in a woman's heart?"

"Wolf Lance, Tewa's father, is the truth I fear," Sparrow Woman replied.

"He rides the backbone of the world," Lone Walker said.

"Are you so certain?" Sparrow Woman's brown eyes studied the writhing flames.

"No," Lone Walker said, unable to lie to the woman who knew his heart so well. He rose from her side and knelt by the fire, added a few chunks of wood and rearranged the stones to better reflect the heat. The firelight played on his naked torso as muscles rippled the length of his battle-scarred flesh. He gathered a piece of charcoal, crushed it, moistened the ashes with spittle and shreds of boiled meat, smeared a stone with the black paste, and dropped the stone in the center of the fire. The spittle boiled away, the meat sizzled and burned, the crushed embers glowed with new life. Then Lone Walker began to chant, softly.

"Great One,
　Source of all surprise,
　You see everything on this earth.
　Hear my song prayer though I have broken your will
　And brought the child out of the Sacred Hills.
　I bind my guilt to you, All-Father.
　To where the sky meets the land
　Let no harm befall my son.
　Among the bones of the rain, protect him."

* * *

Lone Walker's voice trailed off and despite his proximity to the fire, he shivered. He knew the Above Ones had heard him. But as to the will of the Great Spirit, only time would tell. His limbs trembled yet again. Cold Maker stalked the land, stole among the lodges, waited outside the tepee walls. Lone Walker glanced toward his wife. Sparrow Woman's eyes glistened with tears as she opened the blanket to him. Her warmth drew him. Lone Walker returned to her side, slid against her and into her and loved her while the smoke from his spirit fire coruscated upwards and dissipated against the moon's frozen glare.

Jacob waited beneath the cold sky. He wasn't alone among the comical silhouettes of Piegan lodges. He spied other young braves moving silently toward the tepees of the maidens they had chosen to court. Moonlight twinkled like scattered diadems upon the frost-carpeted earth. The starry heavens, like a vaulted ceiling that stretched from ridge to ridge, roofed the entire valley of Medicine Lake. Harsh and chill and lovely lay the night. But Jacob was warm in his heavy woolen blanket as he stood a few yards from the entrance to Two Stars' lodge. Summoning his courage, he drew a reed flute from his medicine pouch. He rubbed the flute between his hands to warm the wood, then with his fingers upon the tone holes he had whittled with his knife, put the instrument to his lips and blew softly.

The sound was faint, almost inaudible. He cursed his awkwardness and tried again, summoning the courage to pipe with more force upon the reed flute. This time the trilling rang upon the still and wintry night. He played upon the reed, letting the lilting tones speak for him, some hesitant, others strong and full of longing.

There were other flutes, other young men with melodies of their own, and the mingling of their music made a joyous cacophony that sparked memories of days past in nodding old men when youth and spring were one.

Jacob played. He closed his eyes; his fingers fluttered over the holes transforming notes from low and throaty to a high, piping caprice. He no longer felt self-conscious. The ritual possessed him now. He was Sun Gift, a Blackfoot, a part of the People. Their ways were his. He only hoped she heard him. He only hoped she would respond.

Suddenly a hand touched his arm. He opened his eyes, and Tewa, sensing she had startled him, laughed and pulling her wolf cowl close around her shoulders, took the flute from his lips. She tapped the flute against his shoulder.

"There, I have counted coup. Now I am truly a warrior woman."

"And too proud to stand in my blanket?" Jacob asked. His right arm, draped with the blanket, swung out.

"Too cold to refuse."

Tewa stepped within reach. Jacob draped his blanketed arm around her shoulders and they walked together. The Hudson Bay blanket formed a cowl that almost completely hid their features as it protected them from the icy air.

"I am surprised Two Stars did not try to drive me off," Jacob remarked.

"He would have," Tewa said. "But I hid his war club and moccasins." She laughed again. Jacob loved the sound of her voice, especially her laughter.

They passed other couples, wrapped and shrouded in the night. Jacob thought he recognized Otter Tail's chunky shape waiting patiently before Good Bear Woman's lodge. The portly brave stomped his feet and slapped his sides in an effort to keep warm. Good Bear Woman was making him wait.

A mongrel pup left the side of a nearby tepee and cautiously approached the hooded couple. Jacob kicked a dirt clod in the direction of the pup and the animal scampered back to its mother's side. Jacob didn't want any distractions.

He glanced at Tewa. Her gaze was fixed on the western rims, and he sensed she walked the High Lonesome in her mind. A star streaked across the heavens, trailing green fire and lost itself beyond the ridge. For a second the darkness was illumined with emerald fire. There was magic here, though Jacob doubted his ability to read the sign. Lone Walker would have had some song for the phenomenon, some prayer chant to invoke the truth in a shooting star. Jacob had not his father's experience, or his wisdom, and he did not believe in the power of the songs. Jacob's truth was the strength of his limbs and a fast horse. His truth was a stout war club, a straight-shooting rifle, and the will to survive. His truth was the impetuousness of youth, and the desire that warmed his limbs and left him yearning for more than this night could bring.

"Do you long for the lonely places?" he asked.

"No. My heart hears my father's hurt and I am saddened. But not enough to leave."

"I am glad."

"Why?"

"I wish to bring horses to your grandfather . . . horses and fine robes and meat for his winter fire."

"What has such generosity to do with me?" Tewa asked, feigning ignorance.

"*Saa-vaa.* I think you know," Jacob scolded. He brushed his blond hair back from his face. His bronze eyes reflected the moonlight as he studied the woman in his arms and read her playful expression. "But I will speak it anyway. We are two called together. I am the Sun Gift, you are Tewa, the Earth Spirit. Surely old Two Stars will see it is good."

"Two Stars is blind," Tewa reminded the young man at her side.

"He will see. Tell him I will bring him gifts like no other. I will speak for you, that this blanket which surrounds us becomes like our lives, holding us together and making us one." Jacob spoke with authority now, clear and strong, for he knew in his heart what must be said. He could not wait months or years but must know now. As when he first saw her, his pulse raced and his breath clutched at his chest. "I will do all these things, Tewa, but first you must say you wish it so."

There. It was done. He would be bound to her from this night forth or he would depart with aching heart and dashed hopes. Let her decide.

Turn to the mountains. Let it be. Be free. Tewa could not hide her feelings any longer. His hunger was hers; his desire, hers as well. His strength called to her, his gentleness too.

"I wish it so," she said and freed him.

Jacob's heart soared among the glittering stars. Tewa's on gossamer wings joined his in the moonlight. Earthbound, their bodies melded one to the other beneath the blanket, and their hands caressed in secret places and foretold the sweeter rewards of the wedding lodge. And then a branch snapped, probably beneath a burden of ice, but Tewa gasped and looked toward the forest. Alarmed by the sound, she searched the impenetrable shadows at the forest's edge.

"What is it?" Jacob whispered. "Do you fear where the Cold Maker creeps among the trees?"

"I fear my father," the young woman replied.

"I pity him," Jacob countered. Tewa stiffened and tossed her head like a willful colt.

"Pity yourself if he rides down from the backbone of the world."

"Let him come. I will bring my fine horses to him. Let him accept my gifts, look into our hearts, and be glad."

Tewa shook her head. "I remember what Lone Walker told us. My father will meet you with his war lance in his hand." Her grip tightened on Jacob's arm. "I fear for you and for my father and what must happen when he rides down into Ever Shadow."

"Nothing will happen," Jacob replied. "I won't fight him. Wolf Lance can howl his challenge to the moon. I won't ride against him."

Tewa glanced up at the one who embraced her. He had found a way out of her dilemma. Her father was much too honorable to fight if Jacob did not ride out to meet him. Her worries ended.

"And what if others say you have the courage of a coyote?" Tewa asked, for Jacob was as proud as any young brave. Yet he only shrugged and remembering a biblical verse from his childhood, spoke haltingly, the memory so terribly distant, and not without pain.

"Tell them . . . to everything there is a season. A time . . . to hate and a time . . . to love, a time of war and a time of peace." Jacob held her close. "Peace will be the gift I bring to you."

On this night of shooting stars anything seemed possible.

29

Unshod hooves of Indian ponies cracked like gunshots, shattering the dry wintry stillness as the horses crunched along the ice-crusted trail. Jacob turned once more to his companions who had helped him track the bear whose paw prints led toward a thicket of aspen saplings and beyond to the dark patch of a cave a hundred yards away.

"You have done enough in cutting the bear sign," Jacob said. Otter Tail and Yellow Eagle had ridden with him the better part of the morning and kidded Jacob unmercifully now that he hoped to ask for Tewa in marriage.

"No, we ought to ride with you," Otter Tail said. "The bear will see your white skin and hide deeper in his cave thinking you are an evil spirit."

"Yes, let us call him out," Yellow Eagle added, grinning. "I have a charmed flute made from the leg bone of an antelope killed by a bear. I need but to blow upon it and old grandfather bear will charge from his lair."

"I must ride alone if I am to ask for Tewa. The gift of a fine bear pelt shall win me a wife from Two Stars."

"And what if the bear kills you?" Yellow Eagle asked, bringing up a distinct possibility. Jacob's aim would have to be true. There was no animal more fierce than a wounded bear.

"Then he can take my pelt to the village and ask for a bride of his choosing." Jacob laughed. "Perhaps even Good Bear Woman." He directed his remark at Otter Tail, knowing the corpulent brave had yet to find the courage to ask for the hand of Yellow Eagle's sister.

"I'd gladly accept," Yellow Eagle said. "It would be an improvement over the one who courts her now."

"*Saaa-vaaa-hey.* I've heard enough!" Otter Tail snapped and spun his horse around. "Someone had better keep watch over the horses you left in the meadow below. Unless you intend them for Kootenai thieves." He rode at a brisk trot back through the forest, retracing his own trail back down the wooded slope. The lofty branches of the ponderosa pines fractured the sunlight and left the hillside checkered light and dark. A man rode across golden gleaming snow into emerald shadow and entered sunlight again. It made for treacherous tracking. However, Jacob Sun Gift had long ago proved his prowess on the hunt.

"My sister may have to one day gather horses and pelts and ask for him," Yellow Eagle said, watching Otter Tail vanish into the woods. He turned, adjusting his weight on horseback. His bad leg often ached after a long ride. "I have ridden with you out of friendship. I leave the same way." He led his own mount onto the path Otter Tail had blazed, lifted his rifle in salute, and rode away.

Jacob watched him leave, sensing the immensity of the landscape loom even larger as he was left alone. He had ridden these woods before and could not understand why such familiar territory suddenly seemed ominous and overwhelming. Perhaps it was the stillness. No wild creature stirred. And on the horizon, the purple peaks were masked with clouds.

Even the noise of his friends' departure ceased to carry on the thin air as if the forest depths had swallowed him whole. Jacob eased the tension by checking his Hawken rifle and adjusting the broad-bladed knife in his belt. His hand closed around the familiar grip jutting from his belt. He carried no war shield. Willow frame and toughened bull hide would not turn the claws of an enraged grizzly. And that was precisely the game he had trailed, an old silvertip whose thickly furred pelt would warm the lodge of blind Two Stars, warm the blind one's heart too, and make the old one happy to accept Jacob's marriage offer.

Jacob studied the deep, five-pointed impressions the grizzly's paws had cut into the snow. They led toward the aspen grove true enough, but Jacob had no intention of plunging into the thicket. He'd skirt the aspens and angle about thirty yards out of his way along the hillside, then cut back and see if the bear sign continued up to the cave on the ridge just above timberline.

An absence of tracks would indicate the grizzly was in the aspen thicket. Jacob didn't relish the task of stalking the animal through that wall of aspen and underbrush. He hoped he wouldn't have to.

Jacob readied himself, marveling at the price a man had to pay to win the hand of his beloved. And what would his natural parents think, to see him courting a Blackfoot maiden. Somehow he felt Joseph and Ruth Milam would have loved Tewa and been proud to call her daughter.

Poor timing for memories. They dulled his sense of caution, preoccupied him with images of long ago, of a boy named Jacob Milam!

He was Jacob Sun Gift now and should never have ridden into the clearing, out of the safety of the pines. Jacob skirted the aspen grove but lost in his reverie cut closer to the aspens than he'd intended.

One moment he was recalling his parents' life of struggle and the next second he was struggling for his life. The thicket exploded in a shower of ice splinters and churned snow. Jacob reined back and his horse reared, pawing the air as a hammer-headed gray stallion charged out from the shadowy underbrush. Jacob kicked free as his horse went down beneath the stallion's onslaught. The gray's rider rose up and seemed to blot out the sky. A mask of hatred beneath a wolf's head cowl split open in a savage grimace, and a demonic shriek filled the air.

Wolf Lance! The name reverberated in Jacob's skull as he caught a glimpse of man and war shield and obsidian-tipped spear. The chiseled-stone spear point missed Jacob's throat by inches. Plunging hooves tore a patch of hide off his hip as the gray stallion vaulted the man on the ground.

Wolf Lance galloped past. Jacob staggered to his feet empty handed and looked in desperation for his rifle. He spotted it in the snow a few yards away. Behind him, his horse struggled to stand and fell back, one of its hind legs broken.

Wolf Lance charged.

"No," Jacob shouted, attempting to reason with the man. "Wait. I won't..." Oh hell, he thought and spun on his heels headed for his rifle. The earth trembled underfoot from the gray charger bearing down on him. Wolf Lance, black war paint smeared across his forehead and eyes, chalk-white paste covering the lower half of his face, brandished a ten-foot war lance, its pine shaft decorated with medicine symbols and black raven feathers.

Jacob reached the rifle, turned, and squeezed the trigger. The hammer slammed down on an empty nipple. The percussion cap had been jarred loose and was lost in the snow. It was an educated guess and all Jacob had time for. Death rode within arm's reach. He parried the spear. The gray stallion clipped his shoulder and knocked him into the snow.

Jacob Sun Gift hit hard, his senses reeling. On sheer reflex he gathered his arms beneath him and rolled to his side, and avoided once again the stallion's unshod hooves.

Jacob willed himself to stand. The aspen was just ahead. He glanced over his shoulder as Wolf Lance brought his war-horse around and drove his heels into the animal's flanks. Steam jutted from the stallion's nostrils.

"*Haaaiiii-yaaa!*" Wolf Lance roared as the gray lunged forward once more.

Jacob stripped off his buckskin shirt and darted toward his attacker. He waved the shirt, shouted and flapped, and the gray stallion pulled up sharply. Wolf Lance had to clutch at the animal's mane to keep from being thrown. That was Jacob's opening. He closed quickly and leapt for the rider. Wolf Lance tried to bring the startled gray to bear.

Too late. Jacob had him. He caught Wolf Lance by the leg and shield arm and held on for dear life as the stallion whirled and reared and bucked. Wolf Lance cracked his spear across Jacob's shoulder but could not dislodge his younger assailant.

Wolf Lance tossed the spear shaft aside and clubbed with his naked hand again and again, raining blows on Jacob who would not let go. The stallion, already panicked by the young man, broke into a gallop yet again. Jacob held Tewa's father in an iron grip. He brought all his weight to bear on the horseman, pulling himself up hand over fist, forcing Wolf

Lance off balance until with a cry of rage the older warrior shifted his stance toward Jacob and both men tumbled from the stallion and went sprawling.

Both men hit, slid over the ice and snow, and came to a rest a few yards apart. Jacob emerged, sputtering, spat a mouthful of dirty snow, and willed the spinning world to stop. *Lock it into place.*

Wolf Lance was already on his feet and closing fast. The older brave was amazing. He kicked out as Jacob rose to his knees. The blow knocked Jacob onto his back. Wolf Lance loosed a cry of victory, drew his tomahawk, and leapt for the fallen man. Jacob coiled up, straightened sharply, and drove a hard right heel into his attacker's groin. Wolf Lance gasped and doubled over and retreated.

Jacob crawled to his feet, stumbled up alongside Wolf Lance, and hit him with a solid left to the jaw. Wolf Lance sank to his knees. Jacob backed away and almost lost his balance. He tried to catch his breath.

"Listen to me," he gasped.

"I'll kill you," Wolf Lance weakly muttered.

"Listen—Tewa and I are called together."

"You . . . die."

"Why?"

"Because it must be so. The All-Father wills it."

"You will it!"

"Yes!" Wolf Lance growled and sprang upright. The whisper of his iron-bladed tomahawk carried on the stillness as it spun through the air. Jacob slipped and fell back against a lone sentinel pine that dominated the clearing. The hawk bit deep into the trunk, nicking Jacob's right ear. It was a superficial cut, but blood flowed down his neck.

Wolf Lance drew the heavy shaft of a war hammer from the beaded belt circling his solid waist and closed for the kill.

Jacob backstepped past the pine and headed toward the aspen grove. He ignored the war hammer and watched instead the man's eyes as Lone Walker had taught him. The eyes would reveal an enemy's intentions. It was a trick that never failed. But Wolf Lance, a seasoned warrior, kept his head deliberately low and he moved with the stealth of his namesake. And when he attacked he moved in close, quick and deadly.

The war hammer, crowned with a chunk of granite large enough to cave in a man's skull, only swiped empty air. Wolf Lance was fast, but Jacob was faster and reached the aspens. The underbrush held him up just a second and the hammer caught him a glancing blow that deadened his left shoulder and catapulted him against a wall of saplings. Jacob, hung up on the branches, saw an ugly red lump swell on his naked bicep. Only a heavy layer of muscle saved the bone.

Wolf Lance wasted no time but pressed his advantage. He plunged forward, the war hammer raised aloft, slashing down to crush Jacob's skull.

Jacob dropped forward and reached for his "Arkansas toothpick." His right hand closed around the rawhide-wrapped grip and whipped the razor-sharp blade from its sheath.

No thought now, the only instinct to survive. Jacob feinted, jabbed, the double-edged knife blade flashing with sun fire. Wolf Lance swung his war club in a mighty arc. Jacob, for all his size, ducked beneath the blow. The mallet head struck one of the saplings and snapped the three-inch-thick trunk like a twig. Jacob struck. He slashed the brave's chest. Wolf Lance gasped at the bite of the blade and leapt back. He chanced to look at the bloody rent in his buckskin shirt. But he was too experienced a fighter to be distracted by the painful wound. Jacob pressed his attack and moved in, his right arm set in a savage thrust. The knife shot out.

But Wolf Lance wasn't finished yet. The war club seemed to come out of nowhere and batted the outstretched knife from Jacob's hand. The granite club swept up and caught Jacob flush in the jaw. Jacob's head snapped back and stars exploded inside his head. The world went dark for a moment, then he turned his back and stumbled through the trees, knowing if he fell, that would be the end. His arm curled about one sapling. He swung around the trunk, gaining momentum. His foot lashed out and he planted a kick in Wolf Lance's belly that knocked the wind out of the brave and left him staggering. But Wolf Lance held on to his weapons, his war club, and now Jacob's own knife. He lashed out at the empty air.

Jacob spat blood and shoved himself out of the grove and into the clearing. An idea formed in the dim recesses of his mind. He retraced his steps, hurrying as best he could back to his rifle. Behind him, Wolf Lance had recovered enough to follow his quarry out into the clearing.

Jacob spotted the Hawken rifle in the snow and dropped to his knees by the weapon. His numbed fingers dug into the pouch on his belt for a percussion cap. Wolf Lance roared in defiance and charged. This was the moment. There would be no other. The two had fought themselves to near exhaustion. It must end now.

Wolf Lance raced across the glittering snow. Strength filled his limbs. The Above Ones were with him. The All-Father had brought him here and when Jacob Sun Gift lay dead then Wolf Lance could return to his people . . . return at last and dream new dreams.

Jacob fumbled with the percussion cap, dropped it, retrieved it from the icy crust, managed to work it onto the nipple.

Wolf Lance raced the distance and held the knife and war club ready to strike. He saw the younger man falter and one last cry of triumph welled from the heart of Wolf Lance. Then he sprang to the kill.

Jacob raised the big .50-caliber rifle and fired.

30

Tewa waited on a knoll in the heart of the village, waited in the sun-drenched afternoon with the glare of evergreen-laden ridges reflected on the frozen surface of Medicine Lake. It had become a custom among the people of Ever Shadow that a maiden would wait upon the knoll for her lover to ride past with his gifts for the girl's family.

Tewa did not wait alone. Sparrow Woman was at her side and Little Plume, wife of Yellow Eagle. Only women who had been taken to wife were allowed on the knoll in the presence of one such as Tewa, a girl waiting for her husband-to-be.

Young girls gathered at the foot of the knoll. Good Bear Woman, who hoped to one day await her own lover, was among them and a dozen or so other young girls including Red Moon, a slight wisp of a girl whose dark eyes smoldered with jealousy as she watched Tewa from afar.

Tewa was unaware of anything but the trail winding off down the valley. Smoke curled from the tops of the Indian lodges and the air was permeated with the smell of wood smoke and the rich aroma of boiled meat and fry bread.

Where was Jacob? The sun already walked a westward path across the sky. . . .

"I have seen his horses," one of the women, Sun Basket, remarked. She was an older woman, gray streaked her braids, and her leathery features were lit by a broad smile. "Many fine horses."

Sparrow Woman beamed proudly and thought to herself, No finer than the one who brings them.

Tewa wore a dress of brushed buckskin and calf-high moccasins. She had wrapped herself in a scarlet woolen blanket. Beadwork adorned her braided hair. But her dress, though fringed, was free of decoration.

Several of the older women of the village had erected a tepee on the periphery of the valley, distinctly apart from the village itself. This would be the wedding lodge. It stood just on the edge of the forest. The hide walls had been decorated with suns and running buffalo and prancing ponies. The lodge awaited its occupants.

"Soon now," Tewa whispered beneath her breath. First Jacob must come with his gifts, which Two Stars was already primed to accept. Then Standing Elk and some of the other tribal elders would conduct the *Two Called Together* ceremony. And afterwards . . . Tewa once again lifted her eyes to the lodge by the forest and envisioned herself curled beneath warm blankets, a fire close by, and alongside her, his head cradled upon her naked breast, Jacob Sun Gift. Man and woman together, made one. Even her father would have to understand and accept and put to rest the All-Father's terrible demands. Let there be children for him to hold, for him to teach his brave wise ways, for him to love and be healed and know peace.

Jacob had promised. . . .

"I see him," Little Plume Woman called out, shading her eyes. Tewa followed her example, shaded her eyes and saw in the distance a single approaching figure. It was Jacob. She knew in her heart Jacob had returned. But where were the horses? The travois of fine robes?

She waited and watched, frowning. What had happened?

"He's afoot," Sparrow Woman observed, her eyes sharp as a hawk's.

"He is leading his horse," Tewa explained. Not that she understood. Had his horse pulled up lame? And then suddenly she recognized the gray stallion he led, and the shock of recognition rooted her in place. Now she saw Yellow Eagle and Otter Tail riding about a quarter of a mile behind Jacob and they drove his horses along the valley floor and out into pasture. And were those robes draped across the back of the horse? No! No! A man, draped face down, his arms and legs dangling limp. She recognized the great black-feathered spear Jacob used as a staff, and her heart broke.

The wives began to drift from the mound sensing something was terribly amiss. Only Sparrow Woman remained and even she shrank back a step at the sight of her bruised and battered son.

Jacob entered the village and walked the horse straight toward the mound, the final steps of his young life's longest journey. Older women of the village recognized Wolf Lance, one of the tribe's bravest warriors, and the wailing began. But Jacob stayed his course and continued to the knoll and the woman he loved and had betrayed. And when he reached the place where Tewa waited, he dropped the reins and stood aside.

"This is the gift you bring to my family?" Tewa asked, her voice trembling but her head held high and shoulders ramrod straight.

"I had no choice," Jacob began. "I did not mean to break my pledge to you."

Tewa walked down from the knoll, unable to tear her gaze from her father's corpse. The slug from Jacob's rifle had gouged a fist-sized hole in the dead warrior's back where the slug exited. Wolf Lance's buckskin coat was stiff with dried blood.

"Jacob Sun Gift has broken no pledge," Tewa replied. "You promised peace between you and my father. I did not know it would be the peace of death."

She took the reins. Jacob reached for her. She drew away, took the great lance from him, and moved to her father's side. She spied her father's wolf cowl and pulled it from around the dead man's features. Tewa slipped the cowl over her own head. She wiped a hand across her father's cold cheek and smeared her face with his war paint.

Then she swung up on horseback and sat behind her father's lifeless form.

"The young men called me warrior woman and so I will be! As my father was first to ride to battle, so I will ride in his place!" Her voice rang out across the people of the village who had come to find out what had happened. Children were hushed quickly away as word spread.

"As my father lived alone, apart from his people, so I will keep my lodge there." She gestured with the lance toward the wedding lodge.

Jacob started toward her. Tewa lowered the spear and the tip of its obsidian blade dug into his chest, halting him in his tracks.

"This is the wolf lance. It is my father's spirit. It will always be between us."

Tewa rose up on the back of the gray stallion and held the wolf lance aloft. "I am Tewa, daughter of Wolf Lance. I am Warrior Woman! *Haaaiiii-yaaa.* All who come to my lodge do so as an enemy."

Tewa wheeled the gray stallion and rode from the knoll and bore her father's body toward the wedding lodge.

PART VI

Ever Shadow

31

April 1840

In the land of Ever Shadow, dreams die to live again. And in the blood of the bear, winter ends long before the geese wing north and snow-draped boughs at last yield their burden.

In Ever Shadow, life lies brittle as a twig and changes with the moon. Bitterroots spring from the soil, uncoil, become firm with bud, with the promise of rebirth.

In Ever Shadow, mysteries reign, for what is life without mystery. Fear stalks the ridges only to explode in the heart and burrow in the mind. It robs reason from the staunchest soul.

Broken-backed ridges, yawning cracks in the earth where the daylight seldom reaches, salt-white peaks that rise in frozen prominence like thrones to the Gods, all are Ever Shadow. All the products of a volatile earth, carved but never humbled by wind and glacier into reaches where a man must walk, if he is to stand in the Season of the Sun.

Tom Milam burrowed as deeply as he could in the niche he'd found between two slabs of granite. Something touched his ankle and for one brief moment he thought, *Rattler!* He would have bolted from cover but for the Blackfoot war party twenty feet away.

The spring winds had a wintry bite here on the divide in the place the Indians called Ever Shadow, but it was the movement by his foot that chilled his blood. He grabbed for the knife in his belt expecting the worst, then a gray chipmunk worked its way out from under Tom's right leg and scampered out of the crevice, and Tom sighed in relief, grateful he hadn't chosen a rattler's den for concealment.

There were five Blackfeet, riding single file along the same deer trail Tom had been following half an hour ago. He had spotted the braves and taken cover as they cleared the woods fifty yards downslope. The wind rushed upslope like a locomotive, kicked grit in his face, and passed on.

The Blackfeet looked to be returning home after a successful hunt. Three horses laden with fresh-killed meat and packets of smoked venison trailed behind the hunting party.

Tom had ascended the treacherous slope on foot. He'd left Pike Wallace with the horses below in the forest. He must have hidden himself well, as there had been no sign or sound of a struggle. No red bastard was going to take Pike's tam for a trophy without a struggle. And no murdering buck was going to take Tom Milam either. Enough Milams had perished in this howling wilderness. Tom Milam intended to live.

Slow as molasses in winter, he drew the percussion pistol from his belt. It was a big bore gun and fired the same hunk of lead as a Hawken rifle, a .50-caliber ball. His high-boned unshaven features blended into the shadowy juncture of the granite crevice. The walls around him blocked the procession of Blackfeet warriors from sight. But the hunting party would pass right in front of Tom's makeshift lair. And if even one brave noticed him, there'd be hell to pay.

Tom listened as the horses drew closer, heard the shale rattle downslope beneath the unshod hooves of the mountain-bred ponies. One of the braves spoke softly as if to his mount, urging the horse over a treacherous stretch of the trail. Tom had to admire Blackfoot horsemanship. He had been loath to try the slope on horseback, but these braves seemed undaunted in their ascent of the precipitous ridge.

Tom Milam held his breath and raised his gun as the lead brave appeared at the mouth of the crevice. He sighted on the warrior's beaded buckskin shirt, leading the hunter until the man rode out of sight. The next man was smaller in size, his thick body firmly astride his mount. The Blackfoot pulled a woolen blanket around his shoulders and cradled his rifle in the crook of his arm.

Tom once again shifted his aim as the third and then fourth warrior filed past. Their features were devoid of war paint, yet Tom felt no trust for them. The Blackfeet were notorious for protecting their tribal territory. They had fought incursions by the Sioux and Cheyenne, by the Crow and Bannock, and by the white man.

The last brave in line caught Tom completely off guard as he brought his gun to bear. He hadn't noticed before, but now he was training his gun sight on a white man. Or at least what had once been a white man.

Blond hair hung to the warrior's shoulders. The hunter's once pale skin had been burned by the sun to the color of bronze. He was long limbed and rode as if he were part of the animal beneath him, at one with the motion of the big chestnut gelding.

Here was a foundling. No doubt his family had been butchered by these Blackfeet and this man carried off as a child.

So, the white man he had been was dead and in his place rode a Blackfoot brave who would no doubt lift Tom's scalp if he got the chance. The kindest fate for him now would be a bullet in the brisket, Tom thought, and his finger tightened on the trigger. Then he realized how foolish he was being. A gunshot would mean Tom's own death as well. The blond-haired brave paused, his horse responding to the merest touch of the reins. The hunter turned and looked directly at the crevice as if sensing something about the hiding place and the menace it contained. The wind whipped the Blackfoot's long blond hair across his features as he studied the niche, the piercing bronze of his eyes as if chipped from the sun was set in a sad stern visage.

Tom ground his back against the rock wall behind him. His thumb poised on the hammer of his pistol, ready to cock and fire if the brave lifted the Hawken cradled in his arm. Tom Milam held his breath and willed himself as one with the surrounding stone. He peered past his gun sight into the face of the white warrior and felt a cold chill creep up his spine. It was an unsettling experience that might have blossomed into full-blown recognition had not the white warrior as suddenly turned away and continued along the trail.

Tom Milam waited and listened to the clatter of the horses recede along the ridge trail. He sighed and lowered his gun, not realizing how close he had come to killing his own brother.

32

Tom Milam sat astride his bay mare on the forested shore
of the Marias River and allowed the animal to drink its fill
upriver of Fort Promise.

Tom studied with open appreciation the accomplishments
wrought by Nate Harveson, Coyote Kilhenny, and the veritable army of men they had brought from Independence.

A great stockade rose out of the lush grassy meadow about
two hundred yards from the river and well out of reach of any
flood should the Marias ever leave its well-worn banks.
Hand-hewn timber walls towered fifteen feet and provided
ample protection for the entire complement of Harveson's
command.

The fort's west wall served as entrance and exit. Two
massive doors swung ajar and a path had already been worn
through the gate, passing beneath a whitewashed plaque that
read FORT PROMISE. Nate Harveson had brought the plaque
from Independence, safeguarding it in his cabin throughout
the long trip by stern-wheeler. Two smaller blockhouses
dominated the cleared ground in front of the fort, arranged in
such a way as to bring an enemy venturing to the front gate
into a crossfire. They were solid-looking structures, built to
withstand attack. Each housed a dozen men. Firing ports
lined the walls. Food and cisterns of water were stored
within. And each blockhouse sheltered a nine-pounder cannon loaded with grapeshot, devastating weapons at close
range. The cannon portals were shuttered and latched from
the inside to conceal the weapons until the proper time.

The fort itself held three more nine-pounders. Their black

iron snouts poked from the ramparts to north, south, and west. Several long, low-roofed barracks had been built beneath the walls to house the men. A stable and corral lay in the shadow of the east wall. In the center of the compound, Nate Harveson had built a two-story log house facing the gate. Stone chimneys rose skyward from the north and south ends and shed-roofed servants' quarters were connected to the rear of the house. Smoke curled from the chimneys.

Pike Wallace and a half-dozen other riders pulled up alongside Tom. Pike dismounted and rubbed his buttocks.

"I got three weeks of ache in me," he groaned. He dropped the reins and his horse sauntered on to the river's edge.

"They finished them two blockhouses since we been gone," another of the men dryly noted. "I'll choose the trail over hauling timber any day."

"These bones ain't suited to neither," Pike complained. "A man my age deserves finer things than a blanket on the ground, jerked beef, and cold coffee." He scratched his scalp beneath his plaid tam and looked up at Tom. "Of course, some of us have got better reasons than corn likker and hot food for coming on in." He grinned at the men behind him. The hardened trappers chuckled among themselves, for it was common knowledge Tom Milam and Abigail Harveson enjoyed each other's company whenever the opportunity might arise.

"We need to run us down some squaws," one of the six grumbled loud enough for Tom to hear, but he was unable to identify the speaker.

Tom ignored the complainer. He didn't care if the man slept alone or with a pack mule. His gaze had centered on Iron Mike, Skintop Pritchard, and the Shoshoni whose name they'd all shortened to Bear. The three men rode a buckboard loaded with empty barrels. Iron Mike steered the team and Skintop Pritchard rode beside him on the seat. Bear sat in back with the barrels.

Traversing the wheel-rutted path to the river took more than a little skill. The wild grasses had been beaten into the sod by all the traffic and the dirt itself churned into mud. But Iron Mike was the best man behind a team of mules and he took pride in his ability to handle the transport wagons. A fistful of reins was more than most men could manage.

"Probably gonna fill them barrels and cart 'em to the blockhouses," Pike observed.

"Better hope nothing spooks his mules," another of the trappers muttered. "Come on you nag, drink your fill. Then I get my rum."

"At noonday? Like hell," cautioned another of the group. His name was Bill Hanna—Dog Bill, men called him, for the peculiar tastes he had acquired in captivity among the Kiowa. Dog Bill claimed he could stew a mongrel until it tasted like buffalo hump. No one disputed his claim. No one had ever stepped forward to make him prove it either. "Nate Harveson don't allow the likker uncorked 'ceptin' after sundown." Dog Bill scratched beneath his brawny arms, grinned, and showed a row of blackened teeth. He was a big heavyset man marked for life by a Kiowa scalping knife that had left a jagged white ridge of scar tissue scrawled across his forehead. "Come to think of it. I'm about tired of Harveson's say-so. Think I'll have a jug all to myself."

"Now you're talking. Tear that key right off Harveson's neck and head for the supply house," the first trapper, Job Berton, replied, relieved he'd have help in bracing Harveson.

"Key, hell!" Dog Bill said. "I'm tired and mean enough to bite the damn lock off and help myself. You with me, Tom?" He knew Milam had a wild streak as wide as the Mississippi and could be counted on when there was some devilment abrew.

But Tom's attention was elsewhere. He studied the water wagon and Iron Mike. And the longer he watched, half a dozen pranks ran through his mind. Iron Mike was a cruel son of a bitch and Skintop Pritchard a bully. And as for Bear, well, everyone knew such savages to be tricksters and back shooters, men who fought without honor. Tom had no use for his kind.

Finding the three together presented too good an opportunity to miss. He reined the bay mare about. The half-wild animal reared and pawed the air, but Tom held on and forced the mare to his will and galloped down toward Fort Promise.

Tom rode at an angle that brought him behind the water wagon.

As yet no one had noticed him. The men on the bench seat had their backs turned and the Shoshoni appeared to be asleep.

Tom untied the blanket from behind his saddle, then gripped the reins and his Hawken rifle in one hand and the blanket in the other. Several of the men in the fort noticed his approach and waved. Tom ignored them and headed away from the stockade walls and toward the wagon. He waited until he'd closed within twenty feet of the wagon, then rose up in the saddle and loosed a blood-curdling yell, fired his rifle, and swung the blanket in a circle over his head. *"Haaaiii-yaaa!"*

Bear, the Shoshoni, jolted awake and slipped down into an empty barrel, leaving only his fingers and feet hanging over the rim. The startled mules stampeded despite Iron Mike's effort to hold them back. Four mules, in their traces, charged as one down an incline that only increased their speed.

Skintop Pritchard, at the crack of the rifle shot, stood and spun around and grabbed for the pistol tucked in his belt. A wagon wheel dipped into one of the ruts and struck with a jolt that knocked Pritchard off balance. The trapper pitched from the buckboard and landed on the single tree between the mules. The pistol jetted black smoke as Pritchard inadvertently fired the gun. The already panicked team continued their headlong rush to the river.

"Whoa! Hold up, damn you!" Iron Mike bellowed. The wagon bucked from side to side. He didn't dare reach for the brake. "Hold up!" The mules rolled their eyes, flattened their ears back, and galloped on.

And Tom Milam urged them on with war whoops and flapping blanket.

"Oh no," Iron Mike groaned as the river rose to meet him. "Whoa!" He hauled on the reins, put his back in the effort. "Ohhh . . . shit!"

The wagon skidded in the mud and hit the river with enough force to send a shower of spray exploding into the air. Iron Mike flew headfirst into the Marias. The mules kicked and fought their harness. Skintop Pritchard dove over the backs of the team to keep from being hit or kicked.

As for Bear, the Shoshoni had just pulled himself halfway out of his barrel when the buckboard careened down the riverbank. The wagon gate dropped and the barrels spilled out the back of the wagon, depositing the hapless brave into the muddy shallows.

Tom Milam turned the mare and headed the animal upslope toward Fort Promise. He felt better than he had in days. Behind him, Pritchard, Iron Mike, and the Shoshoni continued to flounder in their icy bath

Iron Mike heard the laughter and spied Tom riding away. In the distance, Kilhenny's trappers on the walls of Fort Promise cheered and guffawed and taunted the men in the river. Pike Wallace, Dog Bill, and the others rode downriver to add their remarks at the expense of Iron Mike and his companions but were quickly chased back toward the fort.

Skintop Pritchard wrung the water from his beaver hat and hurled it in Tom's direction. He staggered out of the river and shook his fist in the air.

"I'll kill him. The little bastard. I swear I'll kill him!"

"You'll have to stand in line," Iron Mike growled, stumbling up onto the bank. He slipped and sat down in the mud and grimaced as the muck seeped into his britches. He shut his eyes and shook his head in dismay.

Bear crawled out of the barrel for the second time, wiped the water from his dark face, and glanced about in utter bewilderment. He angrily made his way up to Iron Mike, who'd just managed to stand.

"I thought my white brother said he could handle a mule team," Bear complained.

Iron Mike's only reply was a big fist that clipped the brave beneath the chin and flung him onto his back in the sand. The brave rolled over on his stomach, started to push himself off the ground, then settled unconscious against the moist earth.

Skintop Pritchard reached down and dragged the brave back into the water.

"What the devil are you doing?" Iron Mike said, glaring.

"Bringing him around," Pritchard wearily replied. "I don't aim to load these barrels without all the help I can get."

33

Tom had sensed the tension in the fort by the time he'd reached the livestock corral and unsaddled his horse. Spence Mitchell had been shoeing the livestock; he quit when he spied Tom arrive. Mitchell spat a stream of tobacco juice and sauntered over to Tom.

"Coyote wanted to see you as soon as you showed."

"After I report to Nate," Tom answered. He noticed another figure in the shadow of the barn and recognized Con Vogel. The musician had been relegated to stable work and it didn't appear to suit him.

"Kilhenny said to check with him first."

Tom had noticed the change. On the trip upriver from Missouri and during the first few weeks at the Marias landing, Nate Harveson had acted as the sole authority; orders came and went from him, sometimes directly, other times through Coyote.

Yet the farther the stern-wheeler ventured into the wilderness, the more Coyote had begun to undercut those selfsame orders. He'd never openly defied any of Harveson's instructions; he had merely altered a few or made them sound as if they were his own pronouncements.

The half-breed had commandeered a cabin for himself set below the ramparts lining the north wall. Now he'd left orders for men to report to him before they went to Harveson. Soon, Tom figured, he might not need Harveson at all. And what would that portend for Nate?

Or Abby?

Tom glanced up and true to his thoughts spied her watching

him from a second-story window. He looked toward Coyote's cabin, then reached a decision. He'd been on the trail three long weeks. Three long weeks without holding Abby in his arms, without her warmth and easy company.

Coyote would just have to wait. He headed for the Harveson house. Con Vogel watched him go.

"You've seen him then," Nate Harveson said from the doorway to Abigail's bedroom. His diminutive frame was garbed in a round-necked white shirt and black woolen trousers tucked into calf-high black leather boots. His Roman nose was red and peeling from the sun. His cheeks too showed sunburn as well as the front of his scalp, which he had failed to adequately cover even by combing his hair forward. He held a glass of brandy and took measured even sips of the liquor, taking time to inhale the bouquet.

"I intend to spend the afternoon with Monsieur Napoleon," he said, holding up a decanter of French brandy. "So you may freely entertain your brash, ill-mannered young pup."

"More wild tomcat than a pup," Abigail chuckled and folded her arms across her bosom. The blue gingham dress and apron she wore fit her like a glove, accentuating the curves of her bust and hips before flaring out and hanging to the floor. She wore leather ankle boots that buttoned up the side, a laborious task left for Virginia to perform. "Tell me, brother. This newfound tolerance for Tom Milam puzzles me. What's behind such regards?"

"Nothing untoward." Nate Harveson raised the snifter to his sister in salute, drained the contents, and felt the liquor burn a path to the pit of his stomach. "Charm him, dear sister. This isn't Missouri now and we may have need of a wildcat in the days to come. I'll interrupt you two in a quarter of an hour, and have his report."

Abigail started to press him further. The whole wilderness experience was so new and exciting to her she had failed to take note of the strained relationship between Coyote Kilhenny and her brother.

But Nate Harveson had revealed enough for now. He did not want to alarm his sister needlessly. Still, there was something going on with the half-breed—exactly what, Harveson was uncertain.

At least one of the stern-wheelers had remained behind. The ship's captain, Mose Smead, and his crew would back Harveson if trouble erupted. The riverboat was the last link with the civilized world and Harveson had been loath to sever this final bond. Now he was grateful for its presence.

Then again, maybe he was making too much out of Kilhenny's attitude. Kilhenny had certainly driven the men to impressive accomplishments. Fort Promise needed but a little finishing off. There was another barracks to build and the fort needed its own well. With Fort Promise completed, Nate Harveson figured he could rule the vast domain of mountains and game-filled valleys to the west.

"Mine," he muttered as he entered his own bedroom. "I'll drink to that." And that's exactly what he did.

Thalia had just lifted a skillet of corn bread from the stone fireplace out in the summer kitchen when Tom Milam rounded the corner of the house and loosed his best imitation of a Kiowa war whoop. Thalia, for all her plumpness, cleared the wood floor by six inches and raised the skillet aloft as if to save it from the howling savage.

Then she recognized Tom Milam, who had become a regular at her table, and regained her composure. On her rounded ebony features was a patina of flour and sweat. The summer kitchen was her domain—four poles, a wood floor, and a peaked roof, a place without walls where a breeze could cool the hardworking cook and carry the aroma of her labors throughout the fort.

But Thalia served the Harvesons. And woe to the hard-bitten trapper who tried to sample her wares uninvited. Tom Milam was the exception, though she considered him an impudent and mischievous rascal. Still, Thalia loved Abigail like a daughter and Abby had taken Tom to her heart over Thalia's dire warnings. A wild young man like Tom Milam could only bring trouble, Thalia had warned. He makes me happy, Abby countered.

And Thalia had to admit, he was a roguishly handsome

lad, full of the devil. Plus he downright worshiped her cooking. So he couldn't be all bad.

"Tom Milam!"

He laughed and swaggered up to the summer kitchen and perched on the oaken table where he helped himself to a piece of molasses cake Thalia had left to cool.

"Lawd above. You just about gave me the fits," Thalia said, slamming the skillet down on the table to loosen the bread. She flipped it over and the golden brown corn bread flopped out onto a stoneware plate. "Scared me plumb to the bone."

"Don't worry, Thalia. A red heathen'd be a fool to lift your hair. More'n likely he'd cart you back to his wickiup to do his cooking."

"You gettin' sassy with me, boy?" Thalia put her hands on her broad hips. Her huge bosom rose and fell when she sighed.

"As much as I can get away with."

"Last young buck that sassed me, I took him between the sheets and when I got finished with him, he was so weak he'd break wind and fall down." She winked and added, "But the smile never left his face."

"I'll just bet," Tom said, his voice muffled by a mouthful of cake.

He climbed down from the table and retreated from the cook's domain. Abigail waved to him from the top of the steps at the rear of the house and Tom Milam grabbed at the chance to escape the black woman by the table. If she indeed had her mind on sparking, Tom wasn't about to let himself be the tinder.

He walked up to Abigail Harveson. She retreated into the house. Tom followed her into the winter kitchen, a smaller version of the room outside with a narrow pantry and a smaller hearth, stone cold, its ovens and kettles, pots and skillets, already transferred outside as soon as the temperatures had ameliorated.

"You look as pretty as a meadow of columbine, ma'am." He grinned and caught her arm as she tried to lead him toward the front parlor. He pulled Abigail to his embrace and covered her mouth with his. Three weeks had been as long for Abigail and she matched the ardor of his kiss.

His buckskins were caked with dust and smelled of horse sweat and wood smoke. Tom's cheek was rough and black with three weeks of beard. Since departing Independence, there had been time for only the briefest of encounters, always clandestine, always interrupted.

Things hadn't changed at the Marias landing. A tremendous amount of work needed to be done, offering little free time for Tom and Abigail to be alone. Then the area itself had to be scouted, possible enemies located. Three weeks on the trail with Abby on his mind, memories of her that night in Independence, had kept him warm in a cold camp.

But he was home now and the feel of her in his arms stirred his blood, revived his tired limbs. He knew he reeked of the trail, but it didn't matter. First things first.

Abigail felt as if the breath were being sucked out of her. A fire blazed in her lower torso, and her legs grew weak. She hadn't been prepared for such ardor, not in him, and especially not in herself. At last she pushed away, at least enough to end the kiss, though his arms imprisoned her.

"A simple handshake ought to do . . . among friends, that is," Abigail gently chided.

"We were friends in Independence. You're in the wilderness now. Winds blow. Rains fall."

"Oh, I see," Abigail added, her brown hair a mass of ringlets and natural curls framing her pale cream features and mysterious sea-green eyes. "And fires burn?"

"Every chance they get." Tom's embrace tightened anew, drawing her to his lips.

"Excuse me, Miss Abby," Hiram said from the doorway to the dining room. The black man's formal attire of close-fitting waistcoat, white shirt, and black trousers seemed wholly out of place in the rustic confines of log walls. "Mr. Harveson will see you in the parlor, sir."

The interruption had its desired effect. Tom released the woman in his arms. He exited by the hall door and with obvious regret left Abigail in the kitchen.

"Tom?" She called him back. When he turned around, she

held a coffee pot and a cup of freshly poured coffee. "I thought you might be thirsty."

"It's what I'm hungry for that counts," Tom said. "After I report to your brother and scrub the trail off my hide, maybe I'll eat."

"Maybe we'll eat together," Abigail suggested, a knowing smile brightening her expression. Her eyebrows arched in a look of innocence; but her green eyes brimmed with temptation.

34

The parlor was a long, spacious room that included the whole front of the house. One corner served as Nate Harveson's study and contained his desk and a number of bookcases. A piano, a divan, and a variety of end tables and padded Queen Anne chairs dominated the remainder of the room.

Tom reached the parlor ahead of Harveson, who appeared moments later on the rather steep stairway leading to the second-floor bedrooms. Harveson quickly descended and waved Hiram to him.

"Where's Virginia? I haven't seen her about," Harveson said.

"She's in the fort somewhere," the snowy-haired old servant reported.

"Hell, that's no answer."

"She said something about catching fish for supper." Hiram tried to remember when he had seen the girl last.

"Well, have her straighten and clean upstairs," Harveson ordered. He shook his head, sighed, and continued across the room to his desk. He slumped down in his chair and stared at the crudely drawn map of the area. A great deal of blank space was rapidly being filled in with creeks and draws, ridges and valleys and lakes, adding an intimate detail to the map.

"Yours is the last survey party to return," Harveson said, folding his hands across his belly. His stubby fingers toyed with the buttons on the vest he had chosen from his choices upstairs. "I hope you kept accurate notes, my young friend."

Abigail entered the room and sat by the piano. Tom nodded

to her and then joined Harveson at the desk. He started to reply when a pounding on the front door cut him off. The front door, unlatched, swung ajar and Coyote Kilhenny filled the doorway.

He looked broad as a buffalo. His muscled shoulders strained the fabric of his plaid woolen shirt. His thick legs resembled tree stumps wrapped in buckskin. He wore a short-handled ax on his belt; his shaggy red hair hung to his shoulders and blended with his bushy beard. His pistol belt was draped, as usual, across his right shoulder and Tom had no doubt the three pistols holstered on the bandolier were loaded and primed.

Kilhenny stepped inside uninvited, spied Tom Milam, and took a seat by the desk. The chair groaned beneath his weight.

"Spence told me you rode in, Tom. Figured you'd stop by and see me, lad," Kilhenny said. "Being as we're like family and all."

"All survey parties are to report directly to me on returning to Fort Promise." Harveson smoothed his silvery hair and kept his voice low and cordial. "After all, you have your responsibilities, Mr. Kilhenny, and I have mine. We made that clear from the outset and shook on it like gentlemen."

"Civilized agreements always sound better in civilized places." Kilhenny leaned forward and helped himself to a glass of brandy from a table by the desk and gulped the liquid down. He grimaced at the sugary taste and returned the bottle to the table. "I'd as sooner drink mule piss."

"I beg your pardon." Harveson straightened indignantly in his chair. Tom had the image of a gamecock attempting to face down a grizzly. "My sister is present, sir."

"Oh yes, indeed," Kilhenny exclaimed, peering over his shoulder at Abigail. "I mean *horse* piss, ma'am." The half-breed turned his attention once again to the map at hand.

Here on the breaks of the Marias, with the mountains only a good day's ride from the front gates, it was important to know as much as possible about the maze of valleys and snow-patched divides of Ever Shadow. Two of the three riverboats had been sent back to Missouri. Harveson intended to bring up more supplies and an assortment of merchants and tradesmen necessary to transform the outpost into a real community, a permanent settlement supported by the fur trade and later the traffic lured by the mineral riches the mountains surely contained.

By summer's end, Nate Harveson hoped to be able to look out on the beginnings of a real town. Nothing and no one was going to keep him from realizing his dream, especially a troublesome rogue like Kilhenny.

For now, Harveson needed the legendary half-breed. But once those two other boats returned . . .

"Pike drew the maps," Tom said, for once trying to defuse the situation so he could get on with the real reason for his visit. He took an oilskin package from inside his buckskin coat and tossed it on the desk top. "Dog Bill helped as well. He has a steady hand and kept his own record."

"What about Blackfeet? Did you cut any sign of them red devils?" Kilhenny asked.

"Plenty of it," Tom replied. "I think there's a village back in a valley about a five-day haul from here. Pike and I spotted a hunting party. We trailed it as long as we dared."

Tom glanced across the room at Abigail, then returned his attention to the map on the desk. "Pike has our maps. You'll be able to fill in some of those blank spaces," he said.

"Just so long as he brings them to *me*," Harveson pointedly replied.

"Oh, he will. He will," Kilhenny said. "I'll personally see to it. Come along, lad." Kilhenny's bushy eyebrows furrowed and his hard-edged stare bore into Tom. "I'll have a word with you, Tom, my boy." Kilhenny straightened and rapped a scarred fist on the desk top. "We'll have the stockade finished out within the week. Right in time for us to invite our Blackfeet brothers to powwow."

"I still have my doubts about your plan. It does seem a trifle harsh," Harveson said.

"Spoken like a true gentleman," Coyote Kilhenny said. "Let the other fellow make the first move. That works east of the Mississippi. Out here, it only gets you scalped."

"But the final decision will rest with us." Abigail's voice

carried as much authority as her brother's. She was not cowed in the least by Coyote Kilhenny and was determined to prove that fact to one and all. "Our money. Our decision."

"My life, my decision." Kilhenny ran a hand across his grizzled features, nodded in Abigail's direction, and headed for the door. "Tom?" he called over his shoulder as he left.

"Tom?" Abigail repeated the call in her own soft and inviting way.

Young Milam hesitated, torn between the woman by the piano and Kilhenny's shadow stretching in through the open front door where the half-breed waited outside. At last he started to leave. Time and tragedy had cut a pattern he couldn't break.

"Young man," Nate Harveson said. Tom paused, partway to the door. "I should like to talk to you later. My sister has convinced me I've misjudged you."

Tom looked aside as Abigail came to him and placed a hand on his arm.

"Kilhenny is a braggart and an uncouth lout," she said. "What future can you realize by standing in his shadow?" She lowered her voice and looked furtively toward the door.

"I'd like you to be my friend," Harveson added, swirling the contents of his brandy snifter and inhaling the aroma. "A special friend to us both. I'd like to know I can count on you in case of trouble."

"I am trouble," Tom replied, a reckless grin splitting his features. He headed through the doorway.

Hiram seemed to materialize out of thin air and closed the door.

"A disturbing young man," Harveson wryly noted. "Tell me, did he agree or no?"

Abigail had to chuckle. "We'll find out, dear brother, one way or the other. We'll find out.'

She walked to the piano, ran a finger across some middle notes, then turned and peered through the window at Kilhenny and Tom Milam walking side by side. Their shadows stretched forth side by side on the trampled earth and in their wake a dust devil danced and died.

* * *

Con Vogel stared down at his grimy blistered hands, tossed the shovel aside in disgust, and kicked a black clump of dried manure out of his path.

"Enough, damn it!"

Spence Mitchell had to laugh. He poked his wizened profile over the wooden rail to the stall he was cleaning.

"Yup. I been saying the same thing for nigh unto fifty-eight years," he cackled. Mitchell spewed a greasy brown stream of tobacco juice into the straw at his feet. "And here I be." He doubled over, slapped his thighs, and passed gas. "Learn a lesson from old Spence Mitchell, mister fiddle player." Spence wiped his mouth, sighed, and leaned on the stall railing. "Lord, but that's a good one."

Vogel found no humor in the situation. He scowled and stalked off toward the corral, out of the low-roofed long shed that served as a barn. He paused by a water trough and stared at his reflection on the surface of the water.

Was this the son of Hermann Vogel . . . this barn sweep dressed in dirty shirt and worn at knee britches? Were these the hands of a master violinist now callused and cut and blistered? He stared at Harveson's house and replayed, in his mind, a scene weeks earlier when Nate Harveson had agreed to allow Con Vogel to accompany him west.

Harveson has insisted Vogel earn his keep and that meant laboring as something other than a musician. A change had come over Harveson since departing Independence. He had little time in his life for music, being driven by his dream of this northwest outpost.

Con Vogel had only come along in hopes that Abby would come to her senses. But no such luck. Her infatuation with Tom Milam had yet to run its course. Vogel's patience was wearing thin, not to mention the palms of his hands. From the corral, he watched as the front door opened and Kilhenny emerged, followed eventually by Tom Milam himself. The two continued across the compound. Abby appeared in the doorway, her gaze centered on Tom. She never once looked toward the corral.

"Fiddle player, I ain't gonna tend this shed on my lonesome," Spence called out. He stepped from beneath the low

overhang of bridles and bits and leather harnesses dangling
from the pinewood ceiling. "She's as pretty as a picture and
puts a fire under my rocks as much as yours, but that won't
get the stalls cleaned out or put grain in the feed boxes
neither."

Another stream of tobacco juice arced from shadow into
morning sunlight. Vogel lifted his eyes to heaven but what he
intended for Abby and Tom was rooted in hell.

Night, and the bonfire illuminated the sky, and rum and
whiskey flowed free. Fort Promise wasn't entirely completed,
but the work was close enough to finished that the men
clamored for a celebration. Kilhenny heard their pleas. He
blasted the lock off the storage shed and handed out a dozen
casks of liquor to the men gathered round. Skintop Pritchard
and his men had brought in a buffalo carcass. The bull was
skinned and slaughtered and the dark meat spitted and hung
over the cookfires.

Kilhenny's men hooted and hollered and fired their rifles
into the air. Con Vogel had been dragged from his cot and
coerced at gunpoint to fiddle a tune. Vogel's talents began
and ended with the classics, but a minuet played at a furious
pace carried enough rhythm and melody to set the men to
dancing a drunken jig or singing out of tune and improvising
enough off-color lyrics to make a Hun blush.

Beneath the cook-shed roof, by the friendly glow of her
own hearth, Thalia clasped her Bible to her ample bosom and
looked from Hiram to Virginia and shook her head.

"Only God-fearing souls I know is in this here summer
kitchen." She noticed how Virginia kept glancing off toward
the front gates and the hell-raisers gathered outside the walls
of Fort Promise. The Harveson house actually blocked the
young girl's view, but Thalia knew what the girl was thinking. "Child, you ain't got no place among such kind."

Virginia turned on the cook and her eyes flashed with an
intensity that belied her young years. "And just where's my
place? Breaking my back for the likes of high-and-mighty
Miss Abigail or lyin' on it for Mister Nate's pleasure?"

Thalia gasped and glanced in alarm toward the house.
"Hush your voice," she muttered.

"I ain't afeard of Mister Nate," Virginia said. "Not anymore."

"You aren't so old he won't take a switch to your behind." Hiram spoke up from the end of the table.

"Let him try," Virginia said, a proud expression on her coffee-colored features. "Coyote Kilhenny will carve my name on his hide." Virginia ran a hand through her thick black curls and she straightened and stood with her shoulders back and her pointed breasts straining against her cotton blouse. "And if he's not of a mind to, then Con Vogel. Yes. That's right. I've had them both."

"Stay put," Hiram cautioned, a note of sternness in his voice. "And say no more."

"You don't order me," Virginia snapped. She had not meant to sound so peevish; it came natural with trying to defend her conduct. She liked Hiram. He had always treated her kindly. But she was sixteen years old now and had a mind of her own.

"Child, you don't know what you are saying?" Hiram placed a bony black hand on the young woman's smooth, silken forearm. "Mister Nate's treated us good."

"Good enough for you maybe. But there's another high cock of the pen. I heard things. . . ." Suddenly her eyes widened and she clamped a hand over her mouth and retreated toward the yard. Thalia made a grab for the girl, but she easily eluded the cook's grasp and sprang away across the yard, disappearing around the corner of the house. She never broke stride on her way to the bonfire.

And from the window in his room, Nate Harveson watched her run. He spun about and hurled his wineglass at the blanket-draped wall of his room. The glass crashed to the floor. Moments later, Abigail worked the latch on his door and stood in the doorway.

"Are you all right?"

"Yes!" Harveson growled. "No!" he sputtered, trying to put his suspicions into words. Then again, just how much could he confide? He had never spoken of his intimate relationship with the mulatto servant.

"You've found Virginia?" Abigail asked. Her brother nodded. He worked his small fist into the palm of his hand.

"And lost her?" Harveson stared at her, caught off guard by her revelation. "Yes," Abigail continued, "I am aware of your obsession with the girl."

"How?"

"Dear brother," Abigail gently chided. "Being younger than you doesn't make me blind and deaf."

'You never said anything." Harveson crossed to a heavily japanned end table by his bed. He filled another glass with wine. The din of the trappers' jubilant celebration carried through the walls of the house. The wine bottle close at hand was Harveson's own private party.

Abigail crossed the room, knelt by the far wall, and began to pick up the pieces of the wineglass.

"You seem to always be picking up the pieces after I break something," Harveson muttered dejectedly.

"Feeling sorry for yourself, dear brother?" Abigail said. "Come now. Your only failures have been in matters of the heart. For as long as you've worn long pants, you've been in love with the wrong woman."

Harveson chuckled. "That I have." He sloshed another mouthful of wine down his throat and almost choked on the vintage, for his mind was full of painful recollections that somehow struck him as amusing here in this room on the edge of a wild and dangerous country. Ambition was his true paramour, the one love that had never failed him. "You're right, of course. I'm well rid of her. Let her take to the rogues. By summer's end I'll be done with all of them and we'll have a proper town. You'll see."

"Of course we will," Abigail said, standing by the window that looked out upon the entrance to the fort and the glare of the bonfire beyond. The fire beckoned her. The silhouettes of men formed shifting shadows, mysterious by firelight. Their voices were coarse accompaniment to the music of violin and concertina. Abigail heard her brother rise from the bed and start from the room. She followed him into the narrow hall and downstairs to the front room as Mose Smead entered from the back of the house. He held a bowl of peach preserves and a chunk of Thalia's day-old bread.

Smead was a congenial sort in his river captain's coat and

blue woolen trousers. He was of average height and his
friendly features were framed by thick, bushy sideburns. He'd
plied the Mississippi with Nate and Abigail's father and been
a partner in more ventures than he could remember. Nate and
Abigail were family to the captain, like his own children.

He looked up and grinned. "Hope ya'll don't mind. I kinda
helped myself. Didn't see anybody about."

Mose sampled the bread after dipping the end into the
preserves. As soon as he began to chew, an expression of
utter bliss transformed his features. "I swear that old colored
woman can cook." He continued on through the front room
and took a seat by the piano. Captain Smead's other "vice"
was music—listening, not playing.

Nate Harveson and Abigail joined him in the front room.
Abigail bent over and kissed the riverboat pilot on the cheek.

"Uncle Mose, you're always welcome here," she said.

"Good. Then c'mon, Nate. Let me hear something. Perhaps a hymn, eh, to counter the devil's din outside the
gates." He patted the worn leather Bible tucked in his belt,
then resumed eating. Even Nate Harveson had to smile, the
captain's good humor was infectious. And he was grateful for
Smead's loyalty.

"Uncle Mose, you are the one constant in all this troublesome frontier," Harveson said, taking a seat at the piano.
"I'll play for you, old friend."

"And what of you, Abigail?" Smead noticed that the
young woman had taken a woolen shawl from a wall peg and
wrapped herself against the night's brisk breath. "Surely
you'll not be venturing forth with such a hellish commotion
but a few yards without the stockade walls."

"Abby always knows what she's doing, Captain," Harveson
said. Back in Independence he would have been horrified at
the merest suggestion that Abigail go among such men like
Coyote Kilhenny and Tom Milam. Here on the edge of Ever
Shadow, things looked a lot different. Kilhenny was growing
more insolent with every passing day. But Tom had a following as well. He was headstrong and a bit reckless but
obviously a man of courage. Harveson sensed that many of
the trappers liked young Milam and those that didn't seemed

to respect him. Yes, Harveson would rest a lot easier if Tom were brought into the fold.

So Nate Harveson offered no protest as Abigail kissed her "Uncle" Mose farewell and stepped outside. Instead, he secretly wished her well and began to play. And the hymn he chose was entitled *Lord of All Hopefulness*.

35

Iron Mike hunched forward alongside the wooden barrel laid on its side on the buckboard and held a blue enamel tin cup under the spout for Spence Mitchell to fill. The dancing glare of the bonfire behind him caused the shadows of the trappers to lengthen and shrink. Timber split, cracked in two, spilled embers that spiraled skyward to mingle with the stars before winking out. Their temporal tragic beauty was lost on the likes of Iron Mike, who wanted nothing more than to get knockdown, spread-eagle drunk.

Too many of the men had watched his humiliating dunk in the river and those that hadn't witnessed the event heard about it second hand, in richly embellished detail. Before long, Iron Mike had begun to suspect every laugh as being at his expense.

"You've drunk your fill of this snake poison," Spence Mitchell muttered to his former trail partner. They'd ridden the high country together more than once.

"Don't tell me what I've done, you old windbag," Iron Mike growled in reply and banged his cup against the barrel. "Fill it and be damned."

"Likely as not," Mitchell admitted with regret. He spat a stream of tobacco and twisted open the tap.

Gunfire from a dozen guns signaled the beginning of a contest. The trappers jostled and shoved and fought among themselves in position as Dog Bill Hanna and a swarthy-looking hide hunter by the name of Brownrigg squared off against each other. They stood several feet apart as Tom Milam brought a steaming coil of buffalo intestine from the cookfire. The grayish mass, seared by the flames, dripped grease as Tom gingerly carried one end to Brownrigg and the other to Dog Bill. Between the two men stretched more than twelve feet of "boudins," as the trappers liked to call the delicacy.

Tom Milam drew his knife and notched the length of boudins midway between the two men.

"You boys ready?" Tom called out. Both men nodded. "Remember . . . the first man past the cut I made wins a jug of Kentucky Kick Eye all to himself."

The throng around him cheered and began to furiously wager among themselves. Dog Bill Hanna had never lost such a contest. There were few things he loved better than boudins. On the other hand, Brownrigg was a quiet, shifty-eyed individual that no one seemed to know much about, but judging by the size of the belly, which overhung his belt like a bay window, the man could hold his own around a cookfire.

By the buckboard, some distance from the clamoring crew anxious to wager gold, pelts, guns, or horses on the contest, Iron Mike sloshed the fiery contents of his cup down his throat. Spence Mitchell had left to place a bet on Dog Bill.

Iron Mike's mood was much too dark to enjoy the event. Just watching Tom Milam strut like a gamecock among the trappers made Iron Mike's blood boil all over again. His attention rooted on the events by the fire, he didn't notice Con Vogel standing close at hand until the violinist spoke.

"Heard about this morning," Vogel said.

"Go to hell," Iron Mike muttered, ready to drop the young German if he intended to amuse himself at Iron Mike's expense.

"Not me," Vogel replied, holding his hands palm up in a gesture of surrender. "But somebody ought to send Tom Milam there."

"He'd strut for sure, then," the trapper said, his speech slurred from too much drink. He wiped a coarse-looking hand across his features and glanced at Vogel. "You got no use for him?"

"No."

"Then why don't you brace him?"

"Maybe I will," Con Vogel replied.

"The hell you will," Iron Mike chuckled. "You're afraid of him, greenhorn."

"You cut a wide circle around him yourself." Vogel tucked his hands in his pockets and studied the trapper's expression. He wondered if he'd pushed the right button. He didn't have to wait long. Iron Mike crawled to his feet and steadied himself against the nearest wagon wheel.

"I'll show you who's yellow," he said, patting the pistol butt jutting from the wide leather belt circling his waist. He wiped his hands on his nankeen trousers and started toward the bonfire.

Tom Milam announced that the betting was finished. He raised a pistol in his right hand. Dog Bill stared straight ahead, his gaze fixed solely on the length of cooked gut. Brownrigg looked from face to face in the crowd, unable to focus his attention on anyone in particular, his jaws firmly clenched around his end of the "boudins."

Tom fired his pistol and the two men began to eat furiously. They began as one, wolfing down the boudins at a brisk pace, hardly pausing for breath. The men surrounding the two cheered them on. More money had been wagered on Dog Bill and it was obvious from the din that most of the cheers were for him. And slowly, gradually, inch by inch, Dog Bill began to pull closer to the notch. Bite, half-chew, swallow, and bite, chew once or twice, then swallow—he gained on Brownrigg. The cheers for Brownrigg and the shouted encouragements quickly turned to curses. He had promised more than he could deliver.

Just as Dog Bill's teeth closed on the organ meat a full three inches past the notch, the crowd of men swarmed over the two men in the middle and tore the remaining boudins to pieces. Dog Bill was raised onto the shoulders of his friends and handed his jug of Kentucky whiskey before being carried away. Brownrigg was left to double forward and empty the contents of his stomach into the bonfire.

Tom had just started to work his way through the thinning crowd when he spied Abigail coming from the direction of the fort. Several of the buckskin-clad men tried to intercept her; some even moved to block her path. Tom started toward her when Iron Mike caught up to him from behind and spun him around.

One of the riverboatmen had just struck up a tune on his concertina, but his song ended as he backed out of trouble's course.

"I wanna talk to you," Iron Mike blurted out.

"Not now," Tom said and tried to pull free. The man holding him only tightened his grip. His hairy hands closed like a vise. Perspiration showed through his thinning hair, beading his scalp.

"Now! We'll settle it when I say!" Iron Mike bellowed. He was the same height as Tom Milam but outweighed the younger man by fifty pounds.

Tom didn't dwell on the difference or the man's physical advantages. He simply drove his left fist into Iron Mike's face. It was a short, vicious jab that rocked Iron Mike back on his heels. It seemed to sober him up even as the blood began to flow from his swollen nose.

"You bastard," Iron Mike roared and reached for the gun at his waist. Then he froze, realizing Tom had already filled his own hand with a pistol.

"Go ahead. Take it out, Iron Mike," Tom said.

Something in the younger man's eyes compelled the hide hunter to obey. Iron Mike drew his pistol. The two men faced each other, no more than a couple of yards separating the muzzles of their guns. A hush suddenly settled on the throng of men as they hurried to escape the line of fire.

Iron Mike licked his lips and looked down at the gun leveled at his. This wasn't a fight; it was suicide for them both at such a distance.

"Go on, Mike. What's stopping you. Your powder's dry."

Iron Mike's gun began to waver in his hand. He tried to steady it. He was sober now and he finally realized how very dangerous Tom Milam had become. Tom was grinning now, and his blue eyes seemed to blaze with life as if here at the moment of death he was truly alive. There was something horrible in that grin, in the mad light in Tom Milam's eyes, and in the way he seemed to purr as he urged Iron Mike to "start the dance."

Tom walked up to the hide hunter, flush against Iron Mike's pistol, and placed the barrel of his gun to Iron Mike's chest.

"Well?" Tom asked. And Iron Mike lowered his head and dropped his gun. He turned and headed out of the crowd, shoving aside anyone who got in his way. Tom Milam returned his gun to his belt. The concertina player struck up another tune and the crowd of men returned to life.

A cheer rose up from the trappers as a dusky shape flitted among them. Virginia appeared out of the shadows where she'd been waiting and watching, and the trappers raised a great cry of approval. Tom headed straight away from the fire as Abigail vanished beyond the glare. She paused to allow him to reach her side. Then the two of them headed for a grove of trees clinging to the riverbank.

Back at the bonfire, Coyote Kilhenny had arrived with Skintop Pritchard, Pike Wallace, and Bear, and had been given an account of the face-off.

"The lad's full of piss and vinegar," Kilhenny said with pride.

"And maybe you oughta rein him in," Pritchard muttered, his sympathies clearly with Iron Mike. He had to admit, though, Iron Mike had been a fool. "He should have shot first and taken his chances."

"Like you would've done," Kilhenny said, winking at Pike.

Pritchard made no reply. He saw Tom leave with Abigail Harveson and the envy almost choked him. He averted his eyes to the mulatto girl dancing a jig with Spence Mitchell.

"What the heck are we celebratin'?" Pike Wallace wondered aloud.

"Why not celebrate? Look around you, old man. Everything you see is mine!" Kilhenny exclaimed.

"Well, Mr. Nate Harveson may have something to say about that." Pike said. Nothing Kilhenny said surprised him anymore. The half-breed had more twists and turns than a barrel full of snakes.

"Yes." Kilhenny nodded in agreement. "But not much."

They didn't need to tell each other lies to lure each other out into the grove of willows and scrub oaks lining the riverbank. In a secluded clearing a hundred yards downriver of Fort Promise, Tom Milam built a small fire. The night was milder than Abigail had expected. She spread her shawl on the ground in the circle of warmth emanating from the campfire. Tom held up a stoneware jug he had stolen from one of the freight wagons. He uncorked the jug, took a drink, and with a daring expression on his face offered Abigail a drink.

Too proud to refuse, Abigail accepted his offer and tilted the jug to her lips. She hadn't expected a Bordeaux. But liquid fire? She gasped and doubled over, coughing, as the cruel liquor seared a path down her gullet. She sank to her knees and Tom knelt in front of her and laughed as she gasped for breath.

Abigail tried to glare at him, but his laughter and the silliness of her reaction finally won through and she laughed as well, laughed and kissed him. He returned the kiss and Abigail's lips pressed to his yet again. His embrace tightened; her hands searched for him. She lay on her back, the shawl beneath her hips and shoulders as Tom set his guns aside, removed his belt, kicked his trousers away. By the time he stretched himself atop her. Abby's dress was already bunched at the waist. She pulled him to her breast. He entered her with a sudden quick stroke.

They lay together, naked to the warming flames and sated after their passionate union. Tom propped himself up on an elbow and studied the woman beside him. He nuzzled her cheek. She responded with a kiss and then began to search for her clothes.

Tom caught her wrists and forced her to quit and had her lie with him a moment more.

Abigail reached up and traced a line along his jaw, then dropped to his neck and finally his chest. He had been an ardent lover, caressing, touching, kissing, exploring the length of her body. He had brought her to the peak of satisfaction and plummeted with her into the abyss. And yet, lying by him, so warm and blissfully sleepy, she experienced not the golden glow of consummated love but a strangely dispassionate curiosity that tempered her true feelings for him. She was left with a sense of disappointment in herself. She cared deeply for him. How deeply Tom cared for her, she could merely speculate. Would he fight for her? Would he kill if he had to protect her? Of that she had no doubt.

But would he side with her if need be against Coyote Kilhenny? That remained to be seen.

One thing for certain, she'd done all she could to ensure a favorable answer to her unspoken questions. Well, almost all. The night wasn't over yet. . . .

Tom bolted upright and glanced about, searching the grove in the gray light. All was stillness. Then what had awakened him? He reached for one of his guns, the reassuring weight of the pistol soothing his nerves.

"Tom?" Abigail whispered as she was startled awake by his actions. A morning mist shrouded the trees and muted the morning chatter of the birds. "Did you hear something?"

"Yes," Tom answered. "Sort of. I don't quite understand."

"Where?" Abigail said, standing at his side. She faced the same direction as Tom, yet he seemed to be seeing beyond the mist and the trees to the ragged battlements of Ever Shadow and the mountains she knew dominated the western horizon.

"Here," Tom replied and he touched his chest. Perspiration formed along his upper lip. For the first time since he had hidden in the tall grass and waited for a brother and parents who had never returned, Tom knew fear. But he didn't know why. He stood as still as a statue, facing the west, one hand covering his chest, as he listened with his head and with his heart.

The door to the longhouse opened as Abigail reached for the latch, her breath clouding the cool air as she breathed from her exertion. She had hurried across the compound in an effort not to be noticed returning home at such an unseemly hour. She knew her hair was disheveled and reconciled herself to suffer in silence the jokes and innuendos spoken behind her back.

Brownrigg, the bleary-eyed trapper from the night before, all but blundered into Abigail. She barely managed to avoid being knocked down. Brownrigg touched his cap.

"Beg pardon, Miss." Brownrigg was a man with a keen

desire to avoid trouble. "Wasn't expecting to see you," he said lamely.

"Nor I, you," Abigail flatly replied.

"Yes'm. I had business with Mr. Harveson." Brownrigg hurried off toward the barracks built along the walls.

Abigail went into the house. To her surprise, Nate Harveson was waiting for her. He sat on the divan, a pot of coffee and two cups on a tray before him. He had the look of a man who hadn't slept. If the fact that she had been out all night bothered him, he certainly didn't show it. And Abigail, determined to save face, closed the door behind her and kept the color from coming to her cheeks.

"Another musician?" she asked.

"More a songbird," Harveson answered, pouring a cup of coffee for his sister. His cup was already full. "Ignore his rather uncouth plumage. He sings a rather interesting song." Harveson sipped and eased back on the divan. Abigail sat at his side, waiting to hear what he had to say.

"Brownrigg has been in my employ for some time. I hired him on in Independence." Harveson finished his coffee, rose from the divan, and crossed to his desk. "He began reporting to me on the trip upriver, describing how Coyote Kilhenny's been winning over even the men I handpicked for this expedition. Men whose loyalty I thought unquestionable."

"I don't understand." Abigail paused a moment to think. "Or maybe I do." She drained the contents of her cup, the liquid brought warming strength to her limbs.

"He's promised them whole shares of the profits to be realized from our venture, sister. *Our* venture."

"It seems we underestimated Coyote Kilhenny. He is not the simple rogue he appears to be."

"Simple, ha—like Cassius." Harveson slapped his fist into the palm of his hand. "Curse me for a fool. His ambitions are as great as my own, I fear." He stretched a hand out and leaned on the bookcase.

"But what does a man like him know about running a post like this?" Abigail blurted. "He may know bear traps and forest trails, but I warrant profit and loss columns would be beyond even his considerable talents."

"Maybe so," Harveson concurred, smoothing his silver

hair. "But then, one of my ledgers is missing. And a journal I kept during the last year when I was planning all this."

"He still doesn't have your talent. Nor mine."

"We will still have to be on our guard. My authority over these men has dangerously eroded."

"All that will change when the boats arrive." Abigail tried to sound hopeful.

"If we're around to see them. Kilhenny for all his size has a lean and hungry look." Nate Harveson laughed softly. "I can count on Smead and his crew. And there may be others. . . ." He started to suggest Tom Milam and then thought better of it.

"Does Kilhenny have an idea when the boats are due in?" Abigail asked.

"No."

"It can't be too soon." She was concerned, but like her brother, resolute that the likes of Coyote Kilhenny would not prevail against them. Abigail knew her brother wanted to know about Tom. She didn't know what to tell him, other than she had fallen in love with Tom Milam. But would he go against the man who had been his father, who had saved him from the Indians and raised him as his own?

Abigail had plenty of dreams, but answers were in short supply.

Tom allowed Abigail to proceed without him through the open gates of the fort. He waited about a quarter of an hour and then walked from the woods. In these early-morning hours, men were sprawled asleep by the remnants of the bonfire and at their posts, where heavily armed sentries dozed upon the ramparts of the fort.

Tom spied the familiar figure of Coyote Kilhenny sitting in a ladder-backed rocking chair on the flat roof of the barracks at the east wall of the compound. Tom headed straight toward the man on the roof as sunlight gradually warmed the trampled earth and roused the sentries from their illicit slumber.

"C'mon up, lad," Kilhenny said as Tom drew to within a stone's throw of the log barracks. The crisscrossed logs at the corner of the barracks made for an easy climb and in a matter of seconds Tom was on the roof and sat on his haunches in the shadow of the rocking chair. The sky was a limitless azure expanse, devoid of clouds, where the last few stars of evening winked out before the risen sun like candle flames extinguished by a sudden gust of wind.

"Figured you to be asleep," Tom said.

"Someone has to keep watch. Hell, one man could have made off with the stock and emptied the corral and no one the wiser." Kilhenny reached down for the cider jug at his side and sloshed the contents, taking reassurance he still had some drink close at hand.

"I didn't mean exactly asleep." Tom took the jug and helped himself to a swallow of hard cider.

Coyote Kilhenny had been amusing himself with Harveson's mulatto servant ever since the trip upriver. "Naw," he said. "I gave her away. I got what I needed from her."

"What's that supposed to mean?"

"Down below. Underneath my bed. A ledger and a book of notes, written in Nate Harveson's own hand." Kilhenny brushed a tangle of rust-red hair out of his face. "She took them for me, yesterday morning."

Tom's interest was aroused now. What was the crafty half-breed really up to?

"I want you to study on them, lad."

"Me?"

"Sure. You read better than I ever will. There's more to running a trading post than being handy with these," Coyote said, thumping the percussion pistols holstered across his chest. "I want you to study on them, learn about purchasing supplies, figure profit margins, how and what to keep in stock. And laying out land plots. Nate's got him drawn some maps. You need to know them by heart."

"I still don't understand."

"Blast it. Open your ears, laddie buck. You don't think I aim to stand in that little man's shadow for long, do you?"

"You gave your word. . . ."

"There ain't but three people in this whole world I'd stand by—Pike, Skintop, sonuvabitch that he is, and you. No one else counts. And nothing I say to them counts either." Kilhenny held out his hands and Tom leaned forward and passed the jug of cider to the half-breed Scot. Tom's shirt parted and the snake on the chain glinted in the sunlight. "What was that your pa used to say about that ring?"

"Keep the snake on your hand and it'll never coil around your heart," Tom answered, tucking the ring back inside his shirt.

"I didn't have much truck with your pa," Kilhenny said. "But he knew how to die. He had courage. It speaks well for a man." Kilhenny tilted the jug to his lips and drank deeply, lowered it, and wiped his mouth on the sleeve of his flannel coat. "He wasn't afraid of his destiny. And neither am I."

"I don't want trouble for the Harvesons."

"Abigail Harveson's got you wound up tighter than Methuselah's pocket watch. I better not let her lead you into the woods alone, again."

"We walked together," Tom corrected.

Kilhenny chuckled. "Every man says the same thing. I said it once myself."

"This is different."

"It's always different. Always the same." There was a note of wistfulness in the man's voice. Tom realized there was more to Kilhenny than he would ever completely learn. "I aim to have my way in this matter. What Harveson does is up to him." Kilhenny sighed and began to rock back and forth. The chair creaked with every forward motion, the joints protesting the trapper's solid, heavy burden. Kilhenny had seen Brownrigg exit Harveson's house. He wondered what Harveson was up to and decided to have a talk with Brownrigg. He looked at Tom and smiled in satisfaction remembering how Tom had looked at ten years of age, scared but proud, standing all alone on the prairie. He saw himself reaching down to the boy and lifting him up to ride behind him on the saddle.

"Comes a time, a man needs to know he'll leave something more behind than his bones," Kilhenny said. Eleven years ago seemed like yesterday. "That wasn't just a boy I brought out of the wilderness. You were my future. I aim to build something before I go under. And leave it for you, to carry on for me."

Tom met the half-breed's stare. "Well, I'll be, so there's

some chinking loose in that rough bark you call skin. I'd never believed it."

"Wait and see, laddie buck," Kilhenny said gruffly. "You live long enough, you'll lose a little mud along the way, mark my words." With that sage advice, Kilhenny clasped his hands behind his head and relaxed in the sun, let the warmth leach the winter from his limbs. He'd do what needed to be done. And so would Tom.

36

Lone Walker looked east through diaphanous veils of prayer smoke swirling against the sky. He added leaves of elk mint to the fire and a few dried Juneberries and wafted an eagle feather through the smoke, fanning the flames of the prayer fire.

> "All-Father,
> It is good the sun upon the hills
> And Cold Maker has left us that
> Our young men might hunt and
> Bring food to our lodges.
> Happy are your people yet
> Still is my heart.
> I have dreamed that all of
> Ever Shadow lay between my son
> And I.
> And our spirits could not speak."

Lone Walker sang his prayer song apart from the village. He had built his medicine fire by the shore of the lake. His voice would have carried across the glassy still waters, but he sang softly. His keening voice just carried enough that the people of the village knew he was singing, making medicine with the All-Father. Every morning he made his prayer smoke. It was a ritual the Blackfeet of Medicine Lake not only accepted as natural but took comfort in.

"All-Father,
  Glad are we for the swiftness of the horse
  And the warmth of the Life-Giver Above.
  My Prayer Smoke rises from Beauty into Beauty."

Jacob led his horse down to the lake. He'd just ridden the
big gray mare for the first time only a day ago and he
anticipated trouble the moment he swung a leg over the
animal's back. But a temperamental horse was the least of his
concerns as he listened to Lone Walker, a few yards away.

"The song is like the smoke," he said aloud. "It soon
vanishes." Jacob had little use for his father's rituals. He
could see no purpose in lifting his prayers to a God who if he
existed at all was a capricious deity, deaf to the world of men.
Maybe such things were lost to him, feelings and beliefs he
could never understand. After all, he was a white man,
braided hair, beaded buckskins, and all. At least there were
those men and women in the village who had begun to make
him feel apart from the tribe. Ever since the death of Wolf
Lance, five months past, Jacob felt just as exiled by their
attitudes as Tewa was exiled through the course of her own
action. She was of the People yet kept to her lodge on the
hillside, a solitary warrior woman who had been touched by
tragedy and the Great Spirit.

"Why do you sing?" Jacob asked.

"I sing that we might know and understand the way of
things," Lone Walker replied. "And I sing that the world will
not end."

Jacob looked toward the lodge nestled back in the pines
upslope from where Lone Walker had built his sacred fire.
My wedding lodge, Jacob wryly reminded himself, and to
Lone Walker replied, "Perhaps you are too late." He walked
away, following the lakeshore.

Lone Walker watched him leave and his heart was filled
with sympathy for his adopted son. There was talk in the
village of driving Jacob out of Ever Shadow and forcing him
to leave the People behind, never to return to Medicine Lake.
Of course, such talk always reached Lone Walker second-
hand and rose infrequently at best. The death of such a noted
warrior as Wolf Lance had upset the tribal elders, but none of

them had demanded banishment for Jacob. Lone Walker wondered if even the scattered outcry against Jacob would have occurred had the young man been born a Blackfoot.

As for Tewa—men called her Warrior Woman. She had ridden with raiding parties and captured Kootenai ponies and added Kootenai scalps to her war lance. She had decorated her lodge with symbols of charging horses and the figure of a woman carrying an elk horn bow loosing arrows at her enemies. Already, the people of the village held her in reverence, as one touched by the Above Ones and led onto a special path. They kept their distance from her and accorded her the deference shown the tribe's most honored warriors or medicine men. Still, Jacob was drawn to that lodge on the hillside, like a moth to a flame perhaps, or, even more so, like the hunter drawn into the mysterious heart of the forest where the wild wolf waits.

Jacob walked his horse into the lake until the icy cold surface of the water lapped at the mare's underbelly.

"Gentle now." He kept his voice low and soothing to the wary animal. "Gentle now." The water served a twofold purpose. It would cushion his fall if the mare bucked him off. It would also make the mare work harder to dislodge him once he mounted up.

Jacob grabbed a handful of mane and swung up onto the animal's back. Jacob's legs tightened as the animal shied, then plunged forward, kicking up spray and soaking herself and the white man. The mare reared, arched its back, kicked its hind legs out, fought the man and the water for all of five minutes and then as abruptly quit, tossed its head, and waited, obedient to the reins and the soft-bit hackamore.

Jacob, eager to take his chances on hard ground, rode the mare out of the lake. The mare had had its fill of fighting; the strong, sturdy animal only wanted to run. And Jacob gave her the lead and rode at a gallop toward the entrance to the valley.

Tewa stood before her lodge and watched the spectacle of man and beast vying for dominance, and in her own heart felt a kinship for the gray mare. She too struggled, tried to battle free of the burdensome shadow of her father's death. She warred with the feelings in her heart as she watched Jacob emerge from the lake and head off down the valley. She wanted to run to her own fierce charger and ride with him and suffered guilt anew that she should even consider such an act and with her father's killer no less.

A twig broke behind her and she spun around. Sparrow Woman emerged from a thicket of fir trees that had screened the woman's climb. Though no man might approach Tewa's lodge, Sparrow Woman was under no such taboo. She carried a parfleche freshly filled with elk mint and bitterroot and dried chokecherries and handed the parfleche to Tewa, who pretended she hadn't been watching Jacob from afar. Sparrow Woman knew different but said nothing of the matter.

"What do you want of me?" Tewa asked gruffly. She brought out her scraping stones and squatted down by a rack on which she had fixed an elk skin. She began working the pelt with the stone scraper, smoothing the skin to make it more pliable.

"I want nothing of you . . . only for you." Sparrow Woman ignored the younger woman's brusqueness. Patience emanated from her as she knelt by Tewa and took up one of the pelts that had already been worked and began to stitch it with a length of sinew. "I have walked your path. It is a lonely journey." She looked across the valley where the far slope was dotted with burial scaffolds overlooking a verdant meadow.

Tewa's eyes were moist when she looked up from her labor and met Sparrow Woman's open, honest gaze.

"When does the journey end?" she asked, sounding more like a frightened girl than one called Warrior Woman.

Sparrow Woman replied matter of factly, "You will know."

Jacob and the Shoshoni saw each other almost simultaneously. Walks With The Bear reined in his bald-faced gelding and the pack horse trailing behind him. The Shoshoni held his right hand palm outward in a gesture of friendship. Even from fifty yards the Shoshoni recognized that a white man in the trappings of a Blackfoot blocked his way to the valley. He was surprised but held his ground.

The Shoshoni and Blackfeet had rendezvoused together down on the Yellowstone in years past. Neither tribe had encroached on the other's hunting grounds, which helped to keep peace between them. Still, a man couldn't be too sure, and Jacob had foolishly left his rifle back in the village. The bowie knife sheathed at his waist was his only weapon. The Shoshoni carried a Hawken rifle in the crook of his arm. However, Jacob didn't have to feel lonely for long. Otter Tail announced his arrival with a loud cry that reverberated off the walls of the pass.

Otter Tail had been guarding the entrance to the valley and from his vantage point on a low hill to the south had watched the Shoshoni draw close to the valley. Otter Tail had remained hidden on the slope until he was certain the brave came alone. Jacob was grateful for his friend's arrival. Otter Tail galloped up alongside Jacob and playfully remonstrated the yellow-haired brave.

"Are you so sick at heart that you would let some enemy lift your hair?"

"This Shoshoni does not appear to be an enemy," Jacob said, trying to save face. But the portly brave wouldn't buy it.

"*Saa-vaa,* and if this Shoshoni were a Crow or Kootenai?"

"Then I would depend on my brave brother Otter Tail to save me." Jacob clapped his friend on the shoulder, and the two men rode side by side toward the visitor.

Bear turned in the saddle and with a sweep of his hand indicated the pack horse trailing behind him. "I bring gifts to the people of Medicine Lake. I come in the peace that lay between our fathers and their fathers. I go in peace as well."

Bear wore the beaded buckskin shirt and leggings of his own tribe, but a wide-brimmed black hat shaded his features. He'd tucked an eagle father in the brim. Despite the years since the massacre of his parents, Jacob still had to suppress the anger that rose to choke him whenever he rode among the Shoshoni. One of these braves might have ridden with those killers, befriended Coyote Kilhenny and the half-breed's treacherous cohorts. Bear sensed the thinly veiled resentment radiating from Jacob and avoided eye contact with the younger man.

"I must speak with your elders, the chiefs of your village." Bear tugged a shiny new knife from his belt and handed it to Otter Tail. "Plenty guns like this one," Bear continued and displayed the Hawken he carried. "I bring important news from the River of Two Bears." He turned and offered his knife to Jacob for inspection. Jacob made no move to accept the weapon. He continued to glower at the lone brave, and wanted nothing to do with him. In truth, he felt he knew the man but could not guess why. So he dismissed his suspicions as a natural disregard for all Shoshoni.

"It is a good rifle," Otter Tail admitted and with customary greediness turned back to the pack horse to see what other gifts Bear had brought with him. The Shoshoni wheeled his horse about and intercepted the Blackfoot brave.

"There will be more when I sit in council with Standing Elk and Lone Walker and the other elders," Bear said, a note of finality in his voice.

Otter Tail scowled and circled the pack horse and drew abreast of Jacob.

"Where are the others of your village?" Otter Tail asked, glancing down the back trail at the lone warrior's tracks switching back and forth through the low hills. It seemed obvious the Shoshoni had ridden in from the prairie beyond the distant divide to the east.

"I do not come from my people," Bear said, sitting relaxed in the saddle, a figure of false composure. He lifted his right hand and pointed directly at Jacob. "I come from his."

37

Bear spoke well and his words fell on receptive ears especially after he'd distributed a half-dozen new Hawken rifles among the tribal elders. The white men had come in peace to their fort to the east. They did not intend to encroach on the land of the Blackfeet. They wished only trade with the people of Ever Shadow, offering rifles and pistols, blankets, knives, and iron arrowheads in exchange for pelts and buffalo hides.

If the white man didn't trade with the Blackfeet, they would merely locate further south and trade with the Crow villages down on the Tongue. Better that the Blackfeet put aside their natural enmity toward the white man than see the Crow, the enemies of Ever Shadow, heavily armed and able to encroach the high country.

"White traders five suns from Medicine Lake," Lone Walker mused aloud. "And none of our hunters have returned to tell us of such a thing."

The Shoshoni shrugged and hooked his thumbs in his belt. "The plains reach as far as a man can see. In such a place, two men may ride and never meet." Bear's expression never wavered as he lied. Nothing in his implacable gaze revealed how eleven days earlier he had helped to ambush a Blackfoot hunting party. Coyote Kilhenny, Skintop Pritchard, a dozen hardcase trappers, and the Shoshoni had followed the sound of gunfire to a buffalo kill. Four Blackfoot braves had been surprised and shot dead as they butchered a buffalo bull. Kilhenny had promptly loaded the meat onto a captured travois.

So Bear, the Shoshoni, spoke of peace and gave his gifts and in the end convinced the tribal chiefs to come with him to Fort Promise. Even Lone Walker saw no harm in at least seeing with his own eyes these white men who had come to establish trade.

The medicine pipe was brought forth once more to the elders circled near the council fire in the center of the village. Feathery wisps of white dotted the azure sky crossed from time to time by formations of geese winging north to summer's nesting lands. The pipe bowl was carved from stone brought from sacred ground to the east and fitted with a stem of willow wood. A mixture of cherry bark, wild sage, bitterroot, and elk mint had been tamped down into the bowl and lit with a coal from the sacred fire.

Lone Walker stood among his peers and proclaimed the elders' decision aloud to the men and women of the village who had gathered at a respectful distance, Jacob Sun Gift among them. Even the children had come to stand with their parents, their normally playful attitudes subdued by the lighting of the council fire and the gathering of the chiefs.

"White men have come to Ever Shadow. Walks With The Bear, our brother, speaks for them. He tells us they come in peace. They send us gifts and offer much for our hides and pelts." Lone Walker's voice rang out over the village.

Jacob shifted his stance, sensing Sparrow Woman at his side. She smiled at her son. Jacob touched her arm, then he raised his eyes and spied Tewa at the rear of the crowd, her features hidden beneath her wolf's-head cowl, her father's war lance carried in her strong right hand. It was only with great effort Jacob returned his attention to the council.

"I will go and see with my own eyes," Lone Walker continued. "What others who sit at this fire will go with me?"

Standing Elk, a much-respected chief of the Bowstring Clan, rose to take his place alongside Lone Walker. Then Tall Bull, tens years older than the rest but straight and proud in stature, climbed to his feet and beside him, Hawk Moon of the Sinapah, the Kit Fox clan, declared himself. These four among all the elders were the heart of the council and, indeed, the entire tribe looked to them for wisdom and judgment.

Lone Walker held the medicine pipe aloft, pointing the stem first to the east, the dwelling place of youth, next to the south, symbol of early manhood when youth and vigor burn in the veins like green fire. Next, he pointed westward; there lay the wisdom of a life well lived, with honor and reverence, and lastly, he faced the north, the happy place of death where all who have gone before waited with the All-Father.

Lone Walker turned once again to the east, beginning the cycle anew, completing the great circle of life that has no beginning or end but is one with the mystery and the Father of all.

Smoke curled from the pipe bowl as Lone Walker faced the Shoshoni. "Smoke the medicine pipe that the path of all you have spoken here lies true and straight."

Bear stared at the pipe, knowing in his own mind that to lie at such a time could result in the gravest of consequences. But he'd drunk too much of Kilhenny's liquor and too often tested the power of the white man's yellow metal to be dissuaded now. Kilhenny had promised him wealth and power and the choicest of Blackfoot squaws to warm his lodge. He took the pipe and smoked and passed it to the brave next to him, blind Two Stars, who would have stood and traveled with the younger men but for his lack of sight.

Lone Walker seemed to sense this and knelt by the blind man.

"Old one, your eyes are dark, but your ears are keen. Will you ride with us and listen to what these white men have to say and tell us what is in their hearts?"

Two Stars sat upright; the years sloughed away and he nodded with surprising vigor. The death of Wolf Lance had been a heavy burden for him. Lone Walker's suggestion pumped new life into him.

"I will go."

Two Stars smoked the pipe and handed it to Lone Walker, who put it to his lips. He studied the Shoshoni through the tendrils of sacred smoke. The Blackfoot had his misgivings but could see no other way out of the situation. The white traders must be reckoned with one way or the other.

Lone Walker looked around at the faces circling the council and found the one he sought. The day Lone Walker dreaded had at long last come. Jacob must ride with them, back among his own kind and not just some liquor-crazed, half-wild trappers at the rendezvous but people like Jacob, traders, men connected to the white man's world that lay beyond the plains to the east.

Perhaps Jacob might want to return to his own kind, to go back to the world of his true father and live no more in the song of Ever Shadow. All things were possible and Lone Walker's mind was filled with turmoil at what the future held, blinding his instincts to the treachery at hand. He looked at Bear and said, "It is done."

Jacob stood in the shadow of the wedding lodge on the hill above the village when Tewa rode up and reined in her own mount. She stared in wide-eyed amazement at Jacob, whose presence had completely violated tradition and custom. As for Tewa, she didn't know whether to embrace him or to kill him.

Sunlight and gentle breezes lay softly on the land. Hawks in lazy spirals scoured the landscape in search of prey. And in the distance a bawling bear cub searched a rotting tree trunk for grubs.

Tewa had just ridden up from the village after a brief visit with her grandfather. She had insisted on accompanying Two Stars to Fort Promise despite his protests. She lowered her war lance and pointed the blade at Jacob.

"Why are you here?"

"It once was my right to be here. And not so long ago." Jacob led his mare through the campsite. He moved past her guard and stepped in close to Tewa.

"I wanted to say good-bye," Jacob said. "I ride with Lone Walker to where the white traders wait. Maybe I shall not return but stay among my own people."

If his words affected her, Tewa did not show it at first. "I, too, am going."

"I hear the sadness in your voice," Jacob said. Her eyes were suddenly filled with sorrow. He hoped it was because she feared losing him.

"My heart is heavy. Because I have not yet learned to hate you."

Jacob's own expression hardened. It had been foolish of him to try to reason with her. So be it. Tewa was lost to him and there was nothing he could say or do. He swung up onto the mare and fixed her in his bronze-eyed stare. "Perhaps you will learn by the time our journey is done." He wheeled his horse past Tewa's mount and rode at a gallop down the slope, leaving the dust to settle in the wake of dashed dreams.

38

An hour before supper, Coyote Kilhenny came looking for Nate Harveson. He found him in the study, alone, and awaiting the trapper's arrival. Kilhenny's stomach was growling when he entered the front room and he hoped Harveson didn't have much on his mind. The half-breed's vision quickly adjusted to the lamplight.

"Good," Harveson said as Kilhenny leaned over him. Harveson was seated at his desk, a journal open before him, a page partly filled with his handwriting. He noticed Kilhenny glance at the journal. "An account of everyday occurrences. I have been forced to begin anew what with the misplacement of a previous record."

"Too bad," Kilhenny said.

"But I didn't ask you here to discuss a missing book."

Kilhenny leaned forward and braced himself on the desk with his brawny forearms. Yet for all his overbearing size, Nate Harveson did not quail before Kilhenny. Harveson merely eased back in his chair and crossed his arms upon his chest.

"Better men than you have tried to intimidate me, sir," Harveson said. "Sit down and quit being so predictable."

Kilhenny laughed, straightened, and backed from the desk. He hooked his thumbs in his belt.

"Speak your piece, *Mr.* Harveson."

"All the cards on the table then," Harveson began. "I know you've turned most the men against me, filled their heads with thoughts of greater wealth than what I'd offer. Of course, I intend to pay off my obligations."

"Greed beats reason any day of the week." Kilhenny no longer felt any need to hide his intentions.

"You won't succeed. This fort and everything in it belongs to me."

"Really? I can muster a small army to debate the issue with Hawken rifles not fancy words."

"Kill me and you'll never have a moment's peace," Harveson said. "My sister or Captain Smead—somehow, some way, word will reach the authorities. I have too many friends. And they will see you hounded to perdition." Harveson closed the ledger. "There you have it."

Kilhenny chewed his lip and ran a set of stubby fingers through his beard as he considered the possibilities. He'd always felt a grudging respect for Harveson, no more so than now.

"For a small man, you cast a long shadow," Kilhenny said.

"Damn right I do." Nate Harveson stood and stepped around his desk to confront the half-breed face-to-face. "Thalia will be serving supper."

"I'm surprised you want me at your table."

"All the better to keep an eye on you."

Kilhenny studied the man, then gestured toward the rear of the house.

"Lead the way, Mr. Harveson. Like you said, the house is yours."

As the sun loomed low in the west, cookfires glimmered and men unfurled their bedrolls amid muted tones of conversation. Nate Harveson sat across from Coyote Kilhenny. Skintop Pritchard, Pike Wallace, and Tom Milam gathered round and took their places at the long table. Thalia brought platters of biscuits and set them down in front of the men. Captain Mose Smead arrived to take his place at the end of the table while Abigail, despite Kilhenny's look of disapproval, worked her way between her brother and Tom Milam. Tom didn't mind a bit having Abigail close by, and when she glanced in his direction, he flashed a wicked grin that let her know precisely what he was thinking. She blushed despite herself and concentrated on the meal at hand.

Thalia followed the biscuits with a platter of antelope steaks smothered in gravy, and a cast-iron Dutch oven filled with boiled rice. An apple cobbler rounded out the repast and the men, with little regard for manners, fell to wolfing down their meal, eyes darting greedily to the cobbler on the table before them.

"Job Berton and Tom here say the redskins'll be riding in about noon. That right, Tom?" Nate Harveson said.

"If they make camp," Tom said. He'd been on the trail again for the last couple of days, making a cold camp at night with Job Berton and shadowing the Blackfeet down from the high country.

"You counted thirty braves?" Harveson asked. "I thought only the tribal elders would be coming."

"Call it an escort," Kilhenny said. "A few representative bucks from each clan, the Buffalo Clan, the Kit Fox, the Bowstring, and such." Kilhenny, reached across the table and clapped Harveson on the shoulder and guffawed, spilling gravy down his chin. "Now don't fret, Mr. Harveson, we figure to arrange a celebration for those red devils they'll never forget."

"I'll play 'em a tune personal on one of those nine-pounders," Skintop Pritchard added and winked at Pike.

"I thought if we captured the tribal leaders, the rest of the poor primitives would stay right in line." Abigail folded her hands on the table and waited for Kilhenny to reply. She wasn't about to let the half-breed Scot bully her. "I see no need for unnecessary bloodshed."

"Look, honey," Kilhenny said, "with the Blackfeet, there ain't no such thing as unnecessary when it comes to killing." Kilhenny pointed to the mountains to the west. "Up yonder there's streams and creeks just teeming with prime pelts. Know why? 'Cause the Blackfeet been murdering and scalping any poor bastard who just so even pokes his nose into their hunting grounds."

"Kilhenny's right, dear sister," Harveson said. "We must demonstrate our resolve to stay here from the outset. The savage must give way to civilization."

"Better we meet the heathen on our terms than his." Pike

Wallace never looked up from his plate but promptly filled his mouth with a gravy-soaked biscuit.

"We'll keep the tribal elders until the remainder of the tribe has been driven out," Kilhenny explained. His ham-sized fist closed around his coffee cup and he drained its bitter black contents down his gullet.

"You shouldn't have sent those men to the south." Nate Harveson had yet to touch his meal, the chunks of meat and gravy congealed in the center of his plate.

"Hunters go where there's sign!" Kilhenny snapped. He held out his cup and Thalia hurried over with the coffee pot and filled it, taking care to slosh some of the steaming liquid on the man's fingers. The half-breed never even flinched, though his eyes glanced up at the cook as if gauging whether or not her clumsiness had been an accident.

"S'cuse me, suh." Thalia waddled back to her stove.

"Anyway," Kilhenny continued, "a dozen men won't make much difference." He smiled and in a taunting gesture added, "You needn't be afraid, Mr. Harveson."

"Oh, I'm not," Harveson replied. "Only a trifle concerned. Still, I'll go as far as you. And one step further." He glanced at Kilhenny's cohorts. "Perhaps you and your men had better get your preparations in order. Tomorrow promises to be a busy day."

Kilhenny intended to do just that, in ways Harveson couldn't even begin to guess. He shoved himself away from the table. He stood and motioned for his companions to join him. Pike Wallace sandwiched a chunk of antelope meat in a biscuit. Skintop Pritchard wiped his mouth on his sleeve, drew a knife, and helped himself to a lion's portion of the cobbler, which he held in his hand for want of a plate.

"I hate to rush a meal," Tom said, his expression impassive as he looked up at Kilhenny. "Never can tell when it might be your last."

"Yeah," Kilhenny said, his shrewd gaze darting from Abigail to Tom. "Take your time, boy. Just so long as you're hid down in the draw with Dog Bill and the lads come sunup."

"I'll be there ready to ride," Tom replied.

Kilhenny, satisfied, headed out into the fort with Pike Wallace and Skintop Pritchard keeping close behind.

"Blessed are the peacemakers," Mose Smead said in a reflective tone. He shook his head and tried to make sense of it all.

"No room for peacemakers in my kingdom." Nate Harveson began to pace the packed-earth floor. Things were coming to a head. He had to figure all the angles so as not to be caught off guard.

"I don't like it," Abigail spoke up.

"I see." Smead adjusted his spectacles with a forefinger; the wire frames had an annoying habit of sliding down the bridge of his nose. The captain looked in Tom's direction. "And what of you, young man? Are the precious thoughts contained in the word of God at all familiar to you?"

"My pa read verse and chapter to us every night, all about the peacemakers. Hell, he *was* one right up until the red savages massacred him, my mother, and probably my brother," Tom snarled. His hand crept toward the snake ring dangling from the chain around his throat. "You can't trust them. There isn't a single trick the bastards don't use."

"Like inviting you in under a flag of truce to the slaughter," Abigail blurted.

Even Thalia, tending another batch of biscuits, glanced around at Abigail, surprised she spoke with such force.

"This is different," Tom retorted.

"No," Abigail said, lowering her voice. "But you'll make it so to keep from having to face the fact that you and Kilhenny and all the rest are no better. For all your talk, tomorrow you'll become what you hate the most."

Tom, astonished by her outburst, faltered, tried to respond, to defend himself.

"I thought . . . my God, Abby," Harveson sputtered, taken aback. "You came to build this empire, same as me."

"But not on a foundation of blood."

"There is no other way," Tom angrily interrupted. "Not here. Maybe in the safety of a drawing room but not in the wild country." Her attack had wounded him and only added to the lingering pain he still carried. His parents were dead. Jacob no doubt was dead and Tom had spent a lifetime building a wall around his heart to pen in the hurt. He slowly rose from his place. Abigail, sensing she had overstepped a boundary with him, reached out to him, but Tom pulled away.

"There's a price to be paid when you cross into wild country and you'd better be willing to pay it." Tom said. "Be willing to pay it or get out as fast as you can."

Tom started to walk away, then hesitated, as if there was something else he wanted to say, a word of tenderness born of feelings and emotions still new to him. Abigail was part of him now, locked deep in his heart, but now wasn't the time to tell her. Later maybe . . . He marched across the compound with quick, fluid strides.

Later, Abigail would remember how in the lengthening shadows of a crimson sunset Tom Milam had straddled that precarious border between the darkness and the light.

Kilhenny dispatched Pike Wallace to one blockhouse, Skintop Pritchard to the other, cautioning each one to be alert come the morning. He promised his companions that tomorrow would see the beginning of a glorious future for them all.

One mission accomplished, Coyote Kilhenny proceeded to the next and veered toward the barn. He rounded the corral and moments later he slipped unannounced through the gap in the barn doors that someone had forgotten to completely close. Kilhenny paused to allow his vision to adjust and, being a cautious man, listened before calling out to Vogel.

He heard a girl's muffled laugh, then a rustle of straw and a man's voice, Con Vogel, groan aloud, "Oh God . . ." Kilhenny pinpointed the sound as originating from one of the stalls at the rear of the barn. He stalked silently down the aisle. He already knew what he'd find when he reached the second-to-the-last stall. There, in the fitful glare of a lamp turned dim and hung from a peg on a post above the sweat-streaked couple, Con Vogel lay on his back on a bed of straw, and the dusky form of young Virginia rode him like a stallion from out of the corral. Her back arched and her pelvis ground forward, and Vogel continued to groan as he lifted his pale arms to caress her sweat-streaked dark limbs. Straw clung to her legs and thighs and showed in stark contrast where a few twigs had caught in her black hair.

"Well, I'll be a cross-eyed son of a seventh son." Kilhenny chuckled aloud. "Fiddle player, if you just aren't full of surprises."

Virginia uttered a cry of surprise, grabbed for her cotton smock and calico dress, and scrambled underneath the rails of the stall. The German bolted upright, face blank, then made an attempt to cover himself and his rapidly shrinking manhood. He glanced around for anything he might use for a weapon. There was nothing, so he scrambled to his feet, brushed the straw from his backside, and tensed as Kilhenny pulled a pistol from his belt.

"Now let's discuss this like gentlemen, Kilhenny," Vogel said, holding out his hands as if to ward off the impending gunshot and lead slug.

"I bleed red, not blue." Then, to Vogel's complete surprise, Kilhenny tossed the percussion pistol to the German. "I heard you can use one of these."

Vogel caught the gun and looked up in disbelief. "In the fatherland, I had quite a reputation as a duelist."

"Hell with that, can you shoot?"

"I can shoot. At twenty paces, there is no one my equal."

"Good." Kilhenny scratched at his beard. His shaggy red hair, framing his fierce features, spilled down his back as he tilted his head back and laughed. Holding a gun on such a man didn't make Vogel feel any less at risk. "You're about to become a red Injun," Kilhenny declared, only further confusing Con Vogel.

Coyote Kilhenny leaned over the railing and peered into the adjacent stall as Virginia pulled her dress over her head. The half-breed loosed a horrible growl and bared his yellow teeth. The poor girl choked back a scream and scrambled out of the stall and darted to safety through a back door.

Kilhenny turned to Vogel, who had yet to so much as twitch despite the fact he held a gun. "Pull your pants on, fiddle player. I've got plans for you."

39

Thirty-one Blackfoot warriors skylined themselves along the low hills to the west of Fort Promise and watched a spring shower track across the rolling prairie that stretched between the hills and the stockade.

Jacob drew up alongside Lone Walker, who studied the lay of the land and the fort and blockhouses. The doors to the stockade were open in a gesture of friendliness. A wagon loaded with trade goods had been brought out in front of the fort. Beyond the wagon, a long oaken table had been placed about twenty yards from the west gate. A half-dozen white men at the table stood when the Blackfeet arrived on the hilltops and arranged themselves on one side of table; they seemed unconcerned by the arrival of the warriors.

Lone Walker's expression betrayed his alarm at the sight of the fort and the riverboat that was anchored downstream. Only a handful of white men patrolled the stockade parapets. Lone Walker marveled that so much had been accomplished in so short a time. He wondered how many of the trappers waited in the blockhouses or aboard the riverboat or were hidden in the draws and behind the trees.

"They have seen us." Bear rose up on horseback and held his hand palm upward and shouted a greeting to the buckskin-clad trappers by the fort. One of the men at table—who alone wore a frock coat and woolen trousers, the formal trappings of a life he'd left behind—stepped forward and mirrored the gesture.

"The white men wait. Are we women, to be afraid of meeting them?" Hawk Moon was brash, if courageous to a fault. No one among the Blackfeet had counted coup more than the war chief of the Kit Fox Clan.

"Even the wolf is cautious before the cave of the bear," Tewa replied. Being a warrior woman, her words carried as much weight as any man's.

"I can hear but the wind," Two Stars scoffed. "And the fear in your voices. But I am not afraid. Who will lead me to the white men?"

Two Stars yanked free of his granddaughter's grasp and started his horse downslope. Lone Walker trotted forward to catch up the reins of the old one's horse. Tall Bull, Standing Elk, and Hawk Moon arranged themselves among the members of their societies who had chosen to ride east with them. A third of the fighting men had left Medicine Lake to escort the elders to the white man's camp.

The Blackfeet approached with caution but with no sign of fear. Tewa angled her mount out of the main body of riders and took up a place toward the rear of the others. Two Stars no longer needed her; his place was with the elders, who would actually approach the table and parlay with the white traders.

It didn't take long for Jacob to gravitate toward the back of the pack. Neither of them spoke. Jacob rode tall and straight, his shoulder-length blond hair streaming in the breeze. He was as proud as any of the rest, for the Blackfeet were lords of Ever Shadow. And he was of the People, if not in blood, then in spirit, which often is the strongest bond.

Jacob remembered enough of his own kind to know that a great and powerful civilization lay to the east, a civilization creeping ever westward. This trading post, no matter how innocent, was the first step in an even greater encroachment. A tide of men and women like his parents waited to be unleashed, to tame the land, to bring order to the frontier's own natural and splendid chaos.

Yet Jacob's foster father had counciled for peace. Perhaps Lone Walker hoped to slow progress and establish good enough relations that he might delay and even redirect the encroachment of the white men.

Jacob glanced at Tewa, caught her watching him from beneath her wolf-skin cowl. She quickly looked away as if breaking eye contact could sever the bond that joined man to woman. She turned her attention to the fort and kept her war pony to a brisk pace, her black hair swept back like the mane of her horse. With the elk horn bow slung across her back and brandishing a buffalo-hide war shield and a ten-foot lance, the warrior woman cut a figure of fierce, proud beauty.

Jacob Sun Gift's heart quickened. If only Lone Walker had a prayer song to heal the warrior woman's hate.

Then again, perhaps the problem lay in the singer, not the song.

"They're comin' in!" Dog Bill Hanna called back down to the men in the draw north of the fort. He craned his head above the rim of the draw as Tom Milam scrambled up to join him.

"As many as Bear claimed?"

"Yeah. Near as I can reckon," Dog Bill said, his broad homely features betraying his disapproval.

"Go ahead." Tom knew Dog Bill wasn't the sort of man to keep his emotions in check for long without exploding.

Dog Bill spat on the patch of earth between his elbows and shook his head in dismay. "Ain't right, invitin' a man to parlay and cuttin' down on him. Leastways an Injun wears his war colors if he's coming to fight." Dog Bill glanced sideways at the young man beside him. "Then again, maybe you're Kilhenny's man and I ought not to be talking so free."

"Maybe," Tom Milam said. He watched the Blackfeet start across a meadow of pink and white bitterroots. He marveled at such a fair land and the price to walk it that a man must pay. Abigail's displeasure weighed heavy on him. Now Hanna added to the burden. It wasn't right and there was no sense in kidding himself. But he'd done a lot of things that weren't "right" by somebody's standard. Kilhenny always said a man had to make his own laws and live by them.

"Better tell the men to saddle up and check their loads," Tom said.

Dog Bill hesitated, studying Tom, who stood and hefted the Hawken rifle he carried. The mountain rifle was a short-barreled, heavy bore gun that fired a .50-caliber lead slug with enough force to drop a charging buffalo-bull in its tracks.

Tom clambered to the bottom of the draw and ordered the men to saddle up. Then he returned to his vantage point on the rim of the ravine. Dog Bill hadn't budged. He lay on his back, shading his eyes with his battered felt hat. The clouds on high looked as if they'd been painted on with quick strokes of the Almighty's invisible brush.

"Won't be long now." Dog Bill rolled on his side and faced Tom. "You might as well know, son. I can't do nothing to stop this, but I don't intend to help it along neither. A man's got to enter his house justified."

"Suit yourself," Tom muttered. He tried to conjure memories of his parents, hoping to fuel his hatred, to give him the will to carry out Kilhenny's orders. Instead, what he had to face was his own life. He'd run wild, and all the time Kilhenny had taught him to ride and shoot and never walk away from a fight until the other man cried "Quit!" and then to back away. Trust no one. And now Coyote Kilhenny was teaching him a new lesson, treachery.

Nate Harveson turned to his sister on the ramparts above the west gate. He wore his finest frock coat, a handsomely brocaded vest, and woolen trousers tucked into shiny black boots. He patted the dust from his sleeve. "Now I'll show these savages a gentleman, eh?"

"In dress, not deed," Abigail said. She had come to the walls determined to witness for herself what was about to transpire.

"Now, Abby, not again." Harveson gently patted her arm. "My place is at the table. I'll not have Kilhenny assume any more of my authority."

"Please, Nate, it's too dangerous." It wasn't like her to behave so, but a premonition chilled her in the warmth of the midday sun.

"Far more dangerous if these men begin to think of me as a coward," Harveson replied.

A hard-looking bunch lined the walls of the stockade. They were crouched down out of sight and cradling their rifles. Some, like Brownrigg, were still loyal to Harveson. A few, he reminded himself—too few. But help was on the way, two riverboats somewhere downriver, winding their way north—

two riverboats with settlers and crews answerable only to Nate Harveson.

"Not to worry, Abigail. I could use a little excitement." He opened his coat to reveal a brace of pistols at his waist. Harveson smiled and started down the stairway to the hard-packed earth. He found Con Vogel standing in the shadow of the open front gate. Harveson paused, surprised at finding the young German so close by.

"Why, Con, what are you doing here?"

"I figured there ought to be someone close at hand to close the gates if things don't work out." Vogel shrugged, thrust his hands in the pockets of his worn, rumpled coat, licked his dry lips, and stared past Nate Harveson, unable to meet the older man's gaze.

"Good idea," Harveson said. "You're quite right. I'm glad to see you've some mettle. None of us can live forever on the good name of our family. We have to stand alone and cast our own shadows." he glanced at the Blackfeet, approaching from the prairie. "There's a good lad. Come by tonight. I am working on a new piece and I'd like you to hear it."

Vogel stepped back into the shadows before his nerves betrayed him.

Harveson stepped through the gates and marched crisply to the table where Kilhenny and a few other men awaited the arrival of their guests.

"Nice and easy," Kilhenny said aloud. "Remember, lads, when the party starts we tip this table on its side." His hawk's eyes gleamed with anticipation. "That'll be the chiefs in the lead. We want them alive if possible, so wait till they dismount. Then I'll give the signal." He'd gone over the instructions throughout the night and by now each man knew what was expected of him. But talking it out soothed his nerves, gave the half-breed the feeling of being in control. And he liked that.

"C'mon, Mr. Harveson, why don't you stand with me out front here," Kilhenny suggested, daring the smaller man. Kilhenny walked around in front of the table and held his hands palm outward.

Nate Harveson noted the derision in the frontiersman's voice and wasn't about to allow Kilhenny to shame him.

"Why certainly," Harveson replied, loud enough for the men close at hand to hear. "I'll stand as long as you." He took his place alongside Kilhenny.

Harveson studied the approaching Blackfeet. How proud they rode, what magnificent savages with their lances and shields and prancing war-horses. Closer, he thought to himself, closer. Come on in, my splendid enemy. They were the lords of Ever Shadow, and they were in the way.

40

So it began, in the time of the Muddy-Faced Moon, the first act of a people's last tragedy. Bold and strong and fearing no one, the last free people rode into Kilhenny's trap. A hundred yards rapidly shrank to fifty as the warriors began to close ranks on the wheel-rutted main trail that led between the blockhouses. Several trappers had arranged themselves on the porch of each blockhouse and waved to the warriors and held up jugs of corn liquor and pouches of leaf tobacco.

Blankets had been draped over each of the cannons and empty crates stacked in front to better conceal their lethal presence. Still, the Blackfeet studied the situation, saw that the white men weren't armed, rode on toward the table. Only Jacob paused before the blockhouse on his right. Tewa noticed his expression and slowed her mount in response. Jacob continued to stare at one man in particular.

Skintop Pritchard.

The trapper held up a jug of whiskey, slapped the bottle, and shouted, "Hey, bub, come and have a drink with your own kind."

"Shut up, Skintop," another of the men on the porch retorted. "He probably don't speak English no more anyhow."

Jacob searched his memory, his mind straining to recall when and where he had seen the man before. And then in came to him, the moment the warriors in front of him spaced themselves in such a way that Jacob had an unobstructed view of the table and the burly red-bearded trapper who stood to greet Lone Walker and the rest with his gesture of peace.

Joseph Milam shot down in cold blood, murdered by the

*guide he had trusted, the man who had led them all into
massacre. Coyote Kilhenny.*

The name rose in his gorge. Jacob began to tremble as the
rage swept over him, consumed him. The hatred, dormant for
so very long, blazed anew. Jacob couldn't even speak the
name. The words choked in his throat. But the sound he
uttered was born of irretrievable loss and unimaginable pain.

The gray mare lunged forward at a gallop and Tewa had to
swerve her mount out of his path to keep from being trampled.

"Aaahhh!" Jacob's blood-curdling cry rent the air and
scattered the braves, who feared they were under attack.

One moment Coyote Kilhenny had everything under control—
the Blackfeet were just about positioned for the kill—the next
second hell broke loose. A wild-eyed, white-skinned renegade came charging through the ranks of the braves right for
Kilhenny.

"Holy shit!" Kilhenny growled and dived over the table
just as Jacob fired his Hawken rifle. The slug fanned Kilhenny's
rump, then plowed a hole through one of his henchmen who
had the misfortune to be standing directly behind the half-
breed. As the mortally wounded trapper crumbled to earth,
the riflemen on the stockade walls rose up and opened fire on
the crowd below. Rifles appeared in the windows and firing
ports of the blockhouses while the cannoneers, who had been
lounging on the porches, kicked away the boxes and cleared
the tarpaulins and blankets from the nine-pounders.

But the Blackfeet, realizing they had ridden into a trap,
scattered as the cannons roared. Lead shot ripped through the
stragglers, dropping men and horses in a tangle of shattered
bone and mangled flesh.

Coyote Kilhenny and the men around him tipped over the
table and crouched behind the thick panels of their makeshift
barricade only to appear seconds later, pistols in hand. Above
them, on the stockade walls, Kilhenny's trappers unleashed a
winnowing fire into the Blackfeet. An overturned table was a
poor substitute for the safety of the stockade walls.

Lone Walker glimpsed the Shoshoni, Walks With The
Bear, bolt toward the fort as the men on the walls opened up
with their heavy bore rifles. Lone Walker hauled back on the
reins of his mount, and his war-horse reared and pawed the

air. Lead slugs riddled the horse, and the animal rolled onto
its back, loosed a pitiful cry, and died. Lone Walker struggled
to pull his leg free, but he was pinned. His quick-thinking
actions had saved not only his life but Two Stars' as well. The
blind man had been riding directly behind Lone Walker,
whose horse had also shielded Two Stars from the trappers'
rifles. The old chief clung to his horse as the animal galloped
from the fray, bullets burning the air all around him. Yet he
rode unscathed through a field of fire.

Lone Walker tried to bring his rifle to bear on the Shoshoni,
but the wily traitor had already ridden to safety. He slid from
horseback and ran, crouched, to a position behind the table.
Lone Walker winced, trying to free himself, but the horse's
dead weight held him fast. Bullets thudded into the ground
around him, and the brave pitched backward as if shot, using
pretense to save his own life. He remained motionless, his
eyes closed, and listened to the cries of the dying and the
thundering gunfire that lasted scarcely a minute in intensity.
A minute was long enough.

Tall Bull rolled from horseback, the top of his skull blown
away. Hawk Moon, riddled with bullets, managed to leap free
as his horse crumpled beneath him. Though dying, the chief
managed to raise his rifle and shoot a man from the stockade
walls before taking his last breath. Standing Elk charged
through a veritable storm of lead. He loosed a wild war
whoop and bore down on the overturned table. One of the
trappers rose up with a brace of pistols in his hands. He
emptied both weapons into the air as Standing Elk's war
lance skewered him.

The Blackfoot leapt his horse over the table, spattering the
men with grit and dirt in his wake. Kilhenny, half kneeling,
snapped off a shot that shattered the warrior's spine. Standing
Elk threw his hands up and dropped from horseback, rolling
to a stop in the churned earth. So died the chief of the
Bowstring Clan. However, he wasn't the last man to die in
the shadow of Fort Promise.

Nate Harveson had almost reached the front gate when Con
Vogel emerged from inside the fort, raised his pistol, and
fired. Harveson, looking over his shoulder at Standing Elk,

was slammed backward by the force of the slug. He sat down hard in the dirt, clawed at his suddenly numb chest and the red stain spreading across his vest. "Sweet Jesus!" he muttered and looked up and saw Con Vogel, smoke curling from the barrel of the gun in his hand. Harveson tried to stand, but his arms had no strength. It was all crazy. Some mistake, yes, that was it, a horrible mistake. His legs were as numb as his arms now. *I'm building an empire. It's just the beginning. Abby! Oh God! Just the beginning.*

And now, quite unexpectedly, the end. Nate Harveson's head drooped and bowed him forward as he died.

A time for killing, a place for dying, and Kilhenny's men would not be denied. Riflemen streamed from the blockhouses and emptied their guns at the remaining Blackfeet. The trappers on the stockade walls crammed powder and shot down the heated barrels of their rifles and loosed volley after volley at the fleeing warriors. An acrid pall blotted out the sun, the stench of powder smoke burned the lungs, eyes watered from the black grit that spewed from the muzzles of the Hawken rifles.

The tribal elders lay sprawled in attitudes of death below the walls of Fort Promise. The corpses of another ten braves littered the trampled earth between the blockhouses. Grapeshot and rifle fire had taken a deadly toll. Yet it could have been worse. The remaining two thirds of the braves who had journeyed from Ever Shadow had escaped Kilhenny's trap and were riding for their lives, right toward Tom Milam and the men hidden in the draw.

Tom watched as the braves charged past the fort and streamed out onto the plain. It was time to bring his men into play, to strike hard and finish off the survivors. It was time, once again, to avenge his parents' death. And yet he gave no command as the Blackfeet attempted to escape the massacre Kilhenny had arranged.

A shadow fell across him and he turned expecting to find Dog Bill Hanna. Instead, reedy old Spence Mitchell spewed a stream of tobacco juice and leaned on his rifle. He cocked a thumb toward the men in the draw. More than half their number were walking their horses up the draw, following the contour of the land and heading toward the woods. Dog Bill Hanna rode at the head of the buckskin-clad column.

"That sumbitch Hanna is taking them others out of the fight!" Mitchell exclaimed.

"I've got eyes," Tom retorted.

"Well, ain't you gonna stop 'em?"

"Why?"

Spence Mitchell stared at the younger man in amazement. "Why?" Mitchell wiped a forearm across his mottled beard and shook his head. "What the hell's got into you, boy?"

"Something I never knew I had." Tom rolled over on his back, folded his hands behind his head, and studied the limitless expanse of sky. The rifle fire had slackened, but the thunder of hooves rumbled in the earth.

"Well, you and your conscience can go straight to hell!" Spence Mitchell scrambled down to the bottom of the draw, where the remaining ten men waited uneasily for someone to give them the word to charge the fleeing braves.

"What's going on, Spence?" one of the men growled.

"Nothin'," Mitchell replied. "Follow me, lads. Let's take us some Injun scalps." The ten cheered and urged their horses up the side of the draw. Tom listened to their wild war cries. He expected they'd get more than they bargained for. Gunfire rattled on the plain.

Tom Milam kept his back to the fray as he climbed to his feet and returned to his horse, ground-tethered in the bottom of the draw. Tom was uncertain of his course for the first time in his twenty-one years.

As the past bound him to Kilhenny, so did the future hold Tom Milam to a fair skinned girl with eyes of the darkest emerald and hair the color of rain glistened earth.

Jacob Sun Gift riding at a gallop, poured a charge of black powder down his rifle barrel and followed the charge with a smaller caliber lead ball that he seated in place by slapping the rifle butt against his thigh. The load would do for short-range work. He didn't have time for anything else, not if he wanted to save Two Stars' life. The blind man could only ride where his horse took him, in this case right toward Spence Mitchell and another grizzled trapper by the name of

Dan Pugh. Neither of the trappers guessed the old one was
blind, nor would it have mattered. As the other men from the
draw pursued the fleeing party of Blackfeet, Mitchell and
Pugh roared in triumph and bore down on Two Stars.

Their horses were fast. But Jacob's gray mare was faster.
The animal plunged across the rolling grassland. The trappers
raised their rifles. Two Stars pulled blindly on the reins and
stopped not twenty feet from the white men. He seemed to
sense the presence of others and stretched out a crooked staff
he carried. The raven feathers adorning the staff fluttered as
he waved it to and fro.

Both trappers suddenly realized their enemy was sightless.
Pugh grinned and sighed on the brave's chest.

Jacob came at them from behind, his gray mare covering
the distance with tremendous strides. Jacob Sun Gift loosed a
wild cry. He caught movement out of the corner of his eye.
Another trapper joining the contest? Three to one made for
lousy odds. But with Two Stars' life at stake, Jacob had no
choice.

Spence Mitchell and Pugh wheeled their mounts and fired
wildly at the white Indian charging toward them. Jacob
crouched low, leaning forward on the neck of his horse. The
trappers dodged to either side, clawing for their pistols. Pugh
was the closest and Jacob raised up, fired, and dusted the
trapper's buckskin jacket with a lead slug. Pugh dropped off
his mount. Jacob reached Two Stars and planted himself
between the blind man and Spence Mitchell's pistols.

Jacob shouted for Two Stars to crouch as low as possible
and struggled to point the old one's mount in the right
direction. Jacob whirled as Mitchell fired. He tensed at the
gunshot, expecting the impact of a bullet.

Instead, Spence Mitchell had fired into the air. A feathered
shaft sprouted from his neck. A few yards off to his right
Tewa notched another arrow, raised her elk horn bow, then
held her fire. Spence Mitchell clawed at his skewered throat
and screeched. It was a horrid sound. The trapper toppled
from horseback and landed on his side. His legs pushed him
along the ground for a couple of feet as he choked on his blood
and then died.

"What has happened?" Two Stars said.

"Everything," Jacob muttered. He led Two Stars' horse to Tewa, who wore a look of surprise when he handed her the reins.

"I've got to go back. Lone Walker, Standing Elk, the others . . ."

"Dead or captured. I saw."

"No."

"There is nothing you can do," Tewa replied. "They are taken and there is nothing you can do but die."

"Then I'll die," Jacob said angrily, loading his rifle.

"Would Lone Walker wish it so?"

Jacob stared at her, suddenly hating this woman because she spoke the truth. And he didn't want to hear the truth. Not now. He looked back toward the fort and saw a heavily armed body of men emerge through the front gate. He didn't know whether Lone Walker was alive or dead. But there was nothing to be done for it now except ride like hell.

"Aayiii!" he screamed, loosing the pain that welled in his chest. The gray mare broke into a gallop. Tewa followed, leading her grandfather in a race against death.

They needed cover and they needed it fast. Jacob spied the draw not fifty feet away and headed for it, drawn by necessity, and the inevitable hand of fate.

Tom Milam kept his gelding to a loping gait as he worked his way along the draw and out of the way of the escaping braves. The heavy exchange of gunshots to the north and west suggested Spence Mitchell and his boys had gotten a lot more than they bargained for. Tom figured the bastard got what he deserved. Then again, they probably all would. Now there was a chilling thought.

Tom studied the tracks left by Dog Bill Hanna's bunch and decided they'd followed the draw all the way to the edge of the forest. Not Tom Milam; he hid from no one. A sharp tug on the reins and the gelding responded, dug its hooves into the soft earth and started up the side of the draw.

Jacob appeared on the rim, and charged down almost on top of the gelding. Tom kicked free as the horses tangled and lost their footing and tumbled down into the bottom, rolling over each other, neighing in terror, hooves flashing in the air.

Jacob launched himself as well and, landing on his side, rolled and allowed his momentum to carry him to his feet. He charged through the dust, eager to revenge himself for Lone Walker and the others. Tom braced himself on one knee, couldn't find his rifle, and grabbed for his belly gun. Jacob moved in for the kill, raised his rifle, and squeezed the trigger.

Nothing happened. His fall must have knocked the firing cap loose! Tom yanked the pistol from his belt. Jacob leapt forward and swung the Hawken like a club. Tom tried to duck and fired off balance. The heavy octagon-shaped barrel slapped his skull and shattered sunlight into an astounding array of colored splinters flung like daggers toward his eyes.

Tom Milam fell backwards into the draw. Jacob tossed his rifle aside, drew his double-edged "Arkansas toothpick," and leapt atop his unconscious foe. The side of Tom's face was shiny with blood. Jacob straddled him and raised the broad blade of his knife, poised to strike.

"Kill him!" Tewa brusquely gave her verdict as she led Two Stars into the draw. She leapt down and gathered the reins of the gelding and the gray mare as the frightened animals struggled to stand, miraculously spared from serious injury. She glanced around at Jacob, arm raised, unmoving. Tewa hurried to his side. "Kill him," she repeated. She stepped around him and for the first time looked into Jacob's bloodless expression, as if he were face to face with one of the Above Ones. In one hand he held his knife, in the other a fragment of Tom's shirt that had torn away in Jacob's fist. As the knife's lethal length flashed in the sun, so did the serpent ring gleam brightly against the fallen man's chest.

"Kill him," Tewa snapped, vengeance in her voice.

"No," Jacob whispered, lowering the knife in his hand.

"Why?" Tewa asked, astonished by his actions.

Jacob looked up at her. "This is my brother."

41

Hiram recited from Jeremiah. The words sounded appropriate to him and he hoped they would comfort the young woman standing by the corpse of her brother stretched out upon the long oaken table in the shade of the summer kitchen.

" 'Let my eyes stream with tears day and night without rest, over the great destruction which overwhelms the virgin daughter of my people, over her incurable wound.' " The black man's voice wavered a moment. But Thalia touched his arm and encouraged him and Hiram continued. " 'If I walk out into the field, look! those slain by the sword; if I enter the city, look! those consumed by the hunger. Even the prophet and the priest forage in a land they know not.' "

"Well spoken," Mose Smead added in a whisper as he stepped past the black couple and crossed to Abigail's side. She looked up as he approached. The riverboat captain was surprised to find her eyes dry, though her features were pale and drawn, the muscles tense along her jawline and neck. The captain reached over and tucked a Bible into the dead man's hands and patted his cold fingers. "Sleep in peace, son."

"Hiram put the fresh suit on him," Abigail said. "All the better to hide the wound . . . the blood."

"Death is never pretty. But it is final. It puts an end to things," Smead said and shifted his stance.

The sound of a hammer and saw continued to break the stillness of the afternoon. Dog Bill Hanna had volunteered to build a coffin for Nate Harveson's burial. The other casualties, like Spence Mitchell and the men who had followed him, were summarily wrapped in blankets and planted six feet under. The Blackfeet had suffered a different fate. Kilhenny, in his wrath that so many had escaped, ordered the dead braves to be stacked like cordwood and burned.

Only Abigail had insisted her brother have a proper coffin and when Dog Bill stepped forward to offer his services, she gratefully accepted.

"A powerful lot of dying happened today," Smead sadly observed. "And now it's all come crashin' down. I've a good crew. You say the word and we'll fire the engines and build us up a good head of steam and be ready to take you out of this cursed country."

"I'm not leaving." Abigail brushed a few strands of hair back from her features, her green eyes afire with determination.

"What? My dear, are you mad? You've lost your brother today, and that young hot spur you'd taken a fancy to."

"Tom Milam isn't dead," Abigail replied. "Mr. Hanna saw him carried off by some of the Blackfeet. Perhaps they intend to trade him for the man they've got chained in the barn."

Even in her grief, Abigail had been observant enough to notice Kilhenny, the Shoshoni called Bear, and half a dozen men bring in a warrior they had dragged out from under his dead horse.

Later, Dog Bill Hanna had passed along information he'd gleaned from Walks With The Bear that the Blackfoot's name was Lone Walker, a revered shaman and leader of his people.

Tom's capture had only added to the day's calamitous results. Yet he hadn't been killed outright. There had to be a reason for his being carried off. Abigail could only speculate that the savages intended to exchange him for Lone Walker. In the face of her brother's demise, Abigail had to have something to cling to, even something as fragile as hope. It was better than nothing. In the span of a few minutes, her whole world had come crashing down around her. And yet Abigail stood, holding back the tears. Now, in view of so many people, it was time to show strength. If her world had crashed, so be it, still Abigail Harveson wasn't broken.

Abigail sensed someone behind her, turned, and saw Con Vogel standing a few feet away. He'd washed the powder smoke from his broad handsome features and donned his best clothes. He'd wet his blond hair with water and brushed it flat against his skull without a part. His eyebrows all but disappeared, so fine and fair were they against his smooth high forehead. He held his hat and reverently moved in under the roof to stand alongside Abigail. He placed a hand on her shoulder.

"I can't believe he's dead. Even seeing him, now, like this, I can't believe he's dead." Vogel sighed, drew close to the body, and lowered his head as if in prayer. After a few moments of silent invocation, he looked at Abigail. "God, I feel as if I'm to blame. I was standing right there. It happened so damn quick. He was running to cover. Why he turned I don't know, but he stopped to look back. I saw him fall. It was terrible."

Abigail gazed at Vogel in open acceptance. She hadn't been able to make out a thing through all the gun smoke and the commotion on the walls. She had descended the stairs and rounded the entrance to find Con Vogel kneeling by Harveson's body. The strong young German had picked Harveson up in his arms and carried him within the walls.

"I know now what he was trying to teach me, Abby," Vogel said. "My father's influence means nothing here. In this country a man makes his own way. He carves his own destiny out of the great dream, casts his own shadow... if only I could tell him."

Con Vogel embraced her. "I'll be here if you need me," he whispered and kissed her forehead. He nodded a good-bye to Smead and then headed out across the grounds of Fort Promise on his way to the barn.

Abigail watched him go, seeing him in a new light. His arrogance seemed tempered at last. He moved like a man who knew where he was going. The rasp of wood scraping along the earth broke her reverie. Dog Bill Hanna rounded the corner of the house.

He was dragging a coffin.

Lone Walker tested the iron shackle circling his right foot and tethered to the back wall by a couple of yards of heavy chain. His hands were free. And why not? Nothing of any use lay near enough for him to grasp in this front stall.

The blacksmith's forge and tools were directly opposite him, tantalizingly laid out. Only he'd need about four times the length of chain that secured him to the wall.

His right leg throbbed; his entire lower torso felt battered and bruised. But nothing seemed broken. He'd gotten off lucky. The memory of his fallen friends sprawled below the stockade walls and blasted into butchered meat by the cannon fire had burned an indelible image in his heart.

Shadows momentarily darkened the entrance to the barn. Coyote Kilhenny, Skintop Pritchard, and Bear sauntered into the barn. The white men closed in. Only Bear held back, fearful of the Blackfoot's vengeance despite the shackle.

"C'mon, Bear, you red-nigger coward. He can't hurt you no how." Skintop Pritchard drew a line in the dirt floor with the tip of his boot. "See here, the chain'll only reach out so far." Pritchard drew his skinning knife, squatted down, and looked the prisoner in the eyes. "Of course, if'n he was to somehow get loose, I'd cut his liver out and feed it to the wolves." He jabbed the knife toward the Blackfoot. The blade passed to within a few inches of the chained man's face. Lone Walker never flinched. His coolness only infuriated Pritchard all the more.

"I think I'll cut me out an eye, then you'll yelp, you sorry bastard." Skintop Pritchard grinned and hunched in even closer. Too close.

Lone Walker sprang forward, caught the man's wrist, and threw him down. He wrenched the man's arm and forced Pritchard's own knife, still in his grasp, toward his own throat. A couple of seconds more would have finished him.

Coyote Kilhenny, teary-eyed with laughter, moved in and planted a kick under Lone Walker's ribs. The force of the blow knocked the brave against the barn wall. Pritchard scrambled to his knees.

"I'll kill you," he shrieked. But he never got the chance. Kilhenny dragged Pritchard off, wrested the knife from his grasp, and tossed it over by the forge.

"What the hell, Coyote?" Pritchard fumed.

"This buck's worth more to me in one piece," Kilhenny replied, slapping the dust and straw from Pritchard's clothes. "The red devils will be back. I figure seeing their big medicine maker alive and our prisoner oughta take the starch out of them bucks.'' Kilhenny glanced around at the Shoshoni. ''That is, if he's as important as Bear says.''

The Shoshoni glumly nodded. He preferred to see Lone Walker dead at the hands of Skintop Pritchard. Now the opportunity was lost. But there'd be another time, when Kilhenny was asleep or gone from the fort. Then Bear would do what needed to be done. And with Lone Walker's own long knife. Bear patted the hilt of the cutlass he had taken off of the Blackfoot.

Coyote Kilhenny squatted down just out of reach of the Blackfoot prisoner. The trapper rubbed his neck and jaw, scratched at his beard, then examined his stubby fingernails.

''Yes sir, I suspect you'd like to lift my hair about now.'' Kilhenny unslung his water bag, a length of buffalo gut stitched with sinew, thumbed the wooden stopper loose, and offered Lone Walker a drink. ''This is just to show I may be a treacherous son of a bitch but I ain't mean. Bear told me you parlay English, so don't try to trick me.''

Lone Walker took the water bag and tilted it to his lips and drank deeply. His leg ached and his throat felt dry as dust, but a sip of water seemed to help both feel a little better.

''The white Injun that came a-charging after me. Who was he?'' Kilhenny liked knowing his enemies.

''My son,'' Lone Walker said.

''Sure, and Thomas Jefferson was mine.'' Kilhenny's lips curled back in a horrible semblance of a smile. ''I'll ask you again. Who was he?''

''My son,'' came the Blackfoot's answer.

''Now will you let me tickle him with a hot iron? He'll sing right enough,'' Pritchard muttered.

''No. Not now. Let him think it over.'' Kilhenny flexed his big, thick hands and then clenched them into fists.

''Your 'son' and a couple of the other bucks rode off with my boy. Any harm come to him, I'll send you to the happy hunting grounds piece by piece.'' Kilhenny stood and led the others from the barn.

Lone Walker didn't hear the threat. Jacob was alive! He'd escaped unharmed! The spirit singer felt the weight of the world lift from his heart. Jacob Sun Gift had escaped. He lived!

Coyote Kilhenny paused just outside the entrance to the barn as Con Vogel rounded the corral and made straight for the half-breed. The aristocratic young German beamed as he approached Kilhenny.

"He looks happy as the camp dog that made off with the guts," Skintop Pritchard said to Kilhenny.

The half-breed nodded. "And smells fresh as a daisy." Kilhenny hooked his thumbs in his waist belt and waited for Vogel to speak.

"They have Nate Harveson all laid out and ready for the box," Vogel informed them. "It would be proper if you stopped by to pay your respects to Miss Harveson."

"That gal has too much grit to lie to," Kilhenny said. "She'd see through me in a second. She'd see how I was plumb satisfied Nate is out of the way. She might even take a notion I gave you the gun that killed him."

Con Vogel's eyes widened in alarm and he looked nervously around as if the man expected Abigail herself to be standing by and able to overhear Kilhenny's remarks.

"For heaven's sake, Mr. Kilhenny. . . ."

"Laddie, you stopped doing things for heaven's sake the minute you killed Nate Harveson."

Again Vogel glanced about and he held up his hands, pleading for Kilhenny to lower his voice. Kilhenny only chuckled and clapped the German on the shoulder. "Not to worry, my lad. You're one of us now. You're among friends. I've got me a jug of rum under my bed and we owe it to ourselves to finish off."

Con Vogel shrugged and tried to maintain his false brava-do. Kilhenny was right. He was among friends. Who was there to overhear? He fell in step with Pritchard, Bear, and Kilhenny, taking comfort that he had won a place for himself among their ranks. It never occurred to him to glance back over his shoulder and up at the open loft door, where a silhouette ducked out of sight.

For all Con Vogel's efforts, someone had listened and learned his deadly secret.

42

Tom Milam was dead. And if hell held a fate for him, it would be seeing his brother Jacob dressed out as one of the savages who had murdered their parents. Tom managed to will the sight away. There was a great realm of darkness to dive into. A place of Stygian gloom. A place of peace. . . .

My head hurts. How can I feel my head when I'm dead. I'm not supposed to feel anything. I don't understand.

"Tom." *Someone calling my name.* "Tom." *Again? Why so insistent?*

"Tom."

Shards of light illuminated the darkness, partitioned oblivion into a patchwork quilt of shadow and brightness.

I hear. I hurt. Then I'm not dead. Cool water bathed his forehead; he opened his mouth and sucked moisture from the cloth. Kilhenny and the boys must have ridden out to find him. Coyote was probably angry as the devil. Well, he'd been angry before. Tom lost consciousness, relieved his earlier vision of Jacob had been like a nightmare, nothing real. He was among friends now. And so blasted tired. Face them later. Later. Later.

Tom Milam woke. He tried to sit upright, winced, and gingerly probed the lump on the side of his skull with his fingertips. He froze in mid-motion with the realization he wasn't in the fort and the likes of Kilhenny and the trappers were nowhere to be seen. In their place, a Blackfoot warrior woman and an old blind brave sat across from him, firelight playing on their features. A couple of rabbits had been skinned and hung over the fire, and from the looks of them they were about done.

Tom dropped his hand to where his pistols should have been.

"I took your guns," a voice said from the darkness beyond the firelight. "Lucky for you. Tewa would have put an arrow through your heart before you could pull your gun. I'd hate to lose you again, Tom." Jacob stepped into the circle of light. He wore buckskin leggings and moccasins; his upper torso, burned bronze by the sun, rippled with muscles; his tangled mane of straw-colored hair spilled across his shoulders and down his chest. He was marked with the ceremonial scars of a Blackfoot warrior.

Tom's mouth hung open. He was speechless. And yet, behind all the savage trappings, this was indeed Jacob, his brother.

"That's about how I felt when I saw that ring hung around your neck." Jacob crossed the clearing to kneel at his brother's side. "When I think of how close I came to..." He shook his head and slowly exhaled. Then he reached out to embrace his brother.

Tom pulled back, his face an angry mask, revulsion in his eyes. "I'd rather be dead than see you riding with them— riding against your own people."

"These are my people," Jacob said. "Blackfeet took me in when I was just about finished, protected me from the Shoshoni that killed our folks."

"Shoshoni?" Tom blurted out.

"Among others, yes. Blackfeet ways are my ways now." Jacob indicated the two sitting by the fire. "The old one is Two Stars. The girl is Tewa. She is close to my heart."

Tom glared at them. Tewa matched his hatred with her own. She had no use for the white man. He was her enemy. But he was Jacob's brother, and this left her confused and uncertain as to what she should do—feed him or kill him.

"Shoshoni, Blackfeet, what's the difference? They murdered our mother and father, and now you've sided with them." Tom propped himself upright. His right arm trembled with the strain.

"Not I," Jacob said. "You look to your own saddle mates. Look to Coyote Kilhenny."

"What the hell are you saying?"

"Kilhenny killed Pa."

"You're lying. . . ."

"I saw him," Jacob said. "I hid in the buffalo grass and watched it happen. He led them into an ambush, just like today. I saw him shoot Pa. That was the signal for the Shoshoni to hit the camp. It was a slaughter. And Kilhenny and a couple of his friends did their share."

"Lies," Tom snapped. "I'll stop you." His hands closed around Jacob's throat in an attempted stranglehold. But Tom's strength faded fast. The world reeled and he slumped back on his blanket. "Lies," he repeated, more a moan this time. His arms dropped to the blanket and his eyes closed.

Jacob sighed and returned to the campfire. He explained to Tewa and her grandfather what had happened.

"I did not understand his words, but I could tell there was much hurt in his voice," Two Stars said, edging closer to the warmth of the fire. Even a cool night caused his bones to ache these days. Jacob rounded the fire and draped an extra blanket across the old man's shoulders.

Two Stars tilted his seamed face up as if he could see Jacob towering over him.

"The hand that saved the father slew the son," Two Stars said. Jacob stiffened, expecting another admonition from the blind war chief. Two Stars caught the younger man's wrist. "Yet it is a good hand," Tewa's grandfather continued. "I sense the All-Father in what has befallen us. To hate this hand is to hate the Great Spirit of Life that guides it."

Two Stars reached out. "Granddaughter, your hand," he said. Tewa moved closer to the old one and stretched forth her own. Two Stars took her hand and placed it in Jacob's. "Your father walks with the Above Ones, Tewa. He rides the wind. Let it be so. And do not walk the great circle of life with a heart full of hate."

Tewa looked down at their joined hands. Then her eyes met Jacob's. A single tear left a glistening trail along her cheek. She did not pull away.

Jacob clung to her. Tewa's slim fingers entwined with his.

She lowered her head, her lustrous wealth of dark hair spilling forward to hide her features. At last, his grasp opened, their hands parted.

"Maybe I better check on the back trail before sleeping." Jacob rose from the fire, took up his rifle, and started off toward the edge of darkness. He paused on the periphery of light, then continued into the woods. Hidden here in the sanctuary of the forest, a mere two days ride from Fort Promise, it wouldn't do to be careless.

"Granddaughter," Two Stars said softly. "Four eyes are better than two in the dark. Go to him."

"But this one . . . his brother?"

"I will call you if he wakes."

"How will you know?"

Two Stars said simply, "Sometimes no eyes are better than four. I will know."

Tewa glanced at the unconscious man, then lifted her eyes to the forest trail leading out of the clearing.

"Go, child. You have followed your hurt. Now it is time to follow your heart," Two Stars said. "And find where it leads."

Moonlight in Ever Shadow . . .

A man and a woman stood together on a hillside where the ponderosa pines fractured the moonlight into beams of purest silver. It was told in campfire tales that men had wandered these paths of light and found the All-Father only to be blinded by the truth.

Tewa and Jacob had heard the stories by Blackfoot campfires and resisted the temptation to follow the moonlight. They were content with earthbound passion. They clung to desire, held and healed each other in the oneness they felt.

Tewa brought her blanket, as Jacob had given his shirt to cradle his brother's head, and his blanket, that Tom might rest in comfort. She knew he was cold.

Jacob said, "It is I who should offer a place in my blanket to you."

"It is the way," Tewa conceded. "But then you might freeze to death before you ever came to me."

"You have said it," Jacob replied. He accepted the blanket, wrapped it around his shoulders and then over Tewa as she drew close.

They faced the valley and the moon-dappled creek that wound through the pass before sinking back into the soil. Jacob half expected to see a column of armed trappers appear in the valley, dogging their trail. He didn't look forward to a last stand on the hillside.

But nothing stirred save the wind in the buffalo grass and a night-hunting owl searching for dinner. Jacob watched and knew comfort in Tewa's closeness. Her presence helped. He had been terribly worried throughout the two-day ride from Fort Promise. Tom had lost a lot of blood from the gash on the side of his head. Now that he'd come around, Jacob had one less concern. But there was still the matter of Lone Walker. Somehow, deep within, he sensed that Lone Walker still lived. And Jacob would not rest until he learned the fate of the man he had grown to love as a father.

"What will we do now?" Tewa was ready and willing to make her stand wherever and whenever Jacob decided.

"I don't know," Jacob admitted. "You, me, a blind man, and my brother, who might just try to kill me when he wakens again. Quite an army."

"I am glad I am here," Tewa said. She lifted her eyes to the starry firmament. High wispy clouds scudded across the moon's cold stare. Was her father there, among the clouds, a rider in the sky? Jacob had not killed him. Wolf Lance had been destroyed by his dreams. Tewa understand that now and she was free from the blood debt, free to walk the circle of life again, free to love, free to stand by Jacob, free to fight and, if need be, to die at his side.

Moonlight in Ever Shadow...

43

Dreams die at sunrise. Tom Milam roused himself from his blankets. Smoke curled from the ashes of the campfire; lazy gray spirals rose up through the branches of the pines. Tewa and her grandfather were huddled in sleep. Jacob dozed as he squatted by the campfire. He'd propped himself upright on his Hawken rifle. His head bobbed on his chest, rising and falling with every breath.

The forest woke quietly to the morning sun. Birds stirred; the creatures of the forest stole down into the valley and made their way to the spring-fed creek.

Tom rolled from his bedroll and crawled on hands and knees to Jacob's side. He chose each movement, moving slowly, cautiously ignoring the ache in his skull. He spied what he was looking for by Jacob's leg, a heavy bore percussion pistol lying on the ground within easy reach of Jacob and now, Tom. He leaned forward. His fingers inched closer to the walnut and brass gun butt. He had to be careful, for the slightest noise would—

"Be careful, it's loaded," Jacob said.

Tom gave a start and drew back. He regarded Jacob with unabashed respect. "You're good."

"I had a good teacher." Jacob picked up the pistol and passed it across to Tom.

"So did I." Tom sensed a second pair of eyes carefully studying him and glanced in Tewa's direction. She peered at him through slitted eyelids. There was no telling how long she'd been awake. He half cocked the pistol, removed the firing cap, and lowered the hammer, all for her benefit. His actions seemed to satisfy her, for Tewa closed her eyes once more and pulled her blanket up to her chin.

It was obvious she intended to allow the brothers a moment of privacy. Tom returned his attention to the white Indian squatting opposite the campfire. Like two strangers thrown together by fate and uncertain of what to say, they hesitated and remained silent, allowing the moment to find its own resolution.

"I had a dream," Tom said, reliving a moment etched into his brain cells. "I've had it before, about being ten and hiding in the tall grass, waiting for you to come back, Jacob. Only you never showed. Kilhenny did though. The dream's always been the same." Tom eased back on his heels and stared down at the smoldering remains of the campfire. "This time his hand was all covered with blood. The innocent blood of my father and mother." Tom met his brother's gaze. "Yet he saved my life. Even Kilhenny isn't all bad." He shook his head. "Just bad enough." He wiped a forearm across his suddenly red-rimmed eyes and cleared his throat. "Hell, I should have known it long ago. Of course, I didn't want to. That made all the difference."

He lifted a water bag to his parched lips and drank deeply.

"I don't know what to say," Jacob admitted.

"Don't," Tom said. "We took different turns a helluva long time ago. What's the use in kidding ourselves; there isn't any going back. You know it as well as I."

"Then what's left?" Jacob asked, stung by the realization that what his brother said was true.

"Vengeance," Tom Milam answered. His eyes glittered with anticipation. Coyote Kilhenny had been a resourceful teacher; it was time Tom put those lessons into practice.

"I don't understand," Jacob replied.

"First of all, I have to escape from you," Tom said, rubbing his hands in anticipation. "And you'll need to tell me as much as possible about the lay of the land surrounding the village." Tom outlined his plan to bring Kilhenny into the same kind of trap he was so fond of setting for others.   It was a chilling experience, listening to Tom coldly devise his plan. He spoke without passion, detailing his deceit. Jacob listened and agreed with the plan. He wanted Coyote Kilhenny to pay for the massacre of the Milam party as well as the slaughter at Fort Promise. He hated Kilhenny and was determined to bring the half-breed to some kind of justice.

But Tom seemed wholly dispassionate. Kilhenny had spared his life, had raised him, and now Tom intended to betray him. He should have been enraged at learning the truth about Coyote Kilhenny. That part of his humanity seemed to have been excised during the night. Perhaps all that remained of the brother Jacob knew was the ring dangling from the chain about his neck.

"With Kilhenny out of the way," Tom said, "the men at the fort will follow me. If there's an empire to be carved out of this land, I'll be the one who does the whittling."

"The fort goes. This is Blackfoot country."

"We'll see," Tom said.

"See it burned to the ground," Jacob said.

"Be a shame for brothers to lock horns." Tom gingerly touched the makeshift bandage circling his skull. "Of course, we already did that once. You won the first round."

"My people will not allow the fort to remain."

"Your people?" Tom said. "My God, look at your skin, your hair and eyes."

"Look at my heart," Jacob replied.

"Then once Kilhenny's out of the way, we might just wind up peering at each other through powder smoke." If it bothered Tom that he might be going up against his own brother, he hid such misgivings well.

"You can tell your woman to open her eyes now. She doesn't need to pretend to sleep any longer." Tom stood, wavered for a moment, then regained his balance. "I'll fetch my horse," he said. "Then I better pack some grub and get going."

It took Tom longer than he expected to saddle his horse. He had to pause now and then to endure a few seconds of nausea. Each time he willed away the attack and pressed on with the task at hand. His mount shuddered and behaved skittishly amid the strange sights and smells of an Indian camp.

Tom looked over his shoulder once and noticed Tewa sitting on a fallen log, watching his every action. She was a pretty thing, he concluded, though he preferred his women without wolf-pelt cowls and ten-foot-long spears. He winked at the Blackfoot woman. Tewa dug the blunt end of her spear into the earth at her feet and pretended not to notice him. Tom laughed and tightened his saddle cinch.

Jacob came toward him from the opposite side of the clearing. He held out a second pistol to Tom, who nodded his thanks and tucked the weapon in his belt. His coat was torn along the side and his knees poked through his trousers. His scuffle with Jacob had taken its toll. He wasn't used to coming off second best in a fight.

"Maybe you ought to rest more," Jacob suggested. "It's been a long time, maybe we could talk."

"Sure. We could talk about old times. Hell, Jacob, we don't have any old times."

"I didn't mean—"

"Or maybe we might discuss the missing years, the time I was being raised by my father's murderer. And I'd sure like to hear how many white scalps you've lifted since you took to wearing war paint!" Tom stepped back and appraised his older brother. "Quit trying to bring something back that can never be. Since the day I waited for you, alone and scared out on the plain, we've cut different trails. And there just isn't any crossing the ground between."

Tom reached out and took the parfleche of dried meat and fry bread Jacob had prepared for him.

"I aim to bring Kilhenny down for what he did," Tom said. "You be watching the trail. I'll lead Kilhenny right to your Medicine Lake. You got a place to trap him?"

"A gap leading to the valley."

"I know the place."

"You do?" Jacob asked, surprised.

"I scouted it," Tom proudly claimed. "Nobody saw me, but I saw you. Darn near blew your head off."

"Lucky you recognized me."

"Lucky I couldn't get a clear shot." Tom swung up into the saddle. "Be seeing you, brother." He walked his mount through the dancing dust of a spring morning. Jacob watched and could say no more. Words held no power over the sense of loss he felt.

44

"**R**ider coming in," the man on the wall shouted down to another trapper lounging by the front gate. The man by the gate straightened and picked up his rifle.

"Who is it?"

"Don't know. He's got the sun at his back."

Indeed, the rider seemed to be coming directly out of the ruby-colored sunset. Molten crimson clouds billowing overhead transformed a simple solitary stranger into a rider of brimstone, a fugitive from perdition.

"Use your spyglass," the gatekeeper called.

"I am, damn it, I am," the lookout retorted.

"Shit. Are you sure there is only one? Could be a whole passel of them Blackfeet." The gatekeeper checked his rifle. Then he propped the rifle against the wall and swung the gates together.

"Hold on, you fool. It ain't no Injuns."

"C'mon down here and call me a fool, you lop-eared mule."

"Well, I'll be a son of a bitch!" the lookout exclaimed. "I don't believe my eyes!"

The gatekeeper stood in the entranceway and shielded his eyes, curiosity getting the better of him. "I can't see a . . ." the complaint died on his lips as the rider materialized out of the sunset's shimmering light. The rider's shadow stretched before the hooves of his horse and at last engulfed the surly gatekeeper, who watched in slack-jawed amazement as if he were seeing a ghost.

* * *

Coyote Kilhenny leaned on the table, his wide girth overshadowing the scraps of food remaining on his plate. His right hand opened and closed in a fist every time he tried to make a point.

"Grieving is one thing," Kilhenny said, exasperated by an argument he'd been pursuing for the better part of an hour. He wanted Abigail Harveson to leave on the riverboat with Mose Smead. She refused to go. "Your brother's been in the ground three days and its tetched you. Even Captain Smead here thinks you'd be better off back in Independence."

Kilhenny leaned back as Thalia took his plate away. A clutter of antelope ribs, gnawed clean, showed he approved of her cooking.

"I'd buy that darky if you'd name a fair price."

Abigail glared at him, her distaste evident. "The Harvesons do not own people. All our servants are free and work for living quarters, board, and wages. It's the way it's always been and the way it always will be."

"You show real beauty when you're on the prod." Kilhenny grinned, then turned serious. "Look. It'll be hard for me to pacify these here savages while having to worry about the safety of a white woman."

"Aaa-hhh!" Thalia screamed and dropped a platter of biscuits. Abigail, Kilhenny, and Mose Smead glanced up in surprise, caught off guard and alarmed by the cook's outburst.

"I'll worry about the safety of this white woman," Tom Milam said, riding up in the waning light of the afternoon. Several of the trappers had followed him through the front gates eager to hear how he'd escaped the clutches of the Blackfeet. He slid out of the saddle and handed the reins to Dog Bill Hanna, standing among the men.

"Blast and by damn!" Kilhenny roared, slammed his fist on the wood, and almost overturned the table as he stood.

Abigail brought her hand to her mouth, both elated at Tom's arrival and horrified at the freshly scabbed gash and discolored flesh marring his features. If they had been alone, she would have run to him.

Tom didn't know what to expect or what he would feel when he came face-to-face with Coyote Kilhenny. Now the moment had arrived and the numbness that shrouded his heart made him feel stone-cold dead, within and without. Kilhenny's hand was stained with the blood of innocents. Tom felt more alone than ever before. His parents were dead. The one man he had grown to trust was a Judas. And Jacob, though alive, had become one of the savages Tom considered an enemy. Tom looked at Abigail, and her eyes settled his weary spirit. He could have watched her for the rest of the evening.

Kilhenny clapped him on the back and draped his arm across Tom's shoulders. "I knew those heathen bastards couldn't hold you. How'd you get away?"

"As quickly as I could. Just like you taught me, Coyote. I came to in that Indian camp, took a look around, and played possum till I could brain one and steal his horse." He held out a cup and Thalia filled it with strong black coffee.

"That-a-boy." Kilhenny said. He spied Pike Wallace and Skintop Pritchard working their way through the trappers. "See here, lads, Tom ain't under yet."

Pike seemed genuinely happy. Tom Milam's capture had been a bad omen to him. Skintop Pritchard, on the other hand, stepped aside and faded back into the crowd. He'd greeted the news of Tom's capture with a perfunctory "Good riddance."

Tom looked up into the face of his father's murderer and smiled. "Good to be back among my own kind."

"Who was that white renegade running with those Blackfeet?"

"Never said his name," Tom said, his expression devoid of feeling. He strode up to Thalia, knelt and picked up the platter, brushed off some of the biscuits, and stuffed a couple into his coat pocket. "Never like to see a man go hungry, especially when that man is me." Abigail brought a jar of honey and a plate and set a place for him at the head of the table. Her eyes were warm and welcoming. She was greatly relieved to see him, battered as he was.

"I didn't run out empty-handed," Tom said. "I savvied enough of their conversation to know the Blackfoot village is ripe for the picking. We could drive them out of the mountains in a single blow."

"You remember the way?" Kilhenny asked. He'd been pondering the same notion himself.

"In my sleep."

"Well, get some." Kilhenny clapped him on the shoulder once again. "We've got a war party to put together come sunup." Kilhenny wiped a beefy forearm across his bewhiskered mouth. "You heard me, lads. We aren't gonna let those bucks regroup. We can burn their village and drive them out for good. There'll be prime trapping this summer."

"Just so long as we don't drive out the women," Iron Mike roared from the periphery of the crowd.

"Naw," another of Kilhenny's men spoke out. "We'll capture then squaws and tie 'em to poles for safekeeping."

"I gotta pole you can tie one onto," a third voice said. Some of the men laughed. But not all.

"I didn't plan on fighting anybody's private war," Dog Bill Hanna spoke up. Several men around him nodded. "We come for pelts not scalps. Me and my Platte River boys figure we've done all the soldiering we intend to." He touched a hand to the leather brim of his coonskin cap. "Glad you made it back, Tom," Dog Bill remarked, then turned and left.

Tom saluted in the man's direction with his cup of coffee. Dog Bill's men broke away from the main body of Kilhenny's bunch and started toward the gate. They preferred to sleep out under the stars, where it was easier to watch their backs.

"There goes a smart man," Tom said aloud. "The trouble is, he'll always be poor."

"Now you're talking," Kilhenny said.

"I think I ought to have a say in what happens," Abigail suggested sternly.

"Say all you want, but you've been voted down," Kilhenny said.

"By who?"

"By me," Kilhenny retorted. "With Nate lying yonder in his grave, I'm putting myself in command."

Tom froze at the news of Nate Harveson's death. "How did it happen?"

"Injuns. Probably that red devil we got chained in the barn," Kilhenny said. "No need for me to tell you. I reckon you'll get an earful tonight," the half-breed answered with a knowing look in Abigail's direction. "Maybe you can talk some sense into her, Tom. Me and the captain have failed."

"Most assuredly," Smead exclaimed. He rose from his bench seat, steadying himself against the table. "Took a little too much port, I fear." The Captain nodded to Tom and Kilhenny, doffed his cap, and made a grand bow in Abigail's direction.

"My dear 'almost' daughter, I remain at your service." The captain patted the wrinkles from his coat and adjusted the dog-eared leather Bible in his belt. "I don't suppose one of you gentlemen would consider showing me to my boat?"

"Come along, parson," Pike Wallace said, volunteering. He took Smead by the arm. The righteous captain didn't imbibe often, but now and then he could be counted on to tie into a bottle with a vengeance. Afterward, he'd wind up weak legged, bleary eyed, and the proud owner of a monstrous hangover that made his skull feel like the boiler on his boat.

The trappers slowly ambled away as Pike led Smead toward some members of his crew preparing to return to the riverboat with a wagonload of timber.

Kilhenny returned his attention to Tom. "You had me worried," he told the younger man. "I'd have blooded these hills if the Injuns had put you under." He patted the array of pistols slung across his chest. "I'd have made them answer for what they done to you, Tom. Be sure of that. An eye for an eye, that what's writ in the Good Book."

"I feel the same way, Coyote," said Tom. And there was something in his voice that might have alerted Kilhenny had he only taken time to watch and listen. But the half-breed had a raid to plan. And the subtle change in Tom Milam went unnoticed by him.

But not by Abigail Harveson. The moment Kilhenny was out of earshot, she drew close to Tom and put her hand on his arm where he leaned on the table. "What's happened to you?" she asked.

"I'm tired as hell," Tom grumbled. He slathered a biscuit with honey and plopped it in his mouth.

"No."

"You'll see. Soon as I scrub my hide and drink a gallon of coffee."

* * *

Con Vogel squatted in the loft; straw clung to his frock coat and dust patched the seat of his pants. He didn't give a damn. He rose up on his knees and peered out the upper window of the loft toward the Harveson blockhouse and the lamplight flickering in the upstairs window of Abigail's bedroom.

Vogel had been prepared to go calling on Abigail as soon as he had his way with the servant girl. Tom's return ruined everything. Vogel had watched from the loft as Tom Milam arrived at the blockhouse. With Virginia at his side he had waited in the stable's hay loft, hoping that Tom might leave. Instead, Abigail and Tom had entered the house together, dooming the arrogant musician's hopes for rekindling his former romance.

"Damn him!" Vogel's breath clouded on the cool night air. Virginia waited on a bed of straw. She had wrapped herself in a shawl to ward off the chill and waited for Con to return to her side.

"What does it matter? I am here," Virginia said. "I have given myself to you alone, isn't that enough?"

"Alone?" Con laughed and turned to look at her, his disdain replacing the passion that had once ruled his emotions. "Who haven't you given yourself to?"

His words, like the bite of a lash, left her wounded and hurting. She lowered her head and began to sob. "I have never given myself. I meant no more to Mister Nate than a good horse or a huntin' dog. White folks like him say I'm free. Sure. I'm free as long as I do what I'm told." She dried her eyes on a corner of the shawl. Hurt gave way to anger, and she rolled from the hay and stood, naked save for the shawl. Her hands closed into fists.

"Mister Coyote took me. I knew I couldn't stop him, so's I just lay back and let him do what he gotta do. Just like everybody else around here. I didn't give him nothing." She walked across the loft to stand at Vogel's side and touched his arm. "You were gentle. And you got dreams like me. You say sweet words. I give myself only to you, Con. You know that, now. Tell me it's so."

Con Vogel stared glumly at the house in the center of the stockade. In his mind, he could just picture the scene upstairs, Abigail all white and naked and writhing beneath Tom

Milam. There would never be any place in Abigail's life for anyone else, not as long as Tom Milam lived. Why the hell couldn't those Indians have finished him?

Anger burned in his breast, welled up to choke him. It wasn't fair. Not again. Fantasies, like a house of cards, came tumbling down and in their ruin naught but smoldering embers of jealousy and hatred remained.

"Mister Con . . ." Virginia softly pleaded.

At last he focused on her, his expression rigid, stone faced. He needed a drink. He wanted to drown himself in rum. Maybe that would blot out Nate Harveson's face, which appeared every time Con closed his eyes.

"I don't know you," Vogel harshly replied. "I don't know you!" He brushed her aside and rushed toward the ladder leading down from the loft. He hurried down, risking a nasty fall on the makeshift rungs. He left Virginia alone in the shadowy loft, her sobs wasted on his hardened heart.

Virginia fumbled for her calico dress and quickly slipped it on, then wrapped herself in the shawl. A night owl screeched and whirred past the loft window. Virginia jumped, startled by the sound, her heart fluttering.

She heard a voice in the momentary stillness that followed. The captive Blackfoot chained in one of the stalls below had begun to sing. It was a mournful chant whose simple, sad words Virginia couldn't understand. But the spirit of the song was as familiar to her as her own pain and that of her entire race, a people enslaved.

Hiram dug his fork into the wedge of pie on his plate and lifted a mouthful of apples and sugar crust to his lips. Thalia sat across from him, nursing the day's last cup of coffee and watching the old black man enjoy his snack.

He closed his mouth around the fork, shut his eyes, and all but purred with contentment. "Man oh man, whoever made this here pie knew what she was about. Ah, who'd you say it was?"

"Don't know," Thalia, refusing to rise to the bait, reached across the table and broke off a piece of the crust and sampled it. "Somebody just left it on my windowsill 'bout noon. Crust ain't bad. Almost as good as mine."

"Almost," Hiram said. "Mister Nate used to love your

pies. . . ." The old man's features drooped. Sugar and cinnamon turned sour on his palate. Hiram lowered his fork and slid the plate away. "He wasn't the best man, but he wasn't the worse neither." Hiram studied his wrinkled hands and tried to remember a time when his leathery black flesh had been smooth, unseamed by age and work and care. He couldn't. "You were right, woman. Comin' out here was a mistake. We all are for the worse."

Thalia shook her head. "Such talk and you the one always claimin' to be so all-fired ready for a change." The cook slid the plate of pie back toward the house servant. "Tears are for the dead. Pies are for the living. It ain't proper to waste neither." Her round dark features were set, a veritable mask of determination.

Hiram studied her. "Where'd you get such wisdom, woman?"

"Maybe it got left on the windowsill, too," she said.

Hiram laughed gently and dug into the pie.

Abigail woke in the early hours of morning. She touched the place beside her in bed but found cold sheets instead of a warm sleeping body. She sat upright and brushed her hair back from her face and saw Tom standing by the window in the moonlight. He was naked and lithe and seemed to her like some primitive animal waiting at the lip of his cave—for what? His mate? His prey? One and the same? She had wept in his arms and they had made love. No, he had taken her, without pause for endearments and tender caresses and arousing kisses. And she had met his fierce demands with her own, clawing at him and taking his hunger and losing herself in the fires of what seemed now a frightening mixture of passion and rage.

She crawled from the bed and wrapped the quilt around her like a toga, which trailed behind her as she padded to his side. She opened the quilt and offered him a place within its folds.

"Among the Indians, that's a way of proposing," Tom wryly observed.

"You'll catch your death."

"I've been trying to for years."

"Well, don't succeed in my room," Abigail replied bitterly.

"I've buried enough of my heart the past few days." She shrugged and closed her wrap when he made no move toward her. In truth, he seemed impervious to the night's chill, as if he were one with the cold and the dark.

"What are you looking for?" She peered through the window, overlooking the front gate and the distant hills like dunes of drifting coal against the horizon of stars.

"Ghosts," Tom said. His right fist encased the serpent ring he wore around his neck. His knuckles shone bloodless and white in the moonlight.

Abigail shivered though not from the cold. "Tom . . ." she leaned closer, "Tom?"

But there came no reply, for tonight Tom Milam kept his vigil in a place where even love could not reach him.

45

"**G**ive me seventy fighting men and I'll cut a path through the heart of the Blackfoot nation," Coyote Kilhenny declared from the sun-drenched yard of the corral. He looked on as the last of his men found suitable mounts, roped the animals, and led them to the corral fence where the saddles were draped across the rails. It had taken a couple of days to arrange and outfit his force, but they were days well spent. Kilhenny had spent the time exciting his men with the prospect of plunder.

"Seventy men, that's my count," Tom replied, standing alongside the man who had raised him. "And the cannon you've hitched to the wagon."

"Insurance, my lad." Kilhenny squinted at the sun's inevitable climb in the sky. "I want us under way by mid-morning, so don't let your 'fare-thee-well' with the Harveson girl slow us down even further." Kilhenny spat in the dirt at his feet and leaned against Tom. "See you keep your drawers cinched up. Save some for those Blackfoot squaws we're gonna find just waiting our pleasure."

Tom continued to play along with the half-breed. He noticed Skintop Pritchard and the Shoshoni leading Lone Walker from the barn. Kilhenny intended to take the Blackfoot medicine man along just in case they ran into a war party. If Lone Walker was as important as Bear claimed, the braves from the Medicine Lake village would think twice before attacking. Coyote Kilhenny didn't miss a trick, Tom thought— well, maybe just one.

"My horse is saddled. I won't be long." Tom left

Kilhenny in the corral and headed straight for Abigail's. All around him, men were checking their gear, arguing over horses, women, Indians, and the prospect of turning beaver pelts into gold. Men carried gunpowder and provisions to the wagons. It was like some scene more suited to a military expedition. Then again, that's just what it was. Kilhenny's army was marching off to war.

Abigail met Tom on the front porch. He took her by the arm and led her inside and there, ignoring Hiram's awkward presence, held her in a last embrace.

"Don't go," Abigail pleaded. "Stay here with me. Dill Hanna's men will hold Fort Promise along with Captain Smead's crew of rowdies. I do not intend to allow Coyote Kilhenny back within the walls." She kissed him.

Hiram cleared his throat and vanished down the hall, moving as quickly and discreetly as he could.

"I can't," Tom said.

"You mean you won't."

"I mean it's one and the same."

Abigail stepped out of his arms, broke the circle of his embrace, and crossed the room to stand behind her brother's desk. Every step seemed to add to the aura of power and command, that unique quality absent in her brother.

"I am expecting my boats any day now. I don't think Kilhenny realizes, but his position is tenuous. When my people arrive, I shall no longer need him."

"Or me?"

"I want you." Abigail patted the wrinkles from the royal blue wool dress whose high-necked collar was trimmed with lace. She looked every inch a lady. Tom would have liked to rip a few of her buttons loose to free the wanton he knew lurked beneath that suddenly icy exterior. "I want you. But I don't need you." She folded her hands upon the desk. "I intend to remain here, to build the settlement Nate and I envisioned."

"Tall order for a woman."

"Not this woman."

He shrugged and started toward the door.

"Tom . . . what is it? You've changed. Something's happened, I don't know what. Ever since the Blackfeet captured you."

She leaned forward, her knuckles digging into the map spread on the desk top. Unable to resist him and against her better judgment, she held out her hands to him. "Let Kilhenny go."

Tom considered the possibility. But, no, he had to make sure. He couldn't rely on blind luck to bring Kilhenny to justice. Tom's role was crucial to the success of the plan. He had to be certain the bait stayed with the trap.

"No." He didn't try to elaborate; it would do no good and only muddy the waters further. Better to keep Abigail out of it and out of his plans.

"I'll be back," he said and winked at her. For a moment Abigail saw the old Tom Milam, the man she loved, grinning at her behind his dark, glassy eyes.

Abigail might have run to him, held him back, and kept him at her side for always. But the desk with its map of a would-be kingdom blocked her path and kept her from him. Tom darted through the doorway and in a second was gone, and Abigail Harveson was left alone.

46

More than a week of hard riding had taken a toll on Two Stars. His shoulders hunched forward, his head sagged, and it took real effort to keep from falling off his horse. Jacob and Tewa had been worried about the blind brave's health throughout the forced journey. So it was with a great sense of relief that they came to the pass leading to Medicine Lake and the Blackfoot village.

Jacob studied the pass with renewed interest now and noted how the gap between the east and west rims narrowed to form an avenue about a hundred yards in length but no more than fifty feet wide. The walls of the pass weren't cliffs, merely a line of steep hills whose forested summits overlooked the pass four hundred feet below.

Jacob searched the wooded hillside for the lookout that should be stationed back in the trees. He was relieved to see Otter Tail's familiar round figure emerge from hiding and gallop toward them at a breakneck pace down the grassy slope. A second rider appeared in the entrance to the pass, but when Jacob hailed him, the brave whirled his horse and vanished the way he had come, leaving a streamer of dust in his wake.

Otter Tail descended the hillside and gained the valley floor. He raced the remaining yards toward Jacob and the others. Otter Tail's brown mare arrived lathered and dust caked from her ordeal.

'Is my friend the only one to guard our village?'' Jacob said, clapping Otter Tail on the shoulder.

The normally jovial brave shook his head, his war-painted

features grim. "I kept watch for you, to warn you against entering the valley," Otter Tail said. He gestured toward the pass with his rifle. Sunlight gleamed on the brass tacks decorating the stock. Otter Tail carried a war shield of buffalo hide, black raven feathers dangled from the bottom of its circular frame.

"Warn me?" Jacob glanced at Tewa who seemed equally surprised.

'You are not the first to return from the white man's settlement. Many braves have ridden in to tell our people of the deaths of so many of our elders and chiefs."

"Then let there be gladness," Tewa said and indicated her grandfather, wearily clinging to his mount. "Two Stars is back with his people."

"We thought you might be captured like Lone Walker," Otter Tail replied.

"Then my father lives?" Jacob gripped the smaller man's shoulder.

"One of the Kit Fox Clan pretended to be killed and watched the white trappers and the Shoshoni traitor bring Lone Walker into the fort." Otter Tail again looked over his shoulder as if expecting an enemy. "Now you must go, my friend. Tewa and Two Stars ride with me to the village."

Jacob frowned. "I don't understand. Why can't I return to my people?"

"Because white men have slaughtered our young warriors and our elders. Because Short Bow, father of Yellow Eagle, was killed with all the others. And he is filled with rage. Because your skin is white and he who was once your friend has sworn to take your life if you return." Otter Tail shook his head and exhaled slowly.

"And all the people feel this way toward me?"

"No," Otter Tail admitted. "But it will only take one bullet to kill you. Yellow Eagle's. Or will you kill another of your brothers as you did Wolf Lance?"

Jacob lowered his head. "No," he said, knowing Otter Tail was trying to keep Jacob alive.

"There is wisdom in what Otter Tail says," Tewa spoke out, fearing for Jacob's safety. "I will leave with you. Otter

Tail can bring Two Stars back to the village." Her grandfather raised his head, hearing his name mentioned.

"Yellow Eagle is hot tempered," Two Stars said. "It makes him behave like a fool."

"Then he is a fool who can shoot straight," Otter Tail replied.

Jacob rubbed his eyes and the bridge of his nose. He shifted and stretched, trying to work the kinks out of his sore muscles. It was a sun-washed land. The earth yielded to the warm, amber rays of gold.

Yet even at noon, patches of gloom lurked below the lofty rims and shrouded the winding passes that waited beyond. The sun was never fully welcome here. And the valleys and canyons were always at war, forever caught, like the hearts of men, in that struggle between darkness and light.

This is my home, Jacob thought. I belong here for better or worse. He passed his rifle to Otter Tail and trotted away from the lookout who had come with his warning of danger.

"I don't understand," Otter Tail said. "Will he fight to stay?"

"No." Tewa watched Jacob ride into the pass. Her heart rose to her throat. She understood what Jacob intended to do. He would face Yellow Eagle unarmed and die if need be to prove his place among the warriors of Ever Shadow.

Medicine Lake seemed to capture a portion of the sky. Clouds, like schooners, drifted on an azure sea surrounded by an emerald shore. Smoke drifted from the Indian tepees circling the lake, dogs chased one another among the lodges, children played and wrestled, impervious to the mourning cries of the wives and mothers whose loved ones had failed to return from Fort Promise.

For ten years and more Jacob had ridden this same trail, had wound his way through the same pass. He rounded the last hillock and reined in his horse to behold in silent awe this loveliest of valleys ringed by its rugged hills reflected, like the sky, on the lake's mirrored surface. Before, he had always sensed welcome, even the first time when Lone Walker had brought him as a frightened foundling to find new life among the Blackfeet.

Now a group of warriors, he counted a couple of dozen, blocked his way to the village. Yellow Eagle waited among them, astride a pinto charger. He wore a buffalo hat, the horns painted black, and the left side of his face was smeared with black war paint lending a nightmarish cast to his appearance.

Jacob sensed Otter Tail, Two Stars, and Tewa drawing close behind him. Tewa wanted to be at his side but in her heart knew he must face Yellow Eagle alone.

Jacob turned toward them and handed Tewa his broad-bladed knife. He pulled off his buckskin shirt and draped it across his horse. He looked at Tewa and tried to smile.

"Jacob Sun Gift," she whispered.

"I am. Wait for me, Warrior Woman. And I will play my pipe outside the walls of your lodge and you will have to drive me away with your war lance."

"I would break it first," Tewa said, her lower lip trembling. She was angry with herself for displaying even the merest hint of weakness.

Jacob smiled and touched his heels to the big gray, and the animal started forward. It didn't take long to close the gap with the warriors blocking the well-worn trail into the village.

Jacob tensed as Yellow Eagle lifted his rifled musket and aimed it directly at the approaching horseman.

"No further, Jacob," he said.

Jacob continued on directly down the trail, swerving neither right nor left.

"White men betrayed us. They have taken the lives of our young men. They have murdered our elders. Perhaps even Lone Walker by now has joined the Above Ones. The white men have done this. White men like you, Jacob."

Jacob paused at least a spear's thrust from the men facing him. He recognized them all. Some had even ridden to Fort Promise and survived the trap.

"A Shoshoni led us into the trap. Red man and white betrayed us. The white trappers are led by a man named Kilhenny." Jacob searched the impassive array of faces opposing him, hoping to read their intent. Each brave was armed with a rifle or long bow. Yet they seemed more onlookers than enemies. At least none of them rode forward to accuse him, only Yellow Eagle, who already had one grievance against the white men, his injured leg. Yellow Eagle cocked his rifle; the mechanism made an ominously loud noise.

"Kilhenny murdered my own parents long ago." Jacob pressed on, wondering which word would be his last. "You say the white men are without honor. I say there are red men without honor as well. And there are men like you, Yellow Eagle, who have allowed their own pain to cause them to forget honor and turn against one who has been at their side on the hunt and in battle. Well, I have shed the blood of Wolf Lance. But I had no choice. Today, I do. I will not raise a hand against my brothers." Jacob looked beyond the line of men. "I see my mother's lodge. I long to offer comfort to Sparrow Woman." Jacob walked the gray a few paces forward until the barrel of Yellow Eagle's rifle was almost touching his sun-bronzed chest. Jacob's mouth felt as dry as glacial gravel, but he was beyond the point of no return. "If I am to die, then so be it. I will die here, among my people. *My* people. *My* home."

He nudged the gray mare's flanks and the animal responded. For one brief moment, Jacob collided with the men. The iron rifle barrel dug into his flesh, then gave way. Yellow Eagle yielded. The warriors parted as Jacob Sun Gift passed through their midst and continued on to the lodge where Sparrow Woman, his Blackfoot mother, waited to embrace her son.

47

Evening and April showers muted the landscape and blanketed the village beneath a canopy of layered clouds. Thunder rumbled in the distance, but the downpour neither increased nor decreased in intensity. It droned on in a soothing monotony that calmed even Tewa's restless spirit.

She knelt before the cheerful fire ablaze in the center of her tepee and braided her hair by firelight. Earlier in the day, Tewa had watched with renewed appreciation as Jacob faced down the braves who had tried to keep him from entering the village. She had felt a twinge of jealousy as Jacob hugged Sparrow Woman and entered her lodge. Tewa had brought Two Stars to his own tepee, left him with Calling Dove, and then turned her mount to the wedding lodge on the hill overlooking the village.

It had been a cold, empty homecoming to her solitary bed and a lonely fire. At least she had put her father's ghost to rest and no longer had to dance to his demands from the grave. She was free now to hate or love whom she chose...free now to wait and watch and wonder if Jacob would follow the rain-washed path to her lodge.

She made a hasty meal of the antelope meat and fry bread that Calling Dove had insisted Tewa bring to her lodge. The past week had taken its toll on the warrior woman and, despite her own resolve, she crawled to her bedding. Peeling off her brushed-buckskin smock, she crawled naked beneath the buffalo robe she used for a covering. Tewa sighed and snuggled deeper into the blanket-covered willow rushes that cushioned her weary limbs. She listened to the spring shower and wished the patter of raindrops were Jacob's footsteps approaching her lodge. The night was young yet. She would remain awake and see. . . .

Music from a reed flute roused her. Tewa opened her eyes and looked about in confusion. Had she just nodded off? No, one look at the shimmering mound of embers where a fire had been told the woman she'd been asleep for hours.

Jacob Sun Gift sat across from her. He was wrapped in a blanket, his blond hair matted from his walk in the rain. His clothing had been spread out on the ground by the fire. He held a reed flute to his lips and softly piped a series of trilling notes. He held the hand-carved instrument for Tewa to examine the markings. A thunderbird and a morning star connected by a water symbol decorated the flute.

"Sparrow Woman gave this to me. It belonged to Lone Walker and works powerful medicine," Jacob explained. He touched the thunderbird. "Man." He placed another finger on the morning star. "Woman," he said and traced the water symbol binding the other two signs. "They are called together. So it will ever be." He touched his lips to the carved mouthpiece and played upon the flute, his fingers experimenting with the holes that altered the tonal pitch of each note. Jacob lowered the instrument. "With this flute, my mother and father made their lives one. I am to play it only for she who walks in my heart, for Sparrow Woman has said no woman can resist its sweet medicine." A smile touched his lips.

"She has spoken the truth." Tewa lifted the buffalo robe as Jacob set the flute on the altar before the remains of the fire and joined her. His mouth covered hers. She guided him into her. Flesh and silhouette became one. Tewa gave herself completely, drawing the fire of his passion deeply within her. Jacob whispered her name over and over again in a litany of love.

Called together in the Great Circle of Life, they entered the mystery and made sweet medicine—Jacob the thunderbird and Tewa the morning star and between them peace, flowing like a river.

Jacob woke and rolled out from underneath the buffalo robe, pulled on his buckskin trousers, and stood by the circle of embers in the center of the tepee. Tewa rose up on her elbows and started to speak. Jacob waved her to silence, put a finger to his lips, and ducked through the entrance flap.

The last of the morning stars glimmered in the west as the sun's amber glow warmed the eastern horizon and dappled the broken battlements of clouds in hues of orange and ruby fire. Jacob sucked in a lungful of high country air, exhaled slowly, and sensed his whole being come to life. He turned toward the village and spied two men watching him. Otter Tail and Yellow Eagle stood among a thicket of firs a stone's throw from Tewa's lodge. They hadn't been waiting long enough for the dew to settle on their rifle barrels. Jacob's mare had whinnied as the men approached. The gray's warning had roused Jacob from his sleep. He wondered if Yellow Eagle had summoned the courage—or enough hate—to shoot him. He knew only one way to find out and would have started toward the grove, but Otter Tail and Yellow Eagle started toward him. So Jacob held his ground and waited, unarmed and watchful. He stretched forth his empty hands.

"Well, my friend, have you come at last to kill me?" Jacob called out.

The two men walked up to him. Otter Tail held back, allowing Yellow Eagle to limp forward and take the lead. Jacob towered over Yellow Eagle, but the latter's big bore rifle more than balanced the odds.

However, the hot-tempered young warrior appeared to have calmed down. He lowered his eyes a moment and stared at the rifle in his hands, then looked at Jacob.

"Two Stars called many of us together in a council of war," Yellow Eagle said. Jacob marveled at the old one's stamina as Yellow Eagle continued. "He told us of how you saved his life. And more. He spoke of your brother. . . ." The brave hesitated, then met Jacob's studied stare. "You and your white brother will bring our enemies to this valley, our valley. You have arranged to lead them into Ever Shadow."

"To destroy them," Jacob said.

"Two Stars also said this," Yellow Eagle replied. "Why would you do such a thing to your own people?"

"I am among my people." Jacob placed his hand on Yellow Eagle's shoulder. "I will fight by your side and die by

your side if need be. Tell me, then, Yellow Eagle, who is
your brother?''

A hawk on high circled lazily in the sighing wind. Shadows shifted on the valley floor, receded from the rims. The
tribal herd grazed contentedly in an arc close to the village,
young stallions pranced before the mares, and frisky colts
raced through the tender spring grasses greening the landscape, dotted with pink-and-fuschia blossoming bitterroots.

Yet it was a threatened country. Men from the east were
marching to take it away. The people of Medicine Lake must
ride to war again. And Jacob Sun Gift would ride with them.

Yellow Eagle, his expression still heavy with grief, glanced
around at Otter Tail, who nodded and then stepped forward to
join the other two, his cherubic features grown serious now.
Let there be a time for laughter again, after the killing, after
the bloodshed.

Yellow Eagle placed his rifle in Jacob's hands. ''Forgive
me, my brother.''

Jacob returned the rifle. ''You will need this. Here's my
plan.''

48

Thunder and rain, sheet lightning shimmering across the sky, ghost light and spirit song. Magic in the night. The shaman prays; the shaman invokes his power. It is his only defense.

Walks With The Bear waited by the fire while the trappers dug down into their blankets and tried to sleep. Above the treetops, electricity scarred the black night and the wind moaned. Bear shuddered. Sweat beaded his lips and the inside of his mouth and throat burned. Still, he kept his vigil until the last of the white men dozed off and he was alone with his fears and his horror.

The Shoshoni kept a tight grip on the cutlass he had taken from the shaman. It was the only weapon he had against the terrible magic. Ever since leaving Fort Promise, Lone Walker had begun his nightly chant. The trappers didn't seem to care. They ignored the medicine man—he was a valuable prisoner true enough, but they considered him helpless.

By all the power of the Above Ones, couldn't they hear? Were they deaf? The Shoshoni heard and he knew the Blackfoot must be silenced, now before the worst happened.

Bear must kill him, tonight, with his own long knife. Lone Walker's medicine was too strong to allow him to live.

Bear hefted the cutlass in his strong right hand and started across the camp to the tree where Lone Walker was firmly bound and supposedly helpless.

Lone Walker saw the man moving toward him, stealing steadily among the sleeping men. *Closer now.* Lone Walker willed him forward while beneath his breath he sang softly.

* * *

"Above Ones, open the darkness,
 Hear me. Black spirit, born
 Of fire, washed in the blood of the wolf,
 Strike now.
 I have said it.
 Let it be so."

Bear gasped and halted in his tracks. Lone Walker repeated
his chant in a low, unobtrusive tone of voice. It might have
been the voice of the wind. He stretched forth his bound
hands and, in the lurid lightning's glare, Bear could see the
shaman held a smoothly polished stone, tapered at one end,
rounded on the other. He pointed the tapered end at Bear as
he sang.

Bear gasped and raised the cutlass as if to ward off a
physical blow. Rain washed his features and glistened on the
length of steel. His hand fluttered to his throat to grasp the
medicine bag every Shoshoni wore and remembered again
with dismay that he had somehow lost it during the battle at
Fort Promise. He felt naked and unprotected without it. But
there was nothing to be done. He could wait no longer. So
summoning the last ounce of his courage, he started forward,
ignoring the rain pummeling his skull and shoulders.

Lone Walker continued to chant. He shifted his stance,
rattling the chain that secured him to the ponderosa pine. He
opened his cupped hands as Bear began his attack. And this
time, in the ghastly ghost-fire cast by the storm, the Shoshoni
saw all that the Blackfoot possessed, not only the spirit stone
but Bear's own medicine pouch. It was this Lone Walker had
been praying over, working his malevolent incantations,
summoning the dire spirits of illness and death.

Bear faltered in his attack, then recoiled from the shaman
in terror as Lone Walker wrapped the leather cord attached to
the Shoshoni's pouch around the length of the medicine
stone.

"Black hound,
 Thunder spirit,
 Strike in water

And in fire.
I call you in vengeance,
Blood for Blood.
Let it be as I have said.
As I have said.
As I have said.''

The Shoshoni gasped and spun on his heels and raced away
from the shaman, unable to bear the brunt of such a terrible
prayer. He darted away like a shadow flittering through the
trees and broke from cover to race beneath the bones of the
rain while all around him voices in the storm called him by
name. Demons rose from the mud-churned ground and wind
whipped stalks of buffalo grass in pursuit of the hapless
brave. He cut and slashed at the specters that swelled up like
a mighty tide to engulf him. He held the cutlass above his
head and screamed. Lightning cracked and a bolt of yellow
fire lifted the Shoshoni aloft, where for a second or two he
danced like a puppet on a string.

Back at camp, Kilhenny and Tom Milam and a half-dozen
other men crawled from their bedrolls at the sound of the
Shoshoni's baleful shriek and the clap of thunder as a sky bolt
struck close to the camp. The rest of the party, sixty-eight
men, stumbled awake, wondering if they were under attack.

"What the hell?" Kilhenny bellowed.

Tom Milam grabbed his rifle, trotted out of the camp, and
headed toward the clearing. He vanished among the trees only
to reappear a few moments later, holding the smoking,
twisted remains of a cutlass.

The rain beat a steady downpour that bowed the branches
and nearly drowned out the grumbling trappers. Pike Wallace
and Skintop Pritchard held their rifles ready and checked the
surrounding forest. Pike saw the cutlass and muttered, "Saints
preserve us."

The storm had begun to ease in intensity and Tom raised
the ruined cutlass for all to see. Everyone knew who it
belonged to. Con Vogel, crouched in his blankets, shivered at
the thought of the Shoshoni's remains. Iron Mike muttered to
the men closest to him that it was too bad Tom Milam hadn't

been holding the cutlass when the lightning struck. Tom shook his head, indicating Bear was dead.

"That's a bad omen." Pike tugged his water-soaked tam tightly down onto his skull.

"Like hell," Skintop Pritchard snapped, more than a little worried himself but damn if he'd admit it. "So the Injun's dead. Seems like we're two days out and off to a good start. One redskin, dead."

"Yeah, but he was our Injun. A good'un," Pike reminded the man.

"Now he's a good'un," said Pritchard and spat into a nearby mud puddle.

Pike Wallace wagged his silver head and gave up talking to his companion. The man was hopeless.

Tom Milam continued over to Lone Walker. The Blackfoot watched him with some interest, for something about this proud, dangerous young man struck him as familiar.

"So now you have had your revenge, shaman." Tom dropped the cutlass at Lone Walker's feet and squatted in front of the medicine man and looked him straight in the eye. "Maybe you'll have another opportunity before long," he said, lowering his voice. "I am Jacob's brother." He thumped the smoldering blade, stood, and sauntered back into camp.

Lone Walker glanced down at the weapon and placed the spirit stone and medicine bag upon the ruined blade.

Jacob's brother? . . . Vengeance! . . . 'As I have said.' Lone Walker's fierce gaze swept across the army of renegades Coyote Kilhenny had assembled. From the depths of the shaman's proud, warrior's heart, the words formed. And he began to sing anew.

In three days the hills lining the Medicine Lake pass had been transformed. Only a Blackfoot would have noticed the difference. To the unaccustomed eye, the forest-fringed slopes appeared choked with a barrier of heavy brush, grown thick and dry a couple of hundred feet above the floor of the pass.

A closer inspection of the bordering tangle revealed a mass of rawhide-bound clumps, dead branches and dry twigs tied into rounded bales like giant tumbleweeds taller than a man and equally as wide. The bales were secured by horsehair ropes to the trees behind them. Sever the ropes and send the bales tumbling down the slope into the pass below.

Jacob looked out upon his handiwork and nodded in satisfaction. Now if his plan worked—no—it had to work! He glanced over his shoulder as Tewa walked her charger along the face of the slope, keeping just back of the ropes. She rode with head held high, a bold, proud woman, skilled in battle and as brave as any warrior. But then, she was the daughter of Wolf Lance and had celebrated her tenth winter with a raid deep into Kootenai country over on the dry side of the Continental Divide. And yet, for all her prowess, Jacob experienced another facet, glimpsed and indeed embraced a different Tewa, a woman of tender seduction and girlish desire, wholly feminine, full of fire. She was a mystery to him. And he loved her all the more for it.

"Jacob," Tewa called out and worked her way through the trees. "Crow Fox has returned to the village."

"I watched him come through the pass." Jacob walked toward her and she dismounted into his embrace. He drew her close to him and his pulse quickened. There was no doubting or, for that matter, hiding his desire. He brushed the wolf cowl back from her features.

"*Saa-vaa,*" Tewa said, "there is no time for this with our enemies only a little more than a day's ride away. Crow Fox narrowly escaped capture to bring us word."

Jacob's eyes widened. "So close? They made better time." He released her and walked back out of the pines to once again inspect his handiwork, the bales of dry underbrush like a wall along the slope. Across the pass on the opposite rims, Yellow Eagle and half a dozen braves were making a similar check of their own barricade.

"Will this stop them?" Tewa asked.

"If not, it'll sure make things interesting for a time," Jacob laughed gruffly. He stepped out from the shadows, and Yellow Eagle, spying him, waved. Jacob waved back.

"I am glad he no longer wishes to kill you," Tewa said.

"I'm glad a lot of people no longer wish to kill me."

A wind, sounding like the onrush of a locomotive, worked its way through the pass, ruffling the yellow-green grass carpeting the valley floor. Jacob brushed his sun-bleached hair back from his face. His eyes gleamed like yellow gold as he studied the woman at his side.

"Yes," Tewa agreed, thoughtfully. "To follow the circle is to be open to the will of the All-Father, no matter how painful." Her expression grew pensive, tinged with regret. "My father still walks in my soul at times." She looked up at Jacob, her eyes moist. "Don't die, Jacob Sun Gift."

Jacob didn't know how to respond at first, so he took her in his arms yet again and stroked her black hair and held her close. His doubts were hers. Love today was all the reassurance he could offer. Violence lurked in the wind. A time of reckoning was upon them all, and who would be left standing amid the bones of the rain?

49

It was the last day of April, the time of the Muddy-Faced Moon, when seventy-one men, five days out from Fort Promise, dismounted at the bottom of a long, narrow draw and waited for the first golden tint of sunrise to brighten the eastern horizon. The men grumbled among themselves, rubbed and stretched their weary limbs, and made a cold camp beneath the Douglas firs towering a hundred fifty feet overhead.

Kilhenny studied the lessening dark. One by one the stars winked out with the approach of dawn. He kicked a pinecone at a bull snake working its way upslope in search of prey. The reptile, which had been roused from its lair by all the activity, hissed and quickened its pace. It was impossible for the men to move noiselessly. Horses would neigh and choose to fight their riders for a time. However, any dust trail churned by the animals had settled during the past hour.

Kilhenny pointed to a solitary star in the northwest. "Lucifer, the fallen angel." It seemed suspended above the range of hills that formed an entrance to Medicine Lake. "He points the way."

"Fitting," Tom muttered.

"You reckon we been spotted?" Pike Wallace asked, walking his horse up alongside Kilhenny and Tom Milam. Pike's eyes were constantly ranging the surrounding hills.

"We'd know by now," Tom said. Pike chewed on the stem of his clay pipe, the tobacco tightly packed and unlit. Tom clapped him on the shoulder. "Don't worry, amigo. I aim to ride on and scout the pass."

"Nerves," Pike said indignantly. "I'll show you 'nerves.' Boy,

I was fightin' my way through redskins when you were still in knee britches.''

"I know. I was there, remember?''

"Oh, uh, yeah," Pike stammered.

"But you're not going with me.''

"Take him," Kilhenny ordered. "One of you stay to keep watch while the other brings word the pass is clear.''

Tom shrugged. He didn't like it. But too much of a protest would alarm a man like Kilhenny and arouse his suspicions. He pointed his horse toward the mouth of the arroyo. "Reckon you can keep up, Pike?''

"Watch my dust, boy," Pike replied cantankerously.

Tom looked back at the rough-hewn parade of frontiersmen who followed Coyote Kilhenny into the high country. Each man was heavily armed with rifle and belly gun and an assortment of knives, hatchets, and tomahawks. A couple of roisters were busying themselves with the cannon under the watchful eyes of Iron Mike, who had assumed responsibility for the weapon. The gun carriage had worked loose and a rock had knocked a spoke loose from the wheel. All around Tom, the men readied themselves to ride into battle after a full night's march. Tom wondered if his brother, Jacob, really had a chance of stopping Kilhenny's army.

"You coming?" Pike called out.

Tom waved to the older man and started out of the arroyo.

"Be careful, lad," Kilhenny said as Tom rode past.

"Like a bear in a beehive," Tom replied.

Con Vogel threaded his way through the trappers and gingerly approached the half-breed, who was dozing beneath the evergreen canopy of a Douglas fir. Kilhenny's eyes were closed. His barrel chest rose and fell in a semblance of sleep.

Skintop Pritchard stepped forward to block Vogel's path. "Where you going, fiddle player?''

Con Vogel bristled at the man's tone of voice. Pritchard made plain his sneering disregard for the young German's talents.

"I intend to speak to Mr. Kilhenny. That is, if it's any of your business." He tried to walk around Pritchard, but

Coyote's henchman moved to block Vogel's path yet again. "Now see here!"

"He's sleeping," Pritchard said.

"The devil never sleeps," Con Vogel scowled. Kilhenny broke into laughter, though his eyes remained closed. "That's good, Con, my lad. Real good."

"I want to talk to you. I want to know where I stand," Vogel said, looking past Pritchard.

"You're standing in the High Lonesome," Kilhenny said, sitting upright and looking directly at the aristocrat. "Blackfeet call it Ever Shadow. I call it mine."

"Thanks to my help," Vogel replied, lowering his voice. "or are you forgetting who put Nate Harveson out of the way? I think I deserve—"

"What?" Kilhenny said, crawling to his feet. He crossed to Vogel and put his face inches from the man's wind-burned features. "You murdered a man. So tell me, what do you deserve?"

"On your orders."

"Did I ever give such an order, Mr. Pritchard?" Kilhenny asked of the man at his side.

"I'll swear you didn't. So will Pike. But we did see the fiddle player here shoot Harveson in cold blood."

"By heaven, that sounds like a hanging offense," Kilhenny exclaimed in mock horror.

"Yes sir. Murder's something they don't even build a gallows for. Any stout branch will do," Skintop Pritchard added with relish.

Con Vogel studied the faces of the two men and with sinking heart realized once again he had cast his lot among brutal and unscrupulous men. But his instincts were that of a survivor. He had made his way across Europe living by his wits. In truth, his quick mind and driving ambition had brought him this far. . . . To the brink of disaster or wealth, it remained for him to insure his fate.

"Look, Mr. Kilhenny, all I want to say is that I have indeed proved myself. I trust my loyalty will not go unrewarded." Though the German towered over the half-breed, it was Vogel who retreated as Kilhenny moved in closer still. Coyote Kilhenny reeked of sweat and bear grease.

His rust-red beard and hair gleamed in the first new rays of sunlight like a wild, tangled mane befitting the king of beasts. Which in truth, Con Vogel silently noted, Coyote Kilhenny had become—a king among beasts.

"Don't worry, fiddle player," said Kilhenny. "I'm a firm believer that a man ought to get what he deserves. Now you better load and prime your pistols. 'Cause the 'devil' has work to do."

Lone Walker sat hunched forward in the powder wagon, staring at the kegs of black powder and shot. His mind struggled to form some kind of plan, some way to ignite the powder and alert his people. He found it incredible that such a large force had approached unnoticed by the people of his village.

He listened to the muted conversation of the men around him. Not all were renegades. There were men simply eager to work the streams for beaver and prime otter pelts unmolested by Blackfoot raiding parties. Wiping out the village seemed one good way to end the Indian menace. All were hard men who followed Kilhenny because he'd proved himself capable. Coyote Kilhenny was one of them, for better or worse. Such men could see no further than prime pelts and a tidy profit at the end of a year's hard labor. It was future enough. They'd leave empire building to men like Nate Harveson and, now, Coyote Kilhenny.

Lone Walker shifted his weight and stretched the kinks out of his legs. He wanted to stand, but the trapper called Iron Mike had already knocked him down for such an effrontery. When Iron Mike wasn't laboring over the nine-pounder or driving the wagon, he was sharpening his knife and threatening to lift Lone Walker's scalp.

The shaman ignored such threats. Bound as he was with his hands tied behind his back, he had no other defense but an icy gaze and his own spirit song. Now, within the heart of Ever Shadow, Lone Walker once more began to sing. The words were almost inaudible. He had no sacred fire, yet so close to the holy places where he had offered prayer smoke in the past, Lone Walker knew the All-Father would hear his softly uttered plea.

He summoned the spirits of earth and fire to rise up and vanquish the men milling about the arroyo, who were taking little enjoyment from their hardtack and nary a cup of coffee.

One of the men, a trapper named Bud Ousley, heard the Blackfoot and shivered. He glanced at Iron Mike, who was greasing the axle on the nine-pounder's carriage.

"What's he singing?"

"This little beauty will have made some sweet music of her own before the morning's through," Iron Mike said, patting the barrel. "Huh?" He looked up at his companion, stood, and walked along the wagon. He leaned on the siding and studied the brave. "Sing all you want, you red nigger, 'cause today, as soon as Kilhenny gives the word, I'm gonna take your hair. You know it, don't you?"

"What's he singing?" Ousley repeated. He was a small man with all the strut of a bantam rooster, though Lone Walker had taken to getting on his nerves of late. Ousley had a healthy regard for Indian customs and Indian ways, even more so since Walks With The Bear's dramatic demise.

"A death chant." Iron Mike drew his knife and touched the point to Lone Walker's throat, then traced a path along his naked chest. The renegade chuckled and returned the knife to his belt. He glanced at Ousley. "A death chant, that's all."

"For him?" Ousley removed his coonskin cap and dried his perspiring face on the sleeve of his Mexican shirt. "Or us?"

50

A red-tailed hawk painted a series of lazy spirals against the azure canvas of the sky. Sunlight peeled the shadows back from the rims and washed the pass in amber light. Hoofbeats shattered the fragile silence and reverberated off the walls of the pass.

The two horsemen entered the Medicine Lake pass with their rifles at the ready. Twenty yards in, Pike Wallace took the lead to prove to Tom and perhaps to himself that he still was a man to ride the river with.

"Mighty quiet," Pike observed and angled toward the slope and out of the center of the pass. "Better we ride the tree line."

Tom studied the lordly ponderosas and the mass of underbrush fringing the hillside. Something . . . someone waited. Pike's eyes weren't as young as they used to be or he would have noticed. Tom hurried his own mount forward and caught up to Pike Wallace and headed the older man off before he'd climbed twenty feet. "What the hell, Tom?" Pike said.

"That's as far as you go."

"What in blazes does that mean?"

"It means I'm giving you a chance to ride out of here. Ride out and head west and don't look back."

"You talk like one of them Hopi Medicine men down in Santa Fe. Plumb crazy." Pike tried to ride past Tom but the young man blocked him again. Pike had to fight his own mount and bring the suddenly skittish gelding under control.

"Look, boy, I don't aim to ride this pass without these here woods. Hell, they could be full—" Pike's eyes widened as a

half-dozen braves led by Jacob Sun Gift walked their mounts
through gaps in the bales of underbrush. Another pair of
braves galloped down from the opposite hills to block off any
escape. "Of Injuns," Pike concluded. He lifted his rifle only
to have Tom snatch the weapon away.

"We've been waiting for you, Tom." Jacob was dressed
for war, his bronze features streaked with red and yellow war
paint. Raven feathers adorned his long yellow braids. He
carried a rifle, though some of the men with him, and Tewa,
carried bows.

"I'm here," Tom replied.

"What about Kilhenny?"

"Waiting for me to lead him in."

Pike Wallace stared at the young man beside him in total
amazement. He couldn't believe his ears. "Tom?" the old
man spoke in a raspy voice, his mouth gone dry. "Laddie-
buck, what have you done?"

"Nothing but what Kilhenny did to my parents on the bend
of the Platte. You remember, Pike, don't you?" Tom said as
Jacob and the warriors closed in. Tom tilted his wide-
brimmed hat back on his forehead and hooked a thumb in the
pocket of his faded, waist-length *vaquero* jacket.

"You always took my part against Skintop back when I
was just a kid," Tom told him. "Here's your chance. The
only one you'll get. Ride out."

"Coyote's gotta be warned," Pike said.

"I'm giving you your chance to live. Take it."

"I gotta hand it to you, Tom. You learned your lessons
well. Coyote couldn't have sold us out no better. You and he
are chips from the same block of wood, yes sir." Pike
reached up as if to scratch his head, but he grabbed his tam
and slapped Tom across the face, momentarily blinding him.
He knocked Tom out of the saddle, whirled his gelding, and
brought the tam down across the rump of his horse. He
reached for the pistol tucked in his waistband. The gunsight
caught as he tried to drag it free. An arrow flew past him,
another pair buried themselves in his back, while a third
pinned his hand to his gut. Pike pulled it free, cried out, and
toppled from his mount. The gelding continued to pitch and
buck all the way down the slope. The brave near the mouth of

the pass cut the animal off, caught its reins, and led the horse away.

Tom Milam stood and brushed the dust from his coat and pants. He looked toward the warriors with their bows and recognized Tewa among them. She was a regular little killer, he thought to himself. Then he walked down the hillside to where Pike lay sprawled on the blood-spattered grass. Pike groaned and opened his eyes a moment and looked up at the young man standing over him. His fall had snapped the arrows and buried the shafts deeper into his body.

"Pike . . ." Tom began.

'Get out of my way," the dying man managed to gasp. He wanted to see the sky, just the sky one last time. He shuddered. His eyes glazed over in death. The shadow of the hawk passed over him.

Jacob brought up Tom's horse and waited in silence for his brother to remount.

"Shit," Tom muttered and swung up into the saddle. Jacob passed him his rifle. Tom nodded his thanks. "You tell your red-heathen friends to let his scalp be. You hear?"

Jacob frowned at his brother's tone of voice. "Heathens? My people walk closer with the Great Spirit than any of Kilhenny's bunch."

Tom watched as Pike's body was carried back into the trees. "Better watch out, Jacob. They'll have you believing all their shell-rattling and prayer fires, mark my words." Tom Milam looked over at Tewa, who held her elk horn bow with an arrow already notched in the sinew string. "You tell your braves I'll be riding in the lead. And we got one of your Injun friends trussed up in the wagon, so mark their targets."

"Lone Walker?"

"Yeah," Tom said. He'd overhead the Shoshoni call their prisoner by name.

Jacob's heart already felt lighter. He turned toward the wall of brush. "Lone Walker is here!" His voice carried to the women hidden behind the dry-brush barricade, Sparrow Woman among them. The wife of Lone Walker closed her eyes and tears of relief spilled down her cheeks. Lone Walker had promised her he would always return. Once again he had kept that promise.

"Lone Walker's that special?" Tom asked.

"He's my father," Jacob answered.

"Joseph Milam was your father or have you forgotten?"

"I have spent half my life with one, half with the other. I cannot love one less, the other more."

Tom dropped his gaze to the blood drying on the sun-washed, grassy slope. "Neither can I," he said. He could sense Jacob's alarm. "Don't worry, brother. I'll do what needs to be done."

Tom swung around and started back the way he had come. He paused once as if plagued by something left unsaid. He looked at Jacob, confused and unsure of what was to be.

For a brief moment Jacob hoped his brother would return. Together they could formulate a new plan to lure Kilhenny into the pass. Yet, even as he wished it so, Jacob realized how the years stretched like an unbridgeable chasm between Tom and himself.

There was no crossing over. And no turning back.

The minutes crawled past. Jacob tried to make them count. He rode among the women hidden behind the wall of dry brush and made sure each wife, sister, or mother was supplied with a lighted torch to set afire the massive tumble-weeds, or a knife to cut them loose and send them rolling down the slope.

Sparrow Woman had brought a parfleche of cold fry bread and dried meat. Little Plume and Good Bear Woman and several other women brought water to the men on the hillsides and when all had drunk their fill returned to their places by the underbrush, finding rest in the lazy morning, taking time to gossip nervously among themselves, dreading the violence to come.

Sparrow Woman embraced her adopted son as he walked past. She seemed more beautiful than he could remember in the emerald-tinted sunlight. Whatever her own fears she hid them well.

"Mother, keep as far back among the trees as possible when the shooting starts."

"I will be where I am needed," Sparrow Woman replied.

Jacob gave up trying to argue with her. She could be as stubborn as a she-bear in a honey grove. He accepted a chunk of fry bread from her. His stomach was tied in a knot, but he knew it made her feel better to feed him, so he ate despite his lack of hunger. And so Sparrow Woman left him, satisfied with herself.

A bee landed on the fringed sleeve of Jacob's beaded buckskin shirt. The insect had alighted for a momentary rest between its hive and the patches of purple-pink bitterroots and crimson Indian paintbrush sprouting from the parched earth. Jacob allowed the insect its moment of respite. The bee as quickly launched itself yet again, then darted through the brambles and out into freedom.

Freedom. Jacob liked the sound of the word. That's what it meant to be a Blackfoot and to roam Ever Shadow . . . to be free.

Tewa caught his attention. She had ridden up from the village after making certain the old ones and children were hidden in the forest beyond Medicine Lake. She didn't come alone: Two Stars was with her.

Two Stars turned his sightless gaze toward Jacob, and Tewa whispered in her grandfather's ear.

"You don't need to tell me," the irascible old chief exclaimed. "I know it's him. Even after all these years he still walks like a white man." Two Stars spoke gruffly, but he followed his comments with a laugh. Then Tewa guided his hands to one of the rawhide ropes tethering a mass of firebrush to a pine sapling. Two Stars seemed satisfied by her placement of him and he patted the knife sheathed at his waist. "I will know when to cut it."

"What are you doing, old one?" Jacob asked of him.

"All that the darkness and age allows," Two Stars replied, turning in Jacob's direction. He stretched out a leathery hand and Jacob stepped within his reach. Calling Dove, the blind man's wife, had marked Two Stars' wrinkled features with war paint. Streaks of white clay covered his forehead and eyelids. Two Stars touched his fingers to his own eyes and then to Jacob's. "You must fight for me, grandson. May you be sharp eyed as I once was and your aim be true. I am old, but the rising sun warms me. And if I am to die, then let it be on such a fine day."

"I had the vision of sight," Jacob said. "Now, Grandfather, you have given me the vision of wisdom."

"There is a time for wisdom and a time to shoot straight."

"I see them! They have started through the pass," Otter Tail called out, trotting up from the barricade.

Half a dozen braves followed him. Jacob knew them all, for they were Crazy Dogs, warriors who would fight to the death rather than flee from battle. Twenty more braves positioned themselves near the bales of underbrush, their rifles loaded and willow-wood longbows held at the ready. Jacob imagined the same scene being repeated on the opposite slope, where Yellow Eagle and the remnants of the Kit Fox Clan joined with the Buffalo Hat warriors and Bowstring Clan. The jaws of the trap were complete.

"Perhaps some of us should block the other end of the pass to keep any of our enemy from reaching our village," Otter Tail suggested.

"Good idea," Jacob said. "I'll go with you."

"And I," Tewa said.

Jacob started to protest, then held his tongue, realizing he'd let his heart rule his head. Tewa's elk horn bow was useless from the hillside. But on horseback and charging through the ranks of the trappers, she was probably more dangerous than any man.

Tewa did not wait for permission. She needed none. Her lithe body vaulted onto the back of her mountain-bred mare and only looked once to see what was keeping Jacob. She was one with him. She would accept nothing less than to charge into battle at his side. It was the way of a warrior woman—Tewa's way and Tewa's love.

And so they rode into the Medicine Lake pass, Kilhenny's army, determined to follow him to heaven or hell as long as there was a profit to be found.

Coyote Kilhenny and Tom Milam took the lead and kept to a brisk pace, for the half-breed didn't like the way the hills rose to either side and the strange barrier of underbrush among the trees unsettled him. But Tom continually reassured him that he and Pike had thoroughly searched the hills right up to the tree line and found nothing to fear. Pike was another matter. Where the devil was he? Toward the middle of the column, Skintop Pritchard cocked his rifle and scrutinized the walls of the pass. Tom claimed he and Pike had silenced two braves stationed as lookouts. That meant the Blackfoot wouldn't know what hit them when the nine-pounder opened up and seventy wild buckskin-clad berserkers cut loose on the village. Pritchard licked his lips in anticipation. It was gonna be a fine day, just fine.

Con Vogel dropped back toward the wagon, taking comfort in the proximity of the cannon. He'd been reassured by Kilhenny that savages invariably feared such a weapon for the havoc and destruction the gun could wreak over a long distance. Now, the only problem with keeping close to the wagon was having to listen to their prisoner's low-voiced chant. Vogel found it difficult to ignore. He heard Bud Ousley curse the Blackfoot as well. Vogel couldn't figure out why someone didn't just silence Lone Walker permanently.

Iron Mike rode the wagon like a chariot. He stood in the back with his rifle primed and ready. Like Coyote Kilhenny, Iron Mike had a sixth sense when it came to Indians. And right now he felt an itch he just couldn't scratch, a premonition, or just plain gut feeling, that there were Blackfeet present. He had to remind himself that Tom Milam had checked out the pass and pronounced it safe. While Iron Mike had no use for young Milam, the trapper in the wagon also knew Tom to be a shrewd woodsman and not one to be taken lightly in a fight. The red devil wasn't born who could fool the lad. So Iron Mike kept his misgivings to himself. He tore a strip of cloth from an empty shot bag and gagged his prisoner and nodded in satisfaction.

"Well done," Vogel said. Ousley, driving the team of horses, breathed a sigh of relief.

The men bringing up the rear of the column raised a cheer and then fanned out, taking care not to bunch together.

"Where the blue blazes are the birds? Even that red tail's skedaddled." Kilhenny shaded his eyes as he sat astride his sturdy roan. "I don't like it." The half-breed glanced aside at Tom. "Where did you and Pike knife them lookouts?"

"One on either rim," Tom lied. They were already well into the pass. He wondered what was taking Jacob so damn long? Nothing stirred save the dust churned by the iron-shod shoes of the horses. No sound save the jingle of harness and the creak of the wagon axle and the muted conversations of the trappers as they rode into the Blackfoot stronghold.

"I smell smoke," Kilhenny declared, wrinkling his nostrils and holding his head high to the wind. He straightened in the saddle. "By damn I do."

"From the village. It's not far now."

"Village? The hell you say. Are you blind, Tom?" Kilhenny pointed at the bundled drybrush that had suddenly begun to smolder and catch flame. Kilhenny spun his horse and shouted to the column behind him. "Pritchard, take some men and flush what you can from the thickets!"

Skintop Pritchard nodded and as quickly dispatched five men toward the west rim and led another four up the east slope. At the rear of the column Iron Mike ordered Ousley to halt the wagon and help him load the nine-pounder.

"I don't like this," Kilhenny repeated as the bordering underbrush burst into flames. The half-breed returned his attention to the trail ahead. His expression betrayed even more alarm as Jacob Sun Gift, Tewa, Otter Tail, and Crazy Dog rounded a low hill and placed themselves directly in the center of the pass but outside the trap.

Kilhenny remembered the yellow-haired, white-skinned renegade who had tried to kill him. He had escaped from Fort Promise and returned to plague Kilhenny once more.

"Who the hell is he?" Kilhenny said, pulling a pistol from his belt as he fought to keep his skittish roan under control.

"Jacob Milam," Tom replied softly in an icy voice.

Kilhenny's jaw went slack. For him, time stood still and a grim realization burrowed into his mind replete with memories of the Platte River massacre—Joseph Milam and the rest of the families who had trusted Kilhenny lying dead in the dust of their dreams. Jacob Milam . . . alive? And if Tom knew that, what else did he know? Everything!

Farther up the pass Jacob raised his rifle and loosed a terrible war cry that reverberated the length and breadth of the pass. At his signal the women on the hills rushed forward, braving the blazing underbrush to sever the ropes while the warriors started the manmade tumbleweeds rolling downslope. They used their spears for levers, and the fiery bales, once pushed into motion, wouldn't be stopped.

Skintop Pritchard and the rest of the men were caught completely off guard in mid-slope. The wall of underbrush burst into flame and then began to move. Pritchard fired into the barrier and the men around him followed suit.

Pritchard tried to turn his gelding out of the path of the fire. He pulled too sharply on the reins. The horse panicked as the flames licked its hooves. He felt the animal falter beneath him and leapt free as the gelding stumbled and slid into another rider, sending man and horse in a vicious head-over-heels, crippling fall.

Pritchard rose up on his knees, looked upslope, raised his hands to his face, and ducked down as a fiery bale rolled over him, setting the trapper's clothes ablaze. Pritchard shrieked and scrambled to his feet and tried to beat out the flames. But his greasy buckskins burned like a torch. He ran and danced and beat at himself to no avail. His course grew more erratic, his motions more leaden. His cries became a guttural whisper, then ended. What toppled to the ground no longer even resembled a man.

51

The fiery avalanche continued down the hillsides, leaving a trail of flames in their wake. The trappers tried to arrange some form of battle line, but the flaming barricade tumbled through their ranks and scattered the riders, destroying any semblance of a defense. As the blaze raged through the pass, the Blackfeet on the hillsides opened up with rifles and bows. Kilhenny's men pitched from horseback, and riderless mounts scurried toward the south entrance to the pass as the grass fire gradually closed off this last avenue of escape.

Kilhenny turned his horse and took in the debacle at a glance. The air rang with the thunder of guns and the screams of the dying and the crackle of flames. War cries rent the air both from the hillsides and the north end of the pass, where Jacob and the others charged the already disheartened trappers.

"I should have left you to die," Kilhenny bellowed, his features grown livid with rage. He whipped his horse into a gallop and ran the gauntlet of pandemonium and death. Tom raised his rifle and for a moment held Coyote Kilhenny in his sights but could not bring himself to pull the trigger, despite his pretense of ruthlessness and his desire for revenge. So he drove his heels into the flanks of his own frightened mount and followed Kilhenny into the hellish conflagration.

Jacob called out to his brother thirty yards away but could scarcely hear himself above the din. Tewa, trying to alert her lover, had to gallop up alongside him and all but shout in his ear to get his attention.

"Lone Walker!" she yelled.

"Where?" Jacob called back.

"The wagon!"

Jacob looked ahead, but the pass was already obscured in billowing curtains of gray smoke as the flames quickly fed on the buffalo grass. Some of the trappers who had been riding to the fore charged through the smoke and made straight for the upper end of the pass leading to Medicine Lake. The Crazy Dogs opened fire. Otter Tail picked a target and knocked one of the renegade trappers from the saddle. A lead slug fanned Jacob's cheek. Another man aimed a rifle at the yellow-haired Indian but died choking on one of Tewa's arrows before he could fire a shot. A Blackfoot brave and a trapper fired into each other at point-blank range and both men dropped from horseback, dead before they reached the ground.

The ragged line of combatants closed ranks. The Crazy Dogs dragged the remaining trappers from horseback in a vicious display of hand-to-hand fighting. Red man and white thrust and parried; fought with long knife and tomahawk, war hammer and rifle butt. A trapper dove for Jacob, who clubbed the man senseless and trampled him in the dirt as he rode from the fray. Somewhere ahead, in the fire-choked passage, Lone Walker was a prisoner and as much in danger as any of Kilhenny's men caught in the Blackfoot trap.

"Rally round me, buckos," Iron Mike roared to the men at his side. He and Ousley had unhitched the nine-pounder and brought it to bear on the western slope. "We'll hound 'em from the hills!" The nine-pounder wasn't going anywhere— two of the horses had been shot dead in their traces.

Warriors on both sides of the pass started down, dodging through a hail of lead. Indian rifles jetted tongues of flame and powder smoke. Willow bows sent arrows arcing into the smoke-obscured passage.

Iron Mike didn't worry about the elevation. Hell, he couldn't even see the damn hill. But he'd already loaded the cannon and all that remained was to touch a flaming brand to the fire part. Black powder flared and the big gun boomed. The trappers cheered and took courage. The explosive shell landed two thirds of the way upslope and blew a hefty crater in the hillside, mortally wounding a trio of braves advancing into the pass.

Lone Walker flattened himself onto the wagon bed as slugs

ripped into the wood siding and the surrounding powder kegs,
showering him with splinters. He sneezed, inhaling smoke
from beneath the wagon. It stung his nostrils and made
breathing difficult. But that was the least of his worries. He
chanced a stray bullet and crawled to his knees and glanced
over the side at the flames lapping at the front of the wagon.

Ousley appeared at the foot of the wagon, grabbed a small
keg of powder, and hurried back to the cannon. In his haste
he paid no mind to Lone Walker. The trappers, with the
natural instincts of all fighting men (and many of them had
served as soldiers in their youth), arranged themselves in an
uneven but effective skirmish line.

Kilhenny arrived on horseback and immediately took command, though only for a moment.

"Beat out the fire, lads," he shouted. His soot-blackened
features were streaked with sweat. "Make your shots count.
We'll whip these red devils." Then he galloped off and no
one had time to realize that the man wasn't just seeing to the
rear guard but fleeing for his life. Only Tom knew, and he
raced past Iron Mike and the skirmishers before they had a
chance to even recognize him.

It was a time for killing and everyone had a job to do.

Lone Walker worked his bound feet under a powder keg
and managed to lever it up to balance on the siding before it
dropped out of sight. Lone Walker stiffened, hoping he had
missed the flames. A mistake would send the wagon up in
smoke. With his hands still bound behind him, the shaman
prepared himself for a nasty jolt and dropped to the ground;
landing on his legs, he managed to break his fall. Still, he
wrenched a knee and a spasm of pain shot up his left side. He
ignored both and kicked the powder keg away from the
flames. He held his ankles over a tangle of burning underbrush. His leggings caught fire, but the ropes binding his
ankles burned away and he managed to extinguish his leggings by rubbing his heels in the dirt.

The shaman switched positions and grimaced as he held his
wrists above the flames. The flesh blistered and seared. The
rawhide loosened. Lone Walker strained against his bonds,
lowered his head, and endured the pain in silence. His jaw

tightened and from deep in his throat a softly uttered prayer escaped. The rawhide parted and Lone Walker crawled clear and rubbed his raw wrists in the dirt. Then he lifted the powder keg he'd nudged out of the wagon and shoved the little barrel into the flames that threatened the wagon. He scrambled to his feet, crouched low, and ran as fast as his shaky legs could carry him.

Back by the wagon, unnoticed by the men at the skirmish line, the flames greedily consumed the powder keg. One of the trappers spied Lone Walker and broke ranks to intercept the Blackfoot before the shaman escaped. Lone Walker tried to outrun the man, but his legs were just too wobbly. The trapper, a raw-boned lout armed with a shotgun, rammed into Lone Walker and knocked him to the ground.

"I ain't goin' anywhere and neither are you." The trapper loomed over the fallen shaman. "'Ceptin' maybe to perdition." He leveled the shotgun at Lone Walker's head.

Twenty feet from the trapper the hungry flames at last wormed their way through a crack in the powder keg and ignited the contents. The smaller keg exploded. Lone Walker ducked and held his hand over his head. He knew what was coming. The trapper spun around. This time the entire wagon erupted in a flash of fire and an earth-shuddering roar. Lone Walker was lifted off the ground and landed another ten feet away while his attacker dropped in the dust behind him, a splintered length of wood piercing the man's chest.

Blood streamed from Lone Walker's nostrils. His ears rang, his entire head felt numb. He spat out a mouthful of dirt and managed to raise himself up on his elbows and knees. A figure moved toward him out of the smoke. A trapper, Ousley, stumbled forward like a man in a trance. His buckskin coat was patched with blood and singed in several places. A sleeve and an arm had been completely blown away. Men galloped past him. The column was in rout and those men and explosion hadn't killed were clearing out. Ousley disappeared into ashen clouds that choked the passage through the hills.

Lone Walker stood and stumbled back toward the smoldering wreckage of the wagon. The skirmishers within range of the blast had all been killed. He counted seventeen bodies sprawled upon the blackened earth. The nine-pounder cannon had been

blown over on its side. One wheel continued to spin. A groan
issued from beneath the cannon, where Iron Mike lay pinned
and dying beneath the gun's crushing weight.

More horses galloped past, a few riderless, the others
bearing the remnants of Kilhenny's army out of the pass and
beyond the reach of Blackfoot rifles.

"Lone Walker!" Jacob shouted and reined back so sharply
that his mount skidded and almost lost its footing on the
hard-packed earth. The gray mare tossed its head as Jacob
guided the animal toward the solitary brave standing amid the
carnage he had wrought. Tewa appeared not far behind Jacob
and followed him to Lone Walker's side.

"Are you all right?" Jacob breathlessly asked. He started
to dismount, but Lone Walker waved him on and swung up
behind Tewa.

"Your brother has gone after the man called Kilhenny,"
Lone Walker told him and gestured toward the south entrance.

"You know?' Jacob said. There wasn't time to ask how.

All that mattered now was Coyote Kilhenny. The half-
breed mustn't escape. And afterwards, somehow, someway,
Jacob thought, he and Tom could try and rebuild their lives
out of the ashes of the past.

"Take care of him," Jacob said to the woman at his side.
"I have to go."

Tewa said, "It is your right." She brushed the wolf-pelt
cowl back and love radiated from her proud features. "I'll be
waiting."

Five minutes later, Jacob galloped into the valley and
sucked in a lungful of sweet clean air. His eyes still stung
from all the smoke, but the big gray had carried him through
all the fire and death unscathed. Now the pass was behind
him. To the east Kilhenny's men fled in a ragged line toward
the distant hills and probably wouldn't stop until their horses
dropped. No doubt they expected a horde of wild savages to
come charging after them.

But it was to the west that Jacob turned his attention. There
two riders could be seen in the distance, one ahead of the
other. Kilhenny was certainly crafty enough to pick the

opposite direction in order to throw off any pursuit. And where Kilhenny went, Tom would have to follow.

The gray mare was fresh compared to Tom's and Kilhenny's. Jacob had no doubt he could catch them. And it wouldn't take long.

Shadows played on the sea of wind-rippled grass. The red-tailed hawk like a harbinger of Armageddon had returned to haunt the sky. Clouds like heaven's feather robes trailed along an azure skyscape, while the sun left its golden scrawl upon the snow-tipped peaks. Distant cliffs were a study in amber and maize and, in their shaded depths, mauve and obsidian.

An hour's ride from the Medicine Lake pass, the thunder of hooves shattered the stillness of a high mountain meadow ringed by forested ridges opening into box canyons and glacial passes.

Coyote Kilhenny's horse faltered as he crossed a narrow ribbon of melted ice, the runoff from a distant glacier. Kilhenny accepted the poor animal's failing with uncharacteristic good grace. The half-breed didn't like running from a fight. The notion galled him. So he halted his mount and let the animal catch a moment's rest. There was no escaping destiny, he figured. Better to make a stand and choose the moment.

Kilhenny watched the horseman round a hill and enter the meadow in pursuit. He knew Tom Milam even from a distance.

Then a second pursuer followed the first and the half-breed's mood dramatically altered. So both brothers had come seeking him. Then it was time to close the curtain on the drama begun more than ten years ago. It had begun with a Milam and would end with the same.

Tom heard his name called and slowed his pace. He glanced over his shoulder as Jacob quickly closed the gap and pulled up alongside his brother. Neither spoke, yet between them passed an unvoiced knowledge of what needed to be done.

Jacob checked his Hawken rifle, placed a firing cap on the nipple, and thumbed the hammer to half cock. Tom Milam thrust his rifle in a saddle scabbard and drew a pistol from his belt. It was a rifled weapon, short barrelled and lethal looking. A second pistol just like the first jutted from his belt.

"My horse can catch him if he tries to break," Jacob said.

"He won't run," Tom replied grimly. "After all, there's only two of us."

Jacob shaded his eyes. The hawk caught his attention, swooping low, rising on the breeze, and alighting on the topmost branch of a towering ponderosa.

"We have an audience."

"Better give him a proper show," Tom said.

Were they strangers after all? Jacob wondered. Had the years indeed broken the bond of blood? Maybe the answer he sought waited in the meadow.

Tom slapped his horse's rump and the exhausted animal managed a loping gallop. The gray mare started forward as if challenged by Tom's mount. And in the meadow by the narrow little stream, Coyote Kilhenny vaulted onto his horse and charged them both.

"Come on, lads!" he shouted. "Let the devil take your soul, Tom!" His horse splashed through the rivulet in a shower of golden droplets.

The meadow was a carpet of emerald and amber stretched beneath the shadows of the mountains. The sunlight here was stark, brilliant. It shone with a clarity reserved only for the lost and lonely places of the world, far from the realm of men. And yet, men had come to beauty today and brought with them violence and death.

Jacob on his gray mare led Tom by several lengths. He waited until he could recognize Kilhenny's determined features set in a seething tangle of crimson hair and beard. Then he slapped the rifle to his shoulder and fired. Blood spilled from Kilhenny's shoulder. Kilhenny howled, leveled a pistol, and fired. The gray mare crumpled and Jacob kicked free and leapt from horseback as Kilhenny swept past. The half-breed, for a single moment, had a clear shot at Jacob's back.

"Kilhenny!" Tom challenged. The half-breed swung around to face this new threat. For a moment they faced each other across their gun sights. For all Kilhenny's villainy, he had spared Tom's life. For all Tom Milam's thirst for revenge, he cared for Kilhenny, who for better or worse had become like a father. Then both men emptied their guns. Kilhenny, although grievously wounded, clung to his saddle, tossed his pistol aside, and tugged another from his bandolier.

"I'll not go under, damn you!" Eyes wild, Coyote Kilhenny looked around for someone to kill. But Jacob sprang from Kilhenny's blind side. Sunlight flickered on the length of double-edged steel gripped in his fist. He'd drawn the "Arkansas toothpick" from its sheath, Joseph Milam's own knife, left to his son. The half-breed did not see him until it was too late. Jacob plunged the blade to the hilt in Coyote Kilhenny's heart and dragged the murderer from horseback. Kilhenny shrieked and clawed at his assailant and writhed in Jacob's grasp. With the last of his great strength he shoved Jacob from him and managed to stand. First Kilhenny wavered, then he sank to his knees, disbelief in his eyes. His hands clutched at the knife's hilt. He groaned and loosed a terrible gasp. Then his eyes rolled up in his head until only the whites showed and he fell face forward in the buffalo grass.

Jacob struggled to his feet, shaking from the ordeal. The man seemed something more than human. He left the knife in Kilhenny's body, fearing to disturb him even in death.

"It's done," Jacob said and looked up at Tom. A look of horror crossed his face and Jacob broke into a run as Tom Milam slumped forward, his shoulders hunched. He looked small and almost childlike.

Jacob reached his side. Tom straightened, and though his chest was covered with blood, he managed a sad smile. His expression softened as if he were truly seeing Jacob and time had not changed them. He reached toward his chest and cupped the blood-stained ring that dangled from the chain. He tore it free and placed it in Jacob's hand.

"Are we always gonna be brothers, Jacob?" he asked. He tensed from the pain, lost his hold, and slid from horseback into his brother's outstretched arms, his final breath, a sigh of acceptance and, perhaps, regret.

"Forever," Jacob said.

EPILOGUE

It was a fair land cooled by a pine-scented wind, a land of sunlight and yet ever wreathed in darkness where the mountains rose to dominate the horizon. To this far country the Harveson riverboats had at last arrived. The boats brought new life and prosperity to Fort Promise. Here was a vanguard eager to claim the wilderness for civilization and, to be sure, profit. Abigail Harveson had immersed herself in the growing community, nurturing it as best she could, and with gratifying success. It had been two weeks since Coyote Kilhenny had marched away. The survivors of his command brought news of the slaughter. As for the survivors, they either took their place in Abigail Harveson's employ or were sent packing.

A settlement was taking root beyond the walls of Fort Promise, and an assortment of buildings was under construction. Even as Abigail's hopes for Tom Milam faded, she took pride in the influx of trappers and shopkeepers and their families. A nation was waiting to tap the riches of a wilderness, and Abigail was only too happy to supply its pioneers. Yet every evening she watched the sunset from the stockade walls and it seemed to her the horizon had been streaked with crimson for far too long. Deep in her heart she knew Tom would never return. He had ventured once too often into the howling wilderness and it had claimed him. Still she kept her vigil, and often the stalwart, homely Dog Bill Hanna stood at her side. He had proved himself an adept replacement for Kilhenny. He knew men and he knew the frontier and he was honest to a fault. And Dog Bill was more than a little in love with "Miss Abigail," though he kept such notions to himself. He usually waited and watched the sunset in silence, content in Abigail's company.

One night nearly a week after the battle, he had blurted out, "Lookee there!"

At first Abigail thought he meant he'd seen Tom, then she noticed the disheveled figure stumbling toward the entrance to the stockade. Abigail gathered her skirt and hurried along the walkway and down the stairs. The broken, exhausted figure passed through the gate and saw Abigail on the stairs. Barely able to hold himself upright, he wavered like a sapling in a thunderstorm. However, his gaze brightened as Abigail drew near.

"Abby," Con Vogel called out in a hoarse voice. His clothes were in tatters; his limbs trembled from lack of food. He was so grateful to be alive, he began to weep. "Abby . . . they're dead. So many dead," he moaned. "Only thing that kept me alive was . . . thought of you."

Abigail Harveson cautiously approached the man. Two of Dog Bill's trappers stepped from the shadows and caught Vogel under the arms for support. The man was almost out of his head from his ordeal, but Abigail felt no pity for him.

"It does me good to see you, Con," Abigail said. She nodded to the men. "Chain him in the barn."

"What?" her instructions caught Vogel completely off guard.

"Virginia confided in me the minute you left with Kilhenny," Abigail said. "She told me everything."

Vogel's features fell; his eyes widened. "No . . ."

"I've been hoping for your return," she said. "Mose Smead will take you downriver to the first court he can find. There you'll be tried and hanged for the murder of Nate Harveson."

"No . . ." His cry sounded scarcely human, yet it hung in the air as the armed guards took him away.

"You can be a hard lady," Dog Bill muttered.

"I can be just that," she agreed. Abigail turned and looked out through the open gates. I'm still here, the young woman told the land, her words uttered only in her mind. It had taken her brother and her own true love, and still she remained.

And there would be a time for tears, after her dreams.

* * *

Jacob walked his wounded mare through the fire-blackened pass. The place still reeked of death and he hurried through at dusk with the western horizon an open wound, a baleful mixture of crimson and ocher and deep-blue light to guide him home. He traveled the pass unnoticed and the cookfires of the village cast a glimmering note of peace and healing to his sorrow-laden soul. On the distant hillside, new burial scaffolds had been erected overlooking Medicine Lake. He was too late for mourning, but then again he had buried his own just two days' past on a scaffold above the sacred earth with the wind to lull Tom Milam in eternal sleep. Jacob had remained in the meadow for a little while, just to be alone with the stars and the memories of a time and a past truly lost to him, now and ever after. Now he returned to the village where life had begun anew.

Jacob watched the village, then lifted his gaze to the lodge on the hillside. Tewa was there. He would go to her and be loved by her.

He waited, listening, and heard the distant chant that rang out over the village like the sheltering wings of the Great Spirit, protecting and restoring. He listened in his grief and experienced deep in his soul a greater sense of belonging than ever before.

Jacob, though yearning for Tewa, was drawn inexorably to this voice at twilight in the season of the sun. Fireflies swirled and filled the air before him. An owl whirred past on wings of night. Jacob's steps were sure in the deepening twilight as he skirted the village. Tomorrow would be time enough to walk among his friends, Otter Tail, Yellow Eagle, and the rest.

Now, this very hour held only one purpose for him. He could no more deny the mystery and the power calling in the night than undo the last eleven years of his life.

Jacob made his way to the low plateau, a broken ledge really, eroded into the side of a hill above the village. He left the mare at the base of the slope and crawled hand over fist in desperation to reach the ledge.

At last he reached the shaman's sacred fire, and Lone Walker, for all his intensity, paused, seeing his "Gift from the

Sun." The medicine warrior's heart gladdened, for he had been unsure whether this young man of two worlds would return.

"You had one brother," Lone Walker said in a voice rich with compassion. He could see into Jacob's heart. "And you have lost him twice."

Jacob sat by the sacred fire and watched the spirit smoke coil and uncoil skyward like a writhing serpent, or souls, dancing, touching, free. Jacob lifted the serpent ring from his pocket and dropped it into the pulsing heart of the spirit fire.

Lone Walker's voice rose softly as he sang of the forest at twilight, the music of the rain, the caress of the wind. He thanked the All-Father for these things and for the Great Circle in which there was no final loss, only a temporary farewell in a oneness without beginning or end.

"Shaman, why do you sing?" Jacob asked, a question he had often uttered in good-natured jest.

"I sing so that the world will not end." Lone Walker's answer never changed.

Tonight, for the first time, Jacob understood, and in that moment sorrow left him. He knew at last the path he must follow. To enter the mystery was to find life. His voice trembled, not with fear but expectancy and even joy.

"Father," said Jacob Sun Gift. "Teach me the songs."

> All-Father,
> With beauty
> Will I walk.
> With beauty
> Will I speak.
> Hear me.
> Heal me.
> It is finished.
> It is reborn
> In oneness, and peace,
> in Ever Shadow.

ABOUT THE AUTHOR

KERRY NEWCOMB's first book under his own name was the best-selling *Morning Star*. Writing with longtime collaborator Frank Schaefer, Kerry's novels have appeared under the names Shana Carrol (*Live for Love, Paxton Pride, Raven, Yellow Rose*) and Christina Savage (*Hearts of Fire, Love's Wildest Fires, Dawn Wind, Tempest*). Kerry Newcomb and Frank Schaefer are also the authors of *Pandora Man* and *Ghosts of Elkhorn*. Kerry lives in Fort Worth, Texas, and is currently at work on a new historical novel.

If you enjoyed Kerry Newcomb's
IN THE SEASON OF THE SUN, you will
enjoy his next novel for Bantam:

SCALPDANCERS

Here is an exciting preview of this new frontier saga,
to be published in the Fall of 1990. It will be
available wherever Bantam Books are sold.

Turn the page for a sample of SCALPDANCERS by
Kerry Newcomb.

Prologue
1814

In the Time of
the Muddy Face Moon

*What do you want of me? Why don't you speak? Above
Ones, send me my dreams, give me my vision. I will follow
my dream quest wherever it may lead.*

*I cannot bear the silence. The stillness in my heart, the
shadows on the wall of the sweat lodge mock this poor
one.*

*I hear the chanting in the village. I hear the water's
song as the ice cracks and life returns to Elkhorn Creek.
And still, Cold Maker, you imprison my spirit. Morning
will soon come to the world beyond the sacred circle of
this spirit fire. Four days have I fasted. And four times this
night I have crawled on hands and knees through the
narrow door of this lodge and brought wood to the sacred
fire. I have sprinkled the flames with cedar. I have made
offerings to the four horizons and prayed and sweated. My
limbs shine with moisture, the breath burns in my chest.*

*Just five mornings past I was in another place where the
earth trembled beneath the hooves of a buffalo. I raced the
wind and the smell of blood was in the air and I rejoiced
to know there would be glad songs in the lodges of a
hungry people, my people.*

Maiyun, do not abandon me. All-Father, my spirit fol-

lows the path of the sacred smoke. Find me worthy, Great One, give me my vision.

A man could get killed...

Sixteen hundred pounds of buffalo bull broke through an ice crusted barricade of Russian thistle and took the first horse on the tip of its short curved horns. A brown mare neighed in anguish and its rider, Waiting Horse, kicked free. The bull raked horseflesh, disemboweled the mare and veered toward a second tormentor, a Blackfoot brave who raised his short bow and loosed an arrow at the enraged animal. The shaft bit deep into the bison's tender hide just behind the shoulder, yet the bull never lost a stride. *Iniskim* was hurt and knew who had done the hurting. The animal bellowed and charged straight for the brave on the mountain bred gray.

Lost Eyes notched another arrow. The gray mare responded to the pressure of his knees and cut to the left to avoid the buffalo's charge. Without warning, the plucky little gray went down, its forelegs buckled; the ground underfoot gave way as a prairie dog burrow caved in on itself.

Lost Eyes jumped free of his mount and tossed his bow aside. The last of his arrows spilled from his otter hide quiver. He landed shoulder down in a patch of snow and rolled to a stop near a draw a few yards from where he had plowed a furrow in the white mantled grass.

He felt the earth tremble against his cheek and willed the world to cease its dizzying spin. Gathering his strength, the brave waited until the last possible second and then shoved himself out of the bull's path. The buffalo rushed past, an unstoppable avalanche of fury, as Lost Eyes slipped over the edge of the draw and slid to the bottom of an eight foot drop in a shower of pink shale and loosened earth.

Two days of sunlight had scoured much of the meadow of April snow, but here in the shadows of the draw, Lost

Eyes sank midway to his calves in a crusted drift. Shaking the grit from his long braided hair, he clawed his way back up the slope and reached the meadow in time to see Waiting Horse, the other young man afoot, attempt to limp out of the path of the buffalo. But the great shaggy beast would not be denied this day and bore down on the helpless youth.

"Ho-hey-a, Iniskim!" Lost Eyes shouted and waved his hand hoping to distract the buffalo.

The animal stumbled and lost a stride then continued its attack. Waiting Horse glanced over his shoulder and cried out to the All-Father. He tried to run, but his leg had been injured by the falling horse. His ankle wouldn't support his weight.

Lost Eyes ran to his bow and searched wildly for one of the arrows he had lost. He found one hidden beneath some trampled grass, fitted the feathered shaft to his sinew string . . . Too late. He looked up just as the bull caught Waiting Horse on the tip of its horns and tossed him high in the air. The young man flopped to the earth and disappeared beneath the cruel black hooves of the beast not a hundred feet from Lost Eyes.

The Blackfoot sighted and launched a second arrow but at that distance the arrow was only a nuisance to the bull. The first arrow had been a killing shot through the lungs. However, the beast refused to die. Iniskim altered its course yet again but quickly lost strength and labored for breath as blood filled its lungs. Lost Eyes, enraged over the fate of his companion, welcomed another attack. He gathered another couple of arrows and hurried to catch the reins of the gray mare as it struggled to its feet. Lost Eyes swung up onto the gray and spied a trio of horsemen coming from the far end of the valley, the other members of the hunting party. They rode at a gallop across the snow-checkered meadow, anxious to be in on the kill. They must hurry, thought Lost Eyes.

The bull, though dying, lowered its head and charged. *Iniskim's* reflexes were dulled now and its speed diminished but it was still dangerous at close quarters.

Lost Eyes leaned forward on the neck of his mount and rode straight toward the buffalo.

"*Ha-hayiia, Iniskim!* Horned killer. This day your flesh will nourish my people!"

Lost Eyes was a young man in his seventeenth winter, built strong and lithe, and he sat his horse as if he were one with the galloping mare. The horse's breath mingled with his own, clouding on the cold high country air. Waiting Horse lay broken and lifeless in the buffalo grass but Lost Eyes forced himself to concentrate only on the deadly beast bearing down on him.

Horse and rider rapidly closed the gap. Lost Eyes' pulse quickened. The young bull bellowed and plunged toward the gray mare. But the horse quickly danced aside, and the bull viciously swiped empty air. Lost Eyes twisted, the bow string snapped his left wrist on release, the arrow flew straight and true. Its hardened sinew warhead passed a rib and pierced the bull's fighting heart.

The beast staggered another twenty yards from the sheer momentum of its charge. Then its legs gave way and the animal collapsed and rolled on its side. The buffalo kicked fitfully for a moment then settled into death.

Lost Eyes rode around his kill and hurried to the side of his fallen friend. He dismounted and kneeled by Waiting Horse. The young brave was still alive, but the light was fading fast and Waiting Horse, seeing the steam rise from his ravaged belly began his death chant.

> "All-Father,
> I have run with the horses
> I have stalked the blackhorn
> And stolen the feathers of the hawk.
> But today *Iniskim* has killed me.

I am young, not old.
A young man should die
in battle—an old man in his lodge surrounded
by his children.
I am in neither place.
Find me, All-Father.
Let me not wander in search of you.
Let me—''

Waiting Horse grimaced. His features were deeply etched in pain. The dying man's eyes opened and for a moment he recognized the brave at his side. Lost Eye's hair was unadorned with eagle feathers. His buckskin shirt and leggings were simple and bore no markings or designs. No spirit symbols linked him to animal or element or to the power of the Above Ones. These were things received in visions. And he was Lost Eyes. He had yet to walk in his soul. He had yet to see what was beyond seeing.

Waiting Horse knew him even through his pain-clouded vision. He reached up and touched Lost Eyes' features, smearing the man's cheek with blood.

"Now you are marked," Waiting Horse said in a dry, rasping voice. He lowered his gaze to his own ripped belly, a curious expression on his face. After all, it wasn't every day a man saw himself from the inside out. Suddenly he arched his back. Lost Eyes struggled to hold him down. Then Waiting Horse relaxed and fought no more and entered the great mystery.

Lost Eyes looked to the ice-glazed ridges lying golden in the sun and the gleaming snowcapped peaks of the Big Belt Mountains stretching across the western horizon. These were barrier ridges of bald faced granite rising above the tree line, a veritable wall of mountains broken by a gap several miles to the south where a high country meadow threaded its way across the Continental Divide, the backbone of the world.

In this meadow the Scalpdancers had settled along the banks of Elkhorn Creek. It was a place of beauty—one that Waiting Horse would never see again. But the mountains in their sun-bright mantle of gold were places of power where a man's spirit might ride with the Above Ones forever. So Lost Eyes looked to the mountains as he waited at his friend's side. The other hunters would be there soon.

The campfire made a beacon in the night and led the last four stragglers out of the darkness of ponderosa pines and barren-limbed aspens. Two travois, one bearing a buffalo carcass, the other, the blanket wrapped form of Waiting Horse, entered the circle of light.

The arrival of the four caused quite a commotion among the half dozen Blackfeet huddled near the flames, especially when one travois' tragic burden was revealed. Waiting Horse had been a popular youth, well liked by young and old. Lost Eyes dismounted and ground tethered his horse while the other braves clustered around the slain man. Only Wolf Lance, who had returned to camp empty handed, made the effort to approach his friend. Wolf Lance was a year older than Lost Eyes and carried an extra twenty pounds on his chunky frame. His moccassins padded across the hard packed earth. Joy and sorrow mingled in his expression.

He asked only one question, how? And listened without recrimination as Lost Eyes recounted the events of the hunt.

Many of the Blackfeet standing by the travois had only grudgingly joined this hunt. Men had died on other hunts, but they believed nothing good could come of keeping company with the man called Lost Eyes. The Above Ones had turned away from him. Why tempt disaster by riding with him? In the end they had listened to Wolf Lance and

Waiting Horse and joined the hunting party. And now, after five days, they had nothing to show for their efforts but one buffalo and one corpse.

Their voices carried on the still night air.

"He counseled us and called us women because we feared," Black Fox said. "See what has happened." He was a burly man of twenty-three, the oldest of the party and a natural leader by strength of arms and cunning.

"Waiting Horse is dead. We warned him," Tall Bull added. A man of average height, he was quick in battle and two Crow scalps decorated his buckskin shirt.

Another brave, Broken Hand, whose deformed left hand had only two fingers and a thumb, carefully tucked the blanket beneath the corpse. He had been closest of all to Waiting Horse, and when he lifted his gaze it was to focus blame on Lost Eyes. He stepped around the travois and started across the clearing as Lost Eyes moved toward the campfire. Broken Hand blocked the other brave's path.

Broken Hand's braided hair was adorned with two eagle feathers and the beadwork patterns on his buckskin coat revealed he had fulfilled his vision quest and could be called by a man's name. He was a proud man.

"No," Broken Hand said to Lost Eyes. "You will not share our fire. You have done enough. We will finish the hunt without you."

Lost Eyes tried to step around the man only to be shoved backward. Lost Eyes batted the brave's hand aside. Broken Hand grabbed for the war club dangling from a rawhide tie at his side. He jerked the weapon free and raised it threateningly.

Lost Eyes made no move toward a weapon of his own. He merely stood his ground, his brown eyes gentle and filled with remorse. Yet there was no weakness in his stance. Though he grieved as much as any of the others, he would not accept blame for the death of Waiting Horse.

"Now will you slay me, Broken Hand, and take my scalp to hang upon your coup stick?"

Broken Hand glanced at the weapon in his hand. Slowly, reason returned to his expression, dimmed the fire in his gaze, dulled the urge to exact a vengeance that wasn't his to seek.

"Strike him!" Black Fox shouted.

"I will not." Broken Hand lowered his war club and shoved the wooden shaft back through the rawhide loop at his waist.

"Strike him. Are you a woman to fear him so?" Black Fox snapped, his hand upon the travois. "He killed your friend."

"*Iniskim* killed my friend," Broken Hand answered.

"Your words, Black Fox, do not fly straight. They are crooked with the jealousy that wishes to keep Lost Eyes from calling your sister to his blanket," said Wolf Lance, seeking to distract the hunt leader.

Two braves by the travois nodded in agreement, and as hunger overcame their sorrow they fell to butchering the buffalo carcass. The animal's organs were quickly sliced away and carried to the campfire.

Black Fox stood silently apart from the others for a while, then followed the aroma of roasting meat back to the fire and sat near Tall Bull.

Lost Eyes squatted near the flames and let their warmth leach the chill from his limbs. He took comfort in Wolf Lance's faithful presence.

"Someone must bring Waiting Horse back to our village," Broken Hand said.

"I will do it," Lost Eyes said and looked up into the faces of the hunters. "Then you may continue the hunt without me and perhaps find good fortune."

No one offered a different suggestion. Lost Eyes didn't expect them to. By virtue of their silence, they assented. In the morning Lost Eyes would depart, taking his ill omens and misfortune with him, riding a lonely trail southwest, with naught for company but dark thoughts and a dead man.

This is a cold trail. I will follow it no longer. It is toward a vision I began. But the path is as fleeting as a shadow and I am the shadow walker, waiting to be made whole, to walk among my people as a man.

Show me my spirit sign. All I see is what has been.

Lost Eyes entered the village at midafternoon. The same cold breeze that tugged at the newly budded aspen limbs ruffled the fringe of his buckskin shirt and leggings. Clouds scudded across the cobalt sky and cast their churning shadows on the valley floor.

The spring that fed Elkhorn Creek flowed from the side of a craggy ridge at the north end of the valley. Icy water seeped from a gaping wound in the slope, wore a furrow in the topsoil, and broadened into a creek about as wide as a young man could leap. The creek followed a course parallel to the bordering hills and meandered out into a meadow of yellow buffalo grass before it petered out a few miles from its source.

The Scalpdancers, a Blackfoot tribe numbering about one hundred seventy families had settled their village against the northern ridge close to the spring. Under attack, the men, women and children could flee upslope to the safety of the pine forest and higher still to the natural battlements of weathered granite ranging the length of the ridge like the exposed spine of some massive primordial beast.

Sometimes it is the sound rather than the sight of home one remembers most, the wonderful country longed for in the solitude of lonely odysseys. For Lost Eyes home meant the bubbling spring that nourished Elkhorn Creek and the noises of children among the circle of tipis in the Blackfoot village.

Horses, grazing along the creek, whickered as the hunter approached on his gray. Boys afield laughed and challenged one another and fired their small bows at an escaping ground squirrel. Women sang as they gathered roots, carried water from the creek, or cooked. The faint rasp of scraping knives on drying deerhides lingered in the air, mingled with the creek's own rippling music and a chorus of barking dogs announcing the arrival of Lost Eyes as he paused on the edge of the village.

For a moment the scene held, one of those brief fractions of a second when the sun seemed to pause in its westward trek, and a wondrous sense of peace filled Lost Eyes' heart.

Then the reality of his world intruded upon his thoughts: He was a man without a vision, and homecoming was not always a time of joy.

Several braves rode out from the village at a gallop, renting the stillness with their wild cries. They would have made a threatening sight to an enemy. Lost Eyes only smiled, he knew them all by name. They were youths on the verge of manhood, their heads already full of glorious deeds and daring days to come. Their enthusiasm faded as they saw Lost Eyes not only led a pack horse ladened with meat but a second horse bearing a dead man. Three of the Blackfeet immediately took up a position behind the travois, forming a makeshift guard of honor for the dead man.

As old men and women, girls and boys, paused to watch, Lost Eyes rode straight toward the cluster of tipis adorned with the arrow markings of the Bowstring clan.

Fool Deer, the father of Waiting Horse saw the travois and recognized his son's horse. He stood, a shaft of wood and a stone tool used for straightening the shaft fell from his grasp. His wife, Many Walks Woman rounded the lodge. She had been bathing with her sisters, and her shiny black hair was plastered to her skull. She entered laughing at some tidbit of gossip her sisters had just revealed, but the merriment ended abruptly and her brown eyes widened with astonishment.

Lost Eyes dropped the reins of the pack horse and then reverently handed the reins of the travois horse to Fool Deer. He was a good natured man, but in this hour his demeanor was as formidable as a thunderhead.

Many Walks Woman ran to the travois. A stifled cry escaped her as she sank alongside the blanket wrapped remains of her son. Her sisters, Berry and Dancing Creek had already begun a lilting wail, a chant soon picked up by other wives of the Bowstring men.

"The meat is yours," Lost Eyes told Fool Deer in a gentle voice. "Your son has given his life that our people might have food."

Fool Deer glanced silently at the pack horse and then back at the man who had brought his son home. Fool Deer's expression revealed his black thoughts, a man without vision brings misfortune. It had happened before, it would happen again.

"My son rides with the Above Ones," Fool Deer said in a hollow voice. "But who, Lost Eyes, will ride with you?"

Beat the drums for me. Play softly the ceremonial drums and face the four winds. And sing for me, Sparrow Woman. Keep within me, and keep me in your heart. I will play upon my flute. I will call you out into the night. I will open my blanket to you, that we might stand together in the night, beneath the glimmering camp fires of the Above Ones.

Breathe the warmth. It flows around me, through me. Sweat stings my eyes and I am blind. No matter. What I seek lies within. Like dreams. Like Sparrow.

**FROM THE PRODUCER OF WAGONS WEST
AND THE KENT FAMILY CHRONICLES—
A SWEEPING SAGA OF WAR AND HEROISM
AT THE BIRTH OF A NATION**

THE WHITE INDIAN SERIES

This thrilling series tells the compelling story of America's birth against the equally exciting adventures of an English child raised as a Seneca.

☐	24650	White Indian #1	$3.95
☐	25020	The Renegade #2	$3.95
☐	24751	War Chief #3	$3.95
☐	24476	The Sachem #4	$3.95
☐	25154	Renno #5	$3.95
☐	25039	Tomahawk #6	$3.95
☐	25589	War Cry #7	$3.95
☐	25202	Ambush #8	$3.95
☐	23986	Seneca #9	$3.95
☐	24492	Cherokee #10	$3.95
☐	24950	Choctaw #11	$3.95
☐	25353	Seminole #12	$3.95
☐	25868	War Drums #13	$3.95
☐	26206	Apache #14	$3.95
☐	27161	Spirit Knife #15	$3.95
☐	27264	Manitou #16	$3.95
☐	27814	Seneca Warrior #17	$3.95

Bantam Books, Dept. LE3, 414 East Golf Road, Des Plaines, IL 60016

Please send me the items I have checked above. I am enclosing $_____ (please add $2.00 to cover postage and handling). Send check or money order, no cash or C.O.D.s please.

Mr/Ms _____

Address _____

City/State _____ Zip_____

LE3-9/89

Please allow four to six weeks for delivery.
Prices and availability subject to change without notice.

★ WAGONS WEST ★

This continuing, magnificent saga recounts the adventures of a brave band of settlers, all of different backgrounds, all sharing one dream—to find a new and better life.

☐	26822	INDEPENDENCE! #1	$4.50
☐	26162	NEBRASKA! #2	$4.50
☐	26242	WYOMING! #3	$4.50
☐	26072	OREGON! #4	$4.50
☐	26070	TEXAS! #5	$4.50
☐	26377	CALIFORNIA! #6	$4.50
☐	26546	COLORADO! #7	$4.50
☐	26069	NEVADA! #8	$4.50
☐	26163	WASHINGTON! #9	$4.50
☐	26073	MONTANA! #10	$4.50
☐	26184	DAKOTA! #11	$4.50
☐	26521	UTAH! #12	$4.50
☐	26071	IDAHO! #13	$4.50
☐	26367	MISSOURI! #14	$4.50
☐	27141	MISSISSIPPI! #15	$4.50
☐	25247	LOUISIANA! #16	$4.50
☐	25622	TENNESSEE! #17	$4.50
☐	26022	ILLINOIS! #18	$4.50
☐	26533	WISCONSIN! #19	$4.50
☐	26849	KENTUCKY! #20	$4.50
☐	27065	ARIZONA! #21	$4.50
☐	27458	NEW MEXICO! #22	$4.50
☐	27703	OKLAHOMA! #23	$4.50

Bantam Books, Dept. LE, 414 East Golf Road, Des Plaines, IL 60016

Please send me the items I have checked above. I am enclosing $_____ (please add $2.00 to cover postage and handling). Send check or money order, no cash or C.O.D.s please.

Mr/Ms _____

Address _____

City/State _____ Zip _____

Please allow four to six weeks for delivery.
Prices and availability subject to change without notice.   LE-9/89

TERRY C. JOHNSTON

Winner of the prestigious Western Writer's award for the best first novel, Terry C. Johnston brings you two volumes of his award-winning saga of mountain men Josiah Paddock and Titus Bass who strive together to meet the challenges of the western wilderness in the 1830's.

☐ 25572 **CARRY THE WIND** $4.95

Having killed a wealthy young Frenchman in a duel, Josiah Paddock flees St. Louis in 1831. He heads west to the fierce and beautiful Rocky Mountains, to become a free trapper far from the entanglements of civilization. Hot-headed and impetuous, young Josiah finds his romantic image of life in the mountains giving way to a harsh struggle for survival—against wild animals, fierce Indians, and nature's own cruelty. Half-dead of cold and starvation, he encounters Titus Bass, a solitary old trapper who takes the youth under his wing and teaches him the ways of the mountains. So begins a magnificent historical novel, remarkable for its wealth of authentic mountain lore and wisdom.

☐ 26224 **BORDERLORDS** $4.95

Here is a swirling, powerful drama of the early American wilderness, filled with fascinating scenes of tribal Indian life depicted with passion and detail unequaled in American literature, and all of it leading up to a terrifying climax at the fabled 1833 Green River Rendezvous.